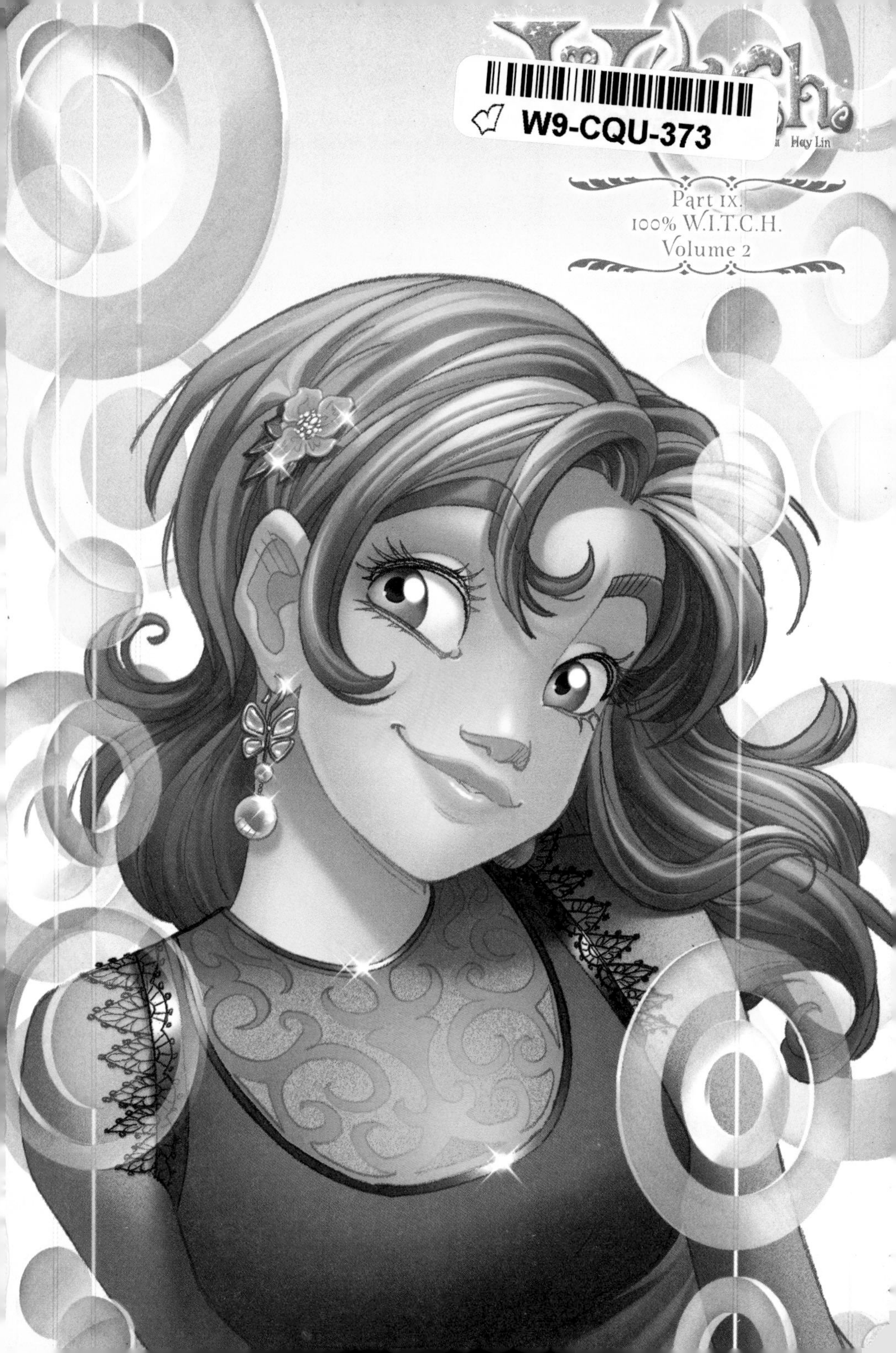
Hay Lin
Part IX.
100% W.I.T.C.H.
Volume 2

W.i.t.c.h

Will   Irma   Taranee   Cornelia   Hay Lin

Part IX.
100% W.I.T.C.H.
Volume 2

CONTENTS

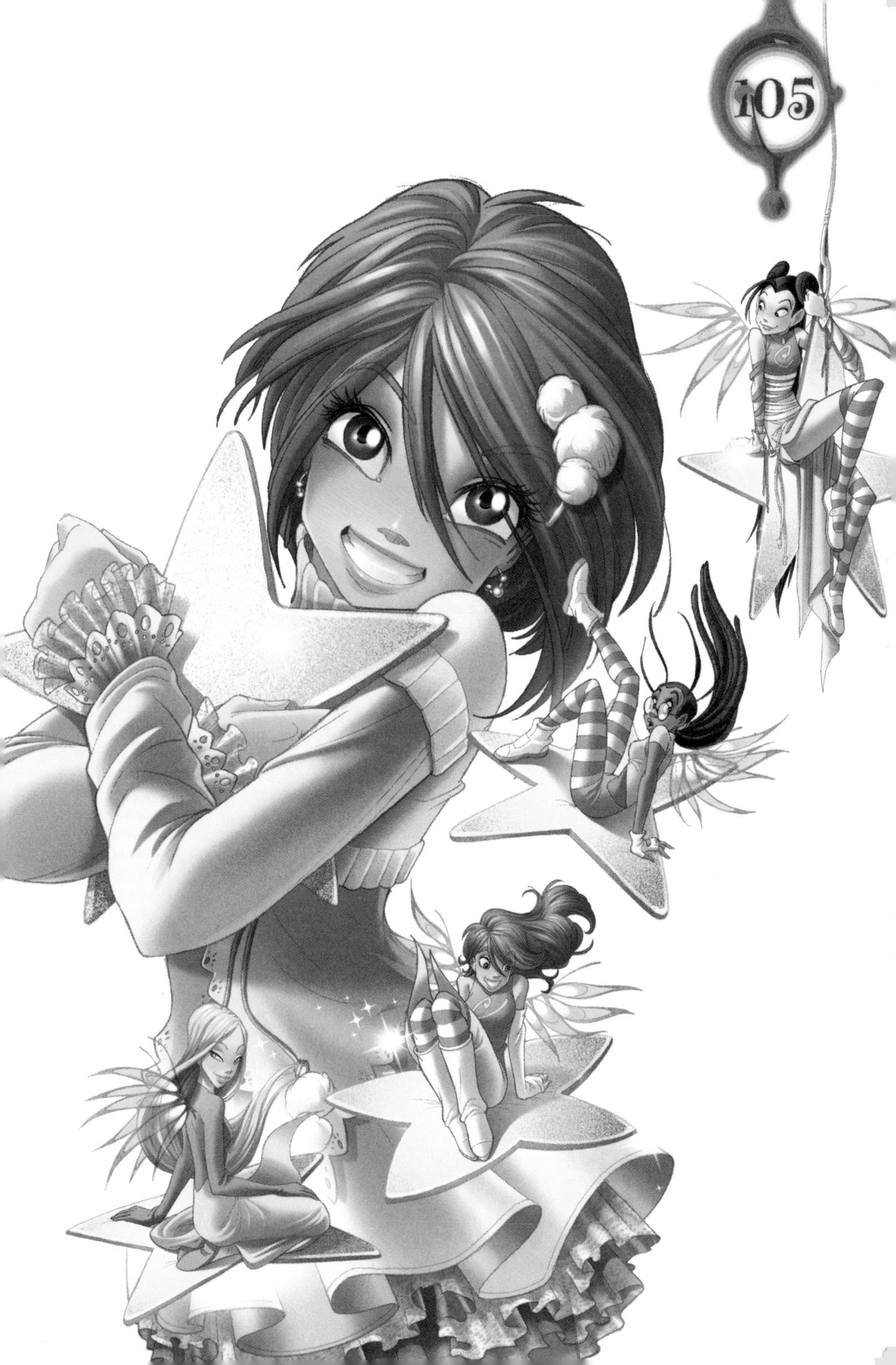
105

Will   Irma   Taranee   Cornelia   Hay Lin

A Special Letter

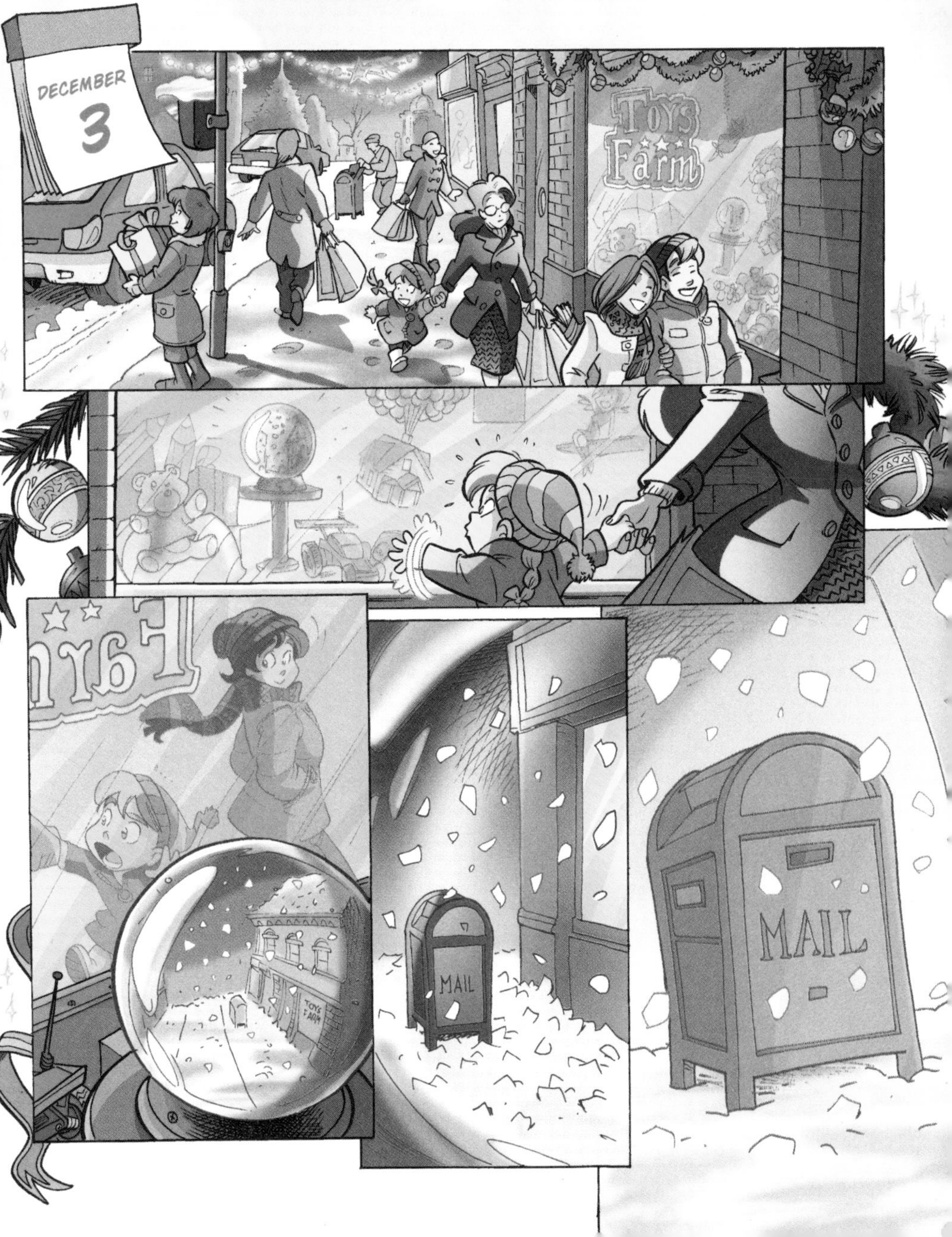
DECEMBER
3
TOYS
FARM
MAIL
MAIL

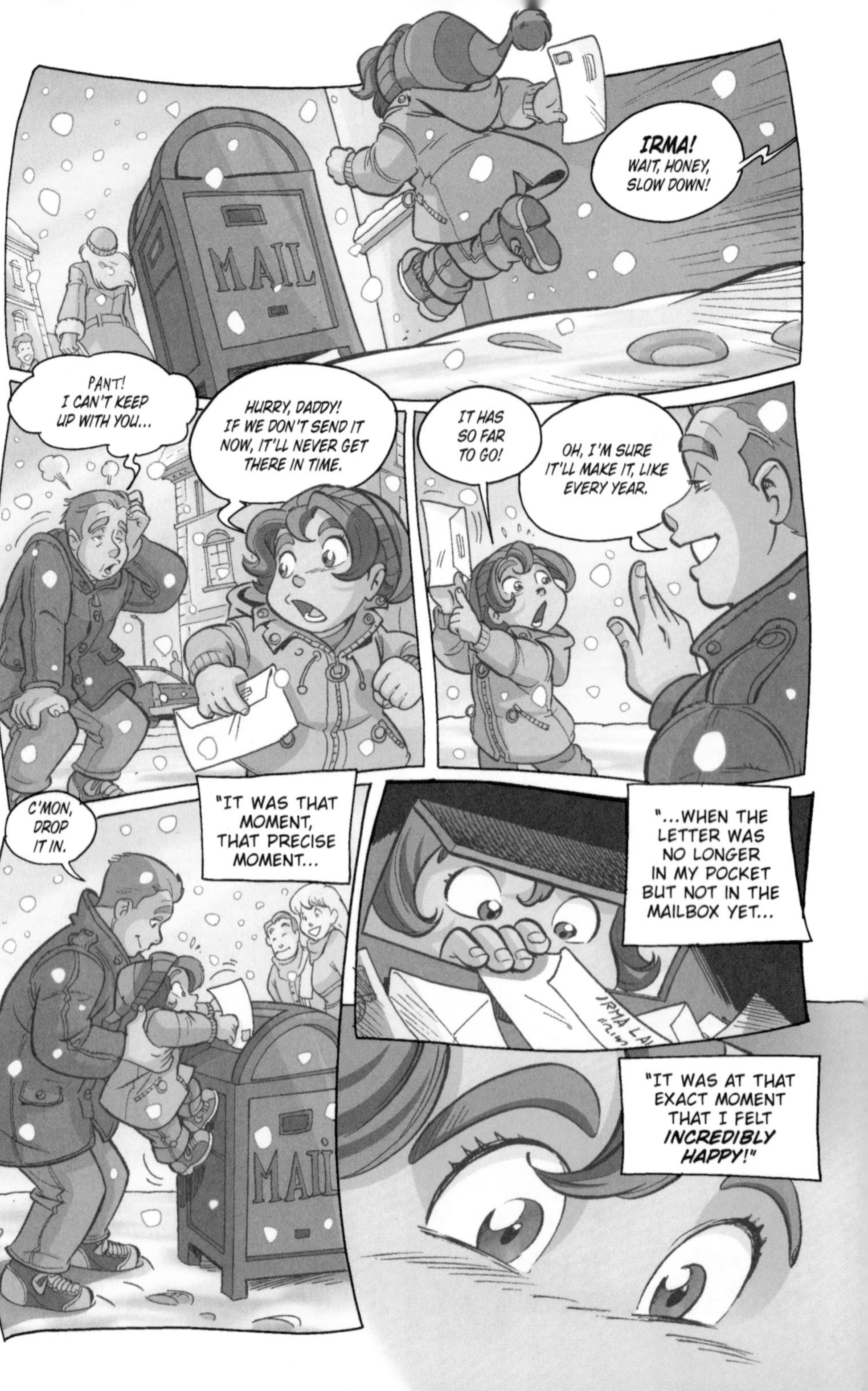
IRMA! WAIT, HONEY, SLOW DOWN!
MAIL
PANT! I CAN'T KEEP UP WITH YOU...
HURRY, DADDY! IF WE DON'T SEND IT NOW, IT'LL NEVER GET THERE IN TIME.
IT HAS SO FAR TO GO!
OH, I'M SURE IT'LL MAKE IT, LIKE EVERY YEAR.
C'MON, DROP IT IN.
"IT WAS THAT MOMENT, THAT PRECISE MOMENT...
"...WHEN THE LETTER WAS NO LONGER IN MY POCKET BUT NOT IN THE MAILBOX YET...
"IT WAS AT THAT EXACT MOMENT THAT I FELT **INCREDIBLY HAPPY!"**

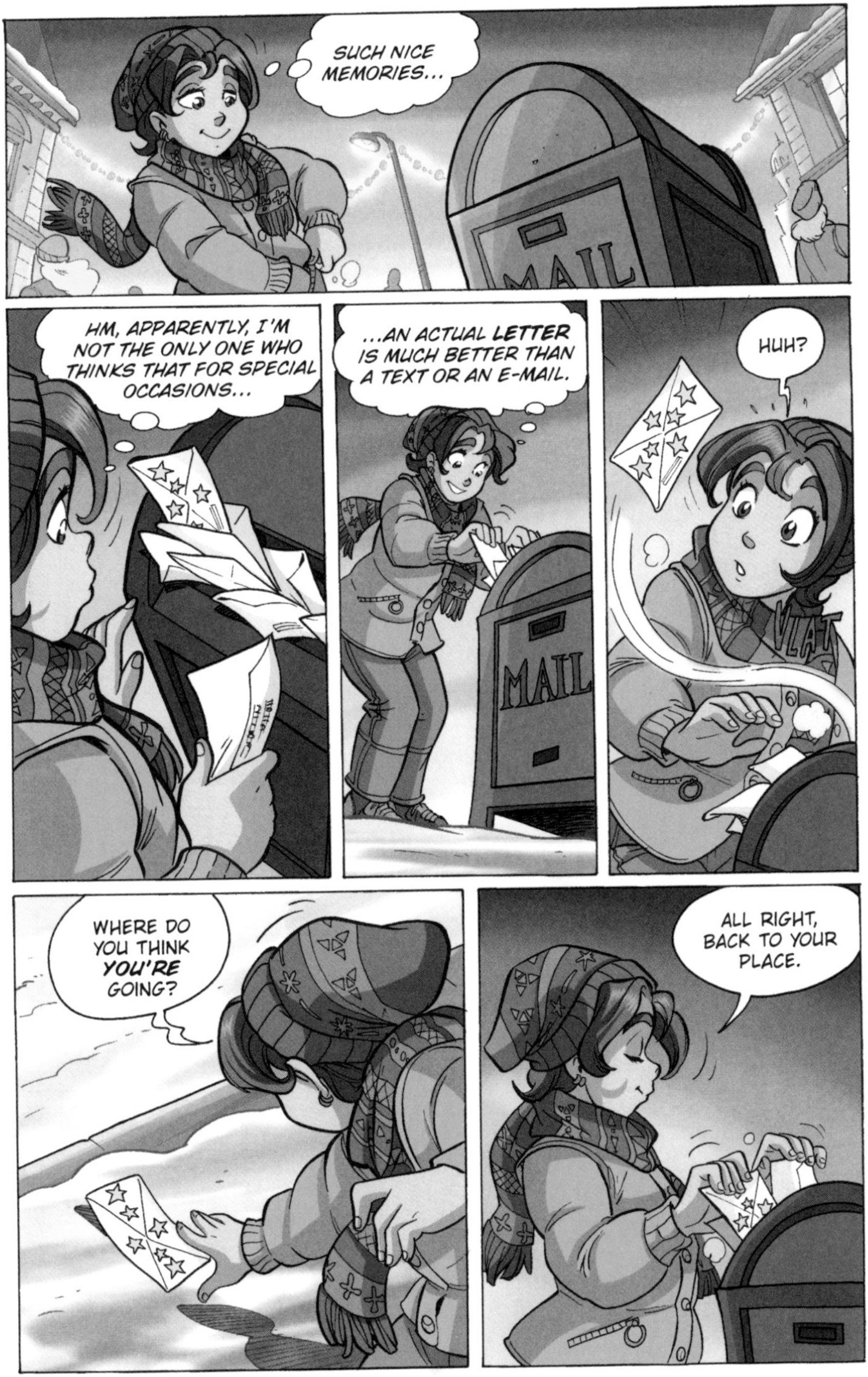
SUCH NICE MEMORIES...
MAIL
HM, APPARENTLY, I'M NOT THE ONLY ONE WHO THINKS THAT FOR SPECIAL OCCASIONS...
...AN ACTUAL **LETTER** IS MUCH BETTER THAN A TEXT OR AN E-MAIL.
MAIL
HUH?
WHERE DO YOU THINK ***YOU'RE*** GOING?
ALL RIGHT, BACK TO YOUR PLACE.

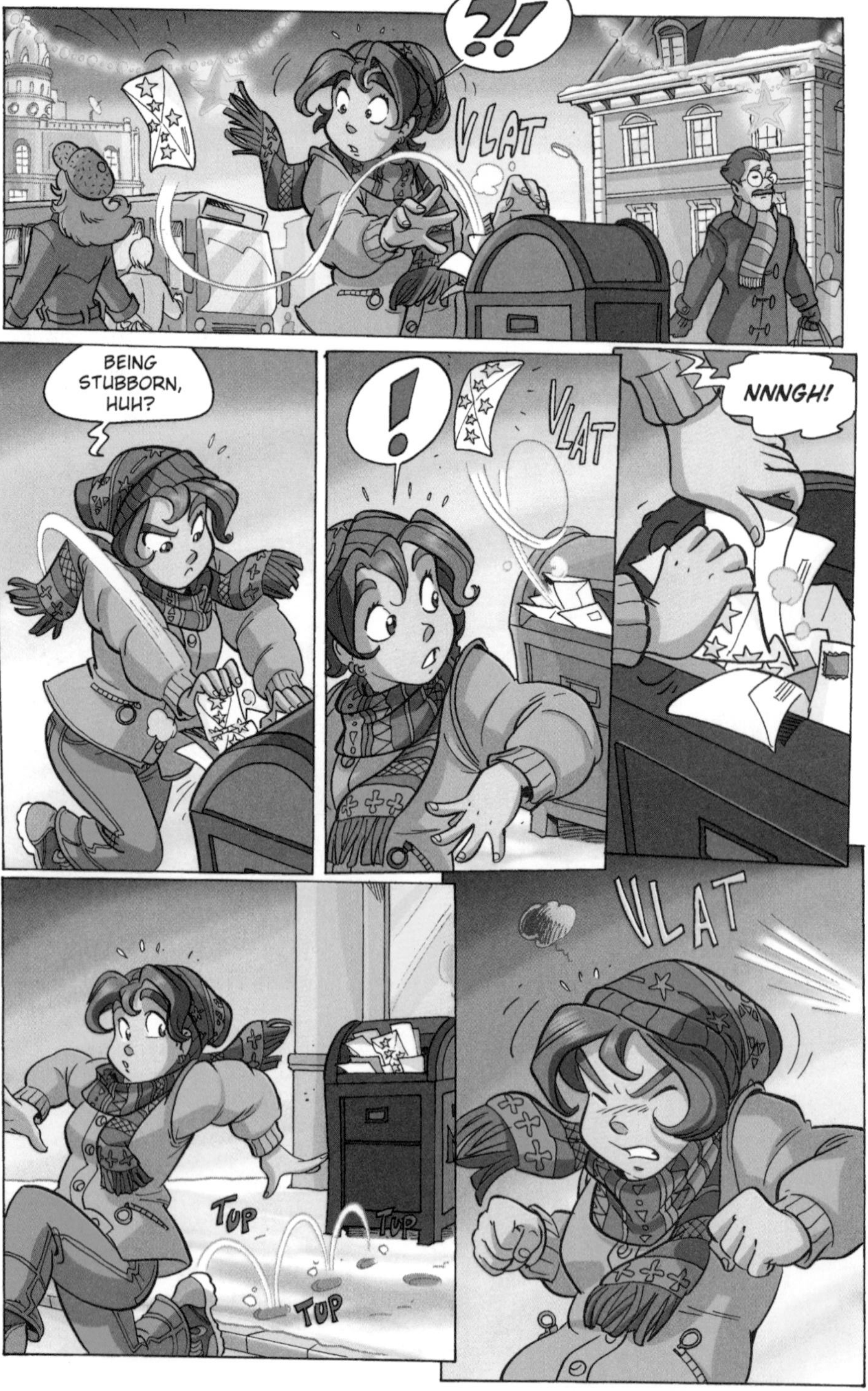
?!
VLAT
BEING STUBBORN, HUH?
!
VLAT
NNNGH!
TUP
TUP
TUP
VLAT

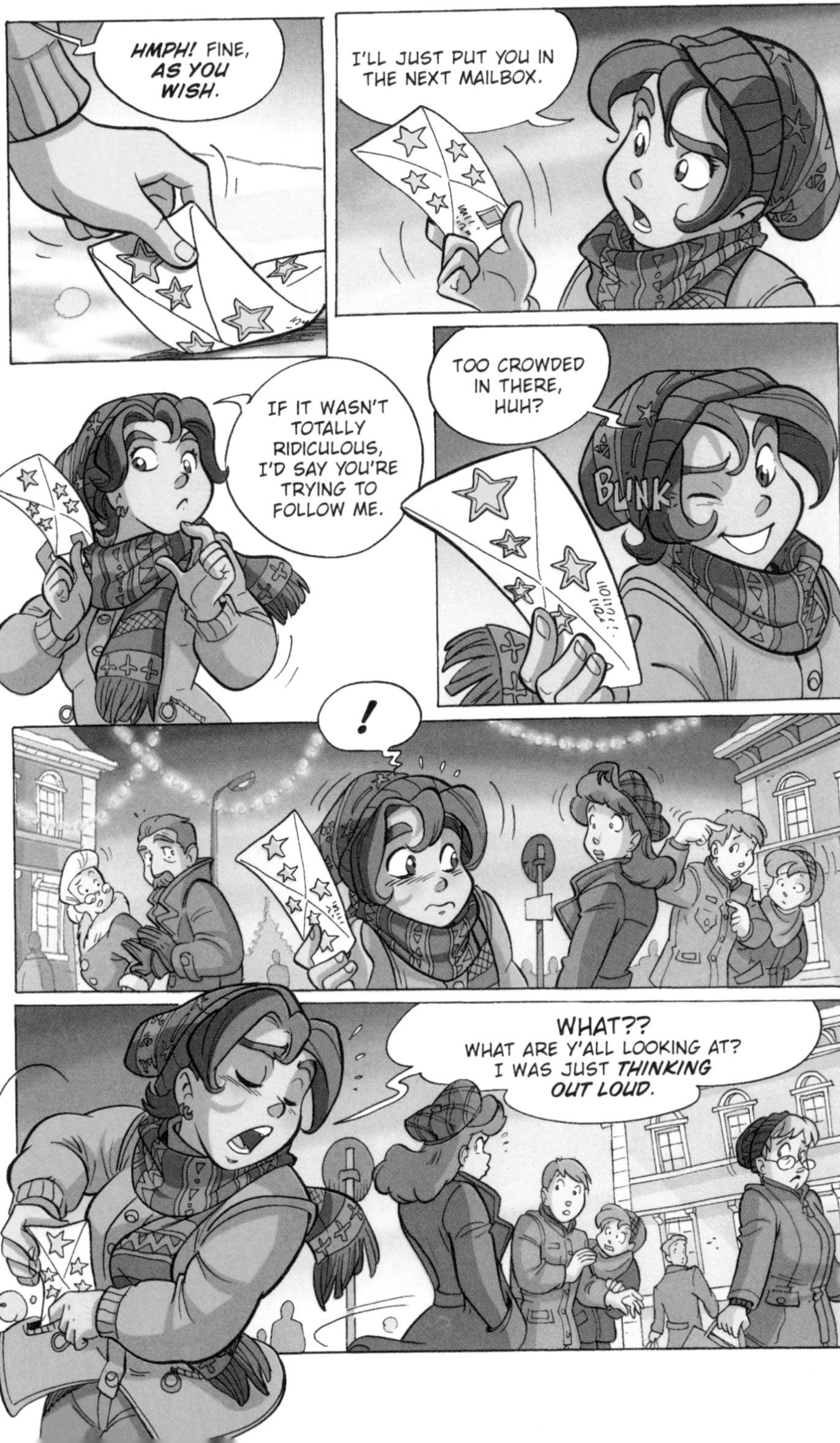
HMPH! FINE, AS YOU WISH.
I'LL JUST PUT YOU IN THE NEXT MAILBOX.
IF IT WASN'T TOTALLY RIDICULOUS, I'D SAY YOU'RE TRYING TO FOLLOW ME.
TOO CROWDED IN THERE, HUH?
BLINK
!
WHAT?? WHAT ARE Y'ALL LOOKING AT? I WAS JUST THINKING OUT LOUD.

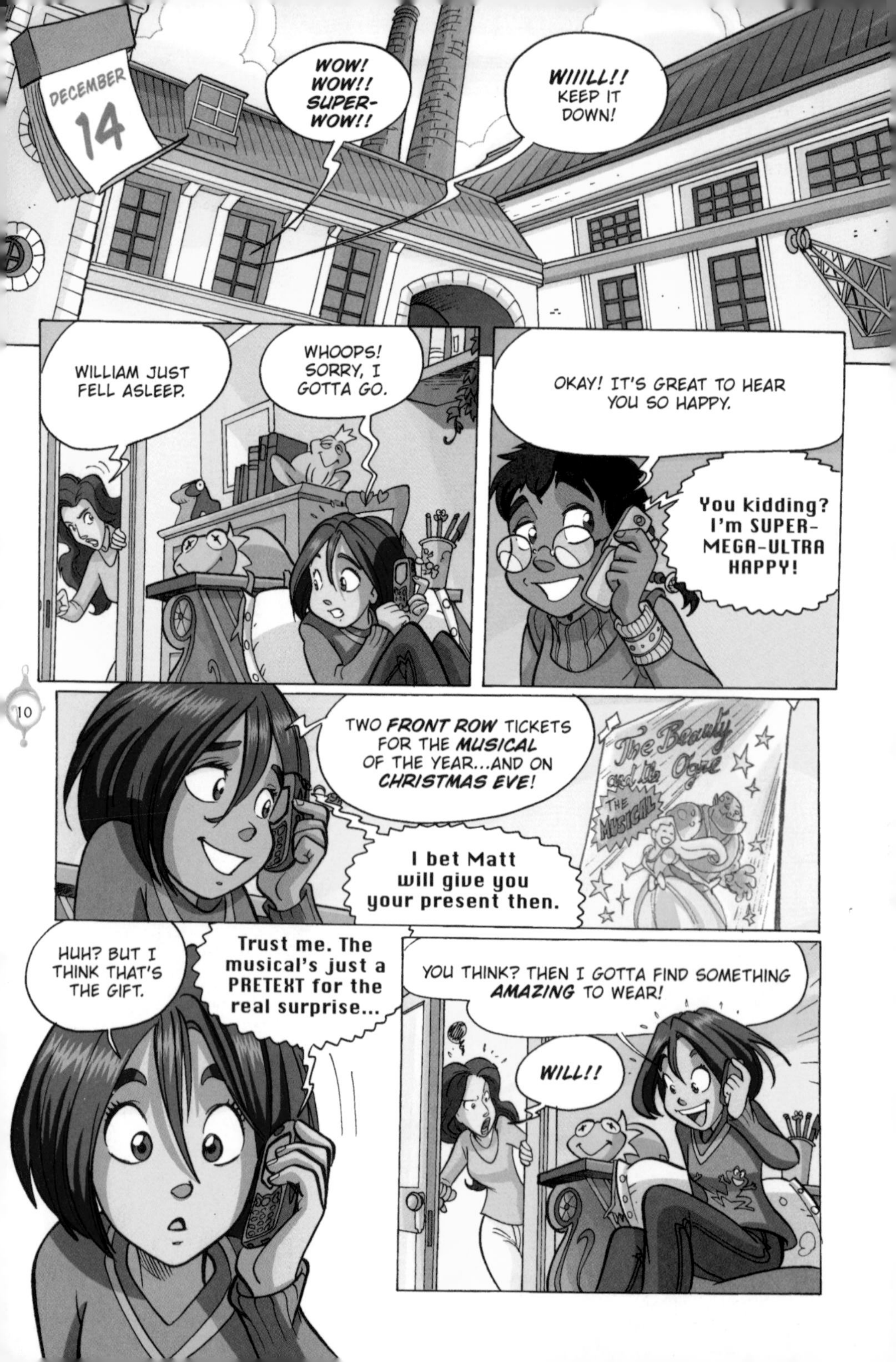
DECEMBER 14
WOW! WOW!! SUPER-WOW!!
WIIILL!! KEEP IT DOWN!
WILLIAM JUST FELL ASLEEP.
WHOOPS! SORRY, I GOTTA GO.
OKAY! IT'S GREAT TO HEAR YOU SO HAPPY.
You kidding? I'm SUPER-MEGA-ULTRA HAPPY!
TWO FRONT ROW TICKETS FOR THE MUSICAL OF THE YEAR...AND ON CHRISTMAS EVE!
I bet Matt will give you your present then.
The Beauty and the Ogre THE MUSICAL
HUH? BUT I THINK THAT'S THE GIFT.
Trust me. The musical's just a PRETEXT for the real surprise...
YOU THINK? THEN I GOTTA FIND SOMETHING AMAZING TO WEAR!
WILL!!

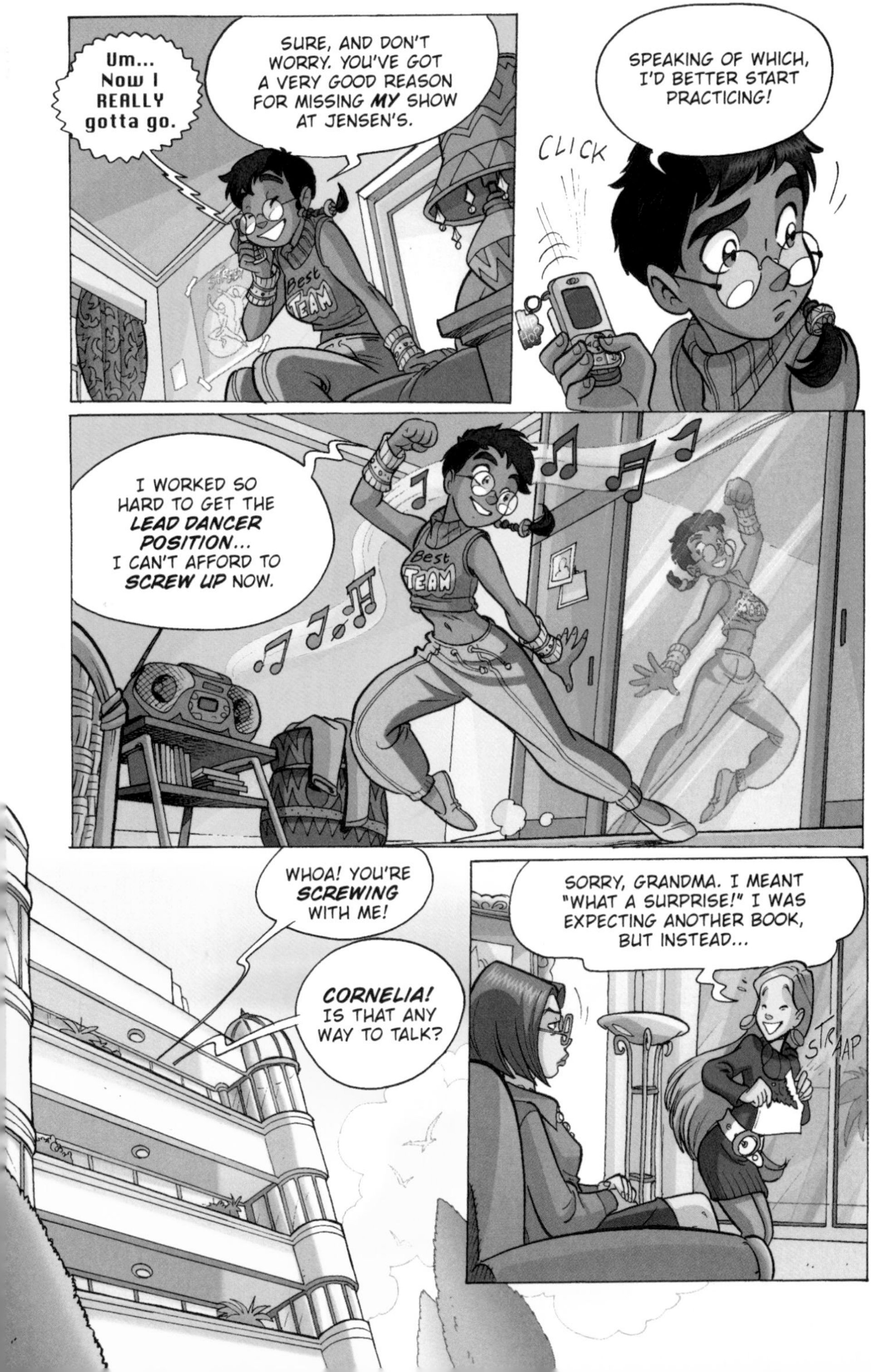
Um... Now I REALLY gotta go.
SURE, AND DON'T WORRY. YOU'VE GOT A VERY GOOD REASON FOR MISSING MY SHOW AT JENSEN'S.
SPEAKING OF WHICH, I'D BETTER START PRACTICING!
CLICK
I WORKED SO HARD TO GET THE LEAD DANCER POSITION... I CAN'T AFFORD TO SCREW UP NOW.
WHOA! YOU'RE SCREWING WITH ME!
CORNELIA! IS THAT ANY WAY TO TALK?
SORRY, GRANDMA. I MEANT "WHAT A SURPRISE!" I WAS EXPECTING ANOTHER BOOK, BUT INSTEAD...
STRAAP

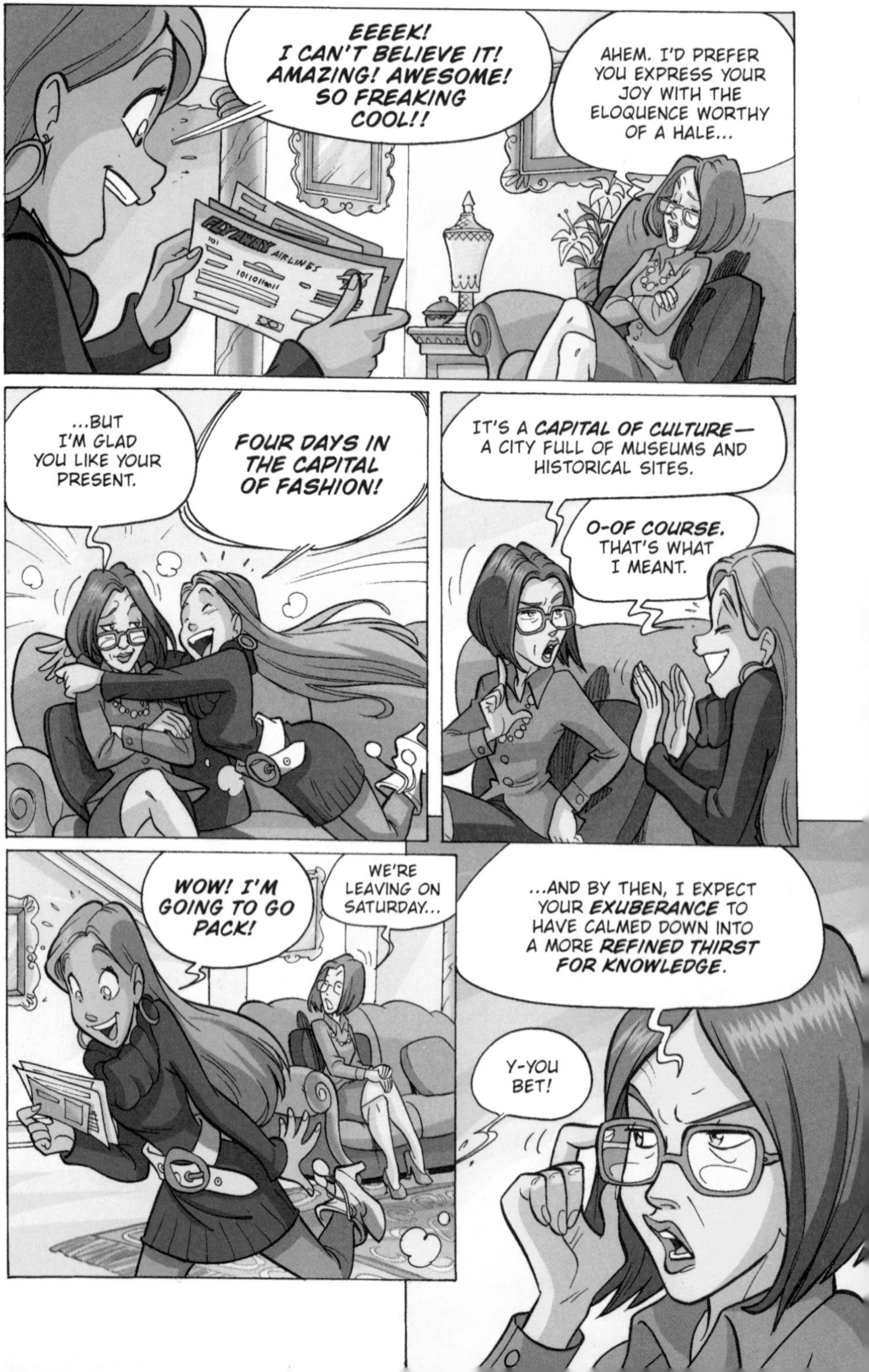
EEEEK! I CAN'T BELIEVE IT! AMAZING! AWESOME! SO FREAKING COOL!!
FLYAWAY AIRLINES
AHEM. I'D PREFER YOU EXPRESS YOUR JOY WITH THE ELOQUENCE WORTHY OF A HALE...
...BUT I'M GLAD YOU LIKE YOUR PRESENT.
FOUR DAYS IN THE CAPITAL OF FASHION!
IT'S A CAPITAL OF CULTURE—A CITY FULL OF MUSEUMS AND HISTORICAL SITES.
O-OF COURSE. THAT'S WHAT I MEANT.
WOW! I'M GOING TO GO PACK!
WE'RE LEAVING ON SATURDAY...
...AND BY THEN, I EXPECT YOUR EXUBERANCE TO HAVE CALMED DOWN INTO A MORE REFINED THIRST FOR KNOWLEDGE.
Y-YOU BET!

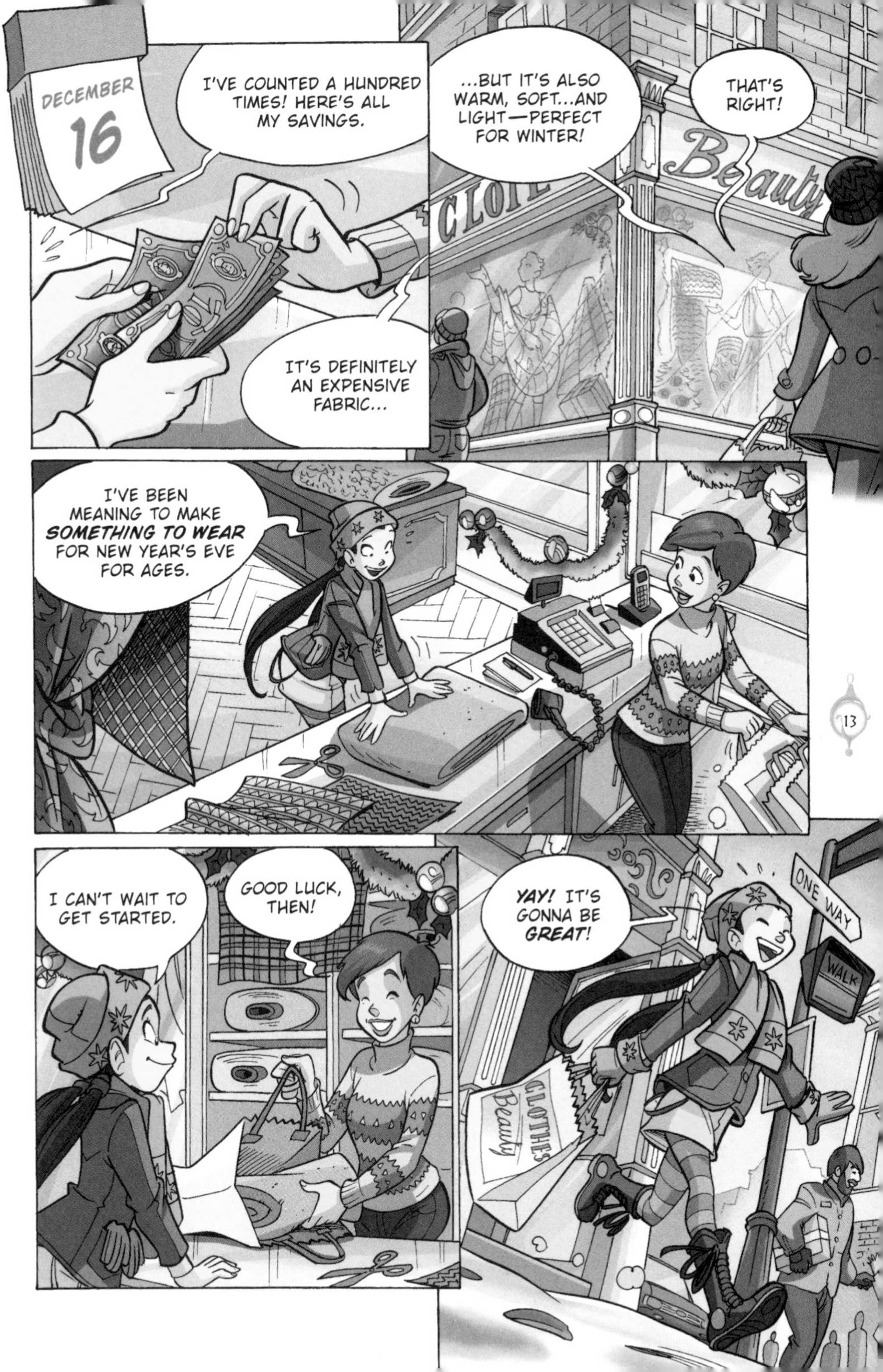
DECEMBER
16
I'VE COUNTED A HUNDRED TIMES! HERE'S ALL MY SAVINGS.
IT'S DEFINITELY AN EXPENSIVE FABRIC...
...BUT IT'S ALSO WARM, SOFT...AND LIGHT—PERFECT FOR WINTER!
THAT'S RIGHT!
Beauty
I'VE BEEN MEANING TO MAKE **SOMETHING TO WEAR** FOR NEW YEAR'S EVE FOR AGES.
I CAN'T WAIT TO GET STARTED.
GOOD LUCK, THEN!
YAY! IT'S GONNA BE ***GREAT***!
ONE WAY
WALK
CLOTHES
Beauty

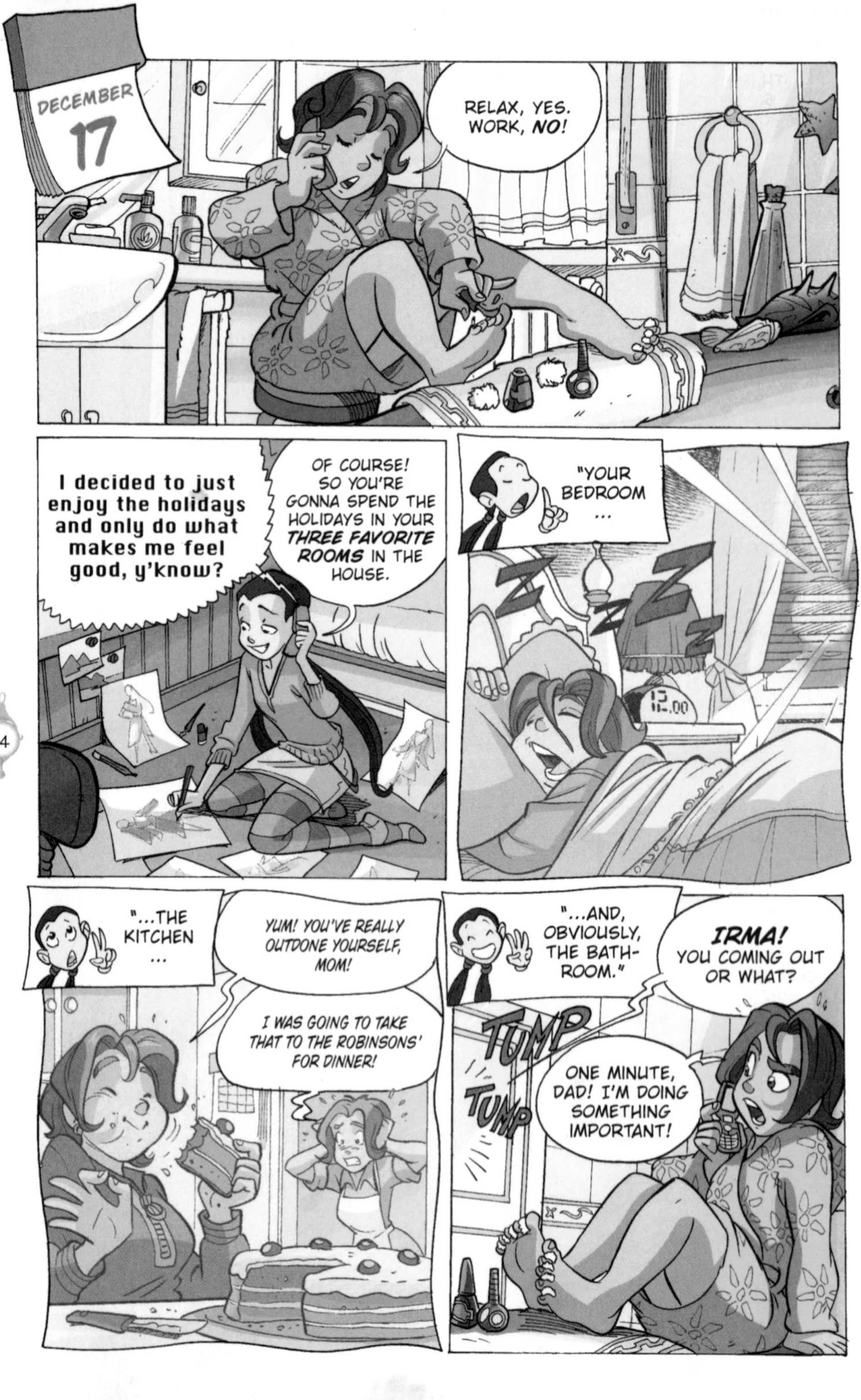
DECEMBER
17
RELAX, YES. WORK, NO!
I decided to just enjoy the holidays and only do what makes me feel good, y'know?
OF COURSE! SO YOU'RE GONNA SPEND THE HOLIDAYS IN YOUR THREE FAVORITE ROOMS IN THE HOUSE.
"YOUR BEDROOM ...
"...THE KITCHEN ...
YUM! YOU'VE REALLY OUTDONE YOURSELF, MOM!
I WAS GOING TO TAKE THAT TO THE ROBINSONS' FOR DINNER!
"...AND, OBVIOUSLY, THE BATH-ROOM."
IRMA! YOU COMING OUT OR WHAT?
TUMP
TUMP
ONE MINUTE, DAD! I'M DOING SOMETHING IMPORTANT!

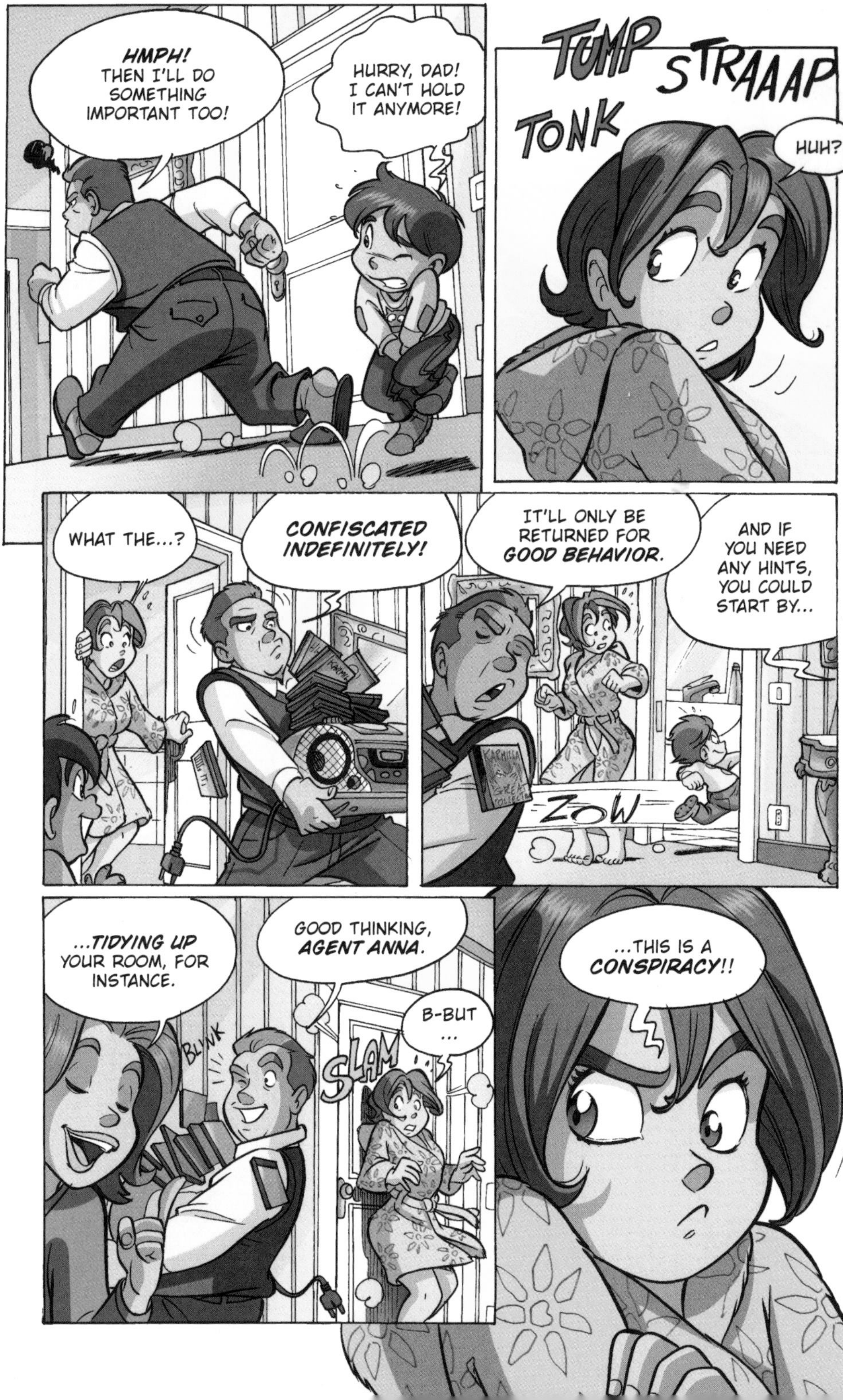
HMPH!
THEN I'LL DO SOMETHING IMPORTANT TOO!
HURRY, DAD! I CAN'T HOLD IT ANYMORE!
TUMP
STRAAAP
TONK
HUH?
WHAT THE...?
CONFISCATED INDEFINITELY!
IT'LL ONLY BE RETURNED FOR GOOD BEHAVIOR.
AND IF YOU NEED ANY HINTS, YOU COULD START BY...
ZOW
...TIDYING UP YOUR ROOM, FOR INSTANCE.
GOOD THINKING, AGENT ANNA.
BLINK
SLAM
B-BUT ...
...THIS IS A CONSPIRACY!!

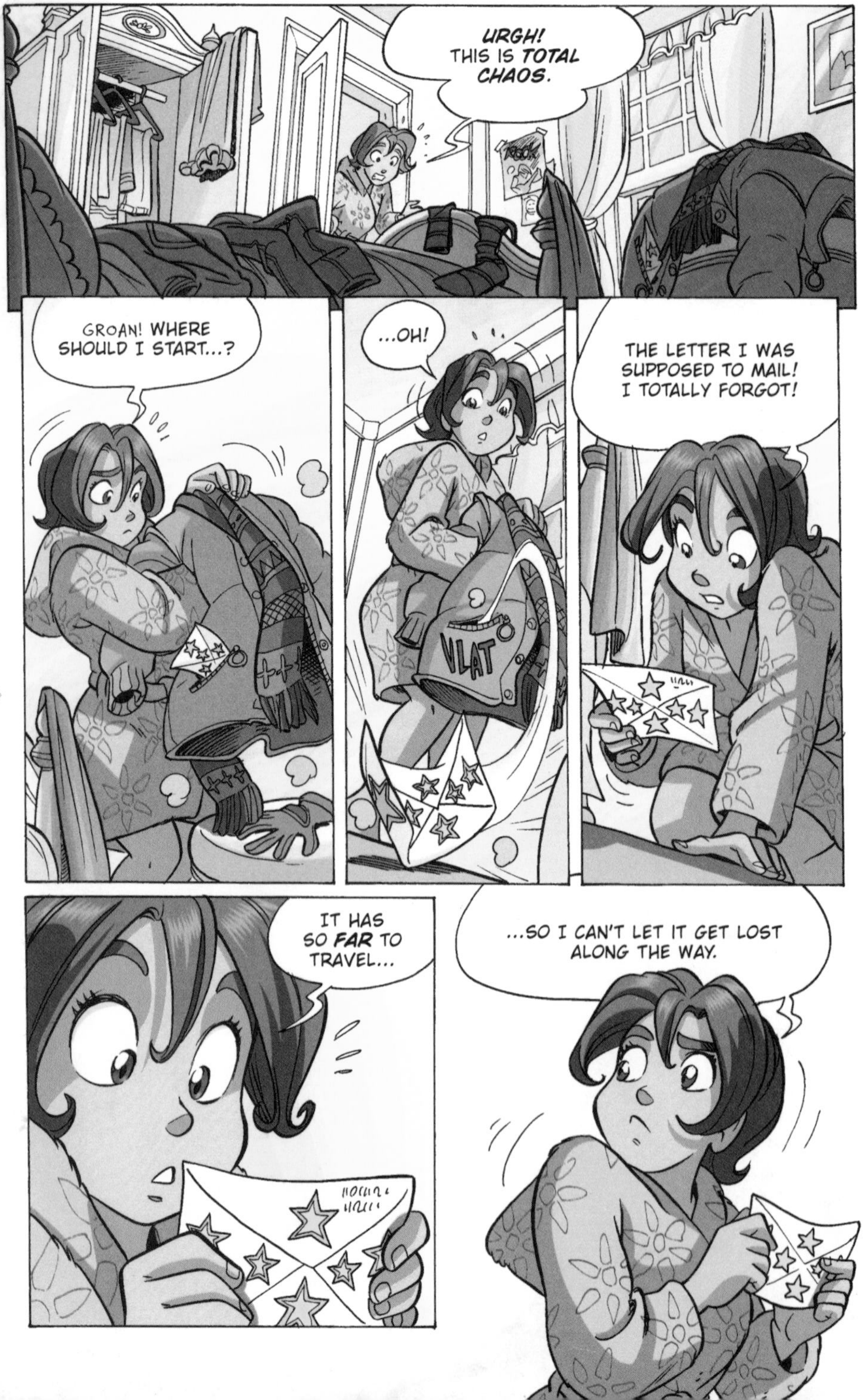
URGH! THIS IS TOTAL CHAOS.
GROAN! WHERE SHOULD I START...?
...OH!
VLAT
THE LETTER I WAS SUPPOSED TO MAIL! I TOTALLY FORGOT!
IT HAS SO FAR TO TRAVEL...
...SO I CAN'T LET IT GET LOST ALONG THE WAY.

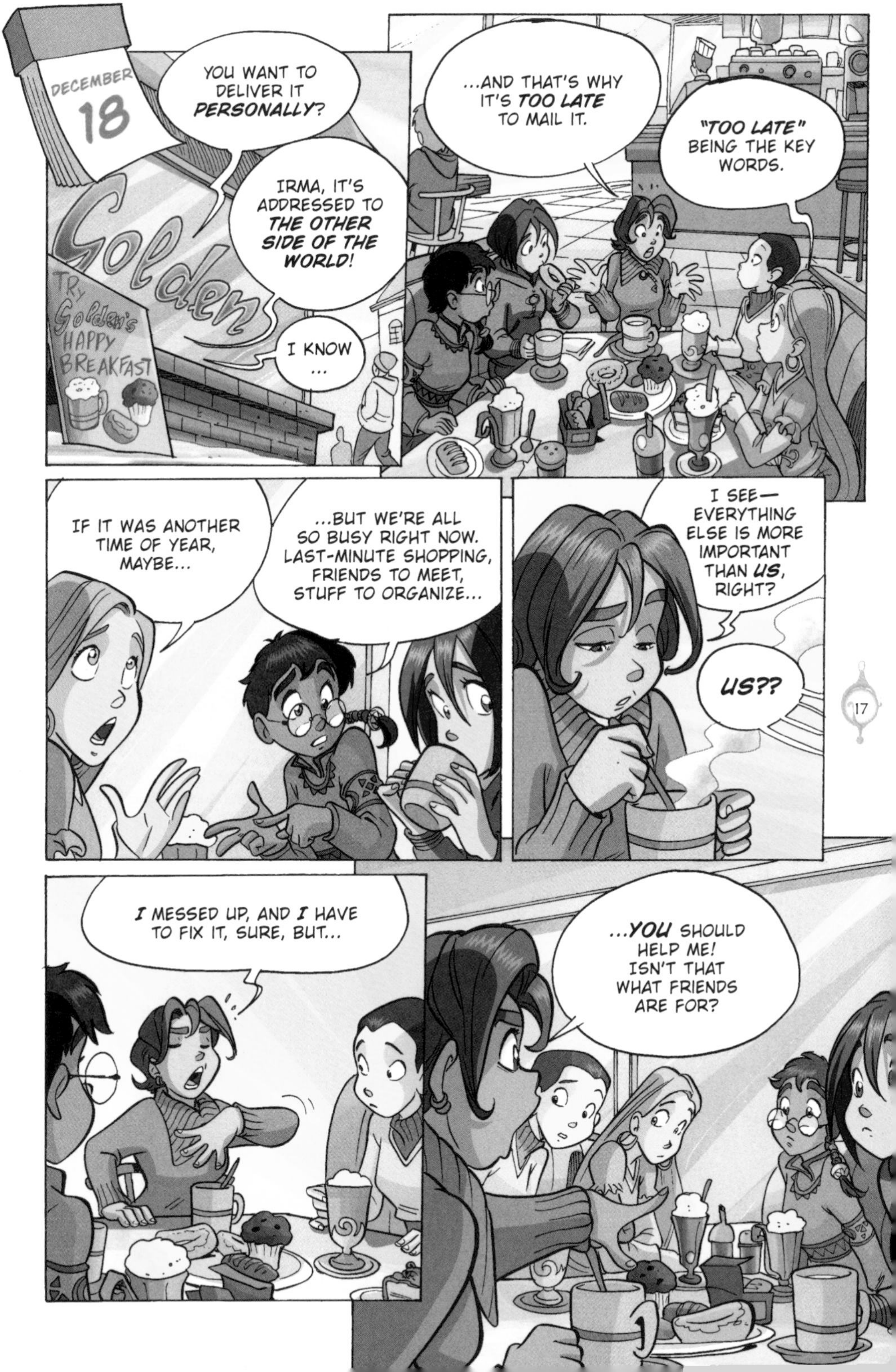
DECEMBER 18
YOU WANT TO DELIVER IT PERSONALLY?
IRMA, IT'S ADDRESSED TO THE OTHER SIDE OF THE WORLD!
I KNOW ...
Golden
TRy Golden's HAPPY BREAKFAST
...AND THAT'S WHY IT'S TOO LATE TO MAIL IT.
"TOO LATE" BEING THE KEY WORDS.
IF IT WAS ANOTHER TIME OF YEAR, MAYBE...
...BUT WE'RE ALL SO BUSY RIGHT NOW. LAST-MINUTE SHOPPING, FRIENDS TO MEET, STUFF TO ORGANIZE...
I SEE— EVERYTHING ELSE IS MORE IMPORTANT THAN US, RIGHT?
US??
I MESSED UP, AND I HAVE TO FIX IT, SURE, BUT...
...YOU SHOULD HELP ME! ISN'T THAT WHAT FRIENDS ARE FOR?

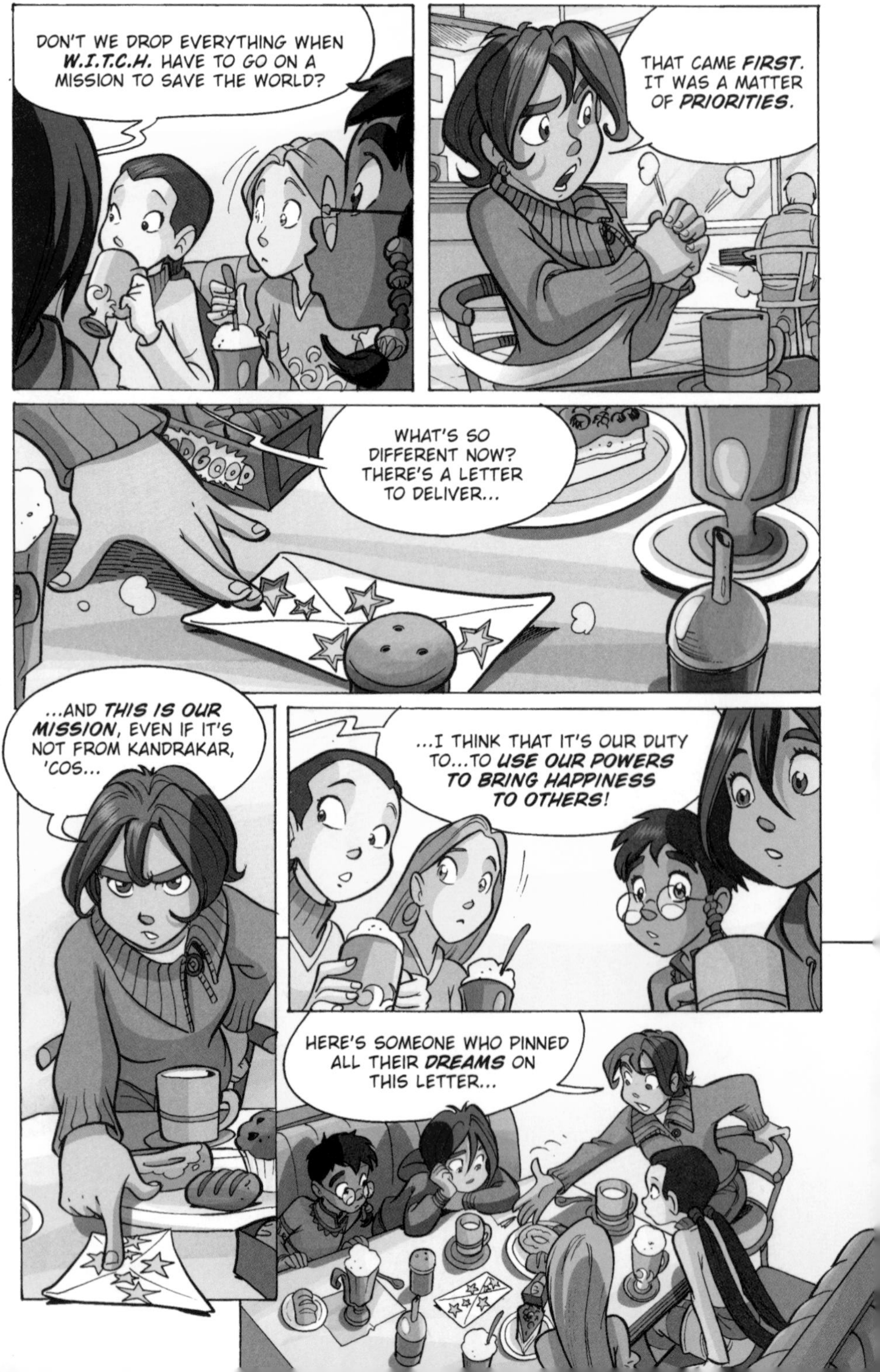
DON'T WE DROP EVERYTHING WHEN W.I.T.C.H. HAVE TO GO ON A MISSION TO SAVE THE WORLD?
THAT CAME FIRST. IT WAS A MATTER OF PRIORITIES.
WHAT'S SO DIFFERENT NOW? THERE'S A LETTER TO DELIVER...
...AND THIS IS OUR MISSION, EVEN IF IT'S NOT FROM KANDRAKAR, 'COS...
...I THINK THAT IT'S OUR DUTY TO...TO USE OUR POWERS TO BRING HAPPINESS TO OTHERS!
HERE'S SOMEONE WHO PINNED ALL THEIR DREAMS ON THIS LETTER...

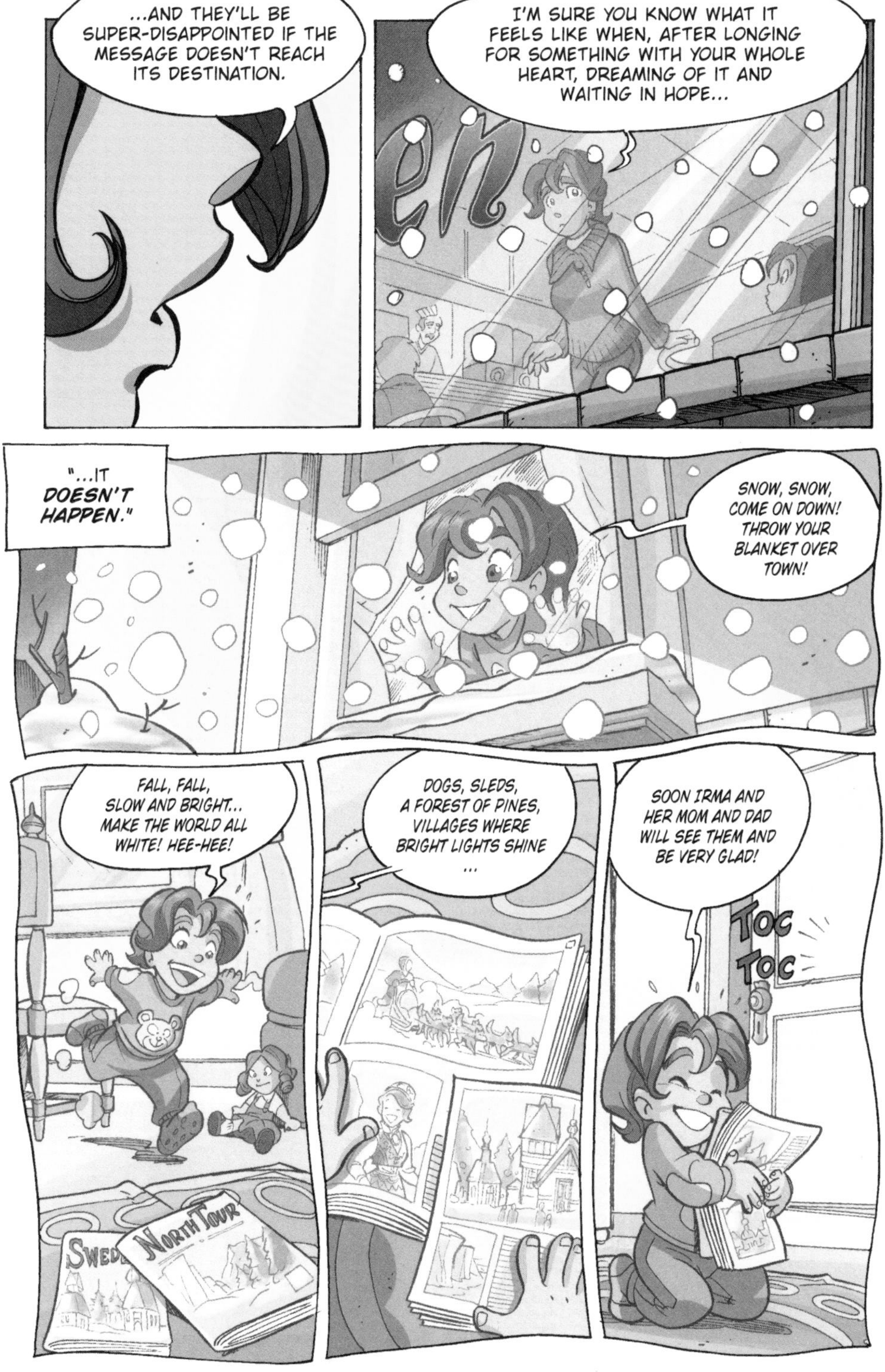
...AND THEY'LL BE SUPER-DISAPPOINTED IF THE MESSAGE DOESN'T REACH ITS DESTINATION.
I'M SURE YOU KNOW WHAT IT FEELS LIKE WHEN, AFTER LONGING FOR SOMETHING WITH YOUR WHOLE HEART, DREAMING OF IT AND WAITING IN HOPE...
"...IT DOESN'T HAPPEN."
SNOW, SNOW, COME ON DOWN! THROW YOUR BLANKET OVER TOWN!
FALL, FALL, SLOW AND BRIGHT... MAKE THE WORLD ALL WHITE! HEE-HEE!
SWEDE
NORTH TOUR
DOGS, SLEDS, A FOREST OF PINES, VILLAGES WHERE BRIGHT LIGHTS SHINE ...
SOON IRMA AND HER MOM AND DAD WILL SEE THEM AND BE VERY GLAD!
TOC TOC

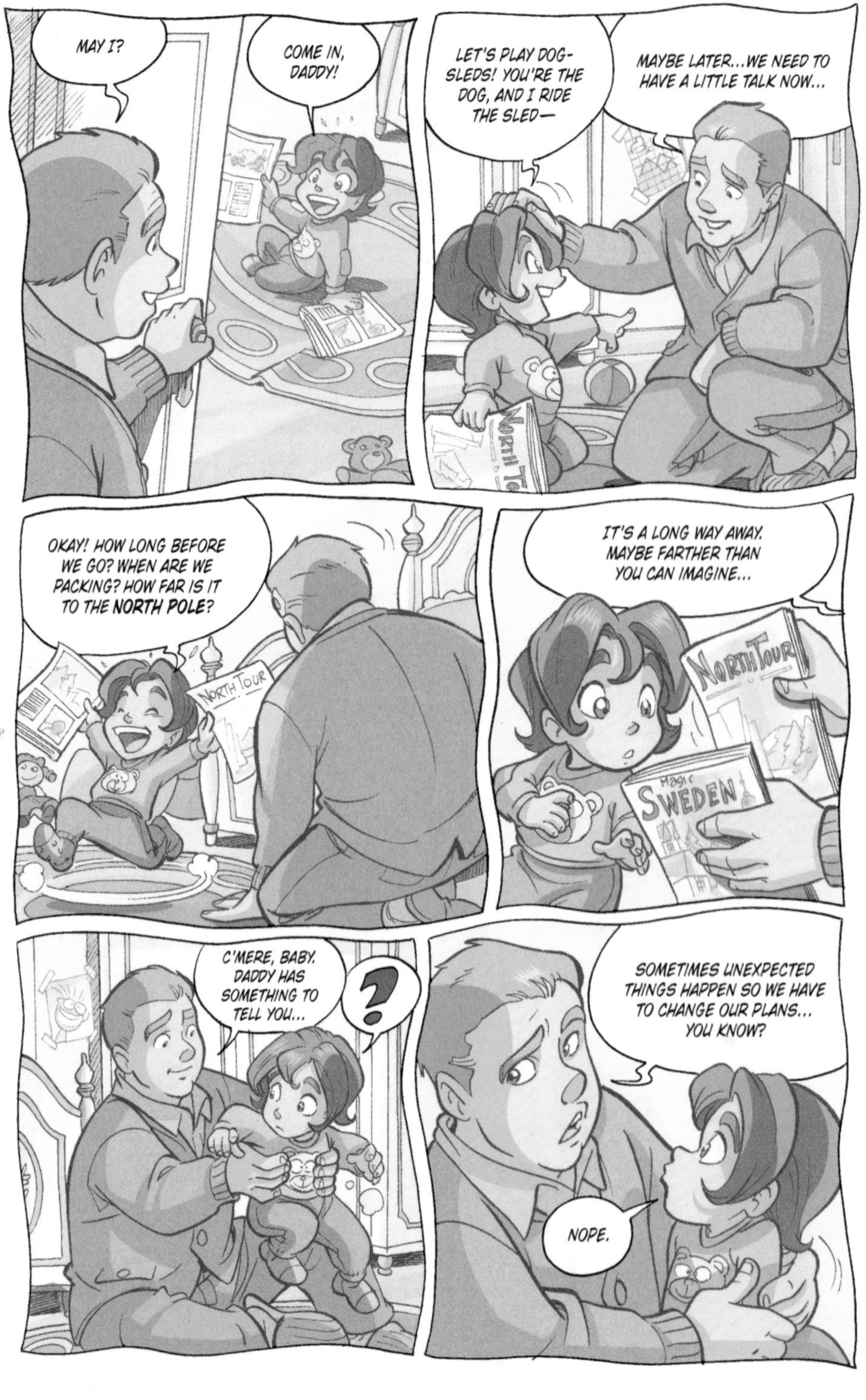
MAY I?
COME IN, DADDY!
LET'S PLAY DOG-SLEDS! YOU'RE THE DOG, AND I RIDE THE SLED—
MAYBE LATER...WE NEED TO HAVE A LITTLE TALK NOW...
NORTH TOU
OKAY! HOW LONG BEFORE WE GO? WHEN ARE WE PACKING? HOW FAR IS IT TO THE **NORTH POLE**?
NORTH TOUR
IT'S A LONG WAY AWAY. MAYBE FARTHER THAN YOU CAN IMAGINE...
NORTH TOUR
Magic SWEDEN
C'MERE, BABY. DADDY HAS SOMETHING TO TELL YOU...
?
SOMETIMES UNEXPECTED THINGS HAPPEN SO WE HAVE TO CHANGE OUR PLANS... YOU KNOW?
NOPE.

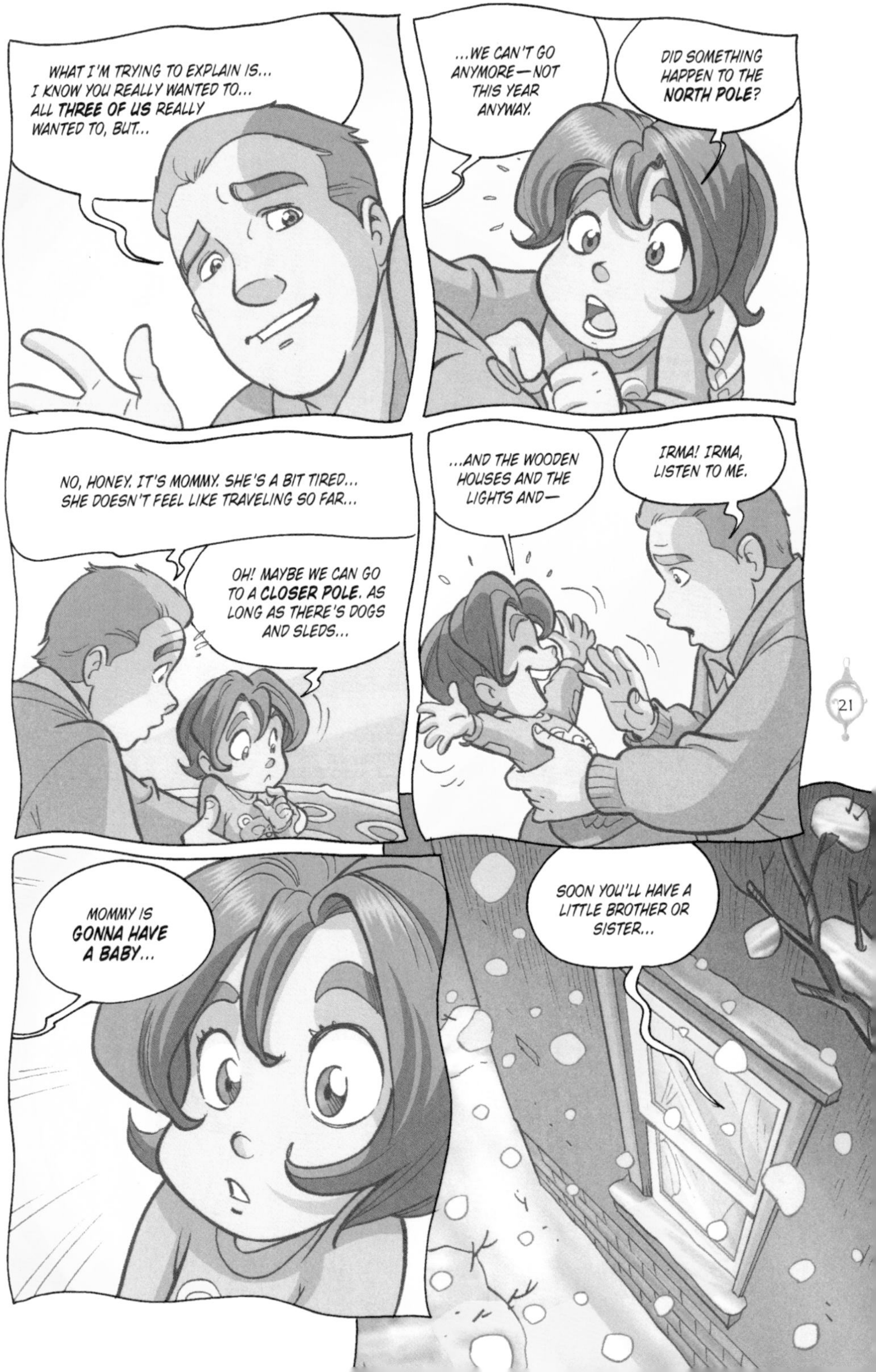
WHAT I'M TRYING TO EXPLAIN IS... I KNOW YOU REALLY WANTED TO... ALL **THREE OF US** REALLY WANTED TO, BUT...
...WE CAN'T GO ANYMORE—NOT THIS YEAR ANYWAY.
DID SOMETHING HAPPEN TO THE **NORTH POLE**?
NO, HONEY. IT'S MOMMY. SHE'S A BIT TIRED... SHE DOESN'T FEEL LIKE TRAVELING SO FAR...
OH! MAYBE WE CAN GO TO A **CLOSER POLE**. AS LONG AS THERE'S DOGS AND SLEDS...
...AND THE WOODEN HOUSES AND THE LIGHTS AND—
IRMA! IRMA, LISTEN TO ME.
MOMMY IS **GONNA HAVE A BABY**...
SOON YOU'LL HAVE A LITTLE BROTHER OR SISTER...

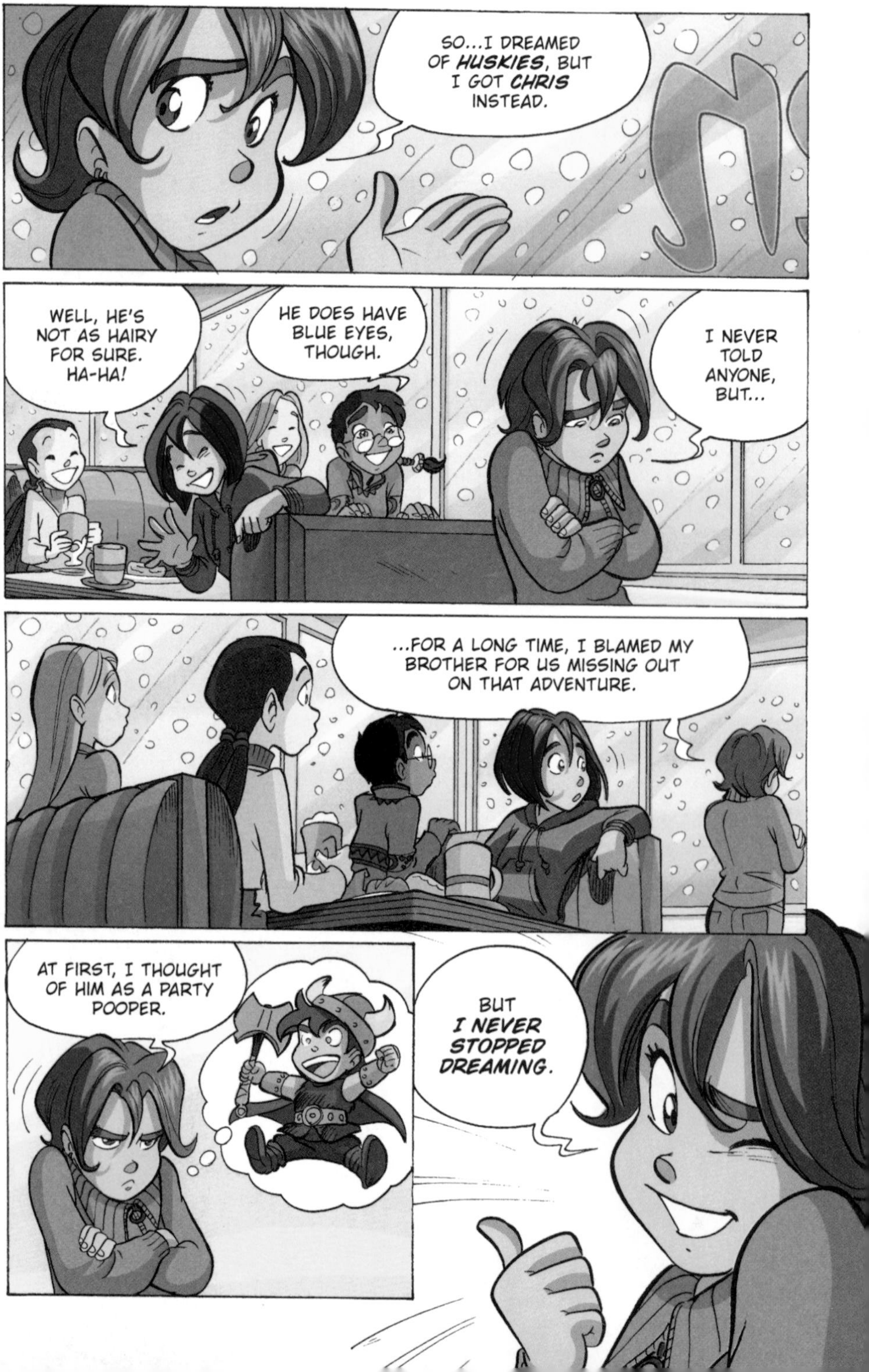
SO...I DREAMED OF HUSKIES, BUT I GOT CHRIS INSTEAD.
WELL, HE'S NOT AS HAIRY FOR SURE. HA-HA!
HE DOES HAVE BLUE EYES, THOUGH.
I NEVER TOLD ANYONE, BUT...
...FOR A LONG TIME, I BLAMED MY BROTHER FOR US MISSING OUT ON THAT ADVENTURE.
AT FIRST, I THOUGHT OF HIM AS A PARTY POOPER.
BUT I NEVER STOPPED DREAMING.

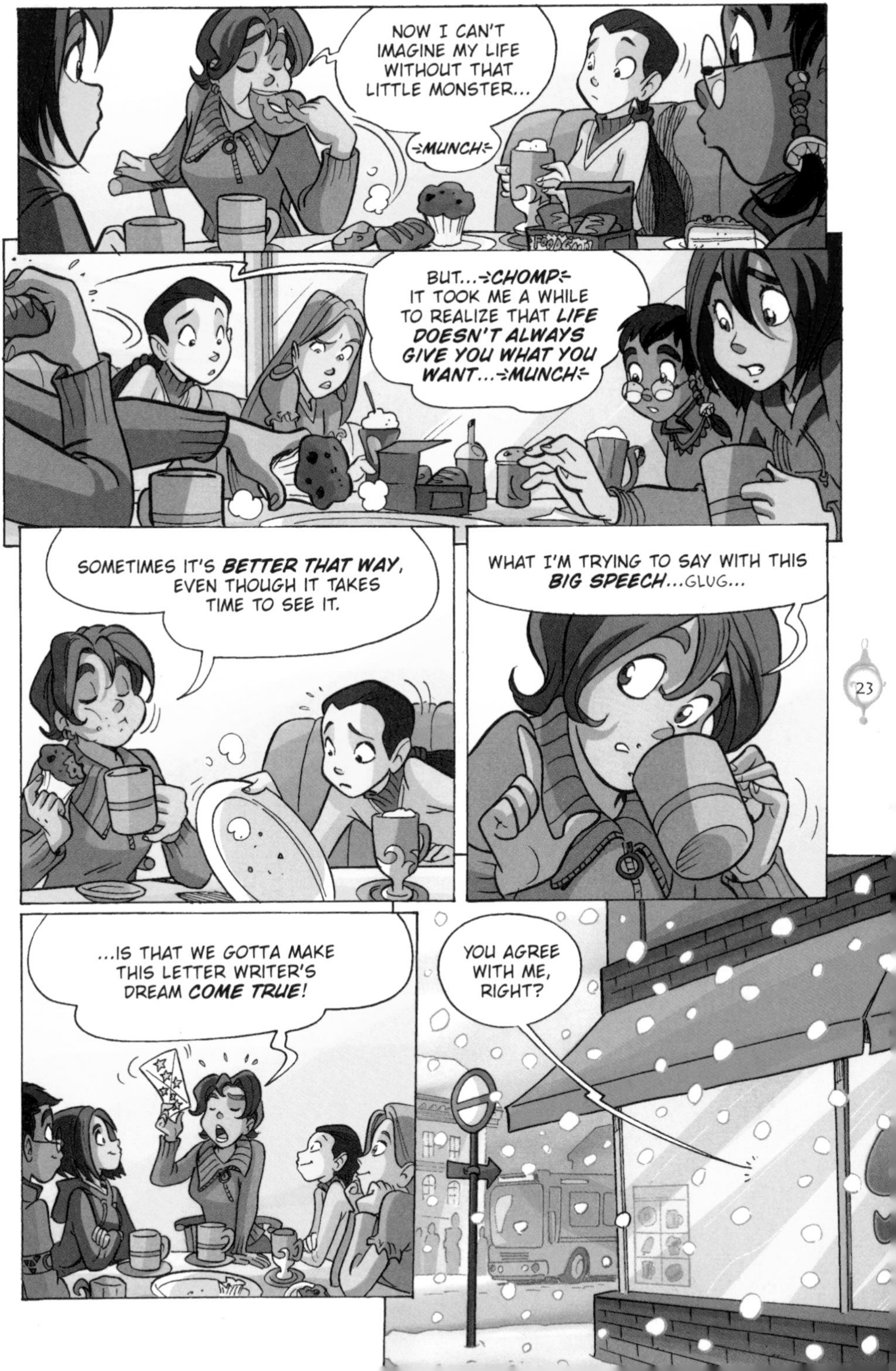
NOW I CAN'T IMAGINE MY LIFE WITHOUT THAT LITTLE MONSTER...
MUNCH
BUT... CHOMP IT TOOK ME A WHILE TO REALIZE THAT LIFE DOESN'T ALWAYS GIVE YOU WHAT YOU WANT... MUNCH
SOMETIMES IT'S BETTER THAT WAY, EVEN THOUGH IT TAKES TIME TO SEE IT.
WHAT I'M TRYING TO SAY WITH THIS BIG SPEECH...GLUG...
...IS THAT WE GOTTA MAKE THIS LETTER WRITER'S DREAM COME TRUE!
YOU AGREE WITH ME, RIGHT?

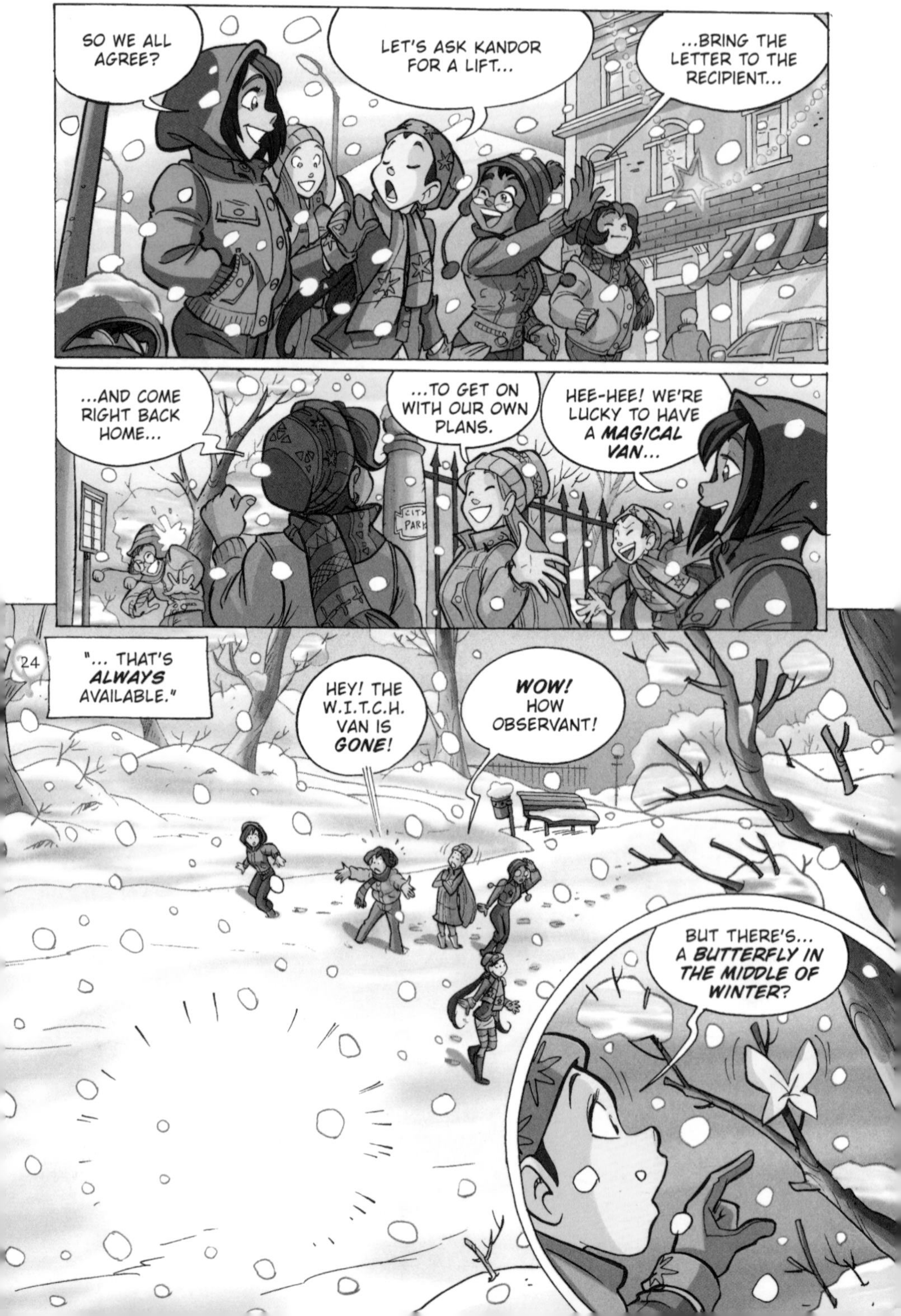
SO WE ALL AGREE?
LET'S ASK KANDOR FOR A LIFT...
...BRING THE LETTER TO THE RECIPIENT...
...AND COME RIGHT BACK HOME...
...TO GET ON WITH OUR OWN PLANS.
HEE-HEE! WE'RE LUCKY TO HAVE A MAGICAL VAN...
CITY PARK
"... THAT'S ALWAYS AVAILABLE."
HEY! THE W.I.T.C.H. VAN IS GONE!
WOW! HOW OBSERVANT!
BUT THERE'S... A BUTTERFLY IN THE MIDDLE OF WINTER?

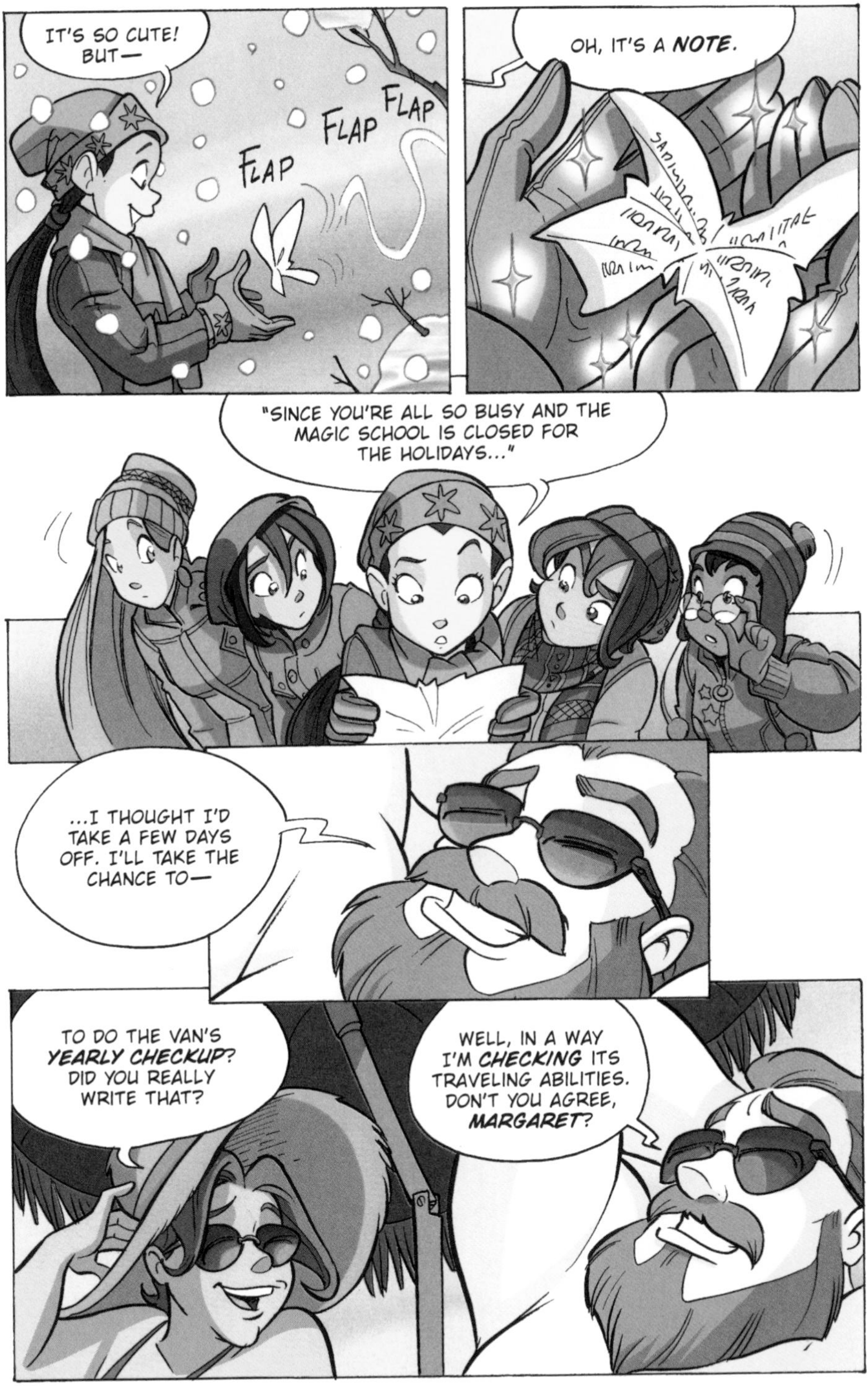
IT'S SO CUTE! BUT—
FLAP
FLAP
FLAP
OH, IT'S A **NOTE**.
"SINCE YOU'RE ALL SO BUSY AND THE MAGIC SCHOOL IS CLOSED FOR THE HOLIDAYS..."
...I THOUGHT I'D TAKE A FEW DAYS OFF. I'LL TAKE THE CHANCE TO—
TO DO THE VAN'S ***YEARLY CHECKUP***? DID YOU REALLY WRITE THAT?
WELL, IN A WAY I'M ***CHECKING*** ITS TRAVELING ABILITIES. DON'T YOU AGREE, ***MARGARET***?

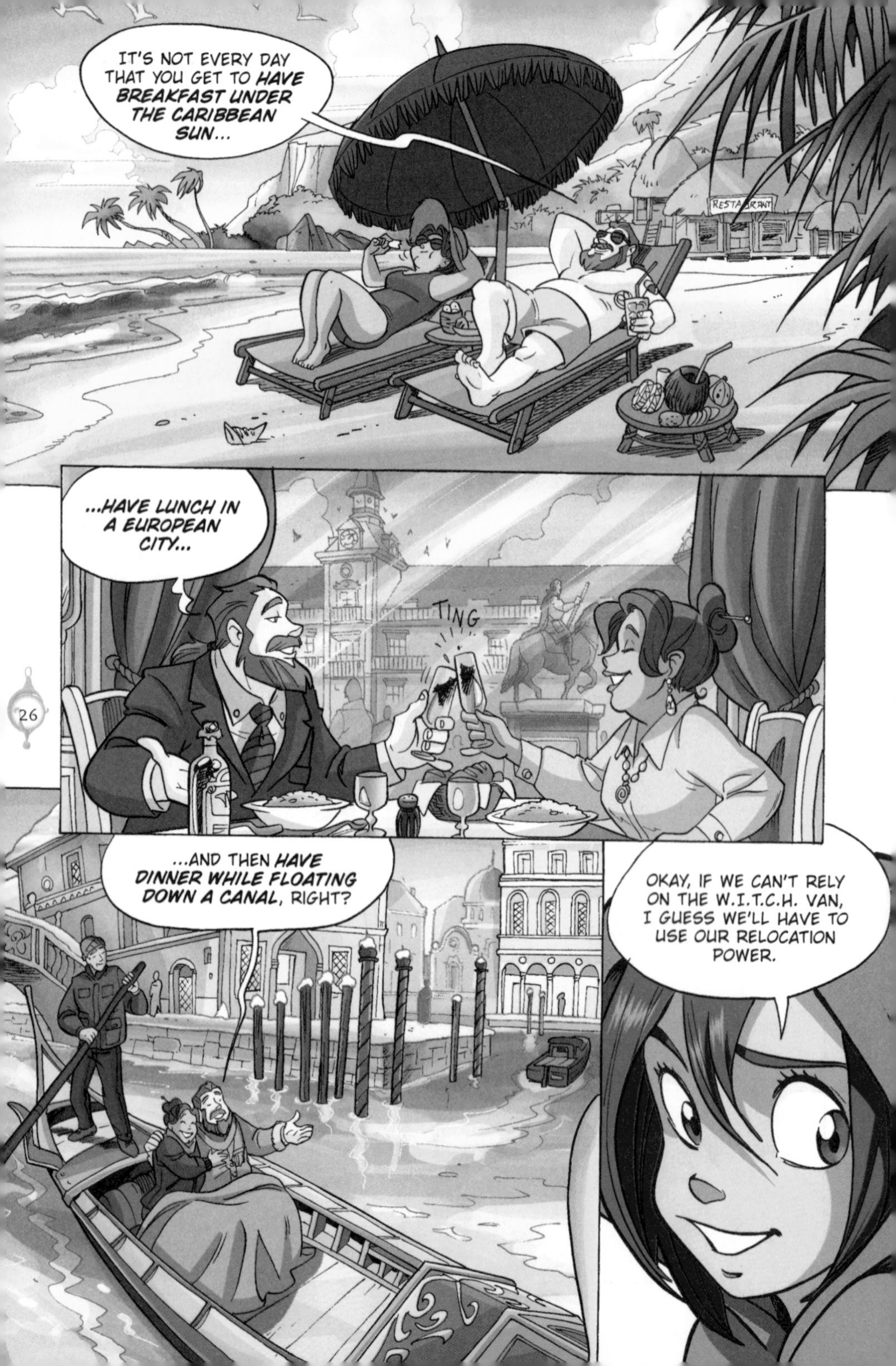
IT'S NOT EVERY DAY THAT YOU GET TO *HAVE BREAKFAST UNDER THE CARIBBEAN SUN*...
RESTAURANT
...HAVE LUNCH IN A EUROPEAN CITY...
TING
...AND THEN *HAVE DINNER WHILE FLOATING DOWN A CANAL*, RIGHT?
OKAY, IF WE CAN'T RELY ON THE W.I.T.C.H. VAN, I GUESS WE'LL HAVE TO USE OUR RELOCATION POWER.

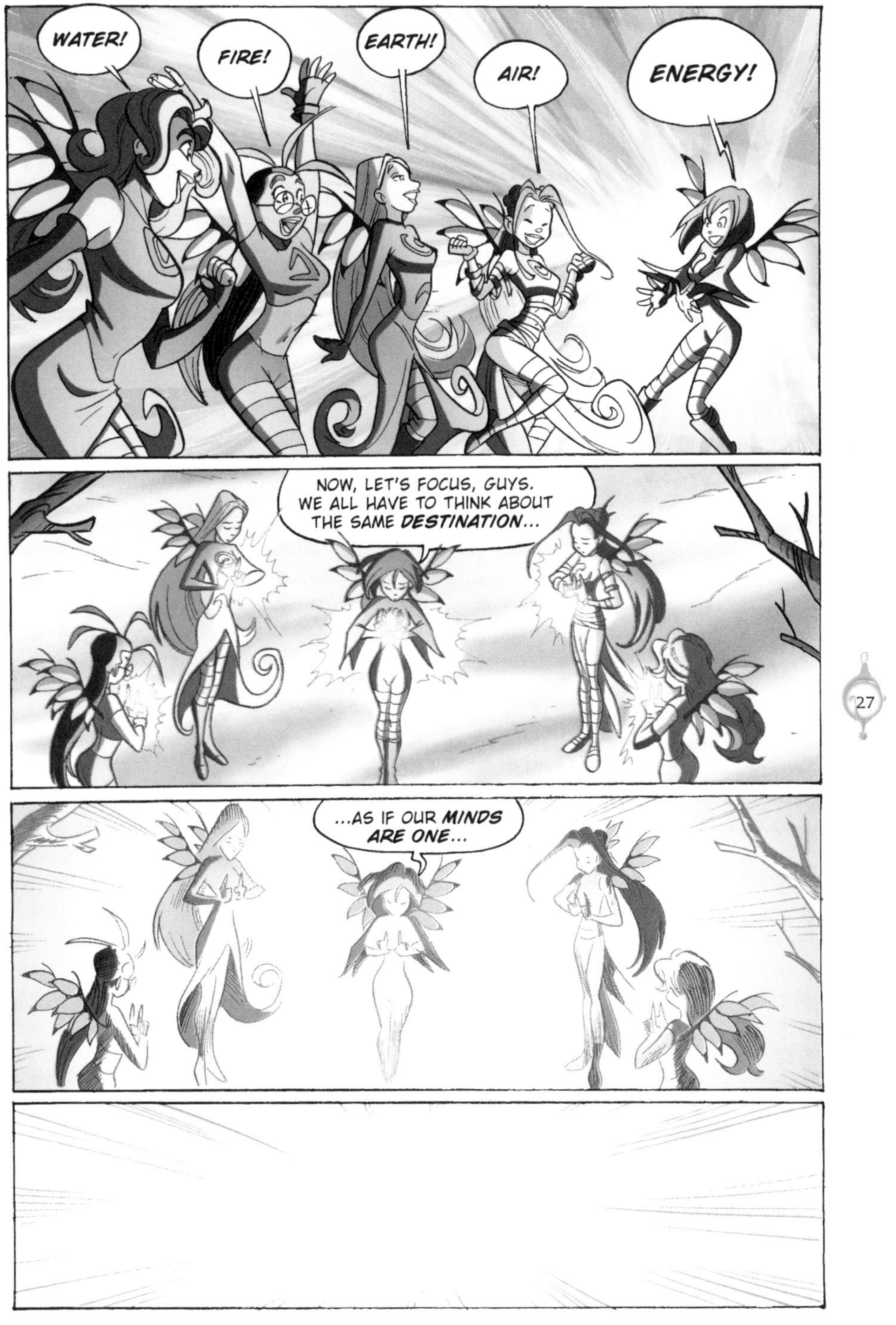
WATER!
FIRE!
EARTH!
AIR!
ENERGY!
NOW, LET'S FOCUS, GUYS. WE ALL HAVE TO THINK ABOUT THE SAME DESTINATION...
...AS IF OUR MINDS ARE ONE...

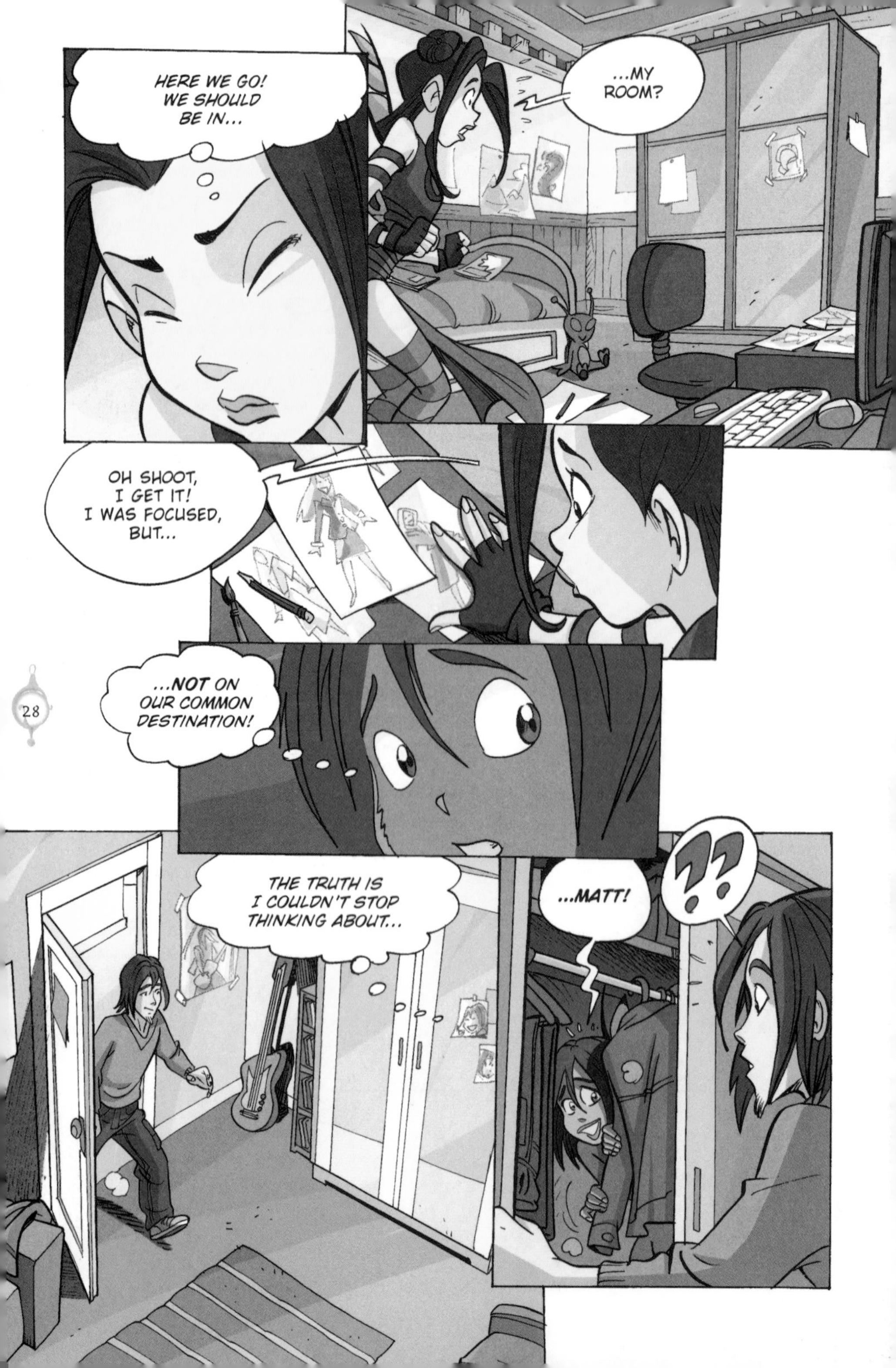
HERE WE GO! WE SHOULD BE IN...
...MY ROOM?
OH SHOOT, I GET IT! I WAS FOCUSED, BUT...
...NOT ON OUR COMMON DESTINATION!
THE TRUTH IS I COULDN'T STOP THINKING ABOUT...
...MATT!
??

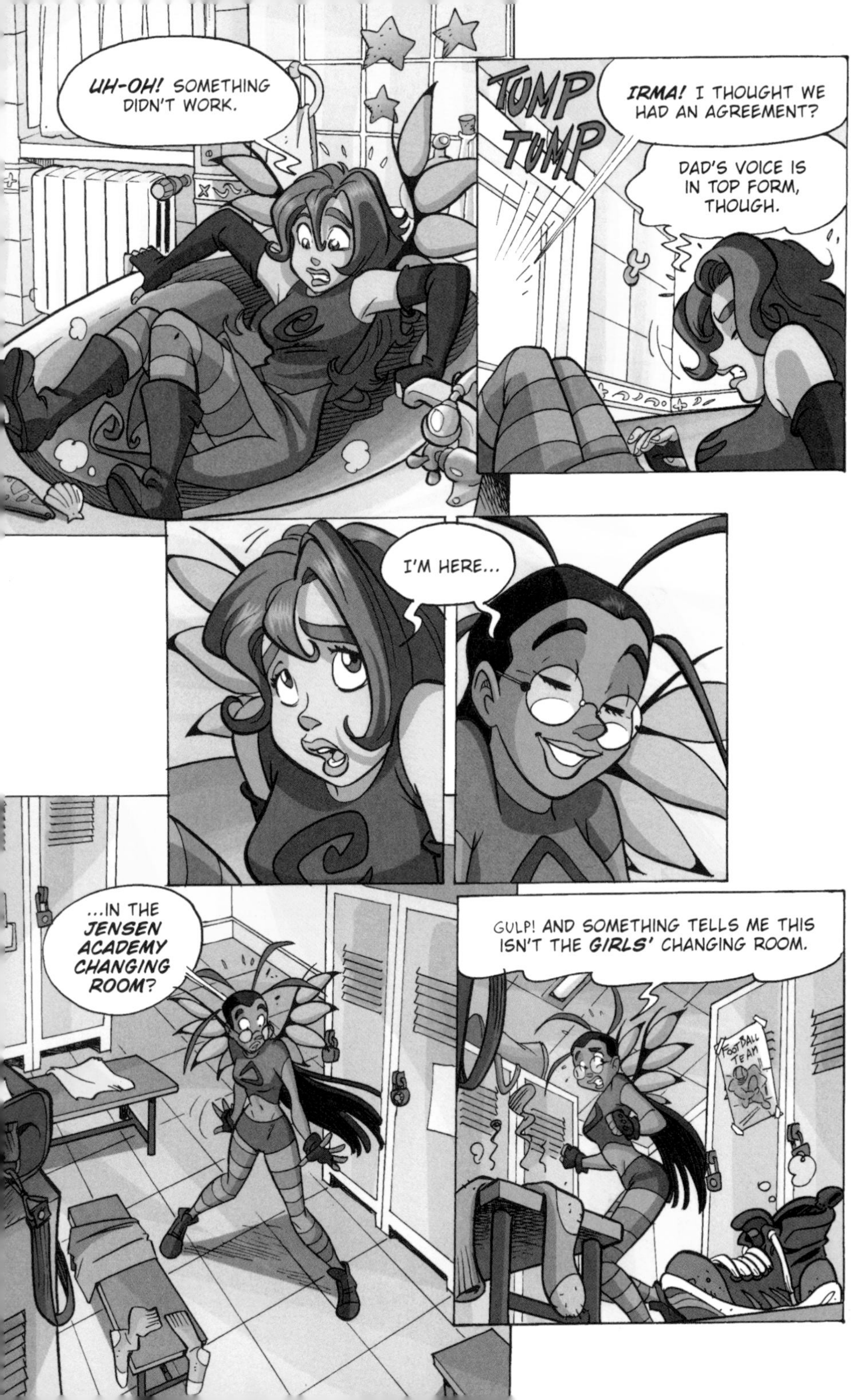
UH-OH! SOMETHING DIDN'T WORK.
TUMP TUMP
IRMA! I THOUGHT WE HAD AN AGREEMENT?
DAD'S VOICE IS IN TOP FORM, THOUGH.
I'M HERE...
...IN THE JENSEN ACADEMY CHANGING ROOM?
GULP! AND SOMETHING TELLS ME THIS ISN'T THE GIRLS' CHANGING ROOM.
FOOTBALL TEAM

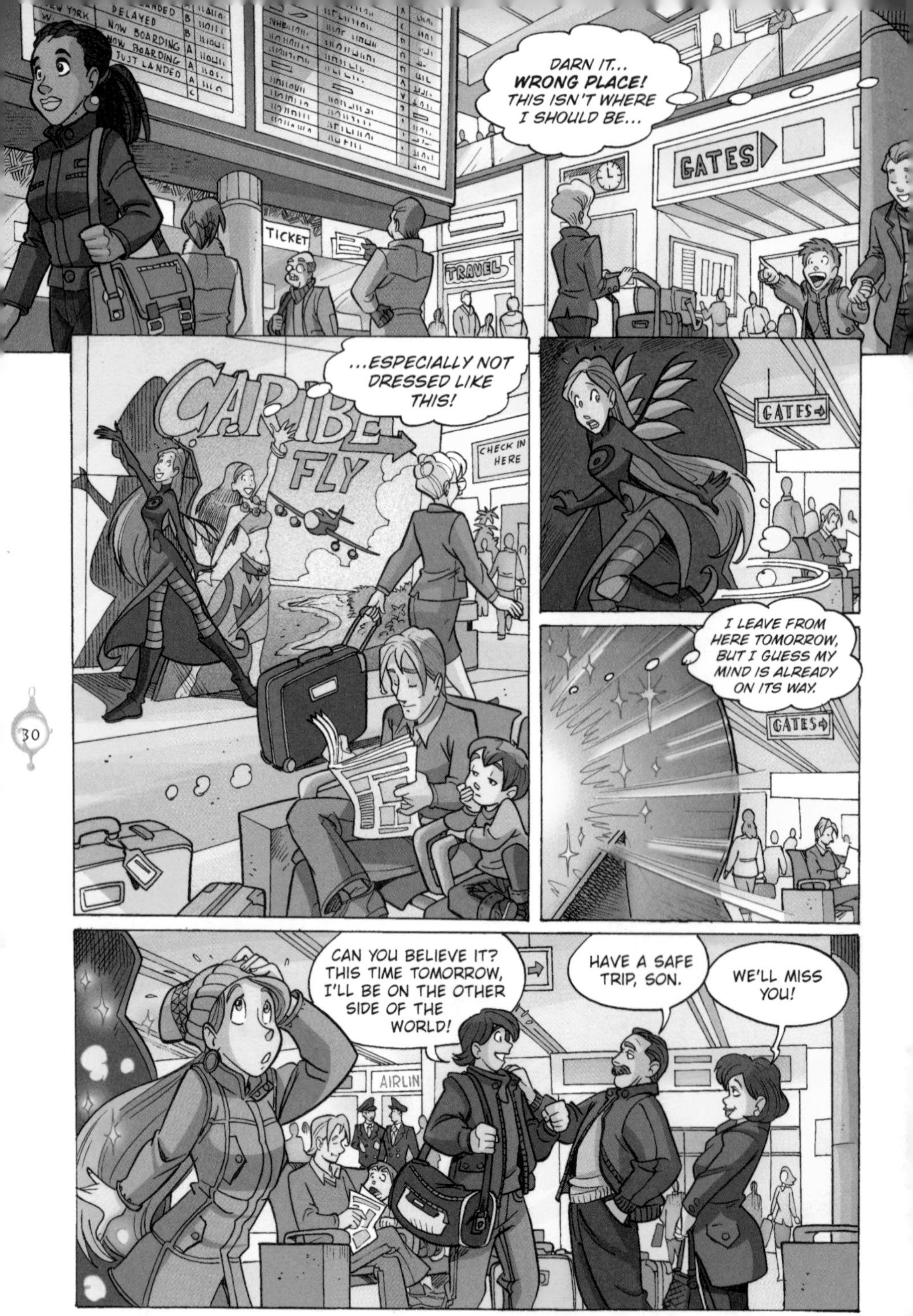
NEW YORK
DELAYED
NOW BOARDING
NOW BOARDING
JUST LANDED
DARN IT... **WRONG PLACE!** THIS ISN'T WHERE I SHOULD BE...
TICKET
TRAVEL
GATES
...ESPECIALLY NOT DRESSED LIKE THIS!
CARIBE
FLY
CHECK IN HERE
GATES
I LEAVE FROM HERE TOMORROW, BUT I GUESS MY MIND IS ALREADY ON ITS WAY.
GATES
CAN YOU BELIEVE IT? THIS TIME TOMORROW, I'LL BE ON THE OTHER SIDE OF THE WORLD!
AIRLIN
HAVE A SAFE TRIP, SON.
WE'LL MISS YOU!

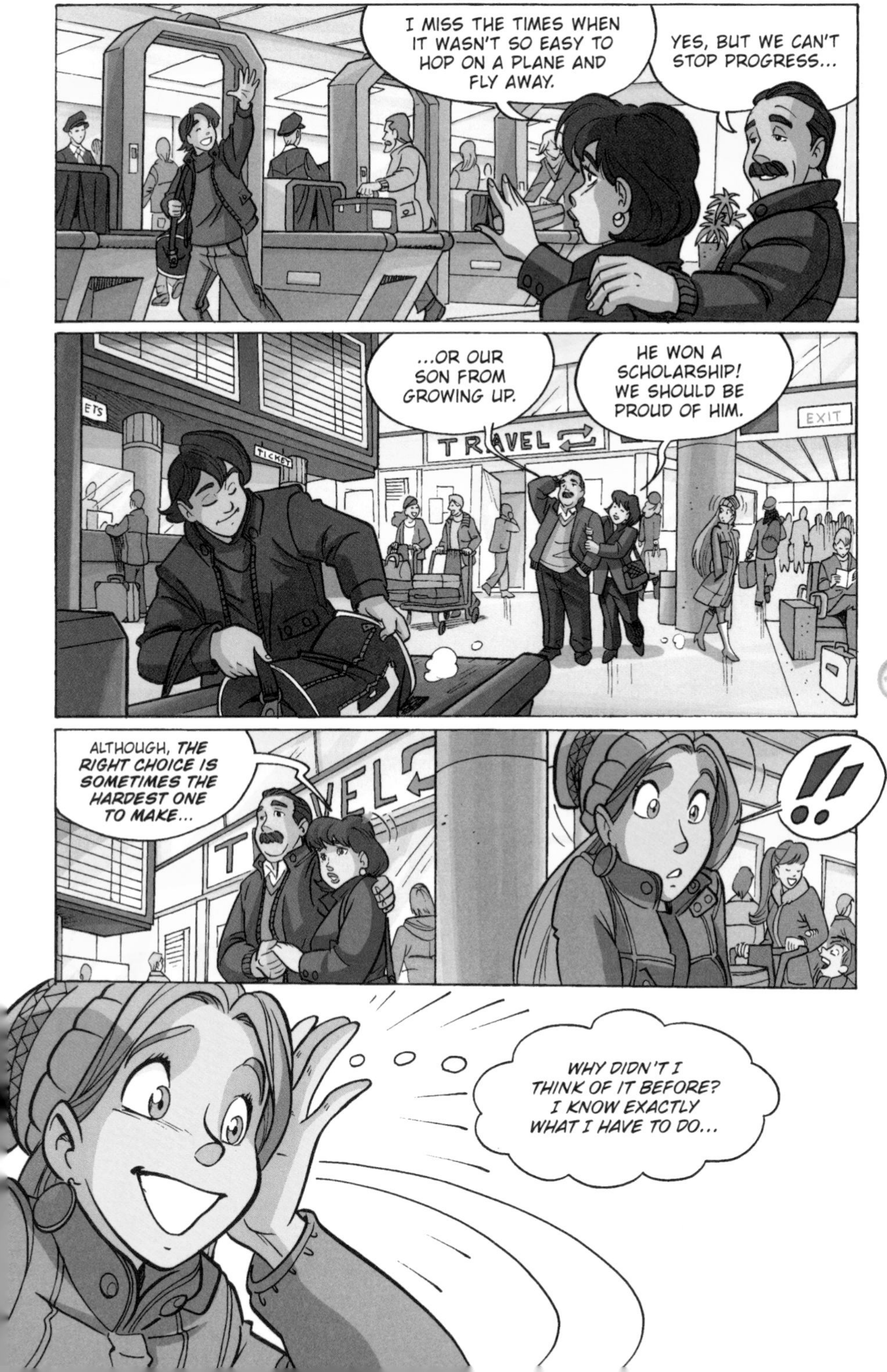
I MISS THE TIMES WHEN IT WASN'T SO EASY TO HOP ON A PLANE AND FLY AWAY.
YES, BUT WE CAN'T STOP PROGRESS...
...OR OUR SON FROM GROWING UP.
HE WON A SCHOLARSHIP! WE SHOULD BE PROUD OF HIM.
TRAVEL
EXIT
TICKET
ALTHOUGH, THE RIGHT CHOICE IS SOMETIMES THE HARDEST ONE TO MAKE...
!!
WHY DIDN'T I THINK OF IT BEFORE? I KNOW EXACTLY WHAT I HAVE TO DO...

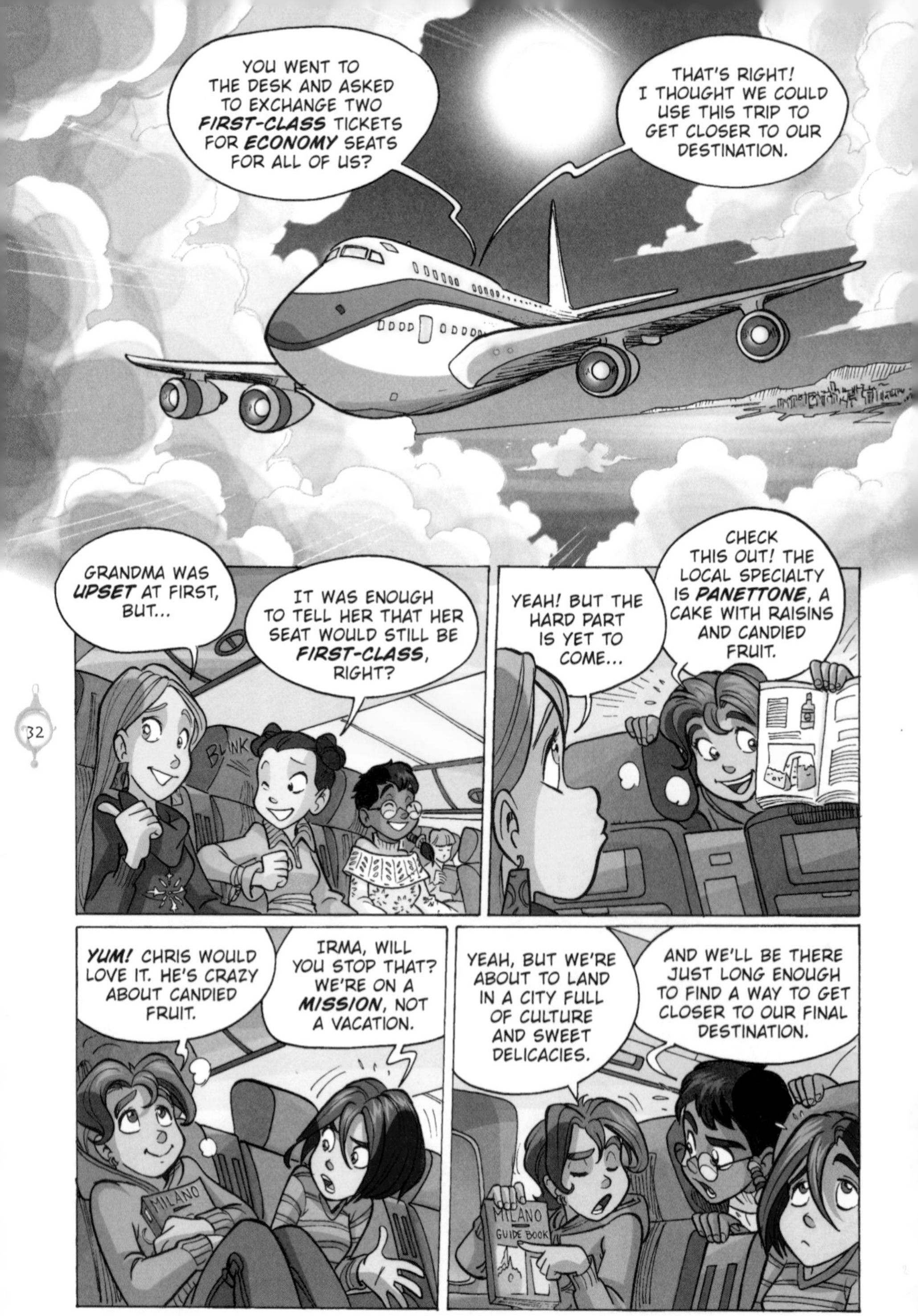
YOU WENT TO THE DESK AND ASKED TO EXCHANGE TWO FIRST-CLASS TICKETS FOR ECONOMY SEATS FOR ALL OF US?
THAT'S RIGHT! I THOUGHT WE COULD USE THIS TRIP TO GET CLOSER TO OUR DESTINATION.
GRANDMA WAS UPSET AT FIRST, BUT...
IT WAS ENOUGH TO TELL HER THAT HER SEAT WOULD STILL BE FIRST-CLASS, RIGHT?
BLINK
YEAH! BUT THE HARD PART IS YET TO COME...
CHECK THIS OUT! THE LOCAL SPECIALTY IS PANETTONE, A CAKE WITH RAISINS AND CANDIED FRUIT.
YUM! CHRIS WOULD LOVE IT. HE'S CRAZY ABOUT CANDIED FRUIT.
IRMA, WILL YOU STOP THAT? WE'RE ON A MISSION, NOT A VACATION.
MILANO
YEAH, BUT WE'RE ABOUT TO LAND IN A CITY FULL OF CULTURE AND SWEET DELICACIES.
AND WE'LL BE THERE JUST LONG ENOUGH TO FIND A WAY TO GET CLOSER TO OUR FINAL DESTINATION.
MILANO GUIDE BOOK

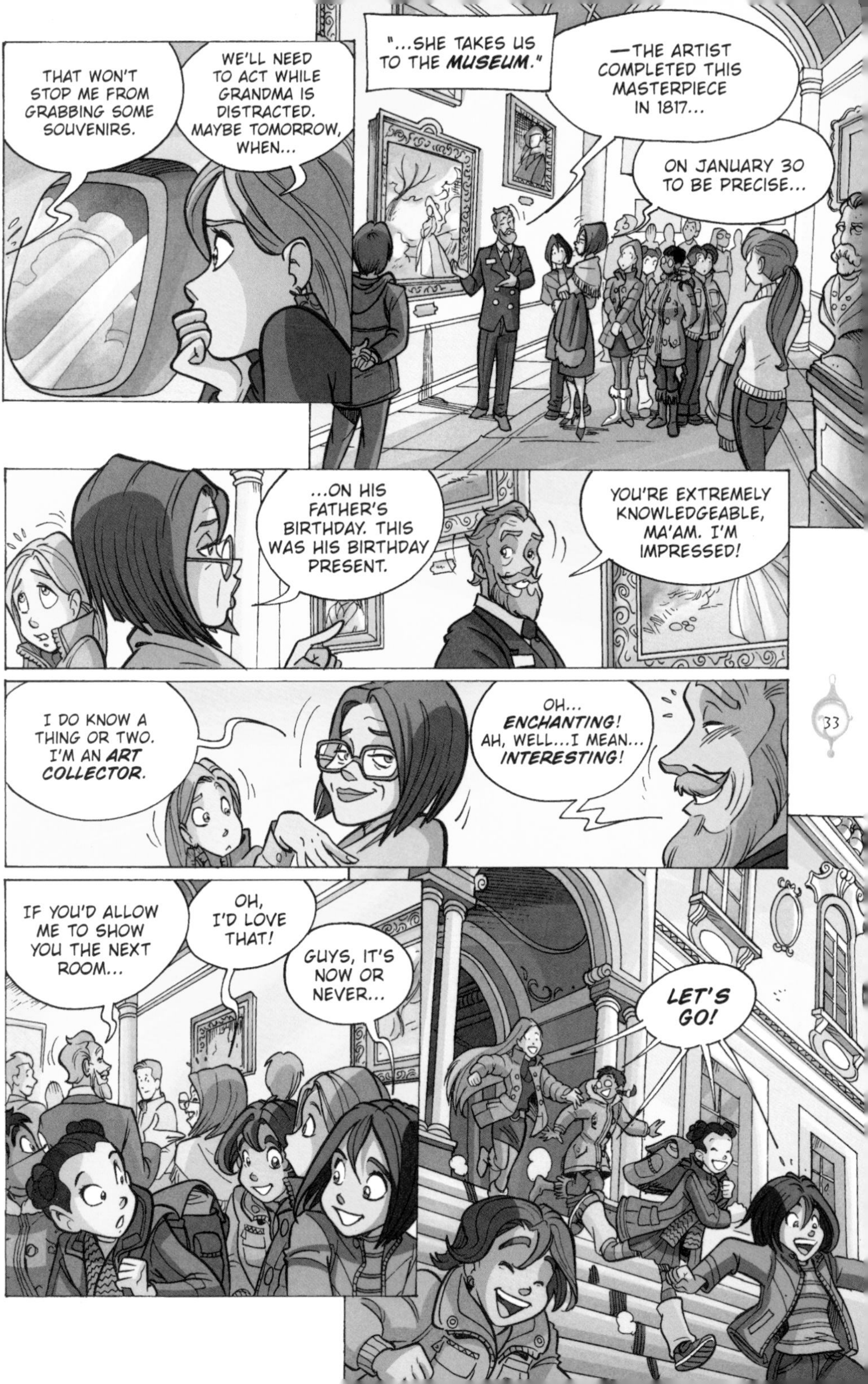
THAT WON'T STOP ME FROM GRABBING SOME SOUVENIRS.
WE'LL NEED TO ACT WHILE GRANDMA IS DISTRACTED. MAYBE TOMORROW, WHEN...
"...SHE TAKES US TO THE MUSEUM."
—THE ARTIST COMPLETED THIS MASTERPIECE IN 1817...
ON JANUARY 30 TO BE PRECISE...
...ON HIS FATHER'S BIRTHDAY. THIS WAS HIS BIRTHDAY PRESENT.
YOU'RE EXTREMELY KNOWLEDGEABLE, MA'AM. I'M IMPRESSED!
I DO KNOW A THING OR TWO. I'M AN ART COLLECTOR.
OH... ENCHANTING! AH, WELL...I MEAN... INTERESTING!
IF YOU'D ALLOW ME TO SHOW YOU THE NEXT ROOM...
OH, I'D LOVE THAT!
GUYS, IT'S NOW OR NEVER...
LET'S GO!

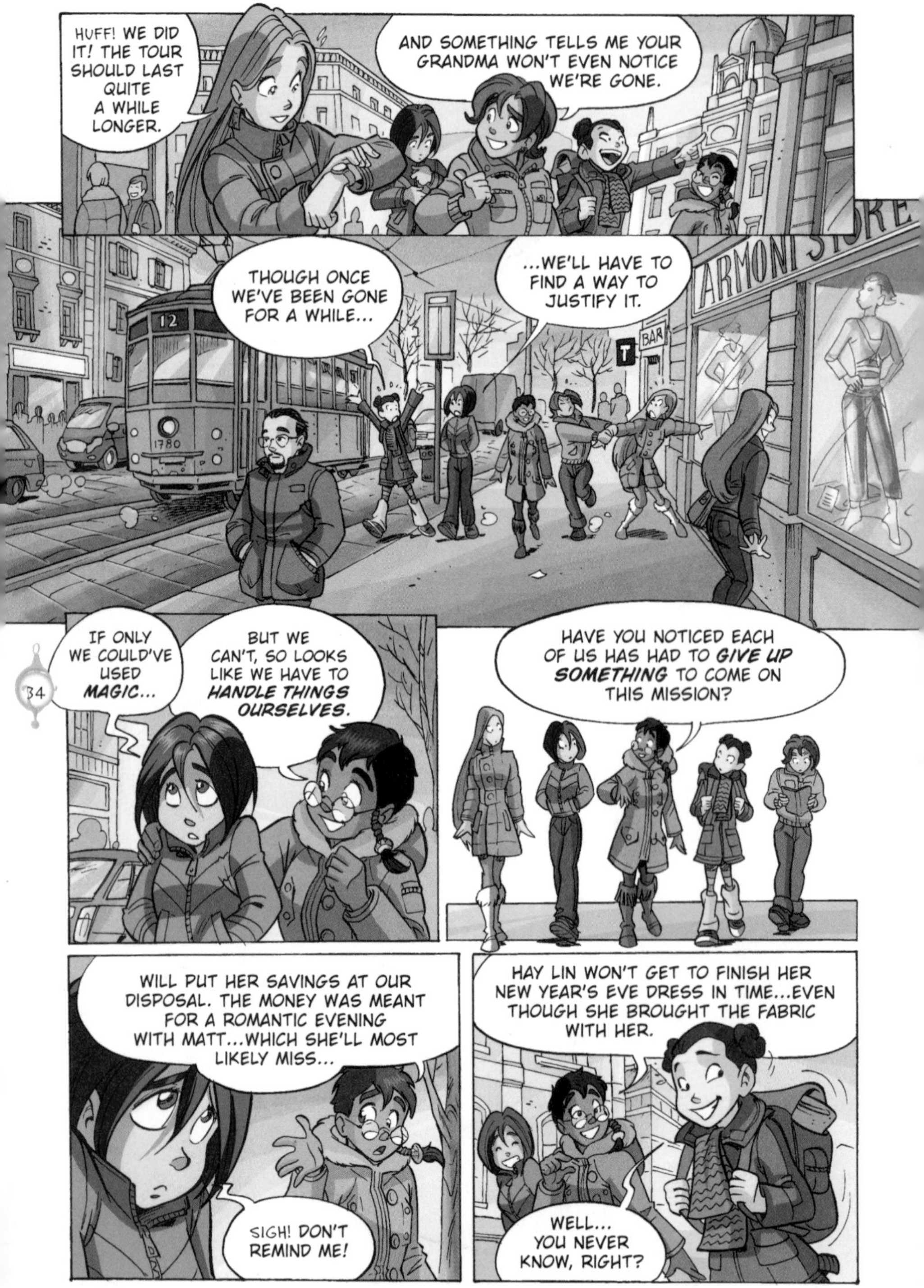
HUFF! WE DID IT! THE TOUR SHOULD LAST QUITE A WHILE LONGER.
AND SOMETHING TELLS ME YOUR GRANDMA WON'T EVEN NOTICE WE'RE GONE.
ARMONI STORE
BAR
T
12
1780
THOUGH ONCE WE'VE BEEN GONE FOR A WHILE...
...WE'LL HAVE TO FIND A WAY TO JUSTIFY IT.
IF ONLY WE COULD'VE USED *MAGIC*...
BUT WE CAN'T, SO LOOKS LIKE WE HAVE TO *HANDLE THINGS OURSELVES*.
HAVE YOU NOTICED EACH OF US HAS HAD TO *GIVE UP SOMETHING* TO COME ON THIS MISSION?
WILL PUT HER SAVINGS AT OUR DISPOSAL. THE MONEY WAS MEANT FOR A ROMANTIC EVENING WITH MATT...WHICH SHE'LL MOST LIKELY MISS...
SIGH! DON'T REMIND ME!
HAY LIN WON'T GET TO FINISH HER NEW YEAR'S EVE DRESS IN TIME...EVEN THOUGH SHE BROUGHT THE FABRIC WITH HER.
WELL... YOU NEVER KNOW, RIGHT?

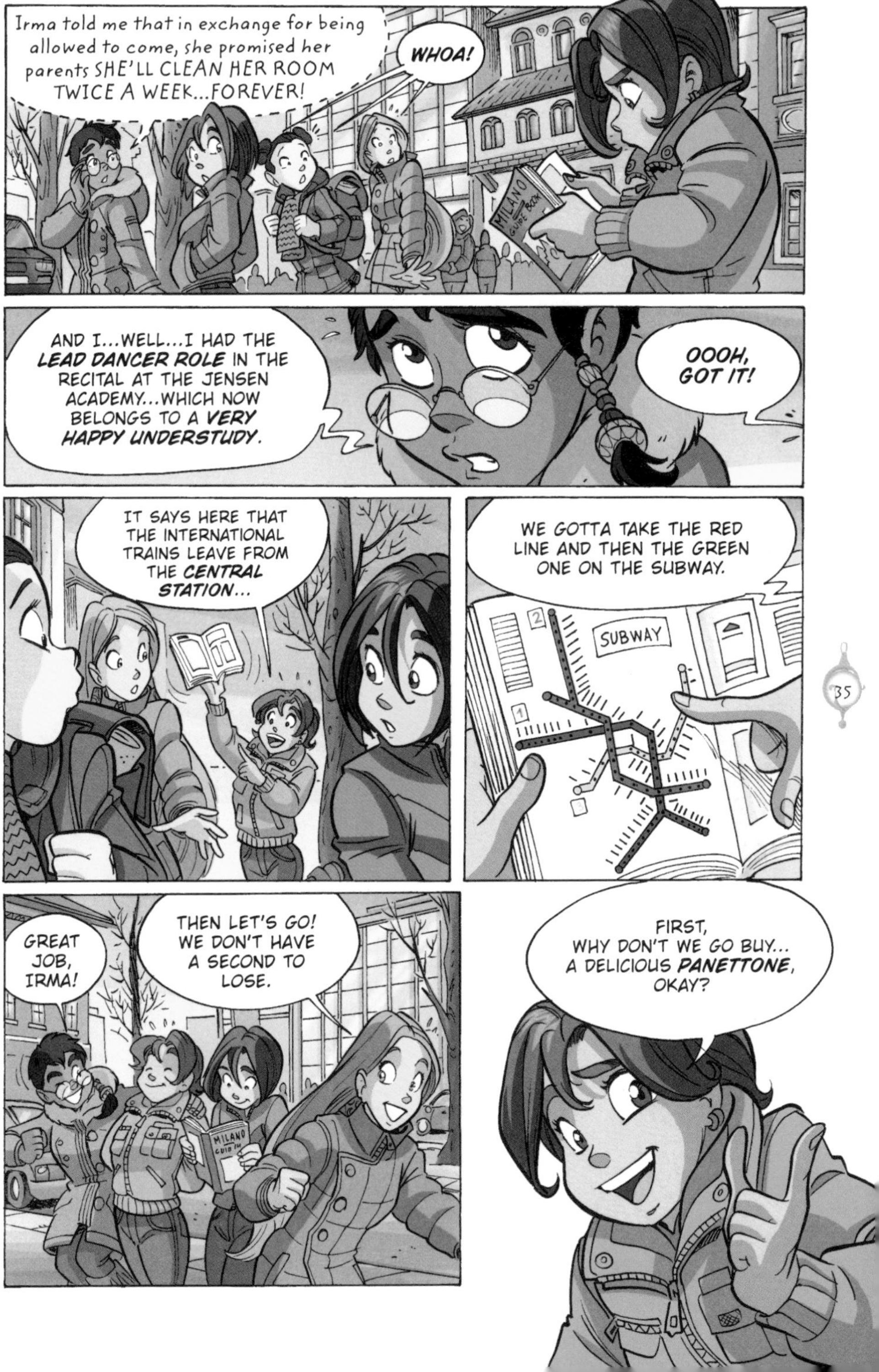

Irma told me that in exchange for being allowed to come, she promised her parents SHE'LL CLEAN HER ROOM TWICE A WEEK...FOREVER!
WHOA!
MILANO GUIDE BOOK
AND I...WELL...I HAD THE LEAD DANCER ROLE IN THE RECITAL AT THE JENSEN ACADEMY...WHICH NOW BELONGS TO A VERY HAPPY UNDERSTUDY.
OOOH, GOT IT!
IT SAYS HERE THAT THE INTERNATIONAL TRAINS LEAVE FROM THE CENTRAL STATION...
WE GOTTA TAKE THE RED LINE AND THEN THE GREEN ONE ON THE SUBWAY.
SUBWAY
GREAT JOB, IRMA!
THEN LET'S GO! WE DON'T HAVE A SECOND TO LOSE.
FIRST, WHY DON'T WE GO BUY... A DELICIOUS PANETTONE, OKAY?

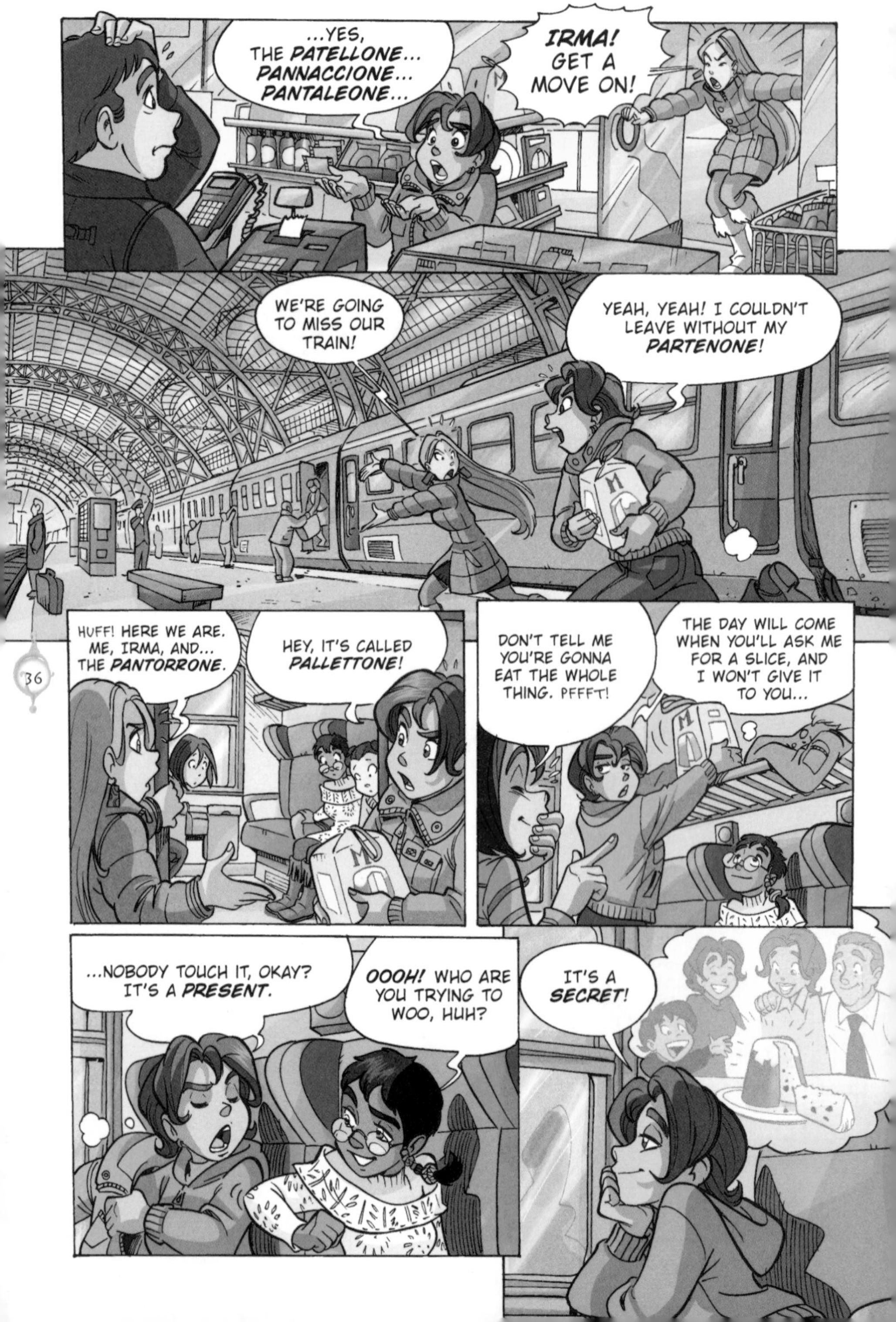
...YES, THE PATELLONE... PANNACCIONE... PANTALEONE...
IRMA! GET A MOVE ON!
WE'RE GOING TO MISS OUR TRAIN!
YEAH, YEAH! I COULDN'T LEAVE WITHOUT MY PARTENONE!
HUFF! HERE WE ARE. ME, IRMA, AND... THE PANTORRONE.
HEY, IT'S CALLED PALLETTONE!
DON'T TELL ME YOU'RE GONNA EAT THE WHOLE THING. PFFFT!
THE DAY WILL COME WHEN YOU'LL ASK ME FOR A SLICE, AND I WON'T GIVE IT TO YOU...
...NOBODY TOUCH IT, OKAY? IT'S A PRESENT.
OOOH! WHO ARE YOU TRYING TO WOO, HUH?
IT'S A SECRET!

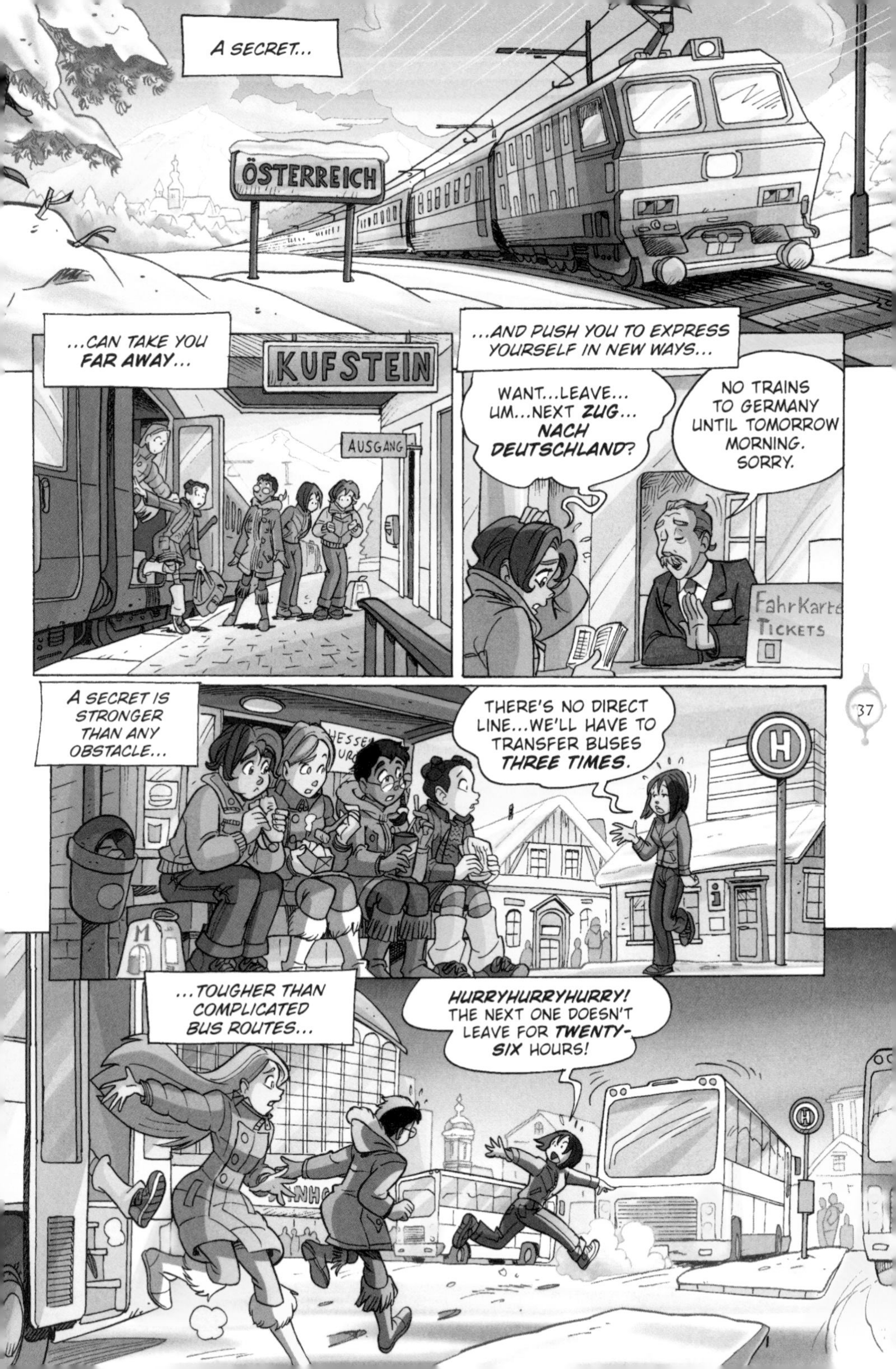
A SECRET...
ÖSTERREICH
...CAN TAKE YOU FAR AWAY...
KUFSTEIN
AUSGANG
...AND PUSH YOU TO EXPRESS YOURSELF IN NEW WAYS...
WANT...LEAVE... UM...NEXT ZUG... NACH DEUTSCHLAND?
NO TRAINS TO GERMANY UNTIL TOMORROW MORNING. SORRY.
FahrKarte
TICKETS
A SECRET IS STRONGER THAN ANY OBSTACLE...
THERE'S NO DIRECT LINE...WE'LL HAVE TO TRANSFER BUSES THREE TIMES.
H
...TOUGHER THAN COMPLICATED BUS ROUTES...
HURRYHURRYHURRY! THE NEXT ONE DOESN'T LEAVE FOR TWENTY-SIX HOURS!
H

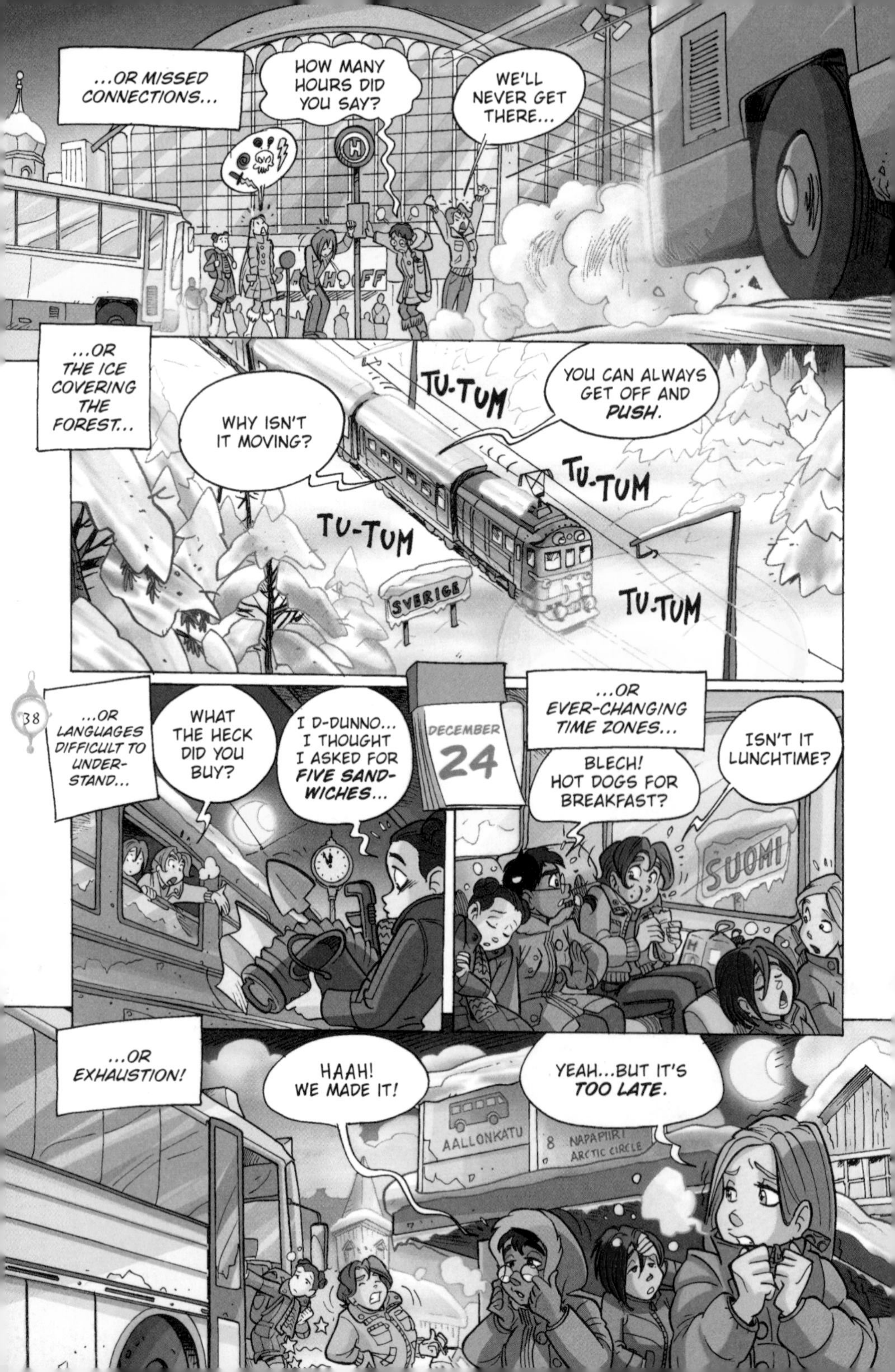

...OR MISSED CONNECTIONS...
HOW MANY HOURS DID YOU SAY?
WE'LL NEVER GET THERE...
H
...OR THE ICE COVERING THE FOREST...
WHY ISN'T IT MOVING?
TU-TUM
YOU CAN ALWAYS GET OFF AND *PUSH*.
TU-TUM
TU-TUM
SVERIGE
TU-TUM
...OR LANGUAGES DIFFICULT TO UNDER-STAND...
WHAT THE HECK DID YOU BUY?
I D-DUNNO... I THOUGHT I ASKED FOR *FIVE SAND-WICHES*...
DECEMBER
24
...OR EVER-CHANGING TIME ZONES...
BLECH! HOT DOGS FOR BREAKFAST?
ISN'T IT LUNCHTIME?
SUOMI
...OR EXHAUSTION!
HAAH! WE MADE IT!
YEAH...BUT IT'S *TOO LATE*.
AALLONKATU
8 NAPAPIIRI ARCTIC CIRCLE

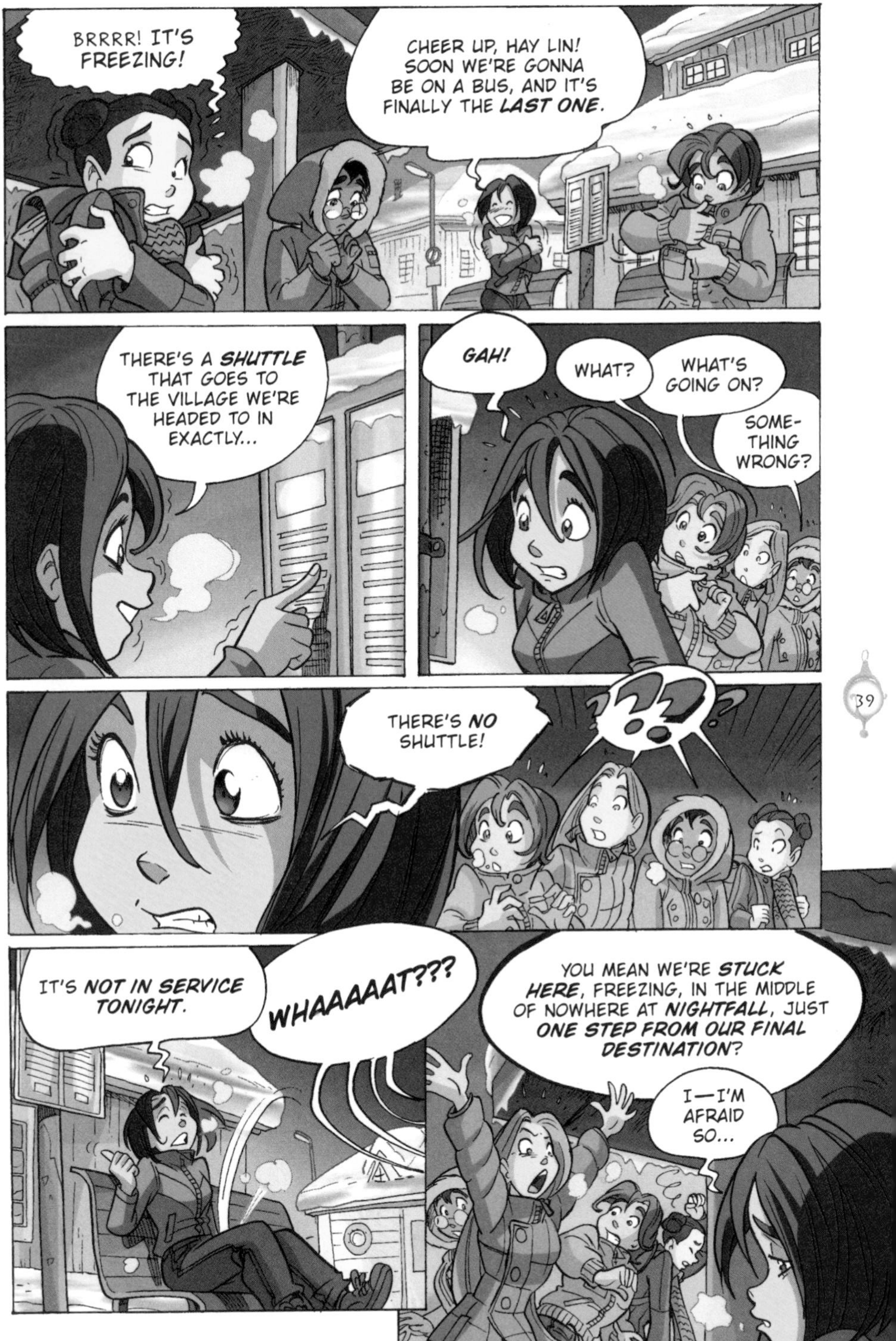
BRRRR! IT'S FREEZING!
CHEER UP, HAY LIN! SOON WE'RE GONNA BE ON A BUS, AND IT'S FINALLY THE LAST ONE.
THERE'S A SHUTTLE THAT GOES TO THE VILLAGE WE'RE HEADED TO IN EXACTLY...
GAH!
WHAT?
WHAT'S GOING ON?
SOME-THING WRONG?
THERE'S NO SHUTTLE!
IT'S NOT IN SERVICE TONIGHT.
WHAAAAAT???
YOU MEAN WE'RE STUCK HERE, FREEZING, IN THE MIDDLE OF NOWHERE AT NIGHTFALL, JUST ONE STEP FROM OUR FINAL DESTINATION?
I—I'M AFRAID SO...

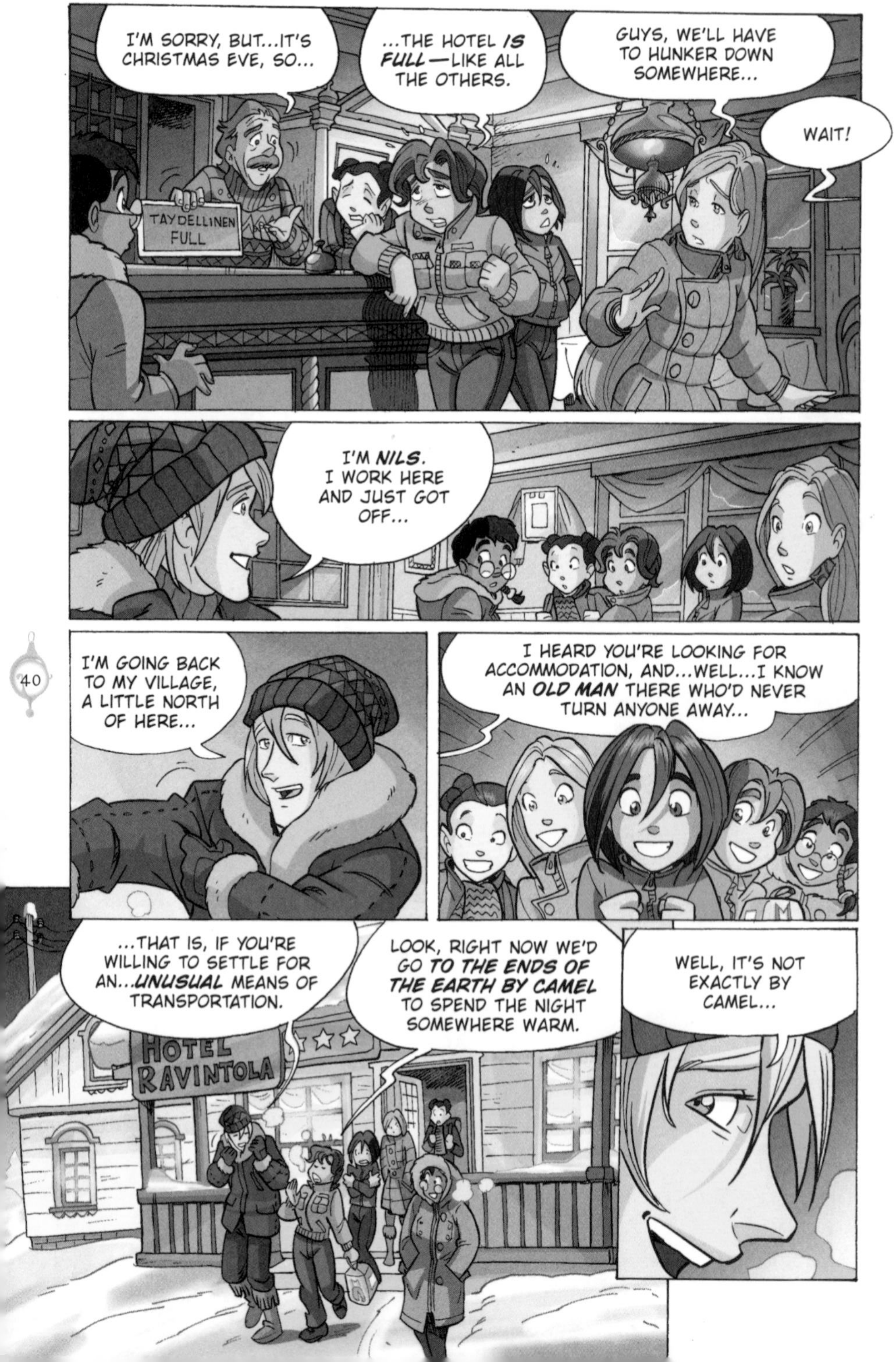
I'M SORRY, BUT...IT'S CHRISTMAS EVE, SO...
TAYDELLINEN FULL
...THE HOTEL IS FULL—LIKE ALL THE OTHERS.
GUYS, WE'LL HAVE TO HUNKER DOWN SOMEWHERE...
WAIT!
I'M NILS. I WORK HERE AND JUST GOT OFF...
I'M GOING BACK TO MY VILLAGE, A LITTLE NORTH OF HERE...
I HEARD YOU'RE LOOKING FOR ACCOMMODATION, AND...WELL...I KNOW AN OLD MAN THERE WHO'D NEVER TURN ANYONE AWAY...
...THAT IS, IF YOU'RE WILLING TO SETTLE FOR AN...UNUSUAL MEANS OF TRANSPORTATION.
LOOK, RIGHT NOW WE'D GO TO THE ENDS OF THE EARTH BY CAMEL TO SPEND THE NIGHT SOMEWHERE WARM.
WELL, IT'S NOT EXACTLY BY CAMEL...
HOTEL RAVINTOLA

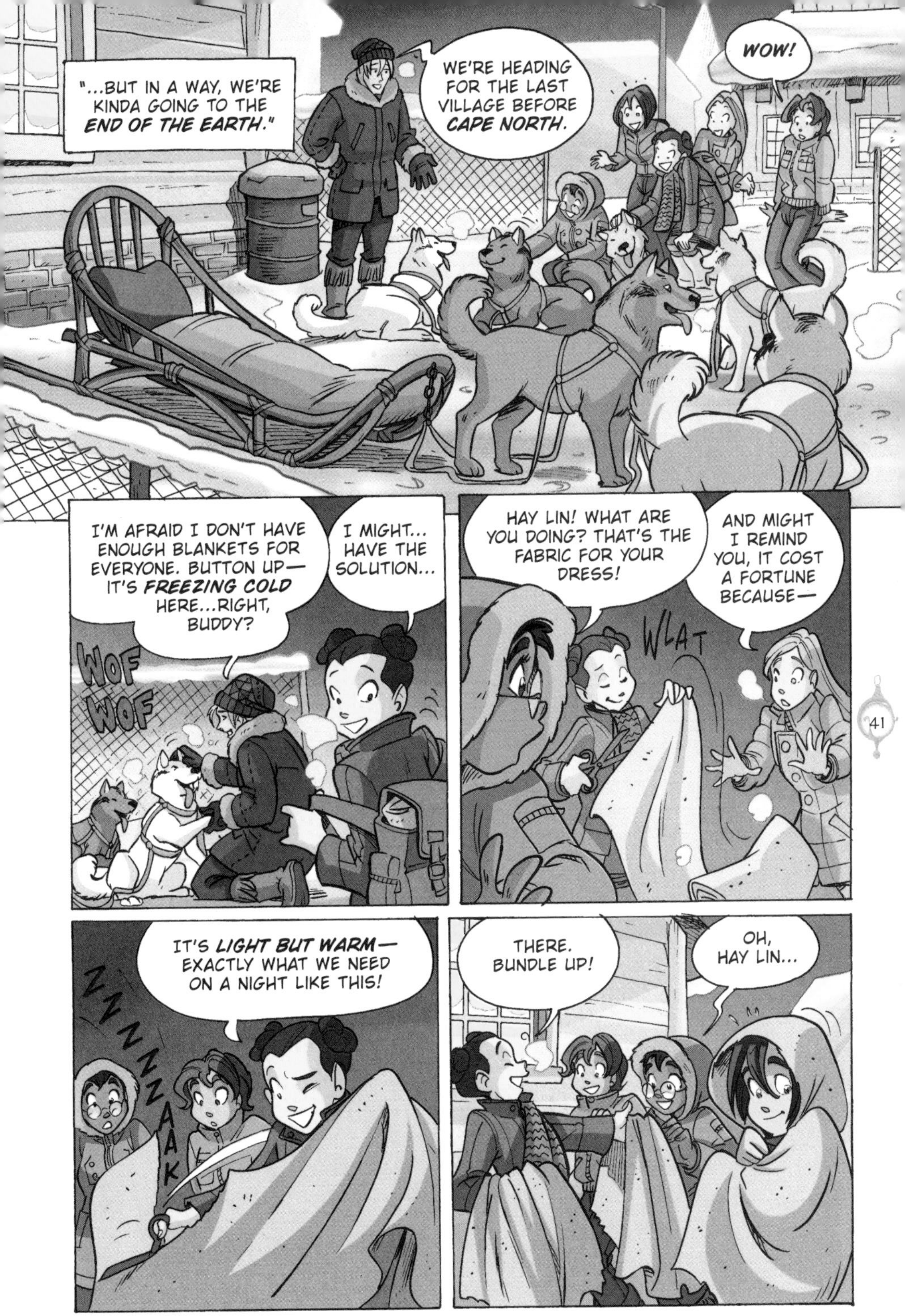
"...BUT IN A WAY, WE'RE KINDA GOING TO THE ***END OF THE EARTH***."
WE'RE HEADING FOR THE LAST VILLAGE BEFORE ***CAPE NORTH***.
WOW!
I'M AFRAID I DON'T HAVE ENOUGH BLANKETS FOR EVERYONE. BUTTON UP— IT'S ***FREEZING COLD*** HERE...RIGHT, BUDDY?
WOF WOF
I MIGHT... HAVE THE SOLUTION...
HAY LIN! WHAT ARE YOU DOING? THAT'S THE FABRIC FOR YOUR DRESS!
AND MIGHT I REMIND YOU, IT COST A FORTUNE BECAUSE—
WLAT
IT'S ***LIGHT BUT WARM***— EXACTLY WHAT WE NEED ON A NIGHT LIKE THIS!
ZZZZZAAK
THERE. BUNDLE UP!
OH, HAY LIN...

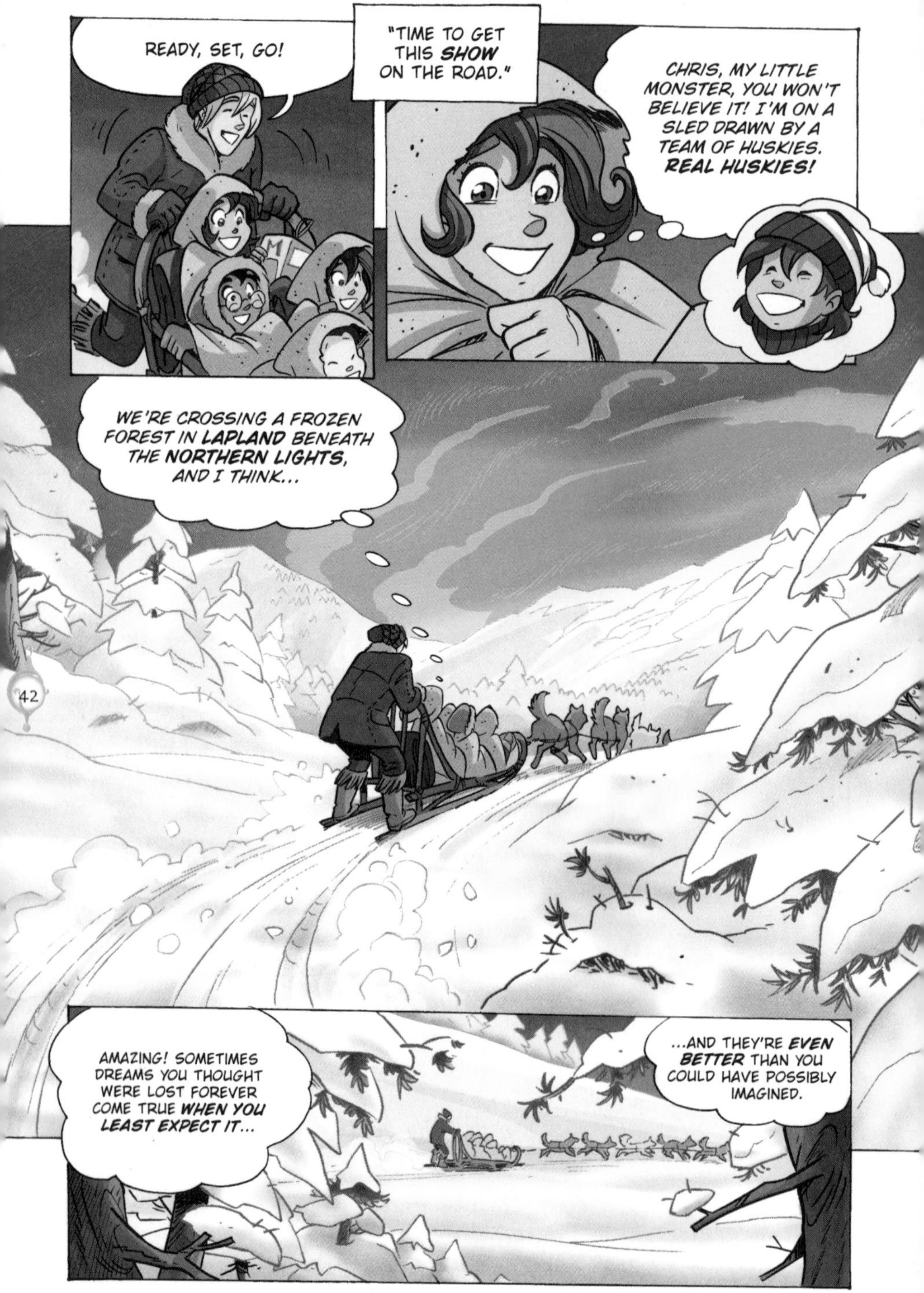
READY, SET, GO!
"TIME TO GET THIS SHOW ON THE ROAD."
CHRIS, MY LITTLE MONSTER, YOU WON'T BELIEVE IT! I'M ON A SLED DRAWN BY A TEAM OF HUSKIES. REAL HUSKIES!
M
WE'RE CROSSING A FROZEN FOREST IN LAPLAND BENEATH THE NORTHERN LIGHTS, AND I THINK...
AMAZING! SOMETIMES DREAMS YOU THOUGHT WERE LOST FOREVER COME TRUE WHEN YOU LEAST EXPECT IT...
...AND THEY'RE EVEN BETTER THAN YOU COULD HAVE POSSIBLY IMAGINED.

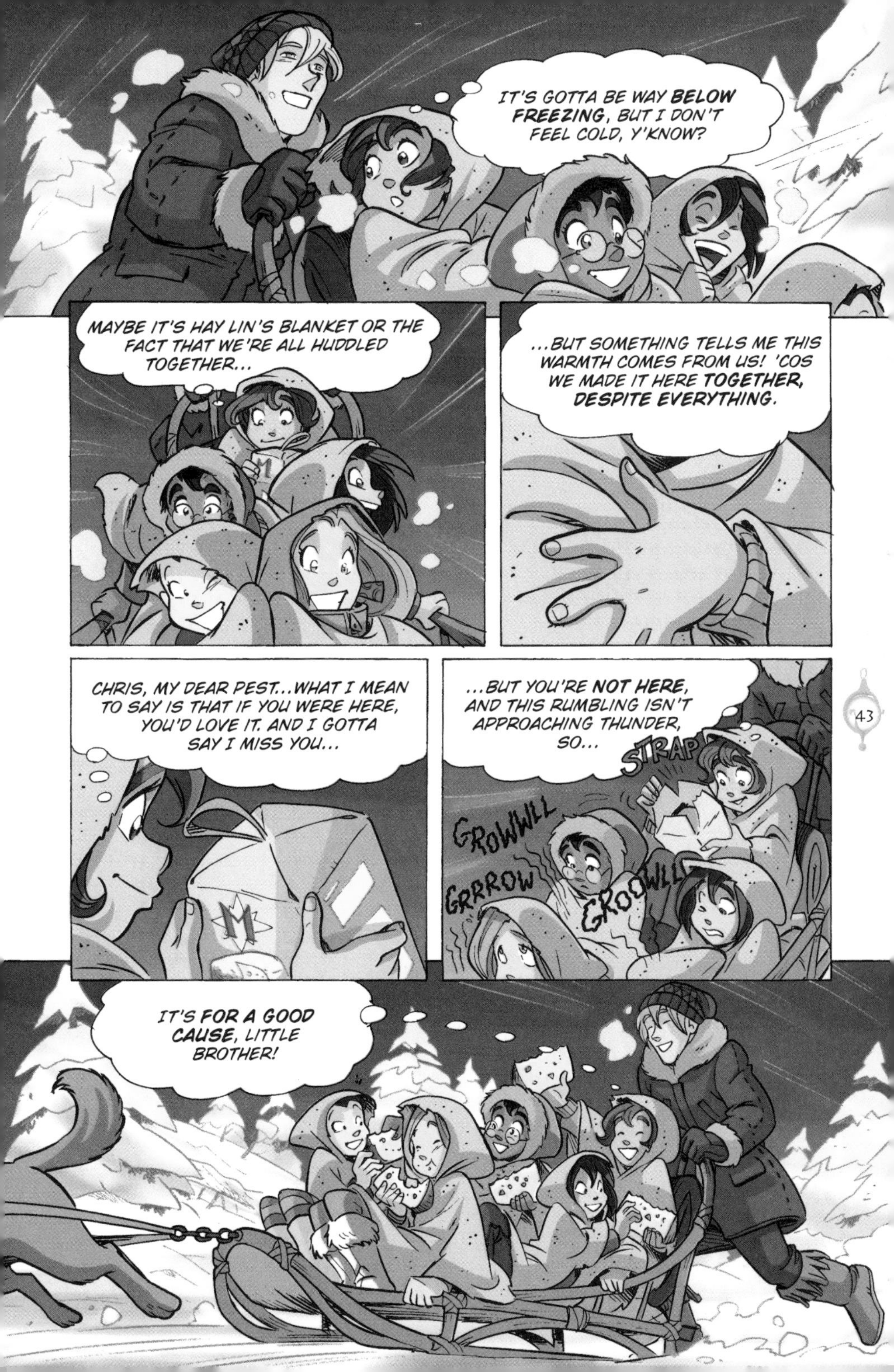

IT'S GOTTA BE WAY BELOW FREEZING, BUT I DON'T FEEL COLD, Y'KNOW?
MAYBE IT'S HAY LIN'S BLANKET OR THE FACT THAT WE'RE ALL HUDDLED TOGETHER...
...BUT SOMETHING TELLS ME THIS WARMTH COMES FROM US! 'COS WE MADE IT HERE TOGETHER, DESPITE EVERYTHING.
CHRIS, MY DEAR PEST...WHAT I MEAN TO SAY IS THAT IF YOU WERE HERE, YOU'D LOVE IT. AND I GOTTA SAY I MISS YOU...
...BUT YOU'RE NOT HERE, AND THIS RUMBLING ISN'T APPROACHING THUNDER, SO...
STRAP!
GROWWLL
GRRROW
GROOWLL
IT'S FOR A GOOD CAUSE, LITTLE BROTHER!

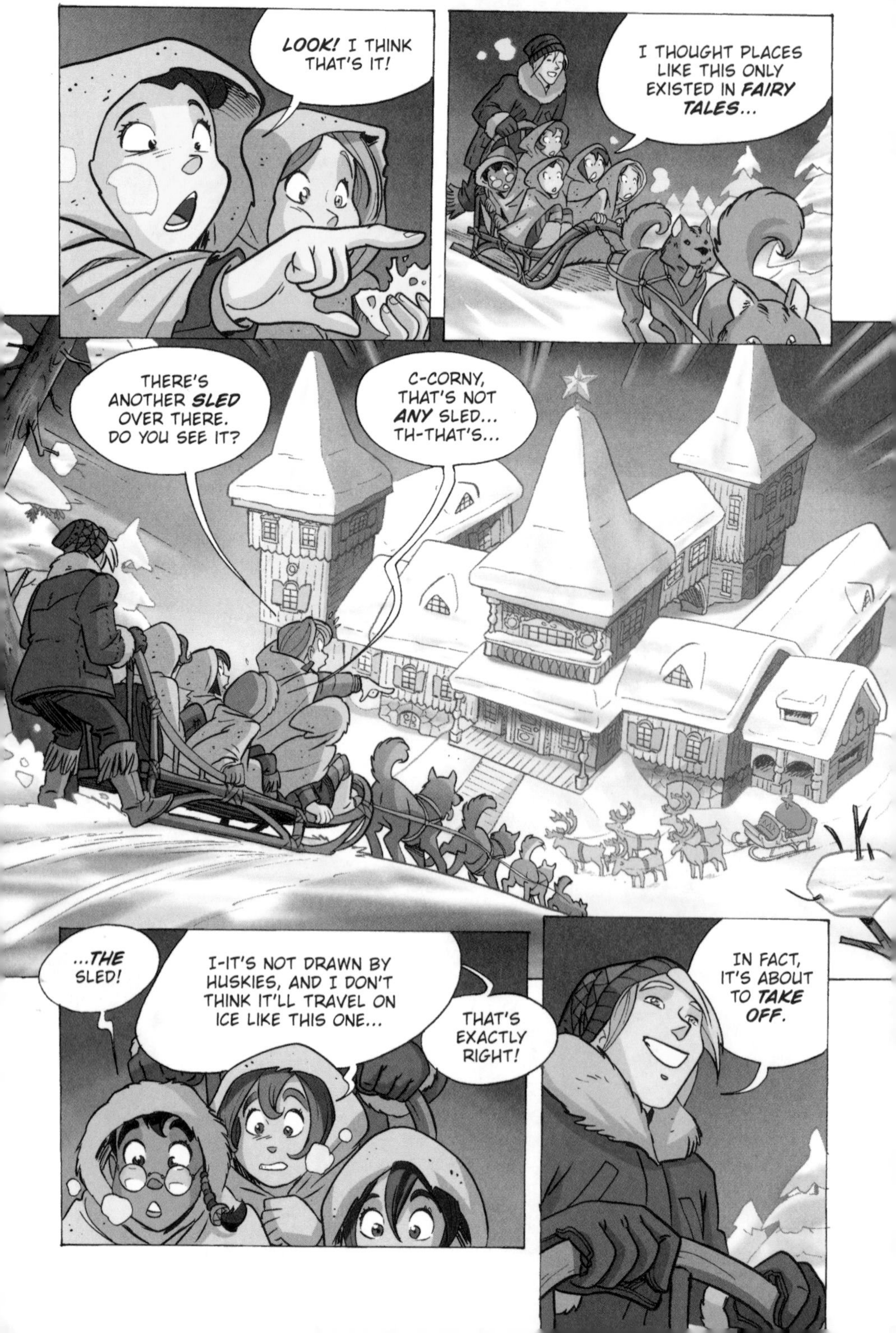
LOOK! I THINK THAT'S IT!
I THOUGHT PLACES LIKE THIS ONLY EXISTED IN FAIRY TALES...
THERE'S ANOTHER SLED OVER THERE. DO YOU SEE IT?
C-CORNY, THAT'S NOT ANY SLED... TH-THAT'S...
...THE SLED!
I-IT'S NOT DRAWN BY HUSKIES, AND I DON'T THINK IT'LL TRAVEL ON ICE LIKE THIS ONE...
THAT'S EXACTLY RIGHT!
IN FACT, IT'S ABOUT TO TAKE OFF.

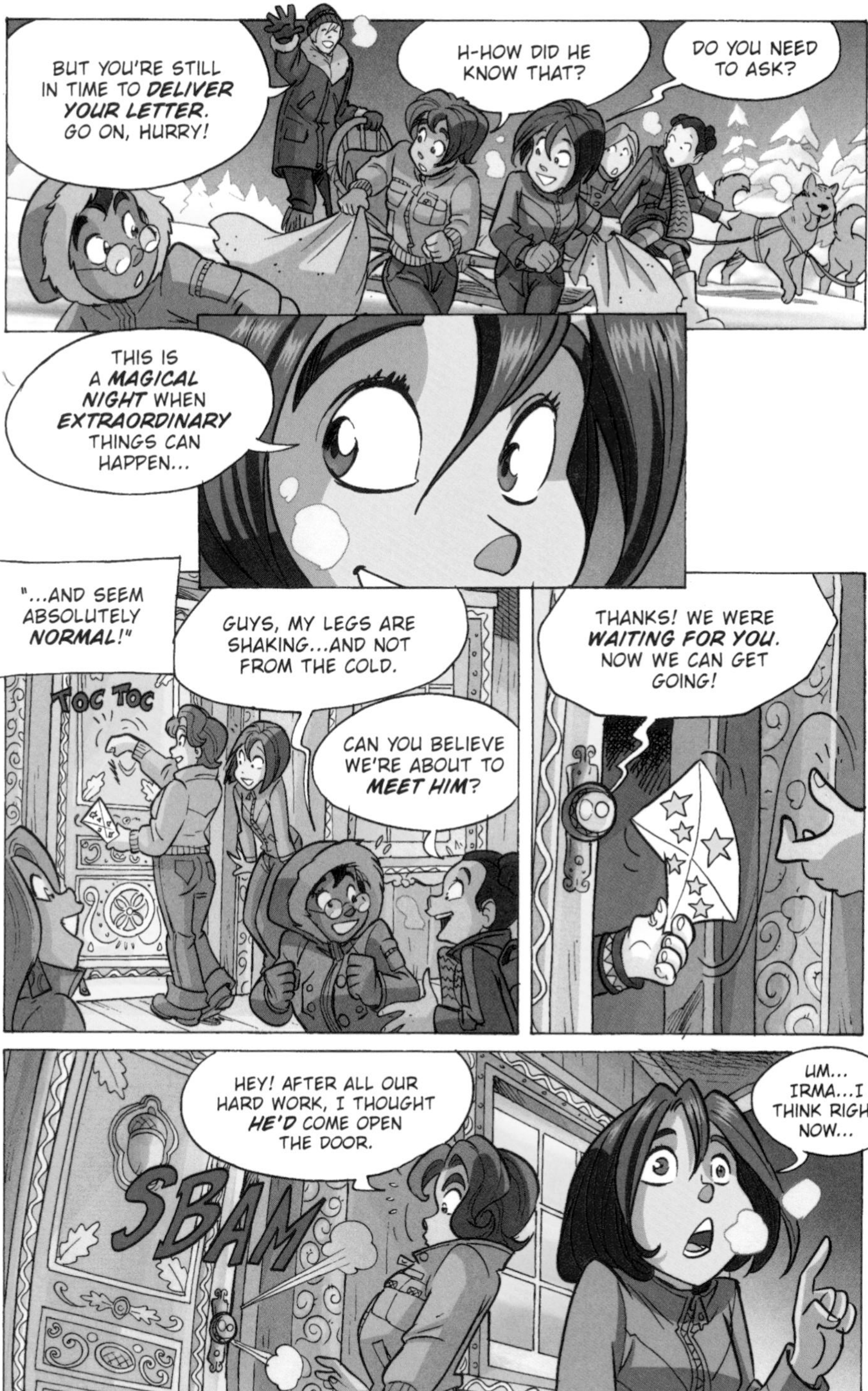
BUT YOU'RE STILL IN TIME TO **DELIVER YOUR LETTER**. GO ON, HURRY!
H-HOW DID HE KNOW THAT?
DO YOU NEED TO ASK?
THIS IS A **MAGICAL NIGHT** WHEN **EXTRAORDINARY** THINGS CAN HAPPEN...
"...AND SEEM ABSOLUTELY **NORMAL!**"
GUYS, MY LEGS ARE SHAKING...AND NOT FROM THE COLD.
TOC TOC
CAN YOU BELIEVE WE'RE ABOUT TO **MEET HIM**?
THANKS! WE WERE **WAITING FOR YOU**. NOW WE CAN GET GOING!
HEY! AFTER ALL OUR HARD WORK, I THOUGHT **HE'D** COME OPEN THE DOOR.
UM... IRMA...I THINK RIGHT NOW...
SBAM

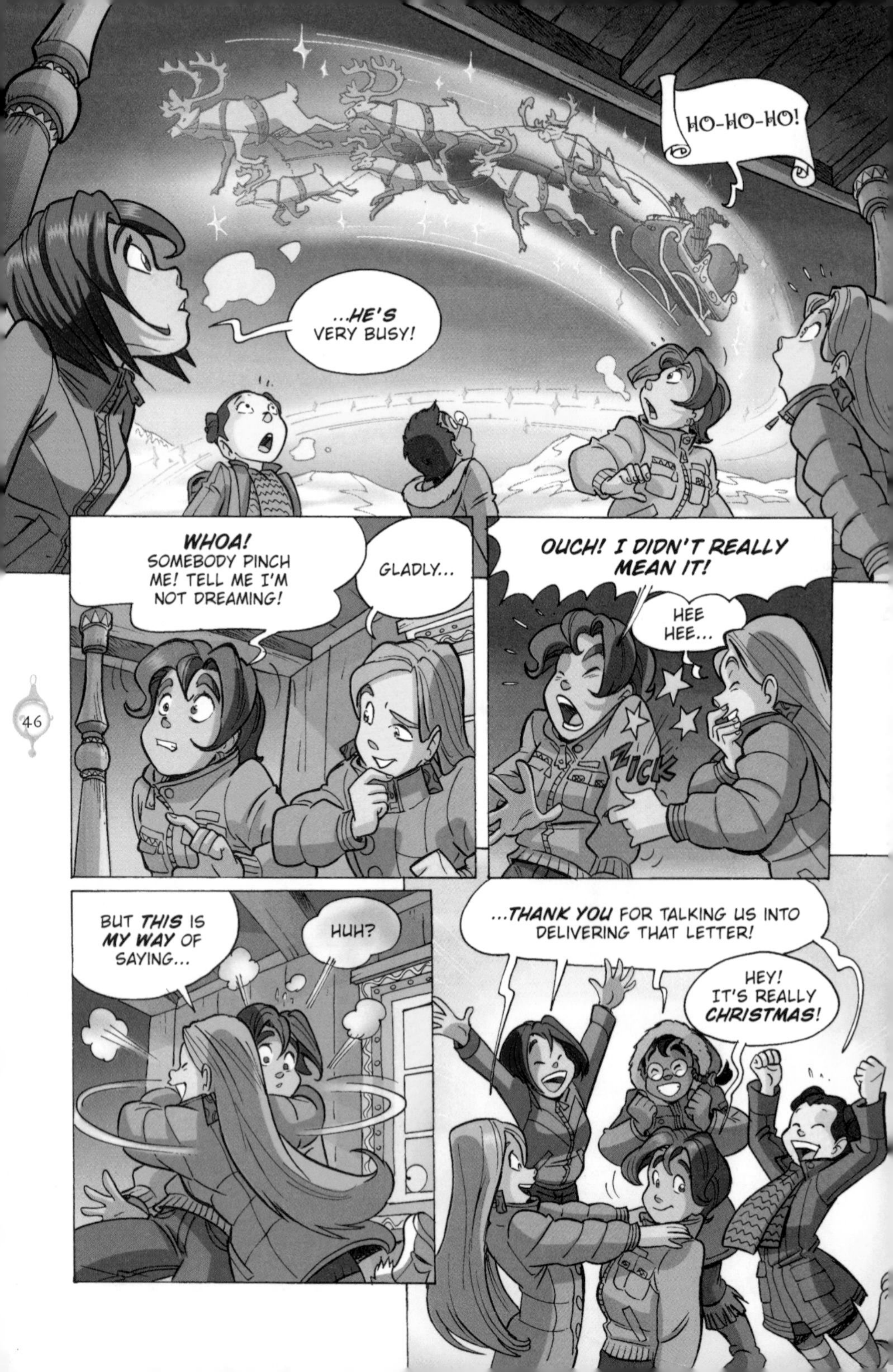
HO-HO-HO!
...HE'S VERY BUSY!
WHOA! SOMEBODY PINCH ME! TELL ME I'M NOT DREAMING!
GLADLY...
OUCH! I DIDN'T REALLY MEAN IT!
HEE HEE...
ZICK
BUT THIS IS MY WAY OF SAYING...
HUH?
...THANK YOU FOR TALKING US INTO DELIVERING THAT LETTER!
HEY! IT'S REALLY CHRISTMAS!

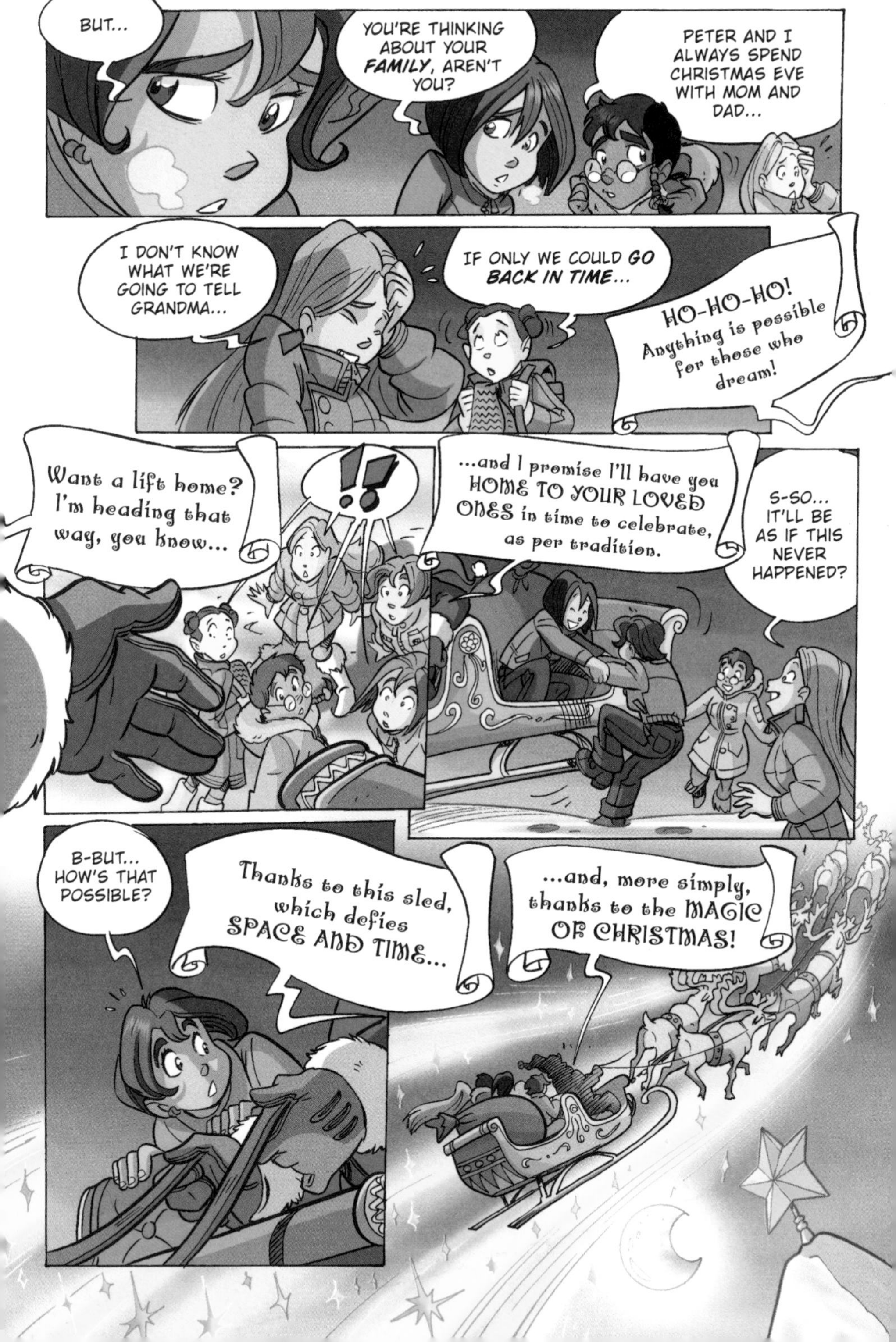

BUT...
YOU'RE THINKING ABOUT YOUR FAMILY, AREN'T YOU?
PETER AND I ALWAYS SPEND CHRISTMAS EVE WITH MOM AND DAD...
I DON'T KNOW WHAT WE'RE GOING TO TELL GRANDMA...
IF ONLY WE COULD GO BACK IN TIME...
HO-HO-HO! Anything is possible for those who dream!
Want a lift home? I'm heading that way, you know...
!!
...and I promise I'll have you HOME TO YOUR LOVED ONES in time to celebrate, as per tradition.
S-SO... IT'LL BE AS IF THIS NEVER HAPPENED?
B-BUT... HOW'S THAT POSSIBLE?
Thanks to this sled, which defies SPACE AND TIME...
...and, more simply, thanks to the MAGIC OF CHRISTMAS!

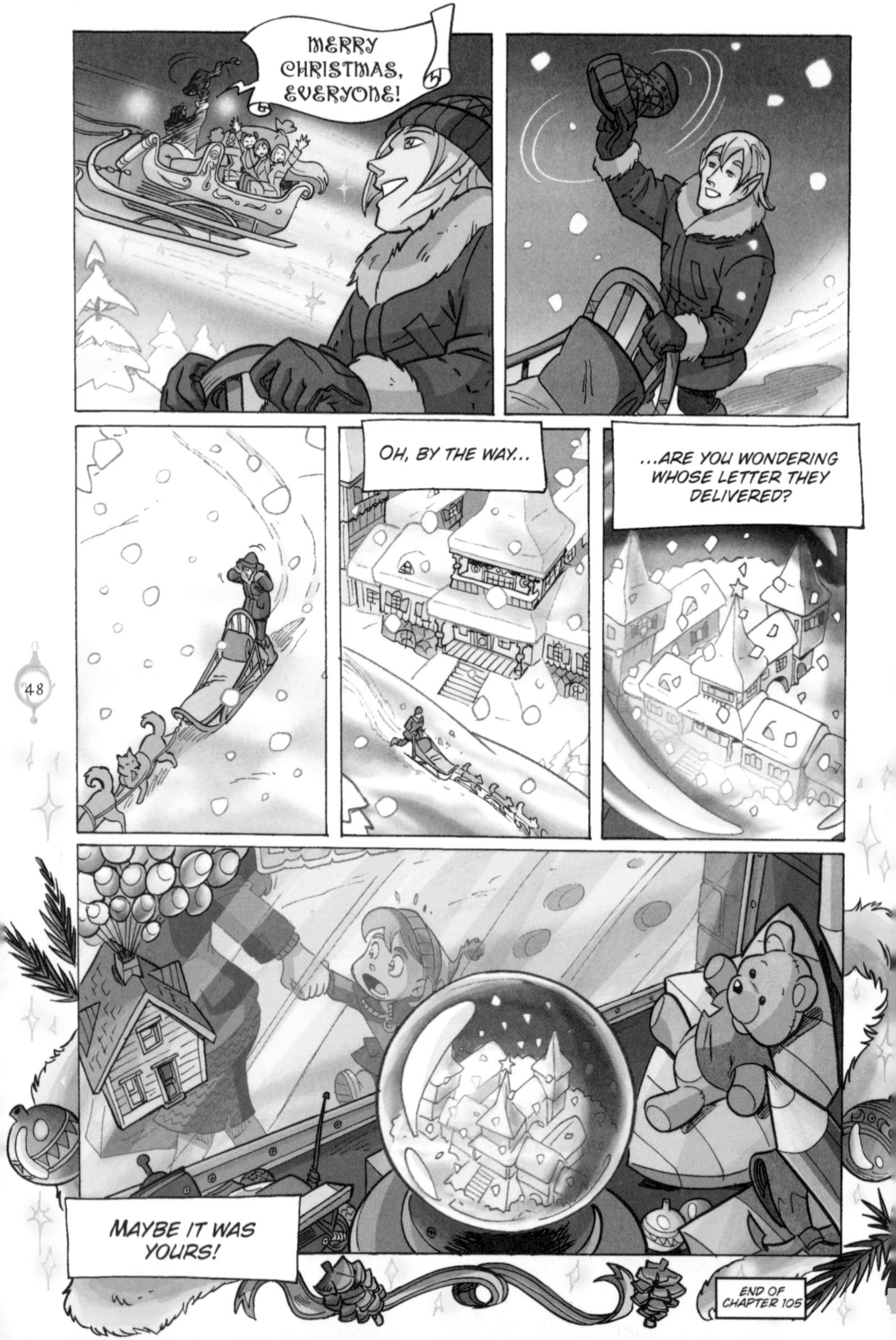
MERRY CHRISTMAS, EVERYONE!
OH, BY THE WAY...
...ARE YOU WONDERING WHOSE LETTER THEY DELIVERED?
MAYBE IT WAS YOURS!
END OF CHAPTER 105

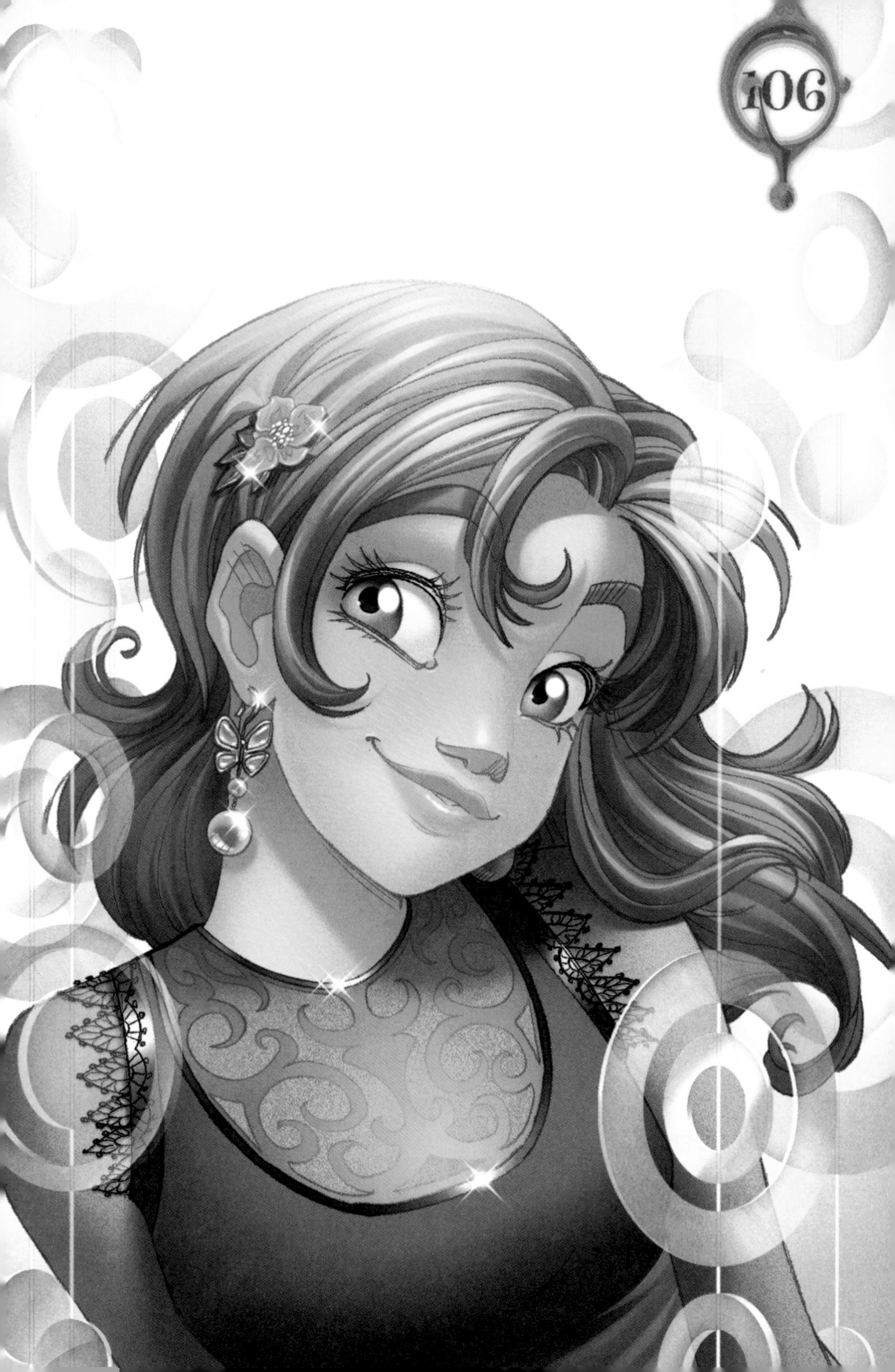
106

Will   Irma   Taranee   Cornelia   Hay Lin

Zodiac

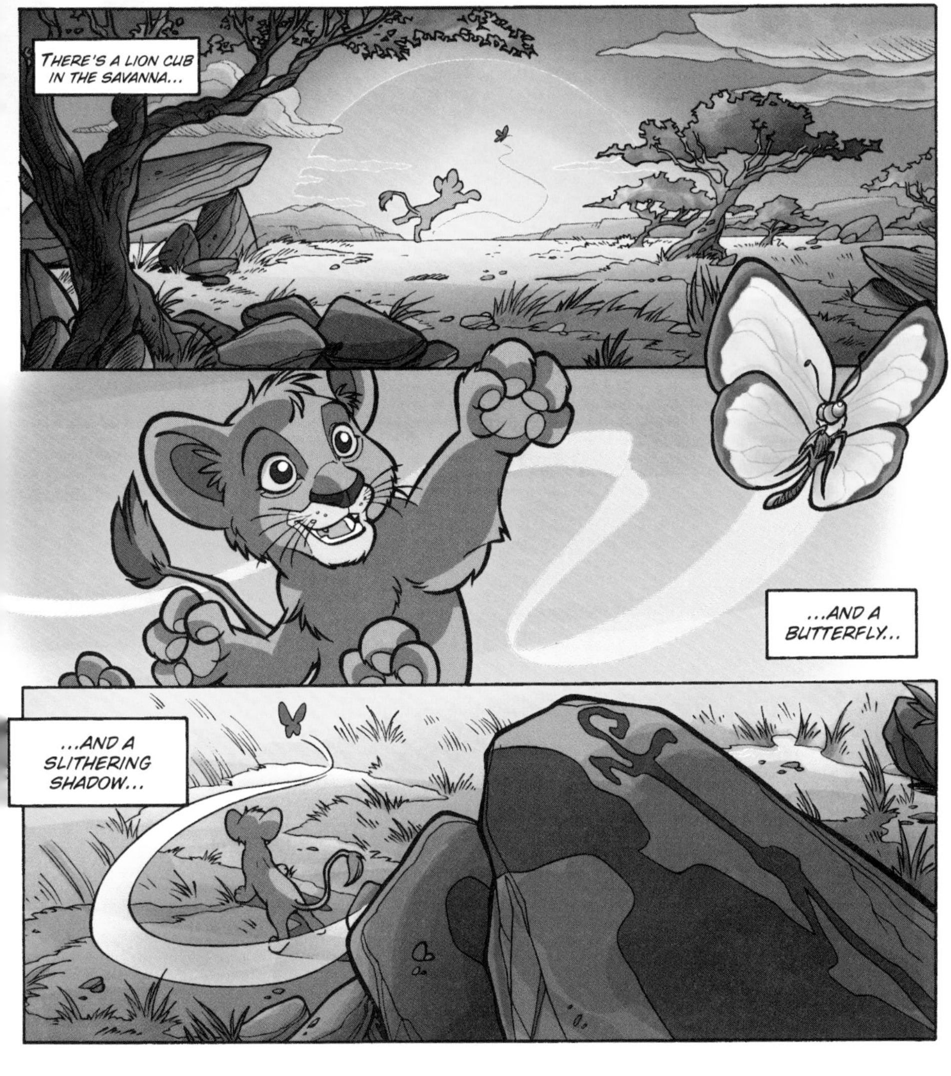
THERE'S A LION CUB IN THE SAVANNA...
...AND A BUTTERFLY...
...AND A SLITHERING SHADOW...

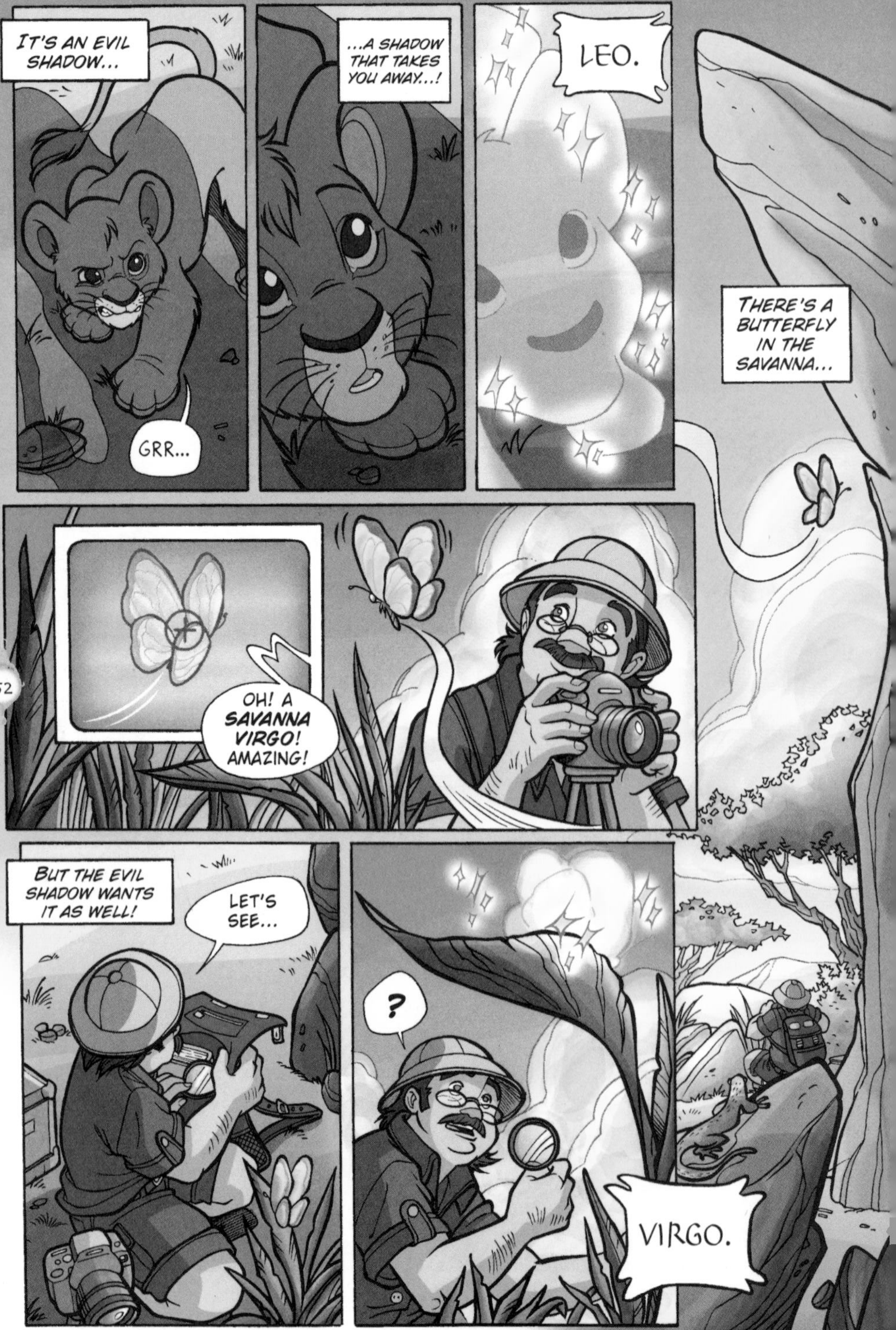
IT'S AN EVIL SHADOW...
GRR...
...A SHADOW THAT TAKES YOU AWAY...!
LEO.
THERE'S A BUTTERFLY IN THE SAVANNA...
OH! A SAVANNA VIRGO! AMAZING!
BUT THE EVIL SHADOW WANTS IT AS WELL!
LET'S SEE...
?
VIRGO.

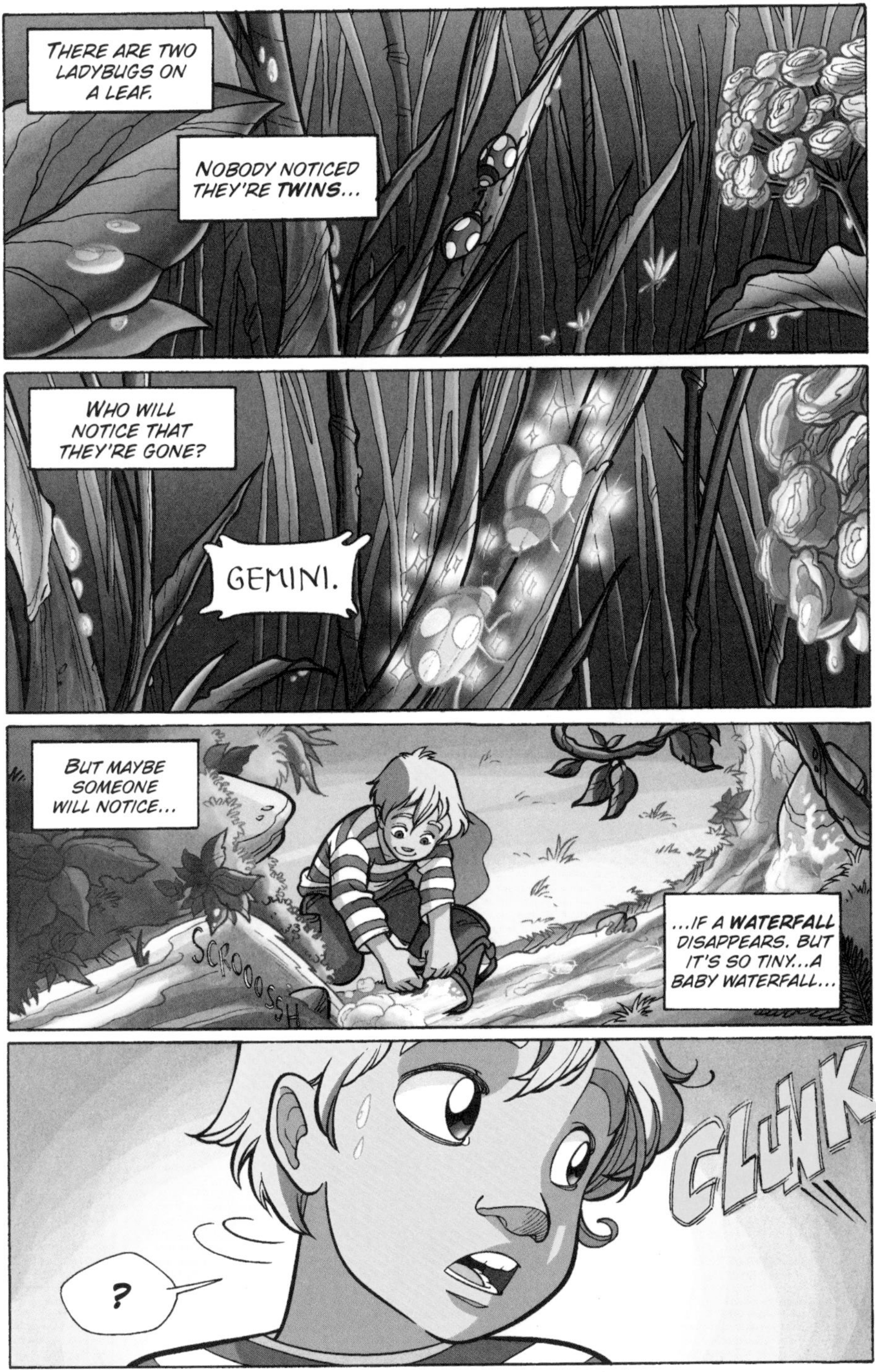

THERE ARE TWO LADYBUGS ON A LEAF.
NOBODY NOTICED THEY'RE TWINS...
WHO WILL NOTICE THAT THEY'RE GONE?
GEMINI.
BUT MAYBE SOMEONE WILL NOTICE...
SCROOOSSH
...IF A WATERFALL DISAPPEARS. BUT IT'S SO TINY...A BABY WATERFALL...
CLUNK
?

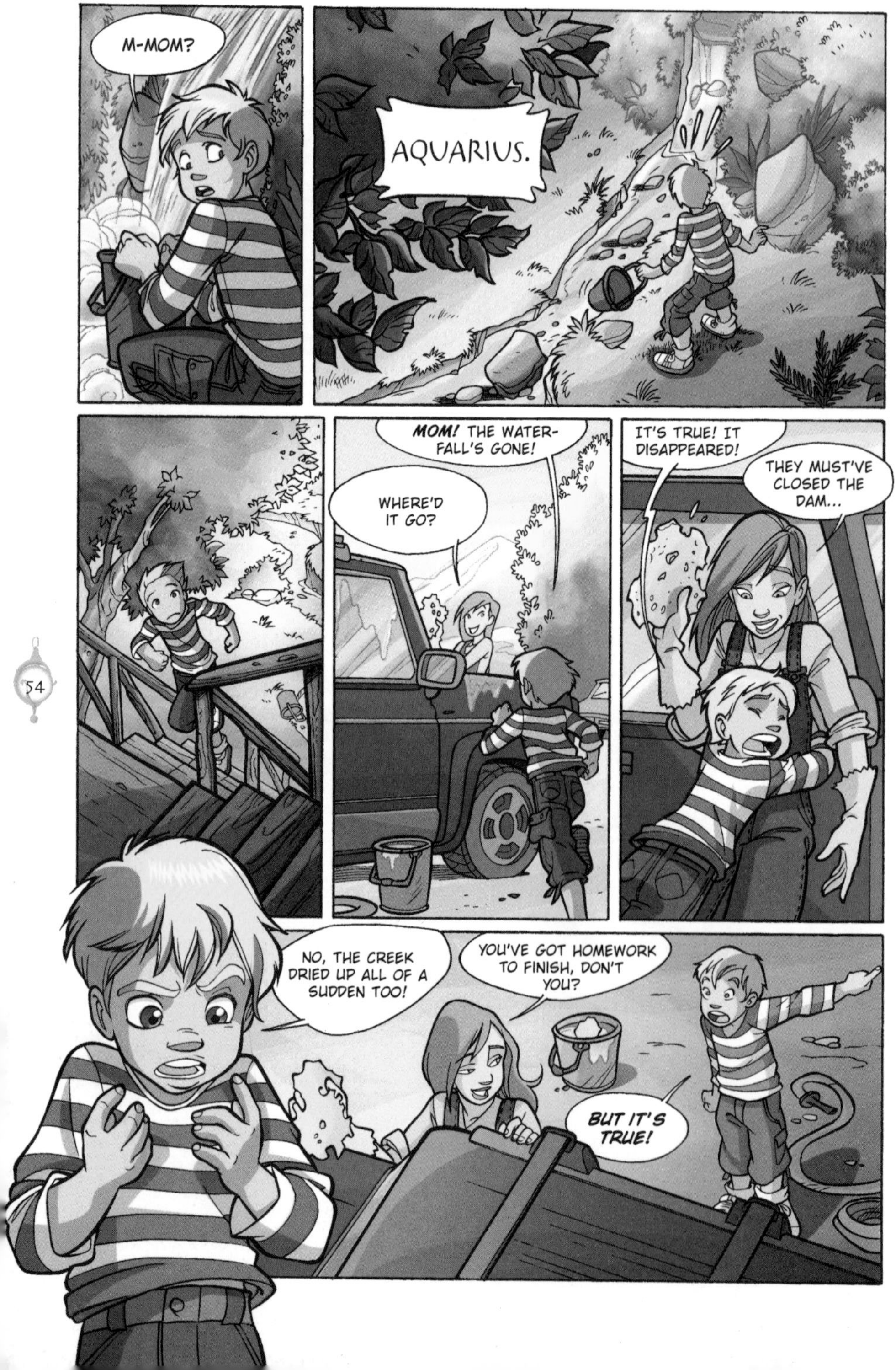

M-MOM?
AQUARIUS.
MOM! THE WATER-FALL'S GONE!
WHERE'D IT GO?
IT'S TRUE! IT DISAPPEARED!
THEY MUST'VE CLOSED THE DAM...
NO, THE CREEK DRIED UP ALL OF A SUDDEN TOO!
YOU'VE GOT HOMEWORK TO FINISH, DON'T YOU?
BUT IT'S TRUE!

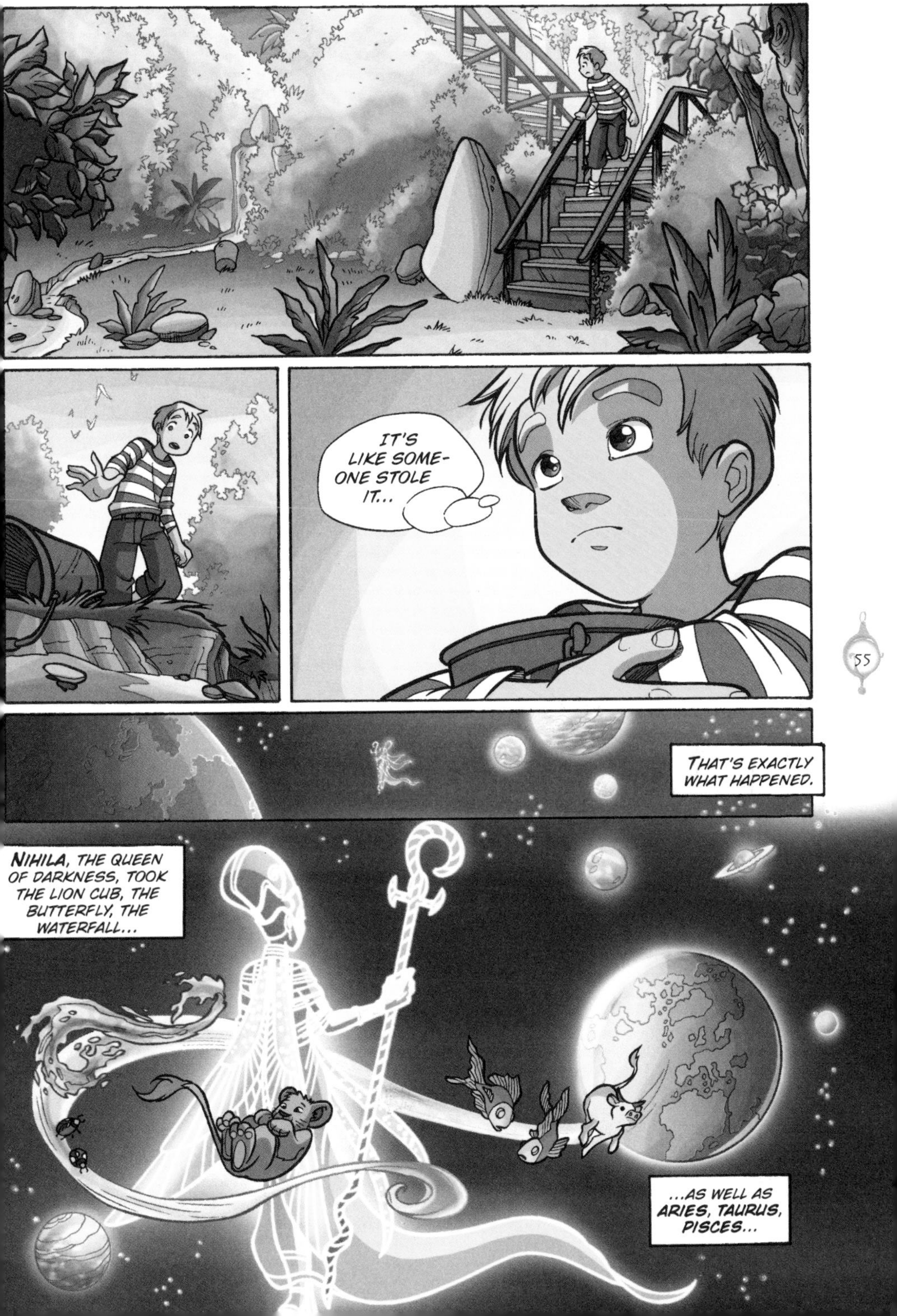
IT'S LIKE SOME-ONE STOLE IT...
THAT'S EXACTLY WHAT HAPPENED.
NIHILA, THE QUEEN OF DARKNESS, TOOK THE LION CUB, THE BUTTERFLY, THE WATERFALL...
...AS WELL AS ARIES, TAURUS, PISCES...

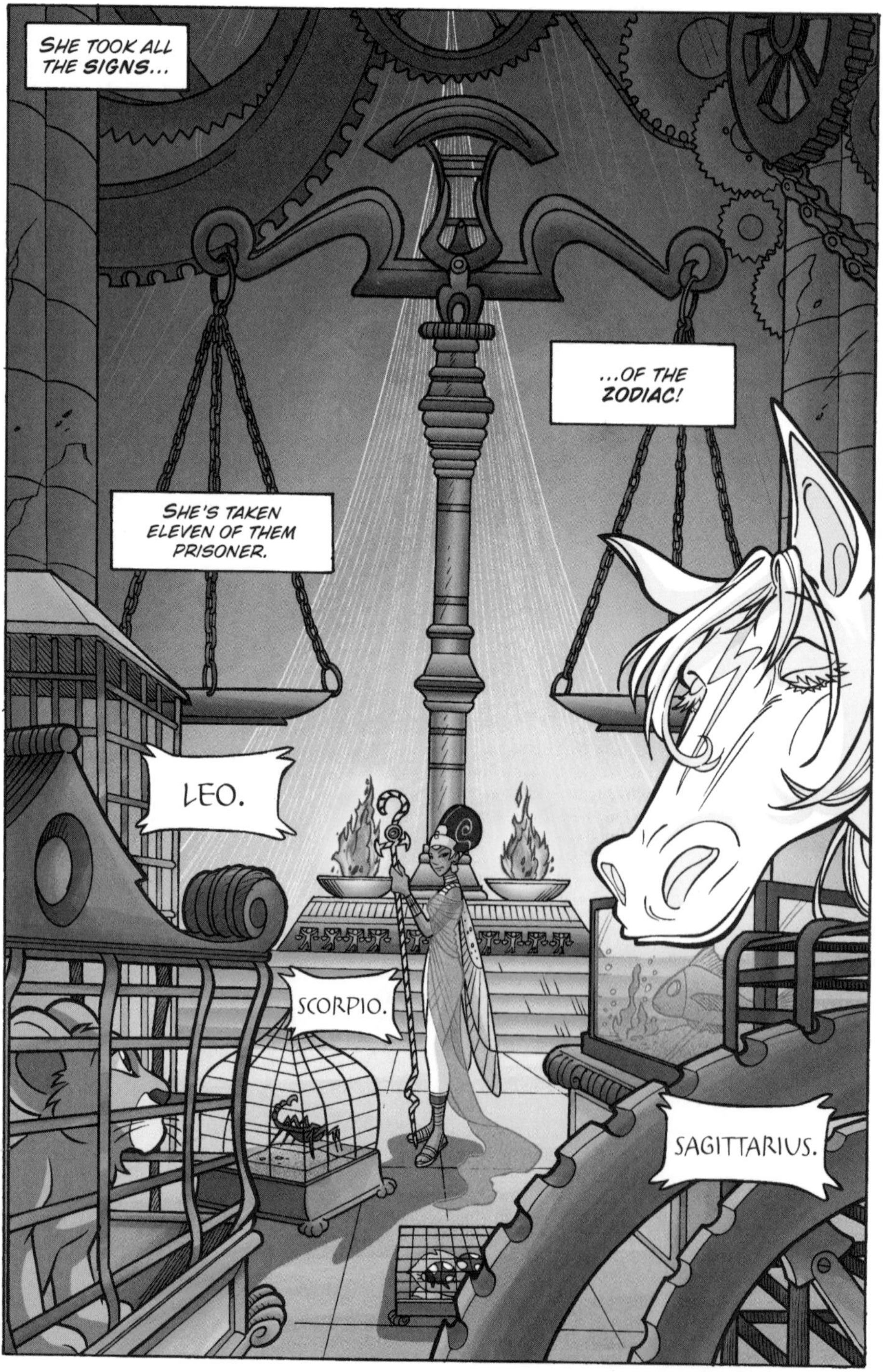
SHE TOOK ALL THE SIGNS...
...OF THE ZODIAC!
SHE'S TAKEN ELEVEN OF THEM PRISONER.
LEO.
SCORPIO.
SAGITTARIUS.

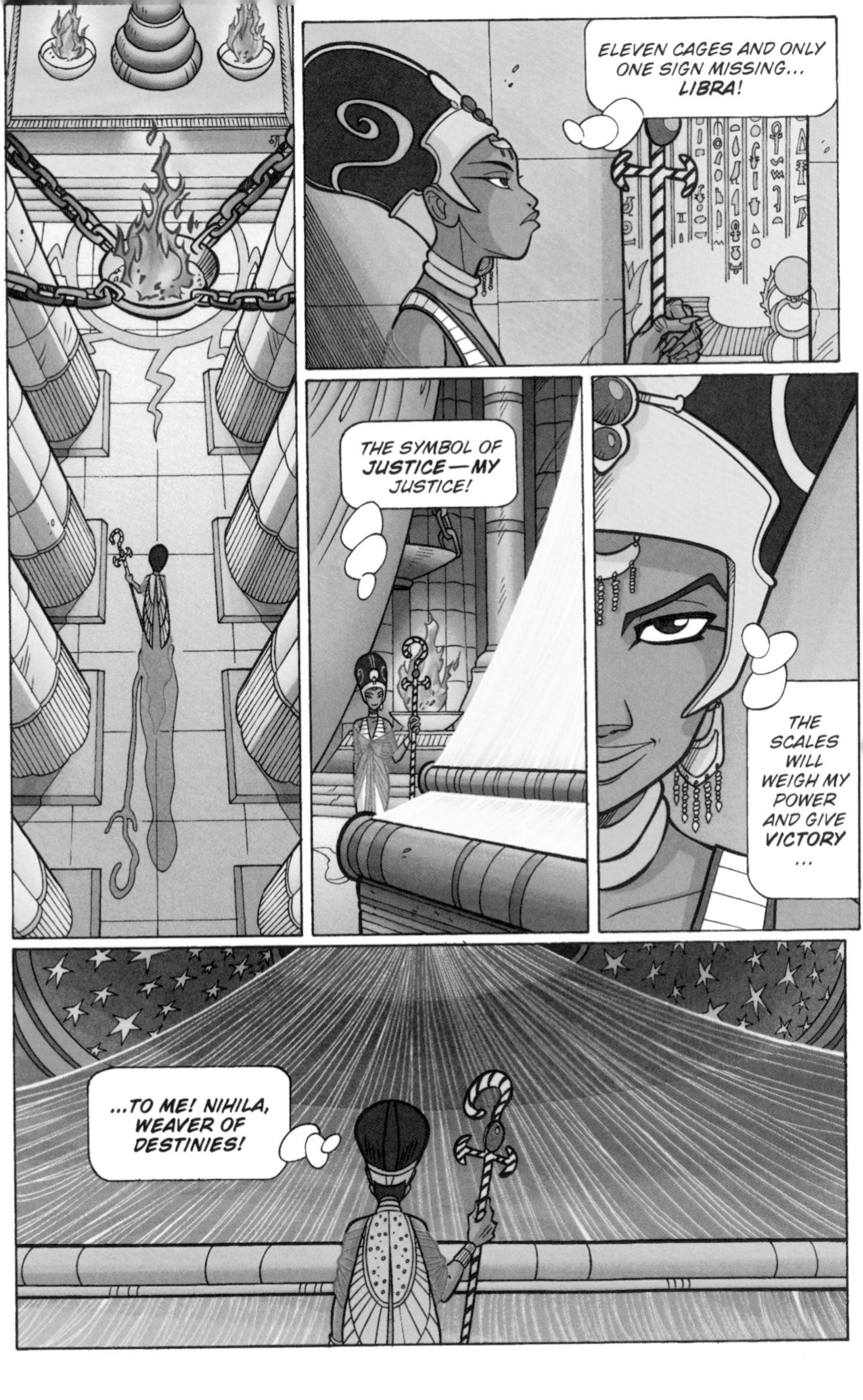
ELEVEN CAGES AND ONLY ONE SIGN MISSING... LIBRA!
THE SYMBOL OF JUSTICE—MY JUSTICE!
THE SCALES WILL WEIGH MY POWER AND GIVE VICTORY ...
...TO ME! NIHILA, WEAVER OF DESTINIES!

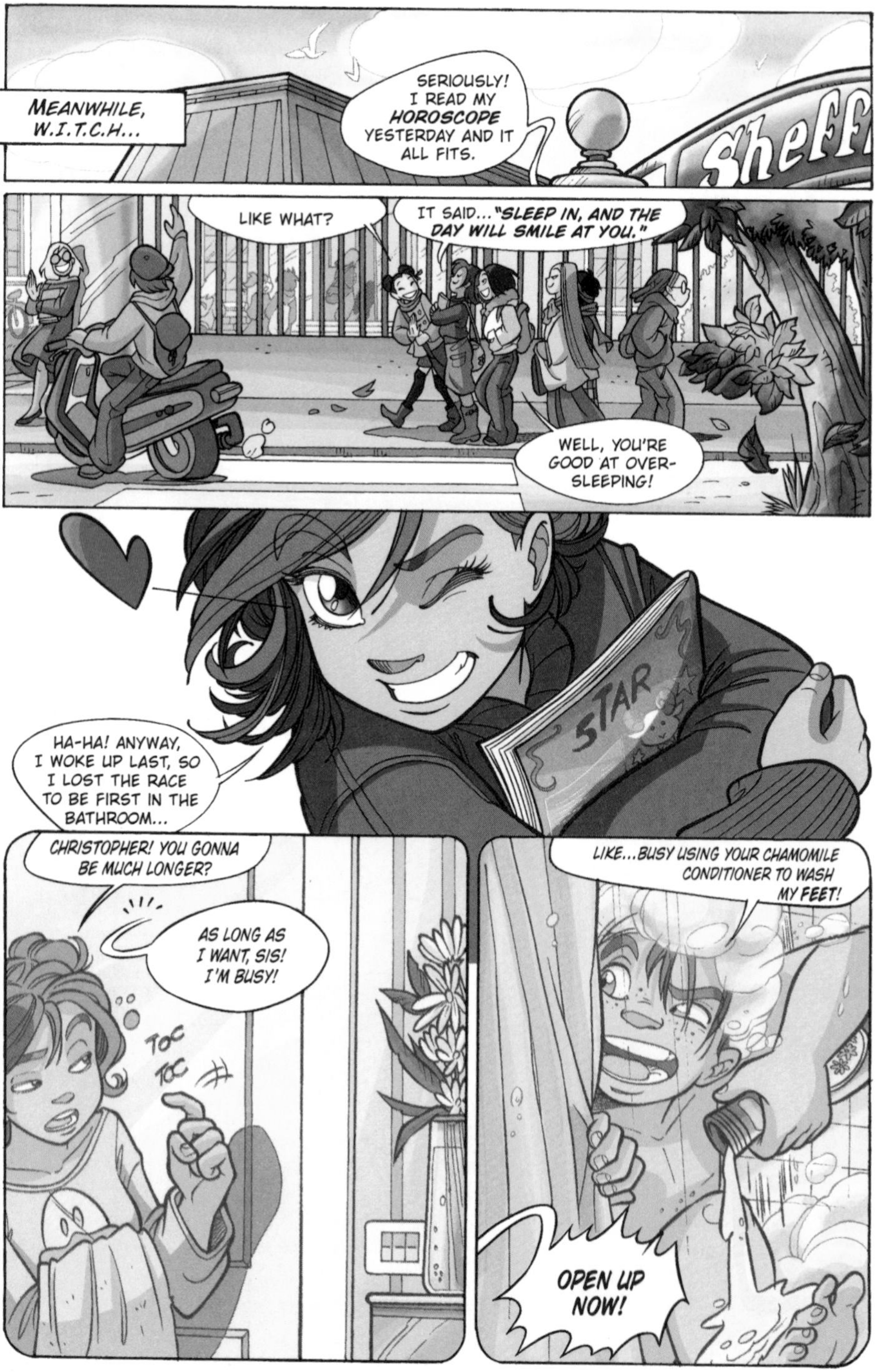

MEANWHILE, W.I.T.C.H...
SERIOUSLY! I READ MY HOROSCOPE YESTERDAY AND IT ALL FITS.
Sheff
LIKE WHAT?
IT SAID... "SLEEP IN, AND THE DAY WILL SMILE AT YOU."
WELL, YOU'RE GOOD AT OVER-SLEEPING!
STAR
HA-HA! ANYWAY, I WOKE UP LAST, SO I LOST THE RACE TO BE FIRST IN THE BATHROOM...
CHRISTOPHER! YOU GONNA BE MUCH LONGER?
AS LONG AS I WANT, SIS! I'M BUSY!
TOC TOC
LIKE...BUSY USING YOUR CHAMOMILE CONDITIONER TO WASH MY FEET!
OPEN UP NOW!

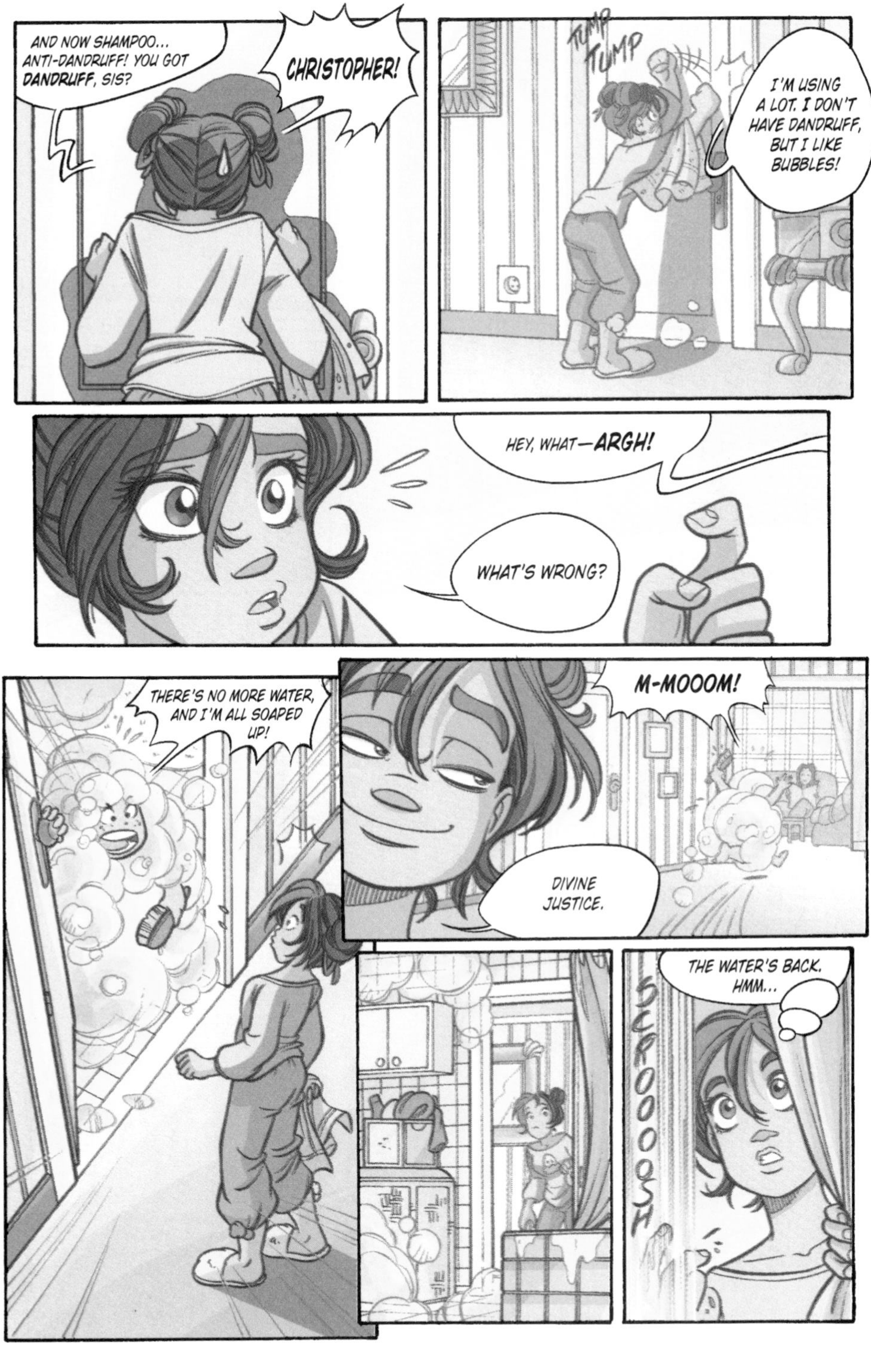
AND NOW SHAMPOO... ANTI-DANDRUFF! YOU GOT DANDRUFF, SIS?
CHRISTOPHER!
TUMP TUMP
I'M USING A LOT. I DON'T HAVE DANDRUFF, BUT I LIKE BUBBLES!
HEY, WHAT—ARGH!
WHAT'S WRONG?
THERE'S NO MORE WATER, AND I'M ALL SOAPED UP!
M-MOOOM!
DIVINE JUSTICE.
THE WATER'S BACK. HMM...
SCROOOOOSH

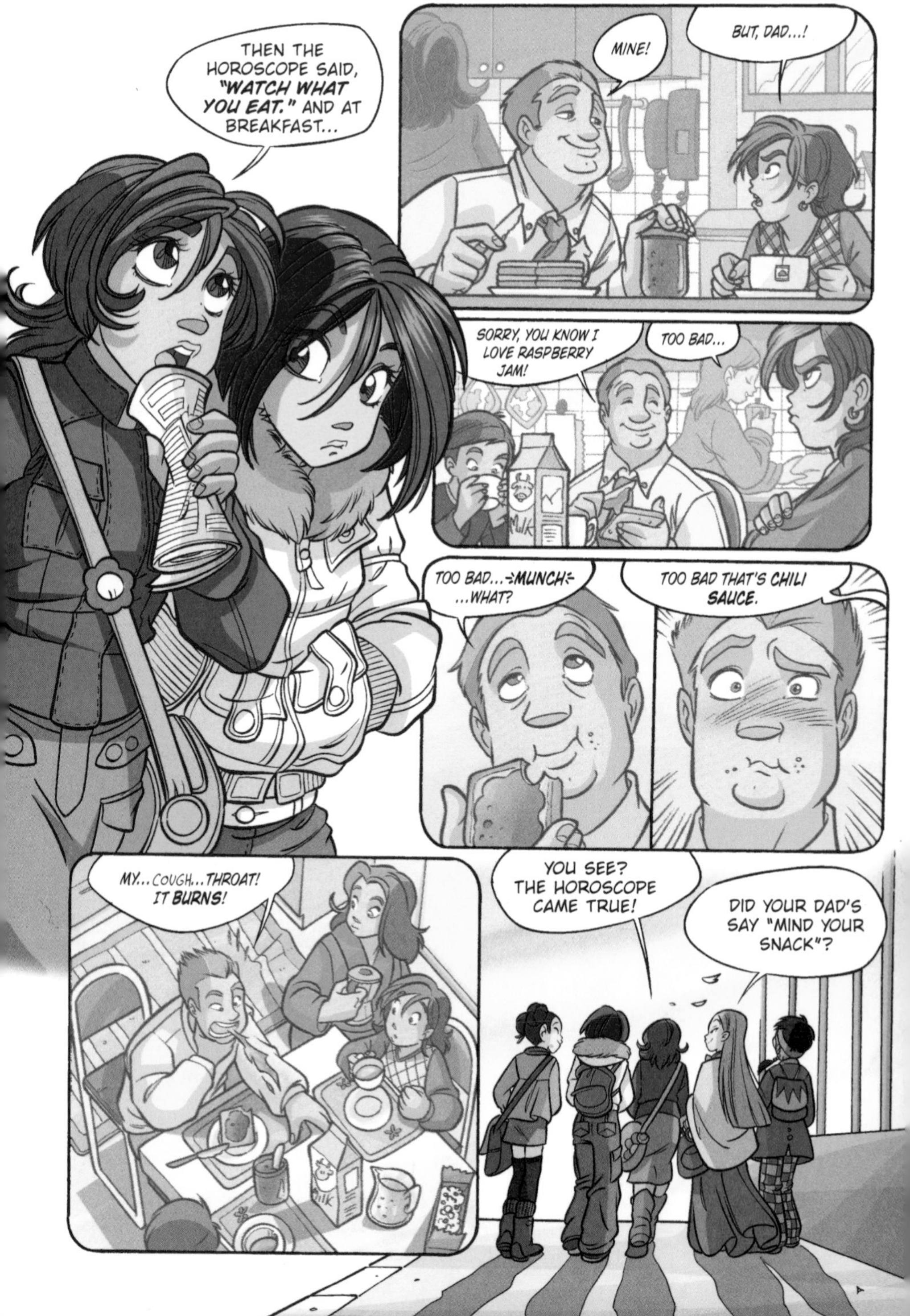
THEN THE HOROSCOPE SAID, "WATCH WHAT YOU EAT." AND AT BREAKFAST...
MINE!
BUT, DAD...!
SORRY, YOU KNOW I LOVE RASPBERRY JAM!
TOO BAD...
TOO BAD... MUNCH ...WHAT?
TOO BAD THAT'S CHILI SAUCE.
MY... COUGH... THROAT! IT BURNS!
YOU SEE? THE HOROSCOPE CAME TRUE!
DID YOUR DAD'S SAY "MIND YOUR SNACK"?

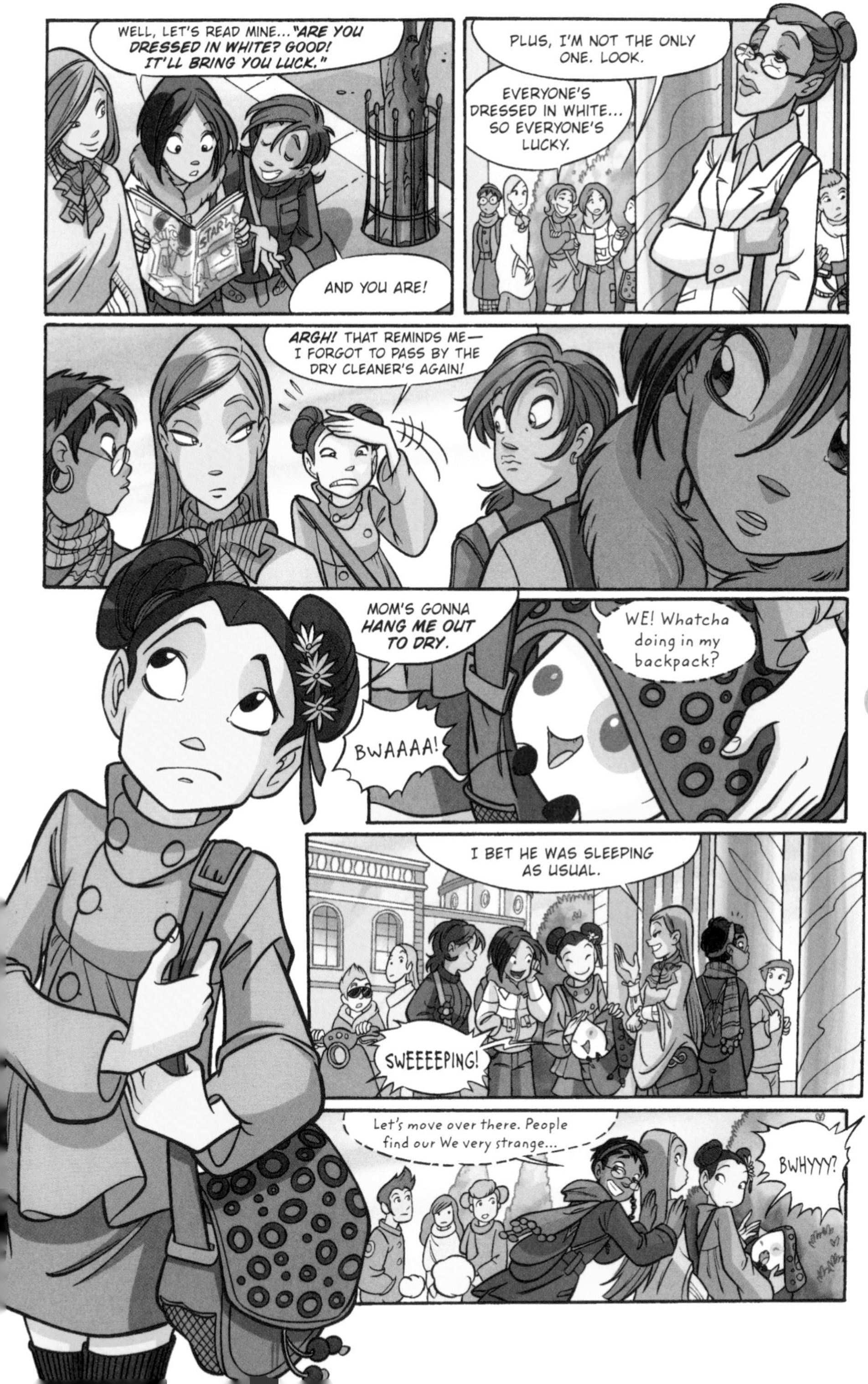
WELL, LET'S READ MINE... "ARE YOU DRESSED IN WHITE? GOOD! IT'LL BRING YOU LUCK."
AND YOU ARE!
PLUS, I'M NOT THE ONLY ONE. LOOK.
EVERYONE'S DRESSED IN WHITE... SO EVERYONE'S LUCKY.
ARGH! THAT REMINDS ME— I FORGOT TO PASS BY THE DRY CLEANER'S AGAIN!
MOM'S GONNA HANG ME OUT TO DRY.
BWAAAA!
WE! Whatcha doing in my backpack?
I BET HE WAS SLEEPING AS USUAL.
SWEEEEPING!
Let's move over there. People find our We very strange...
BWHYYY?

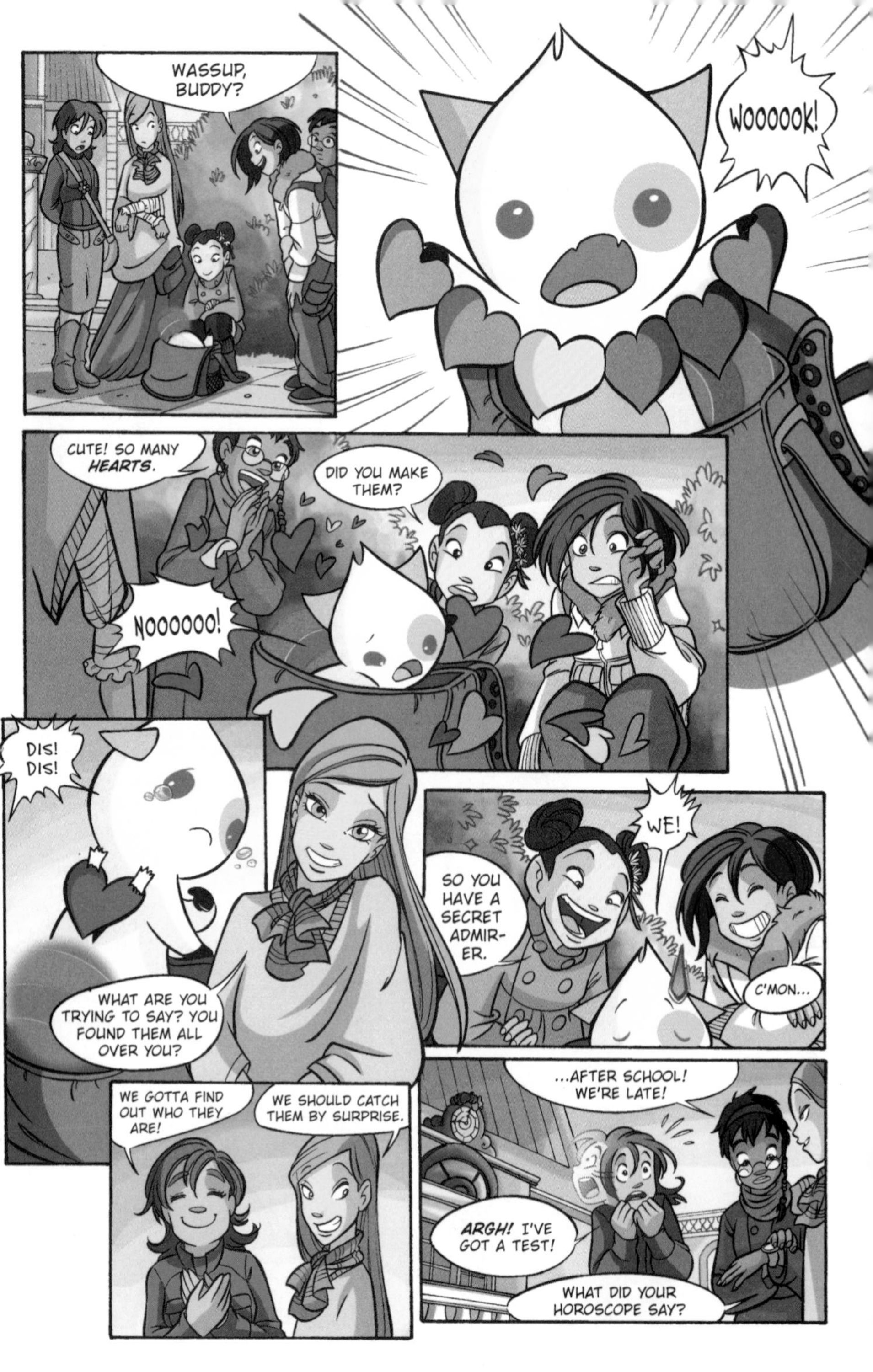

WASSUP, BUDDY?
WOOOOOK!
CUTE! SO MANY *HEARTS*.
DID YOU MAKE THEM?
NOOOOOO!
DIS! DIS!
WHAT ARE YOU TRYING TO SAY? YOU FOUND THEM ALL OVER YOU?
WE!
SO YOU HAVE A SECRET ADMIR-ER.
C'MON...
WE GOTTA FIND OUT WHO THEY ARE!
WE SHOULD CATCH THEM BY SURPRISE.
...AFTER SCHOOL! WE'RE LATE!
ARGH! I'VE GOT A TEST!
WHAT DID YOUR HOROSCOPE SAY?

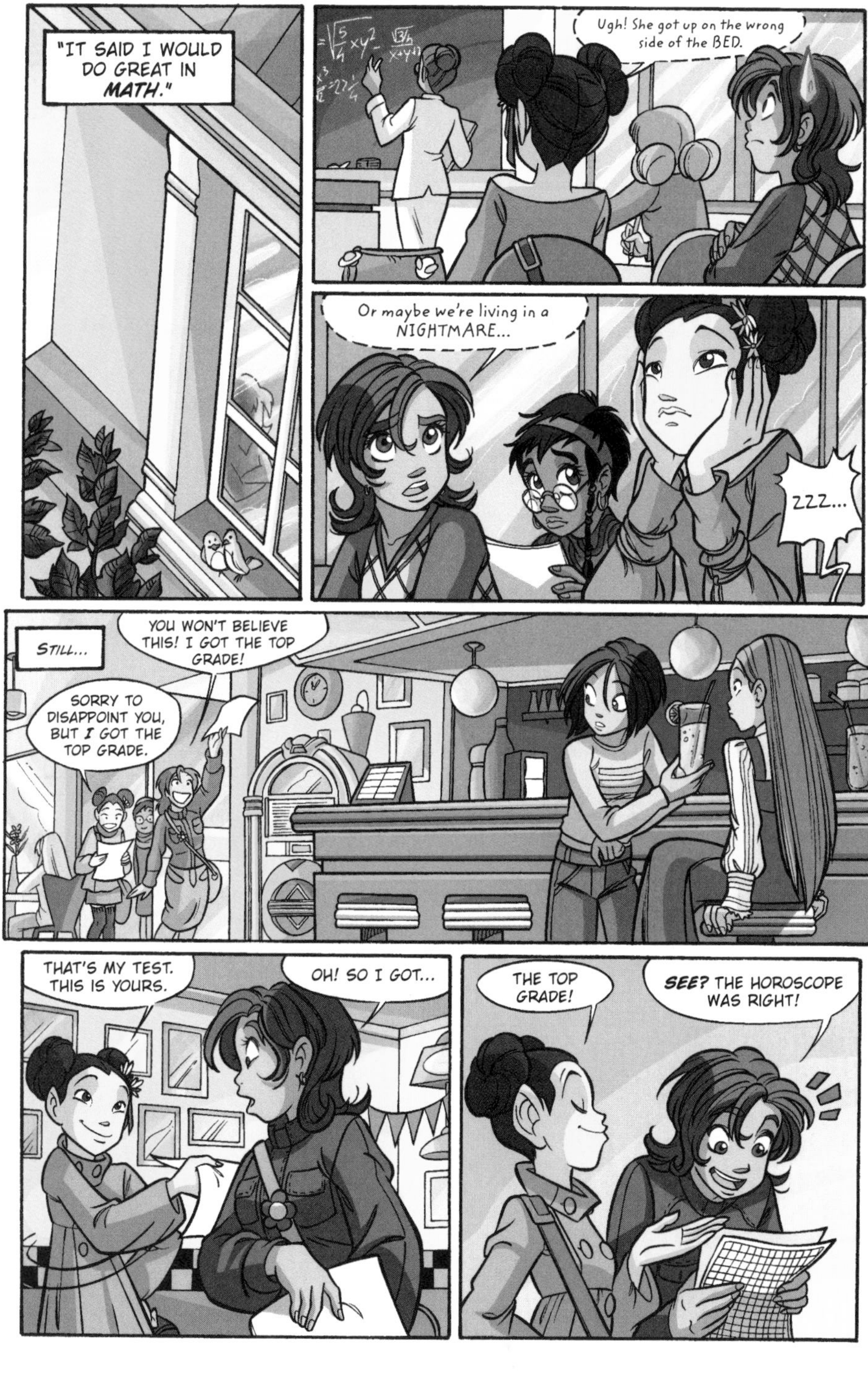

"IT SAID I WOULD DO GREAT IN MATH."
Ugh! She got up on the wrong side of the BED.
Or maybe we're living in a NIGHTMARE...
ZZZ...
STILL...
YOU WON'T BELIEVE THIS! I GOT THE TOP GRADE!
SORRY TO DISAPPOINT YOU, BUT I GOT THE TOP GRADE.
THAT'S MY TEST. THIS IS YOURS.
OH! SO I GOT...
THE TOP GRADE!
SEE? THE HOROSCOPE WAS RIGHT!

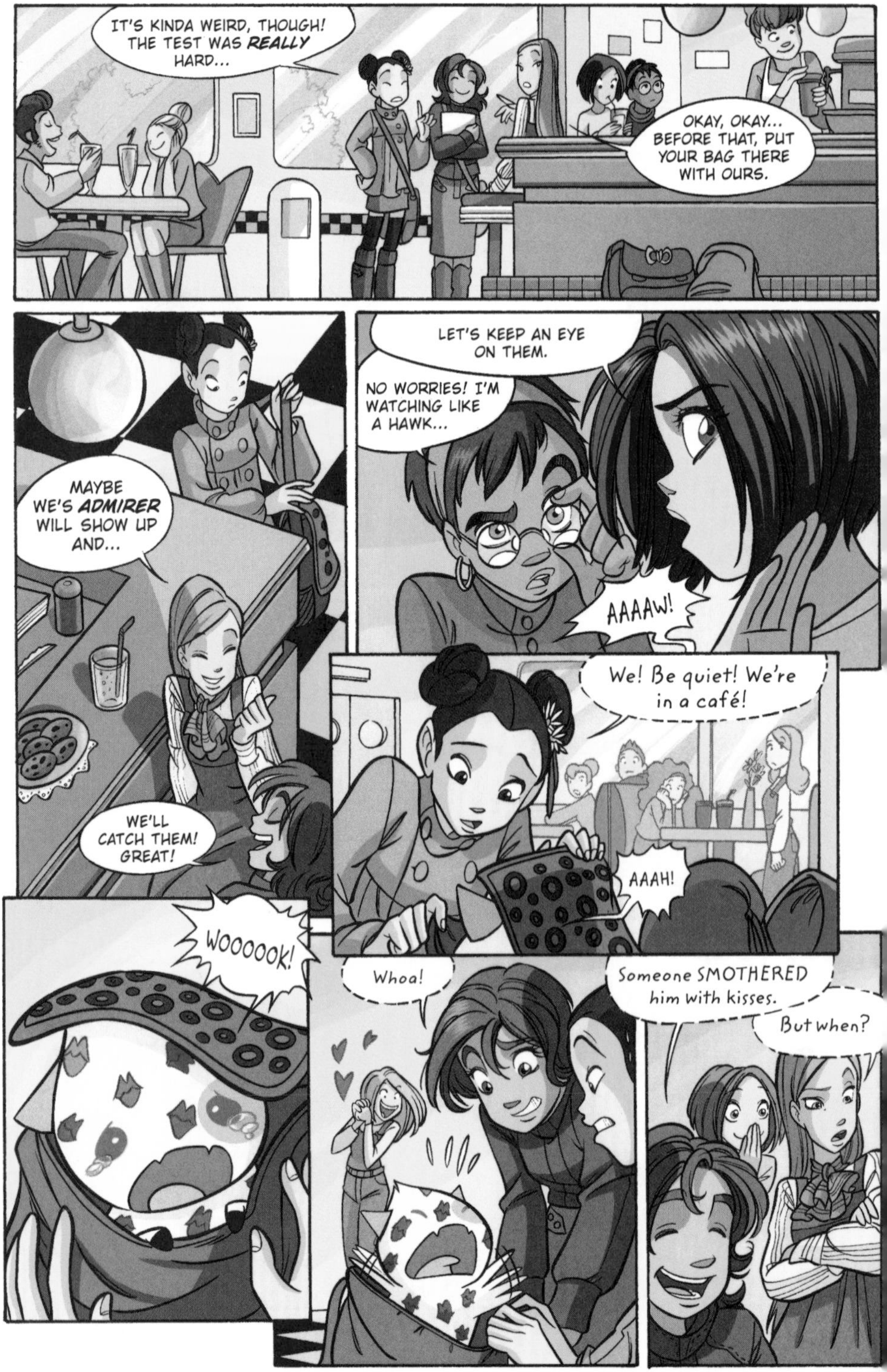

IT'S KINDA WEIRD, THOUGH! THE TEST WAS REALLY HARD...
OKAY, OKAY... BEFORE THAT, PUT YOUR BAG THERE WITH OURS.
MAYBE WE'S ADMIRER WILL SHOW UP AND...
WE'LL CATCH THEM! GREAT!
LET'S KEEP AN EYE ON THEM.
NO WORRIES! I'M WATCHING LIKE A HAWK...
AAAAW!
We! Be quiet! We're in a café!
AAAH!
WOOOOOK!
Whoa!
Someone SMOTHERED him with kisses.
But when?

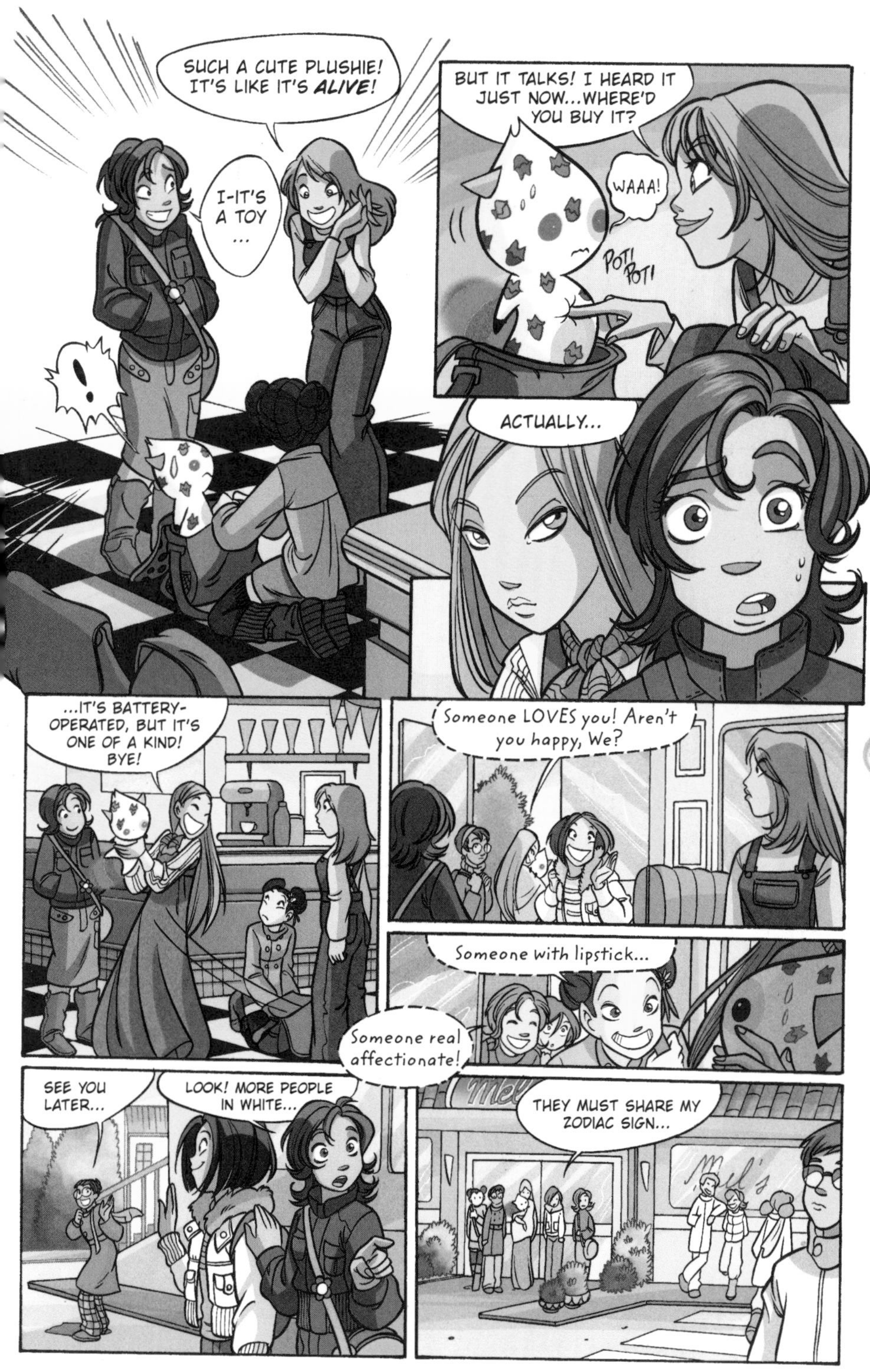
SUCH A CUTE PLUSHIE! IT'S LIKE IT'S ALIVE!
I-IT'S A TOY ...
!
BUT IT TALKS! I HEARD IT JUST NOW...WHERE'D YOU BUY IT?
WAAA!
POTI POTI
ACTUALLY...
...IT'S BATTERY-OPERATED, BUT IT'S ONE OF A KIND! BYE!
Someone LOVES you! Aren't you happy, We?
Someone with lipstick...
Someone real affectionate!
SEE YOU LATER...
LOOK! MORE PEOPLE IN WHITE...
THEY MUST SHARE MY ZODIAC SIGN...

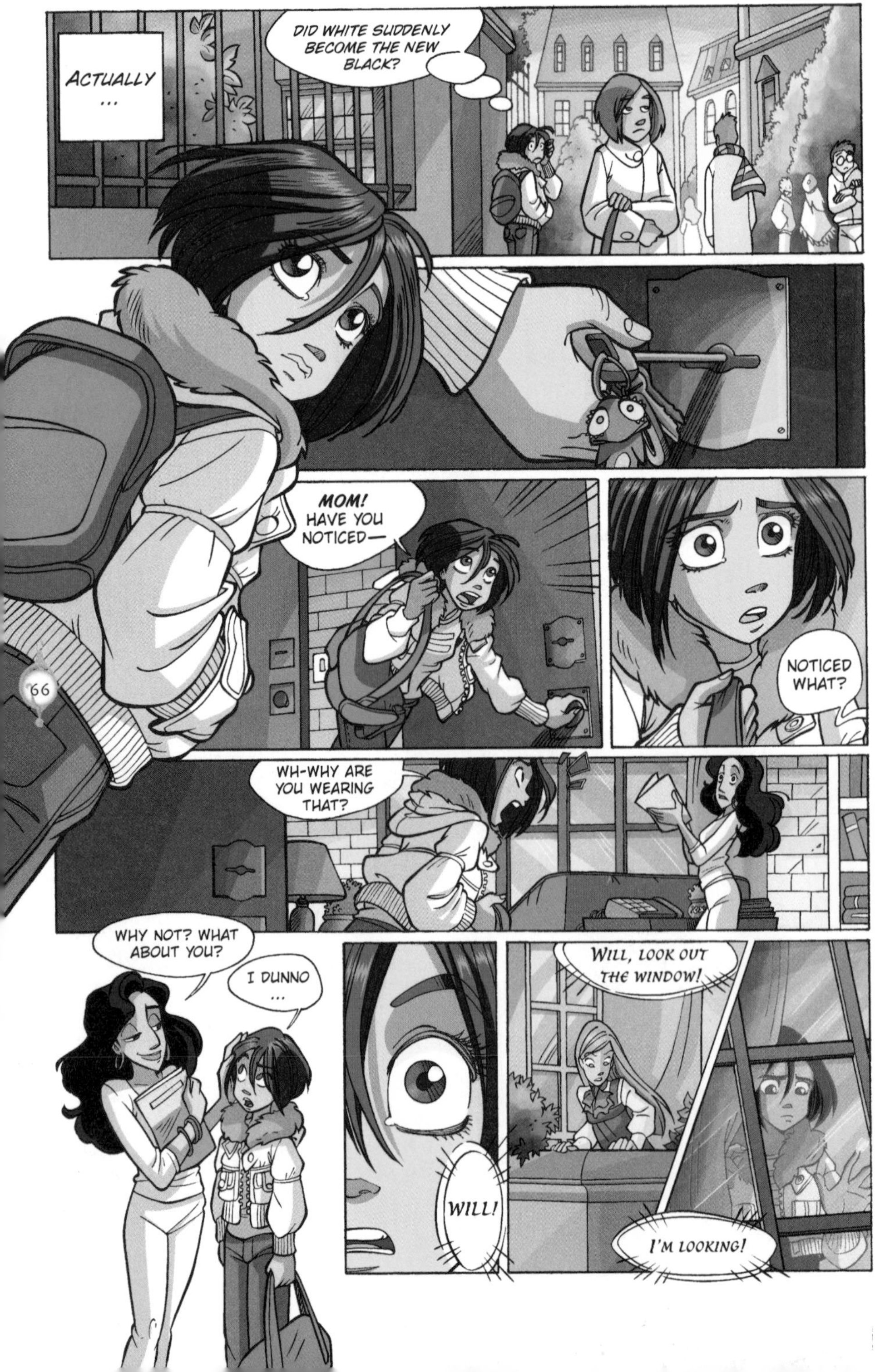
ACTUALLY ...
DID WHITE SUDDENLY BECOME THE NEW BLACK?
MOM! HAVE YOU NOTICED—
NOTICED WHAT?
WH-WHY ARE YOU WEARING THAT?
WHY NOT? WHAT ABOUT YOU?
I DUNNO ...
WILL!
WILL, LOOK OUT THE WINDOW!
I'M LOOKING!

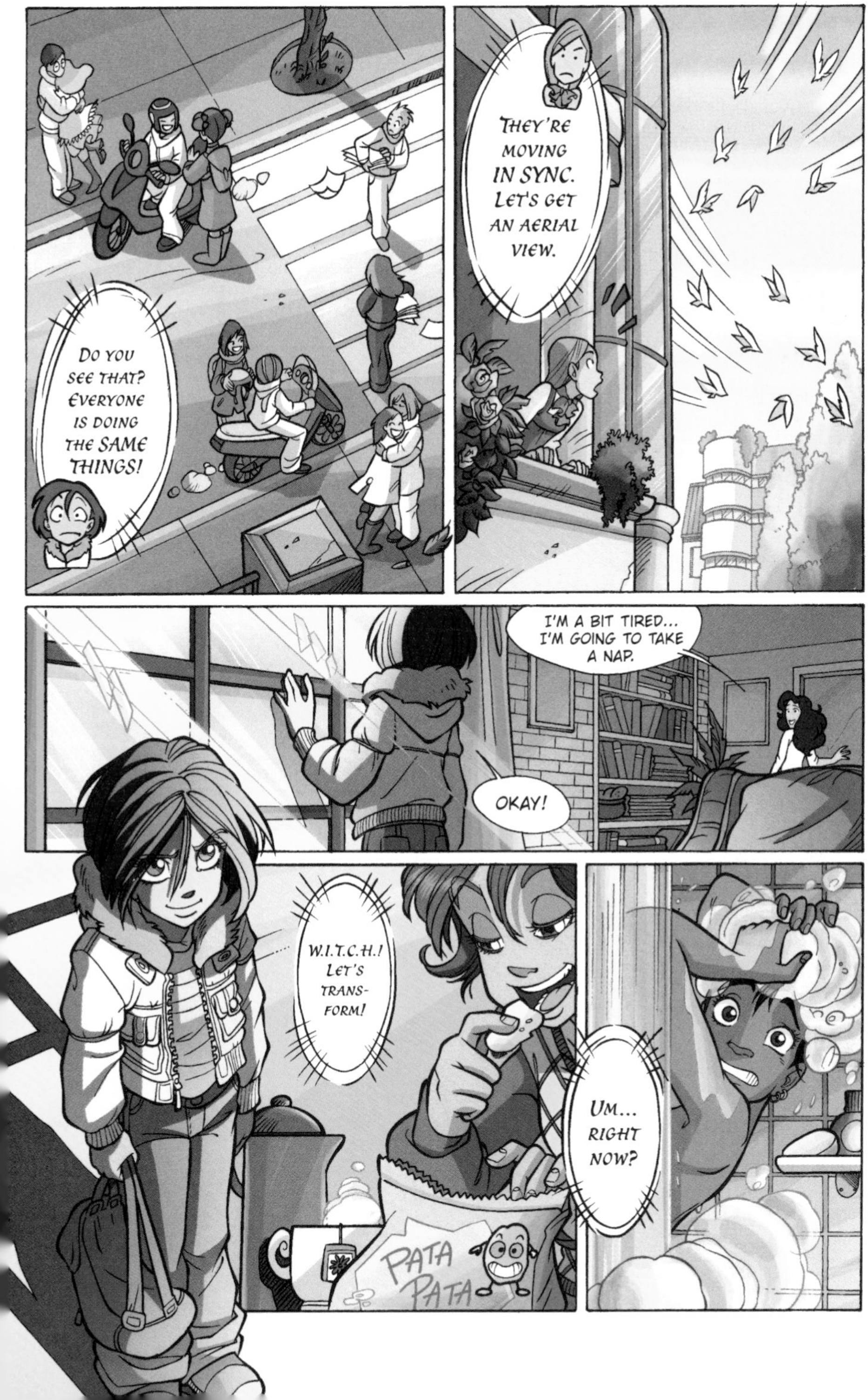
Do you see that? Everyone is doing the SAME THINGS!
They're moving IN SYNC. Let's get an aerial view.
I'M A BIT TIRED... I'M GOING TO TAKE A NAP.
OKAY!
W.I.T.C.H.! Let's trans-form!
Um... right now?
PATA PATA

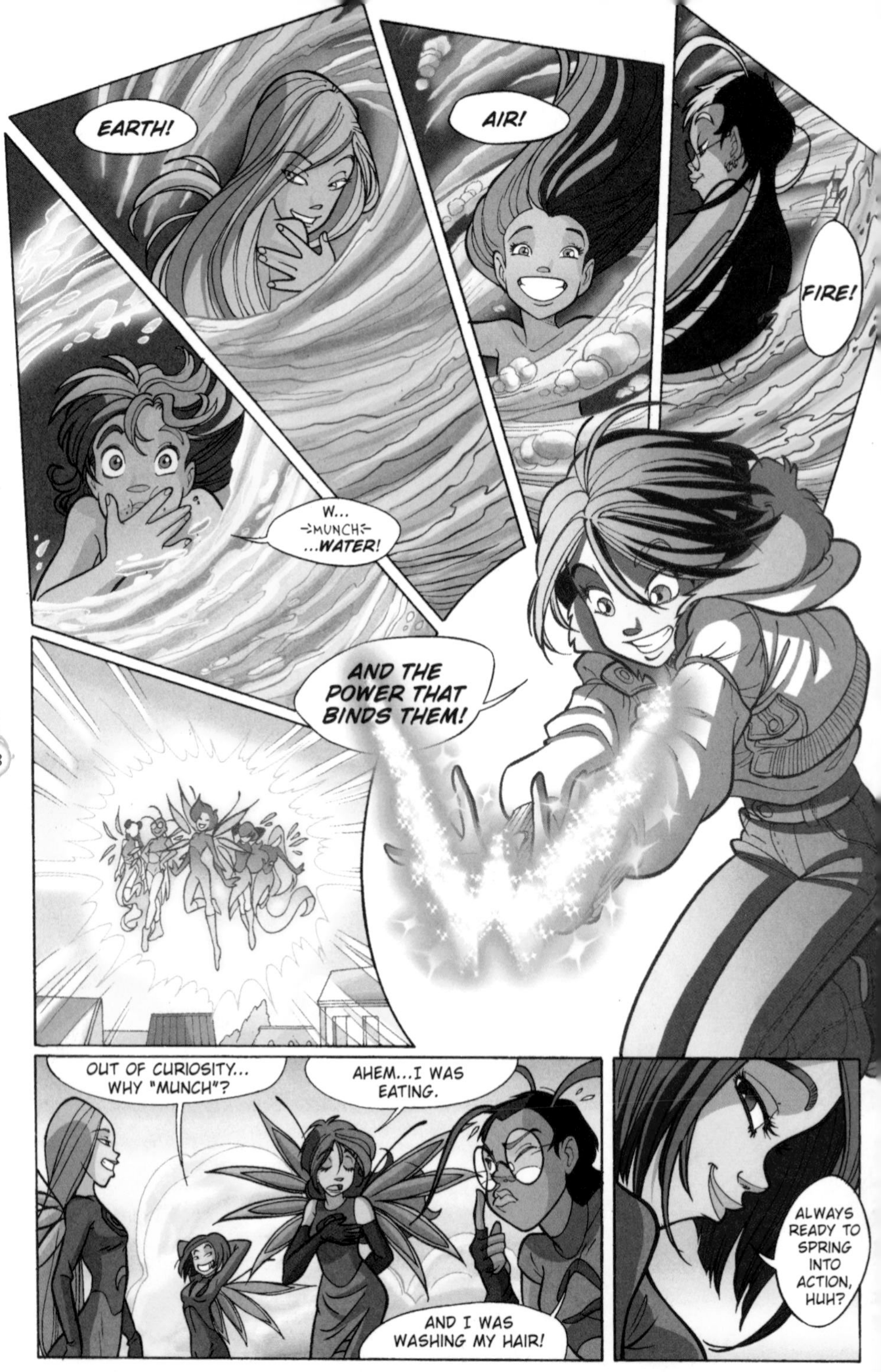
EARTH!
AIR!
FIRE!
W... -MUNCH- ...WATER!
AND THE POWER THAT BINDS THEM!
OUT OF CURIOSITY... WHY "MUNCH"?
AHEM...I WAS EATING.
AND I WAS WASHING MY HAIR!
ALWAYS READY TO SPRING INTO ACTION, HUH?

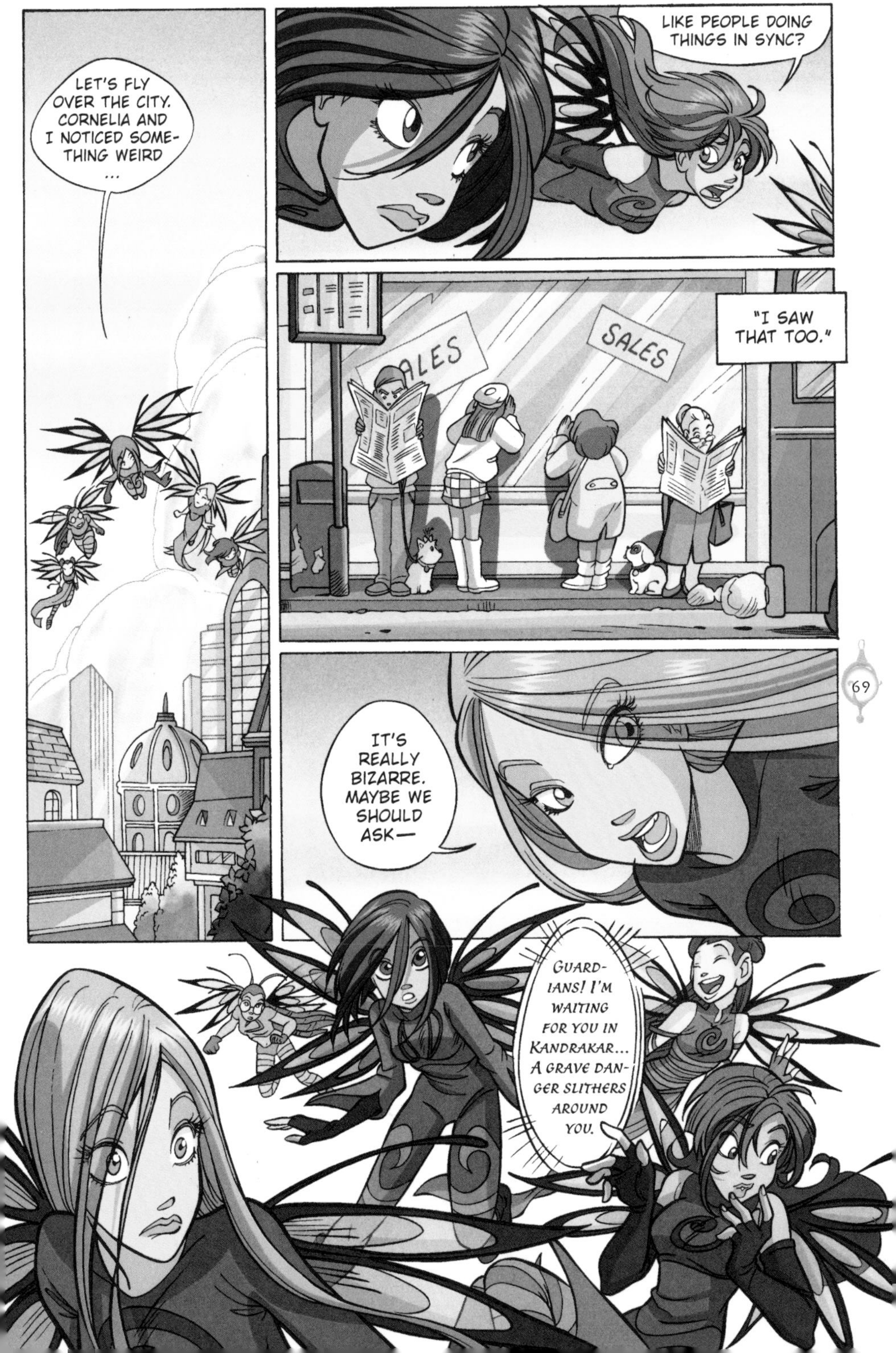
LET'S FLY OVER THE CITY. CORNELIA AND I NOTICED SOME-THING WEIRD ...
LIKE PEOPLE DOING THINGS IN SYNC?
"I SAW THAT TOO."
SALES
SALES
IT'S REALLY BIZARRE. MAYBE WE SHOULD ASK—
GUARD-IANS! I'M WAITING FOR YOU IN KANDRAKAR... A GRAVE DAN-GER SLITHERS AROUND YOU.

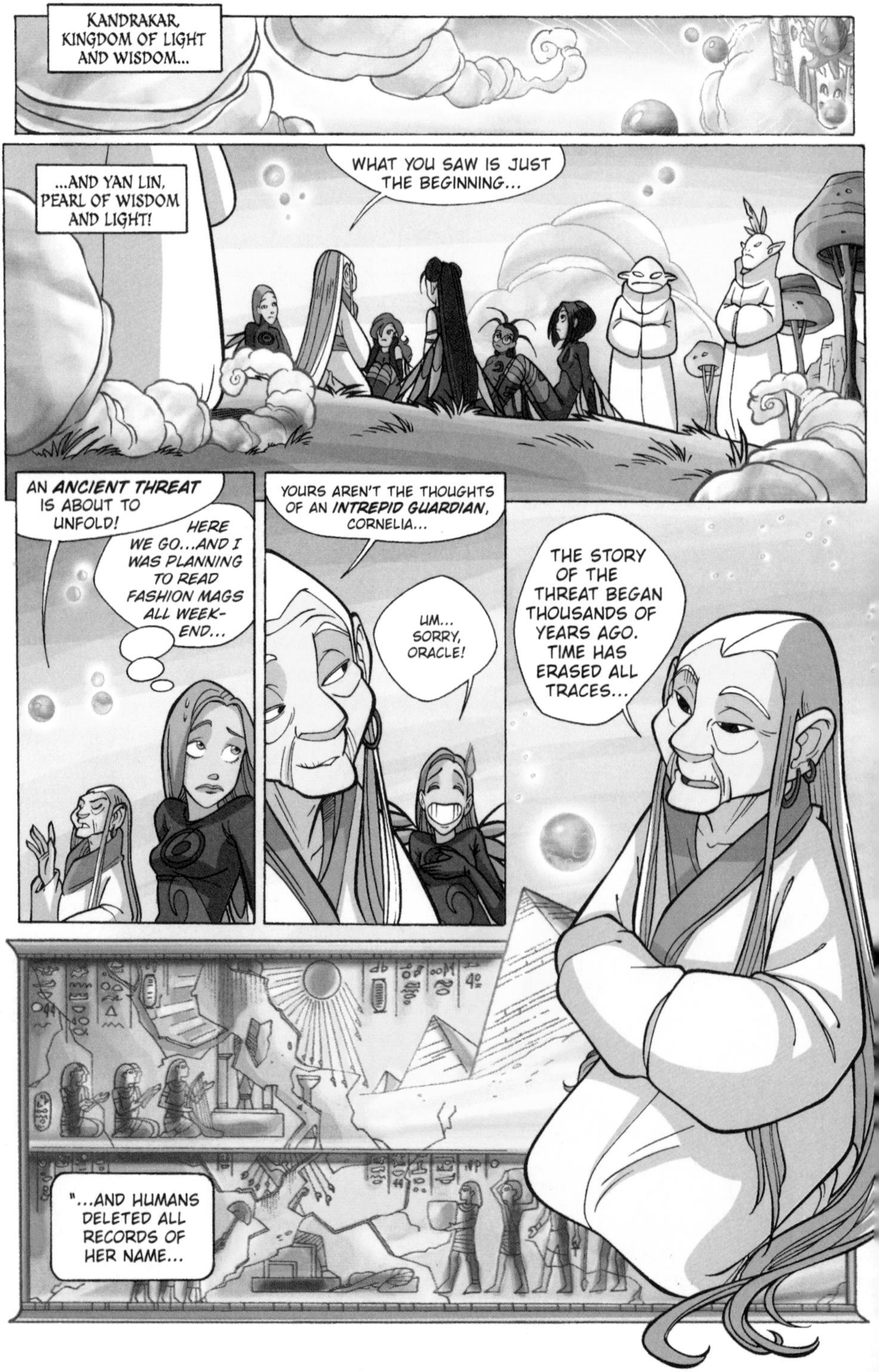

KANDRAKAR, KINGDOM OF LIGHT AND WISDOM...
...AND YAN LIN, PEARL OF WISDOM AND LIGHT!
WHAT YOU SAW IS JUST THE BEGINNING...
AN ANCIENT THREAT IS ABOUT TO UNFOLD!
HERE WE GO...AND I WAS PLANNING TO READ FASHION MAGS ALL WEEK-END...
YOURS AREN'T THE THOUGHTS OF AN INTREPID GUARDIAN, CORNELIA...
UM... SORRY, ORACLE!
THE STORY OF THE THREAT BEGAN THOUSANDS OF YEARS AGO. TIME HAS ERASED ALL TRACES...
"...AND HUMANS DELETED ALL RECORDS OF HER NAME...

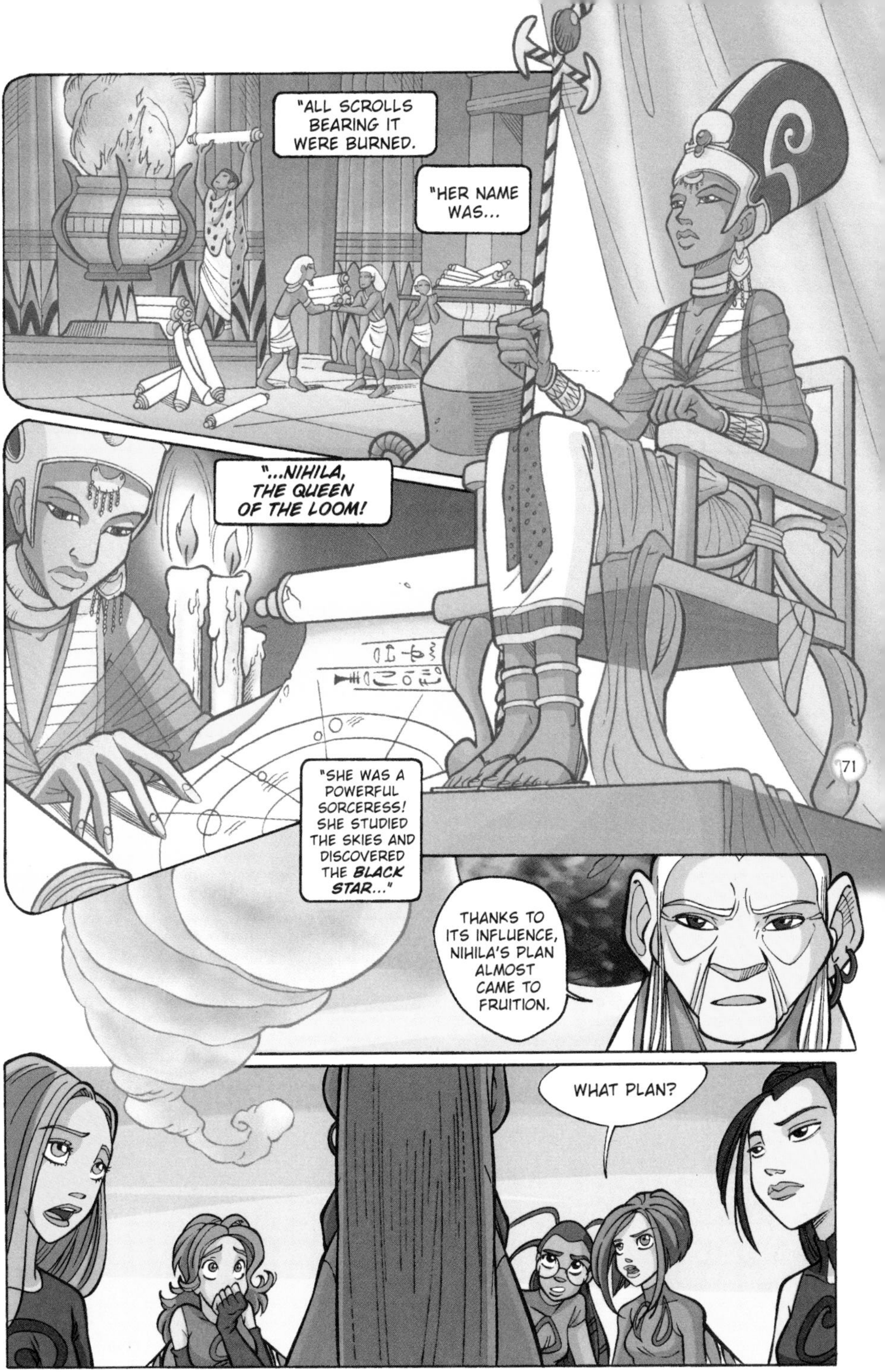
"ALL SCROLLS BEARING IT WERE BURNED.
"HER NAME WAS...
"...NIHILA, THE QUEEN OF THE LOOM!
"SHE WAS A POWERFUL SORCERESS! SHE STUDIED THE SKIES AND DISCOVERED THE BLACK STAR..."
THANKS TO ITS INFLUENCE, NIHILA'S PLAN ALMOST CAME TO FRUITION.
WHAT PLAN?

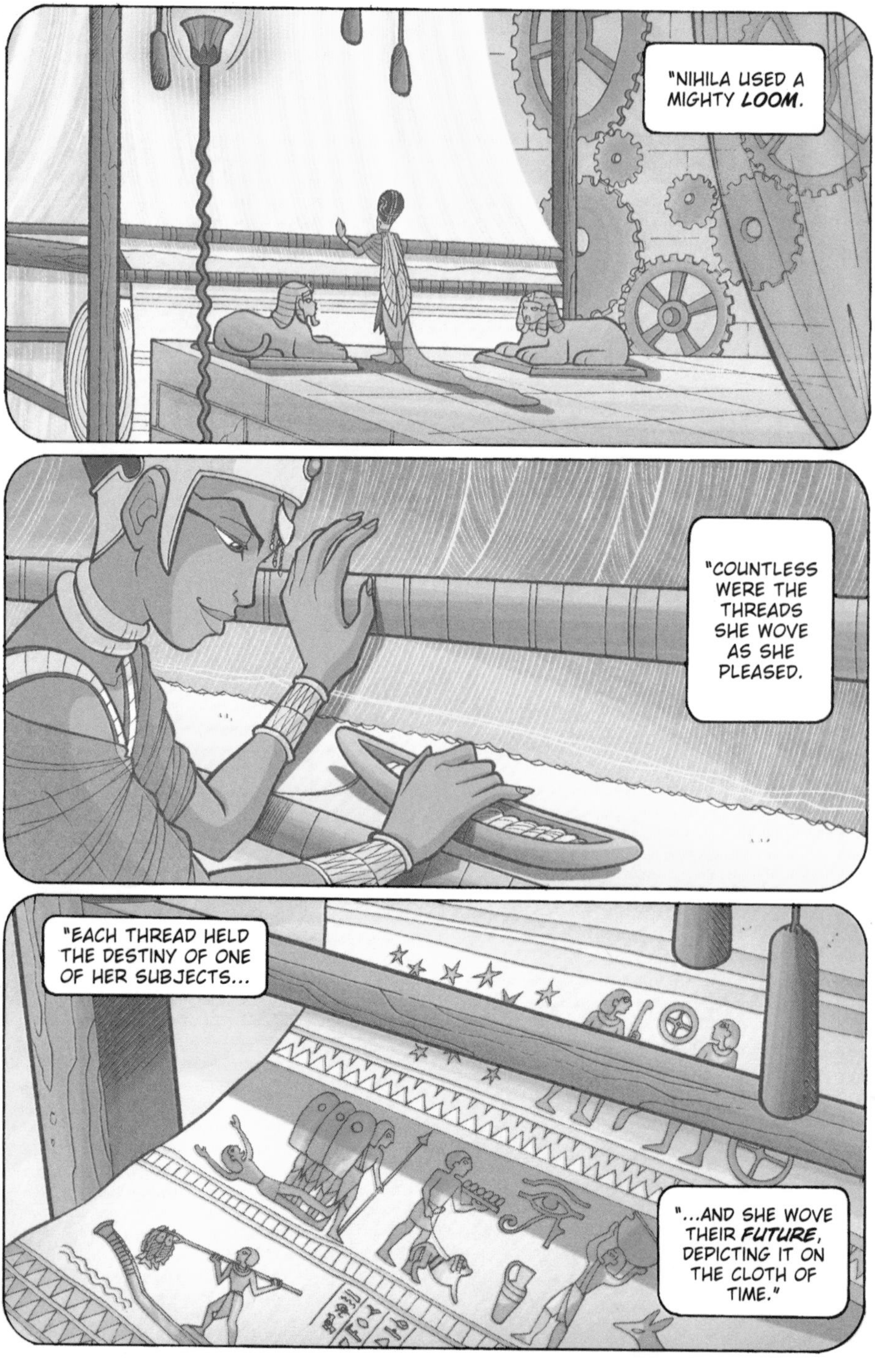
"NIHILA USED A MIGHTY **LOOM**.
"COUNTLESS WERE THE THREADS SHE WOVE AS SHE PLEASED.
"EACH THREAD HELD THE DESTINY OF ONE OF HER SUBJECTS...
"...AND SHE WOVE THEIR **FUTURE**, DEPICTING IT ON THE CLOTH OF TIME."

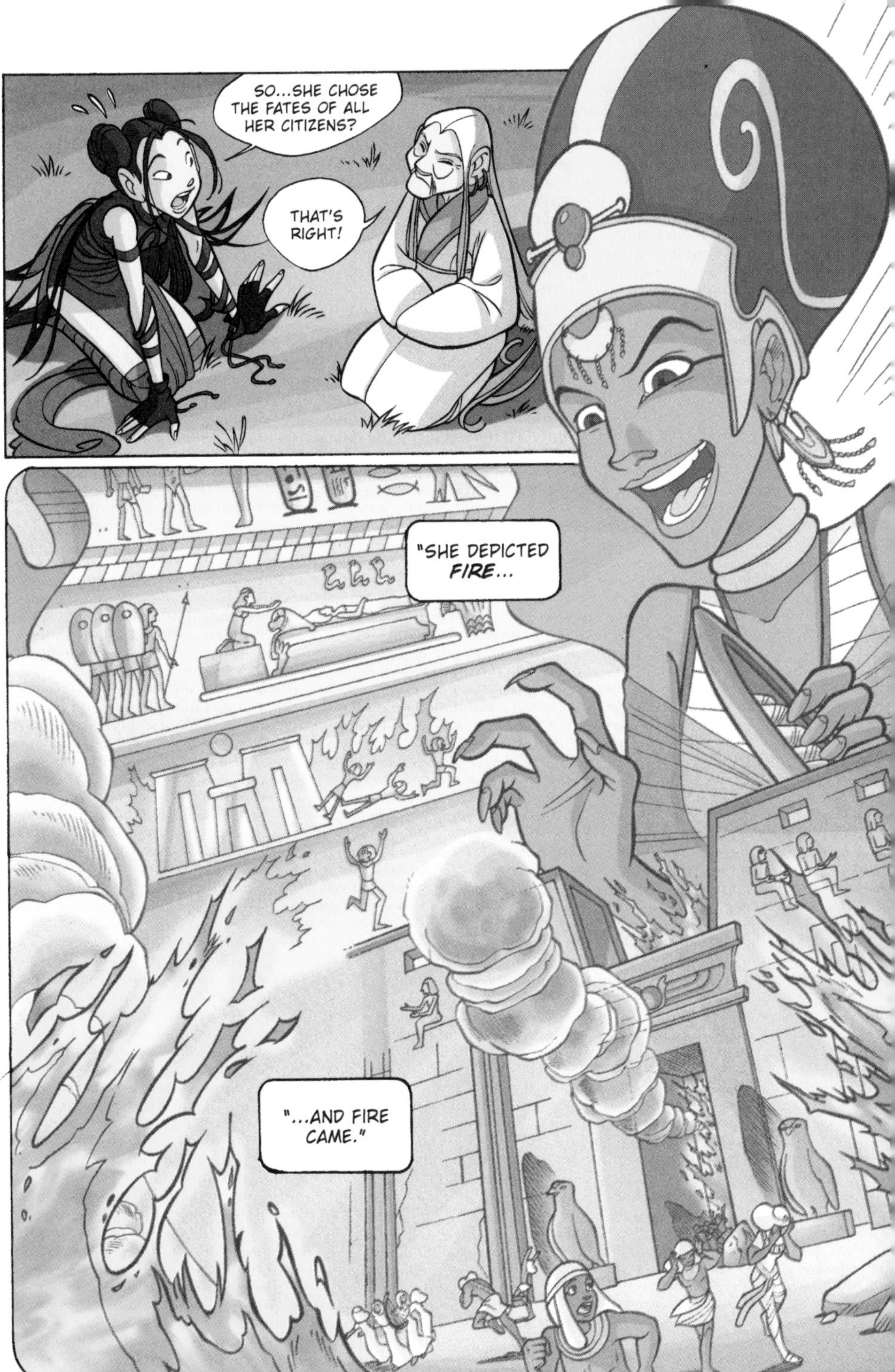
SO...SHE CHOSE THE FATES OF ALL HER CITIZENS?
THAT'S RIGHT!
"SHE DEPICTED FIRE...
"...AND FIRE CAME."

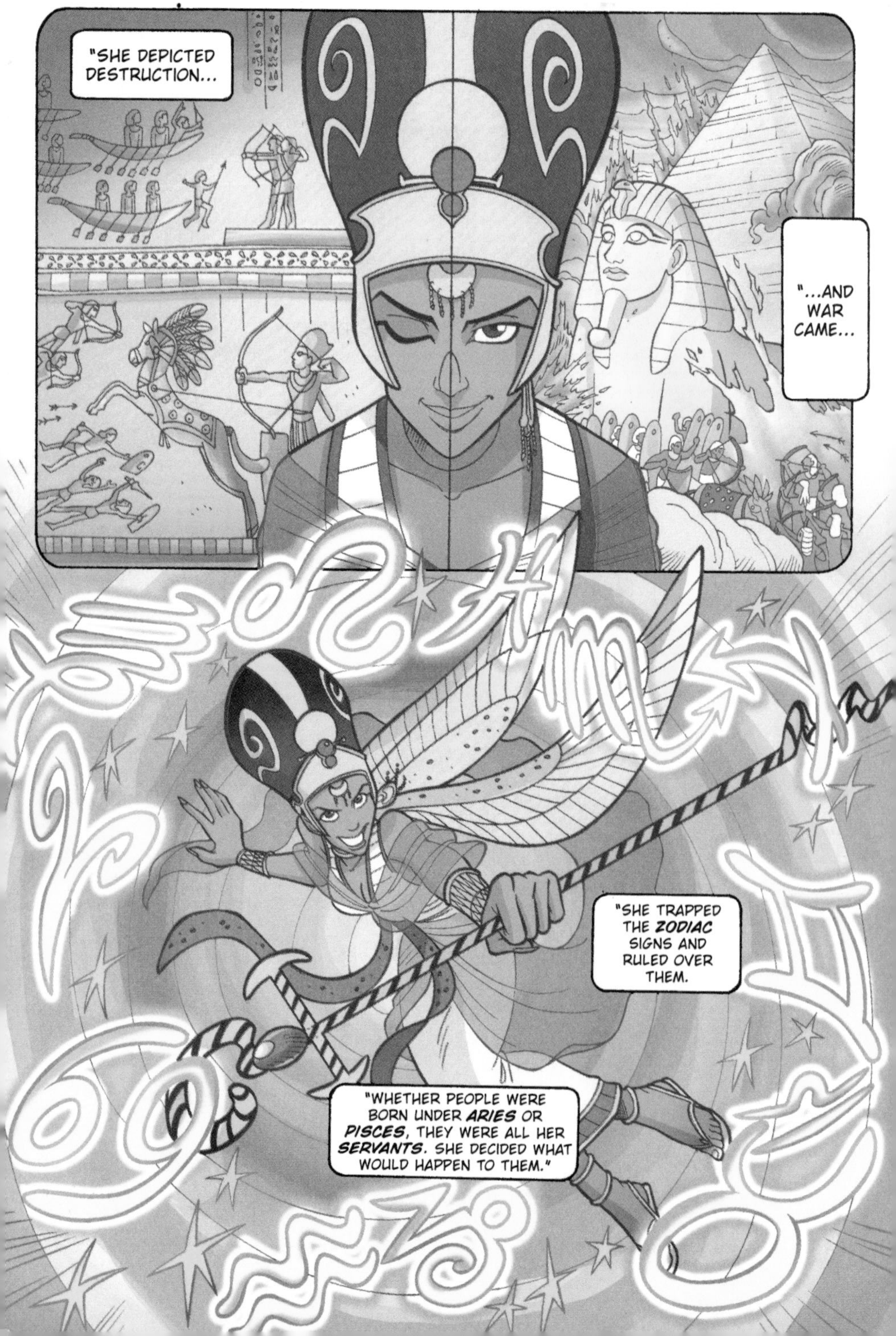
"SHE DEPICTED DESTRUCTION...
"...AND WAR CAME...
"SHE TRAPPED THE ZODIAC SIGNS AND RULED OVER THEM.
"WHETHER PEOPLE WERE BORN UNDER ARIES OR PISCES, THEY WERE ALL HER SERVANTS. SHE DECIDED WHAT WOULD HAPPEN TO THEM."

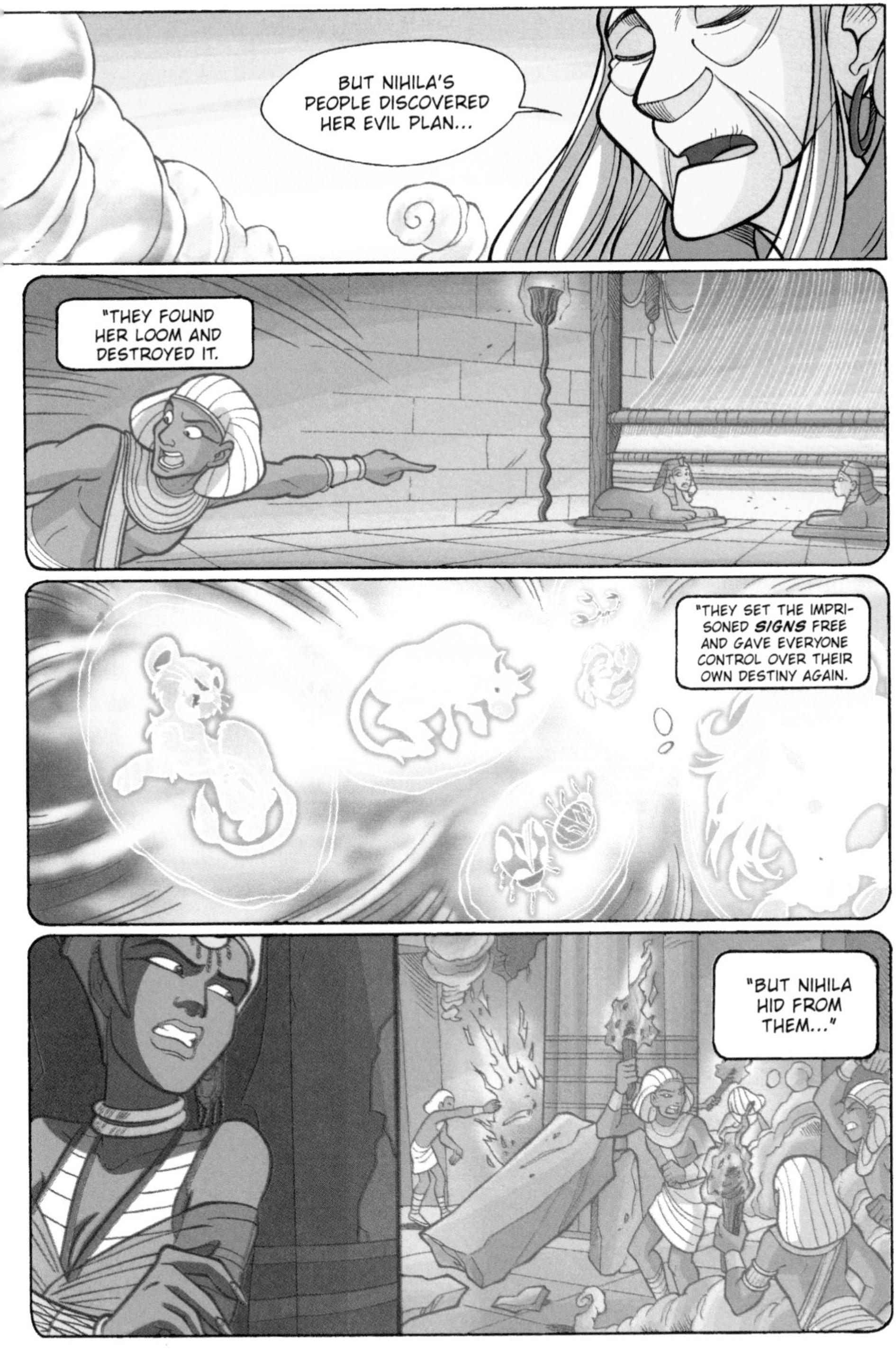
BUT NIHILA'S PEOPLE DISCOVERED HER EVIL PLAN...
"THEY FOUND HER LOOM AND DESTROYED IT.
"THEY SET THE IMPRISONED SIGNS FREE AND GAVE EVERYONE CONTROL OVER THEIR OWN DESTINY AGAIN.
"BUT NIHILA HID FROM THEM..."

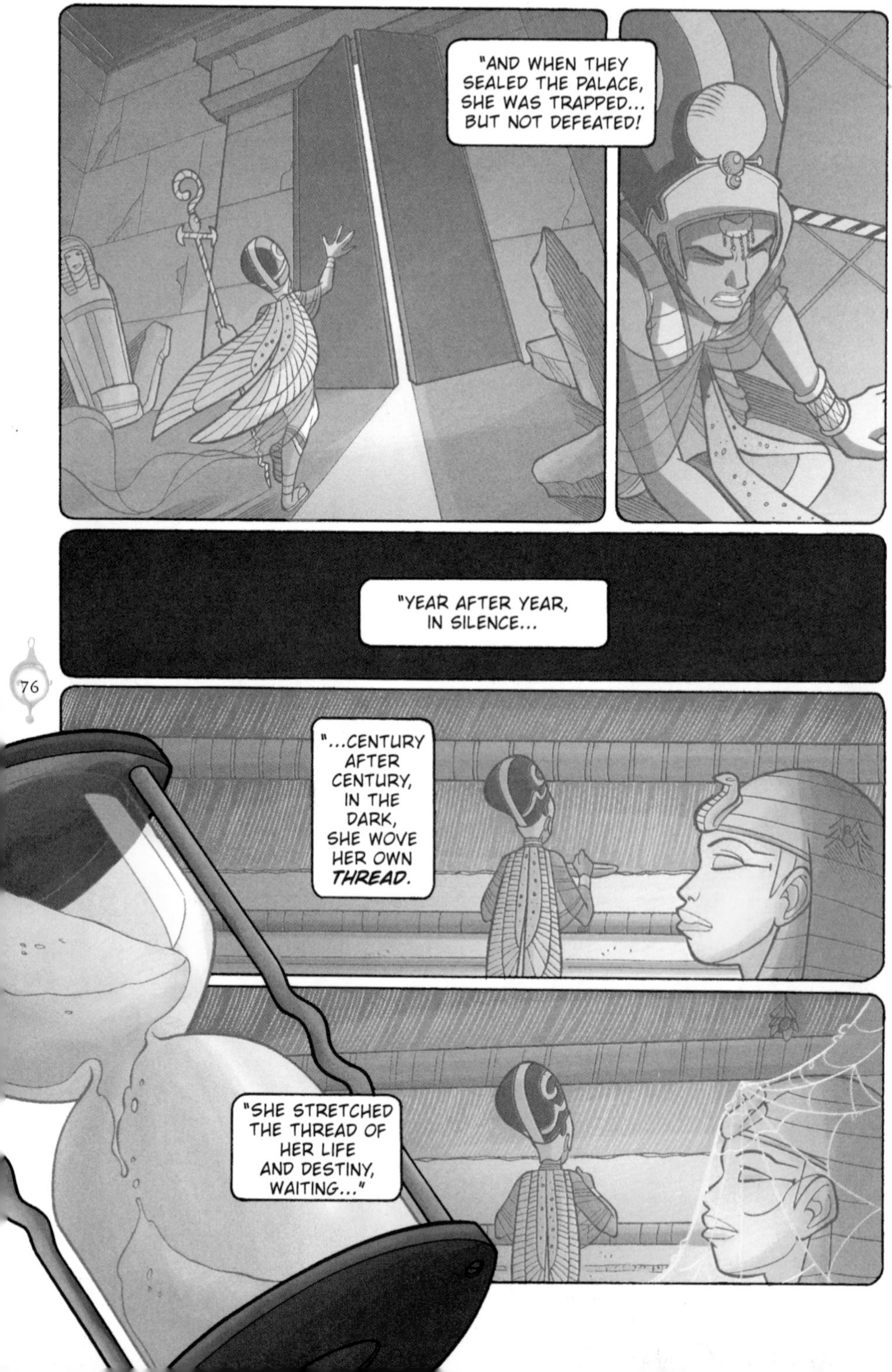
"AND WHEN THEY SEALED THE PALACE, SHE WAS TRAPPED... BUT NOT DEFEATED!
"YEAR AFTER YEAR, IN SILENCE...
"...CENTURY AFTER CENTURY, IN THE DARK, SHE WOVE HER OWN *THREAD*.
"SHE STRETCHED THE THREAD OF HER LIFE AND DESTINY, WAITING..."

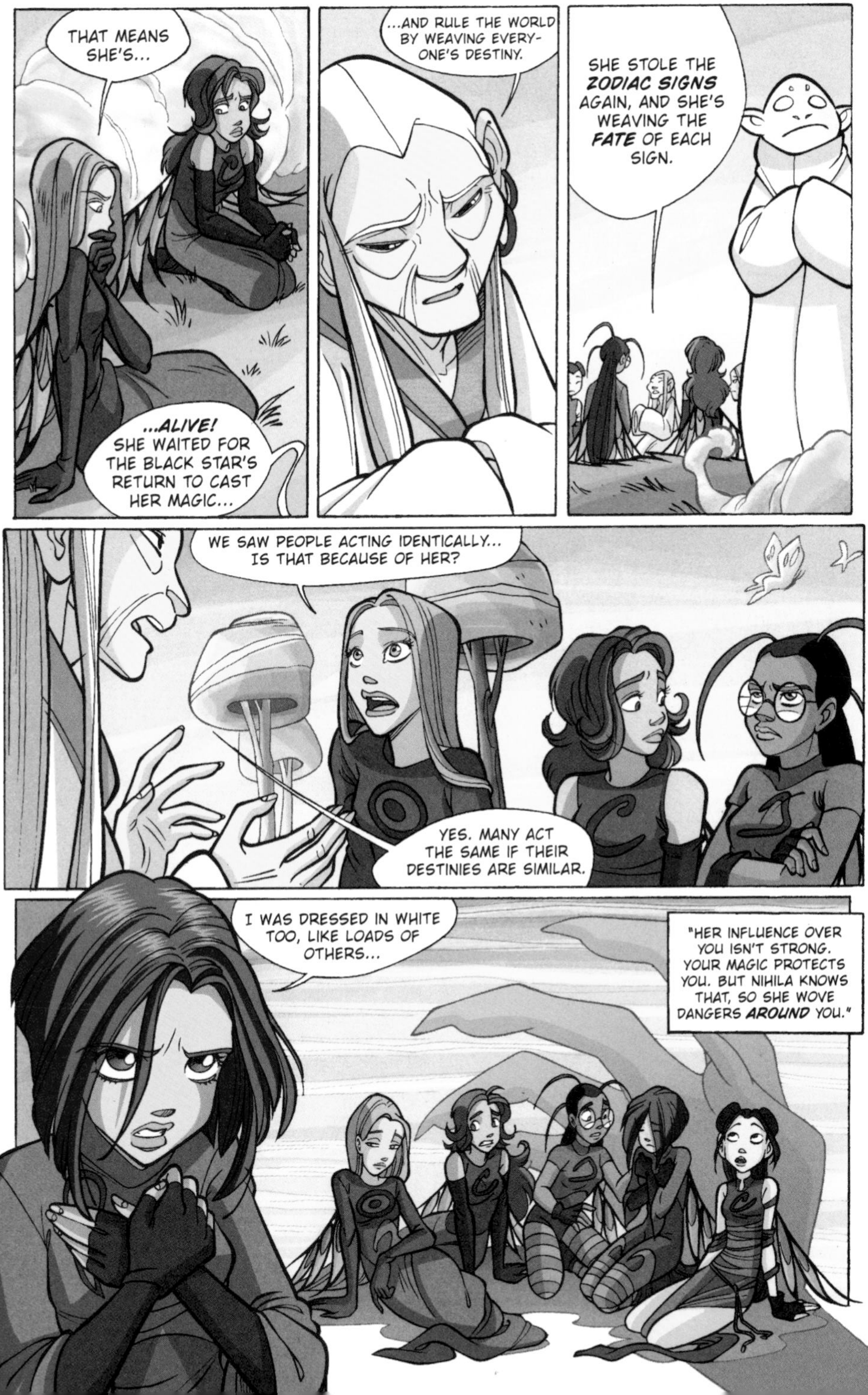
THAT MEANS SHE'S...
...*ALIVE!* SHE WAITED FOR THE BLACK STAR'S RETURN TO CAST HER MAGIC...
...AND RULE THE WORLD BY WEAVING EVERY-ONE'S DESTINY.
SHE STOLE THE ***ZODIAC SIGNS*** AGAIN, AND SHE'S WEAVING THE ***FATE*** OF EACH SIGN.
WE SAW PEOPLE ACTING IDENTICALLY... IS THAT BECAUSE OF HER?
YES. MANY ACT THE SAME IF THEIR DESTINIES ARE SIMILAR.
I WAS DRESSED IN WHITE TOO, LIKE LOADS OF OTHERS...
"HER INFLUENCE OVER YOU ISN'T STRONG. YOUR MAGIC PROTECTS YOU. BUT NIHILA KNOWS THAT, SO SHE WOVE DANGERS ***AROUND*** YOU."

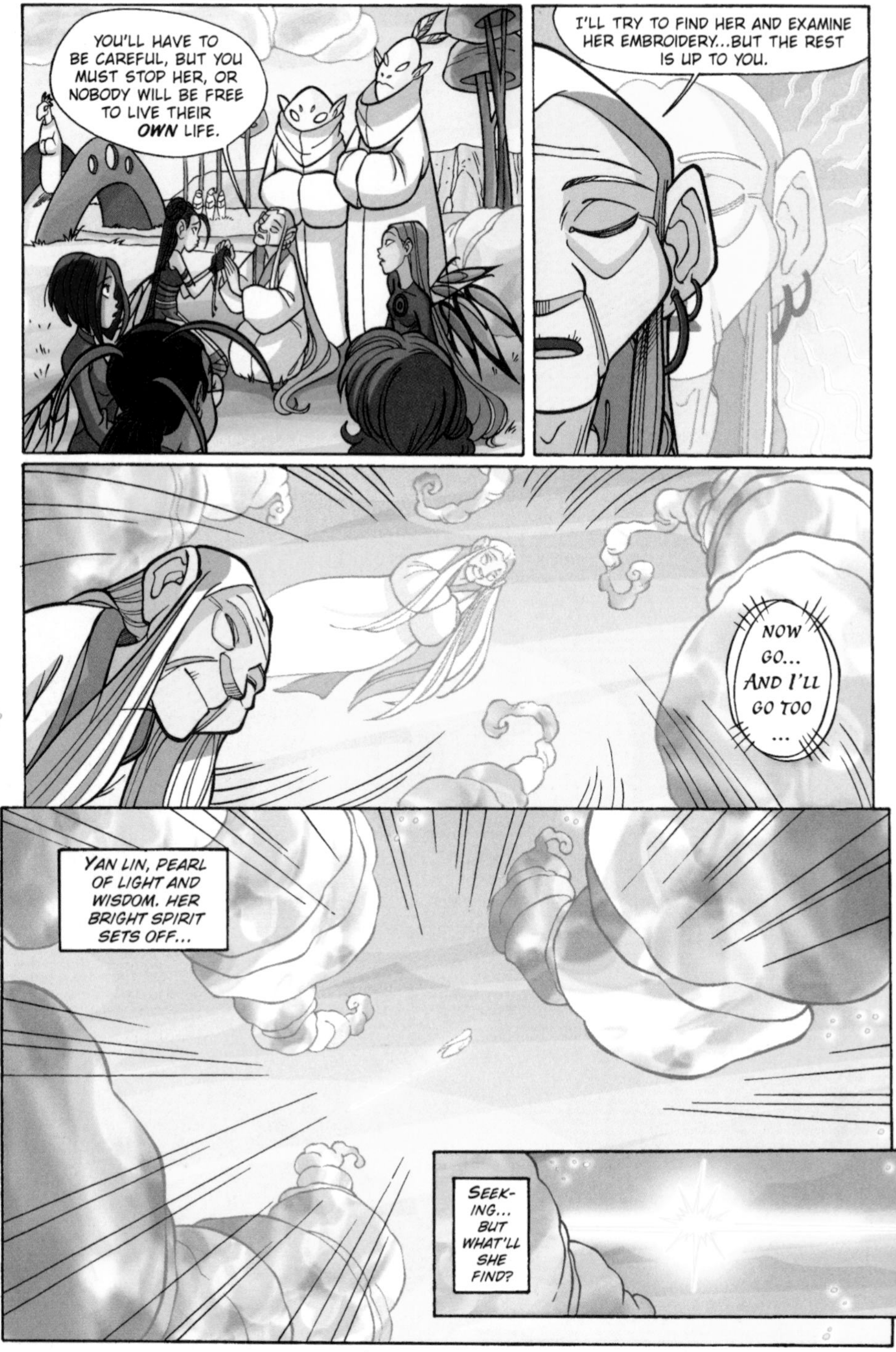
YOU'LL HAVE TO BE CAREFUL, BUT YOU MUST STOP HER, OR NOBODY WILL BE FREE TO LIVE THEIR OWN LIFE.
I'LL TRY TO FIND HER AND EXAMINE HER EMBROIDERY...BUT THE REST IS UP TO YOU.
NOW GO... AND I'LL GO TOO ...
YAN LIN, PEARL OF LIGHT AND WISDOM. HER BRIGHT SPIRIT SETS OFF...
SEEK-ING... BUT WHAT'LL SHE FIND?

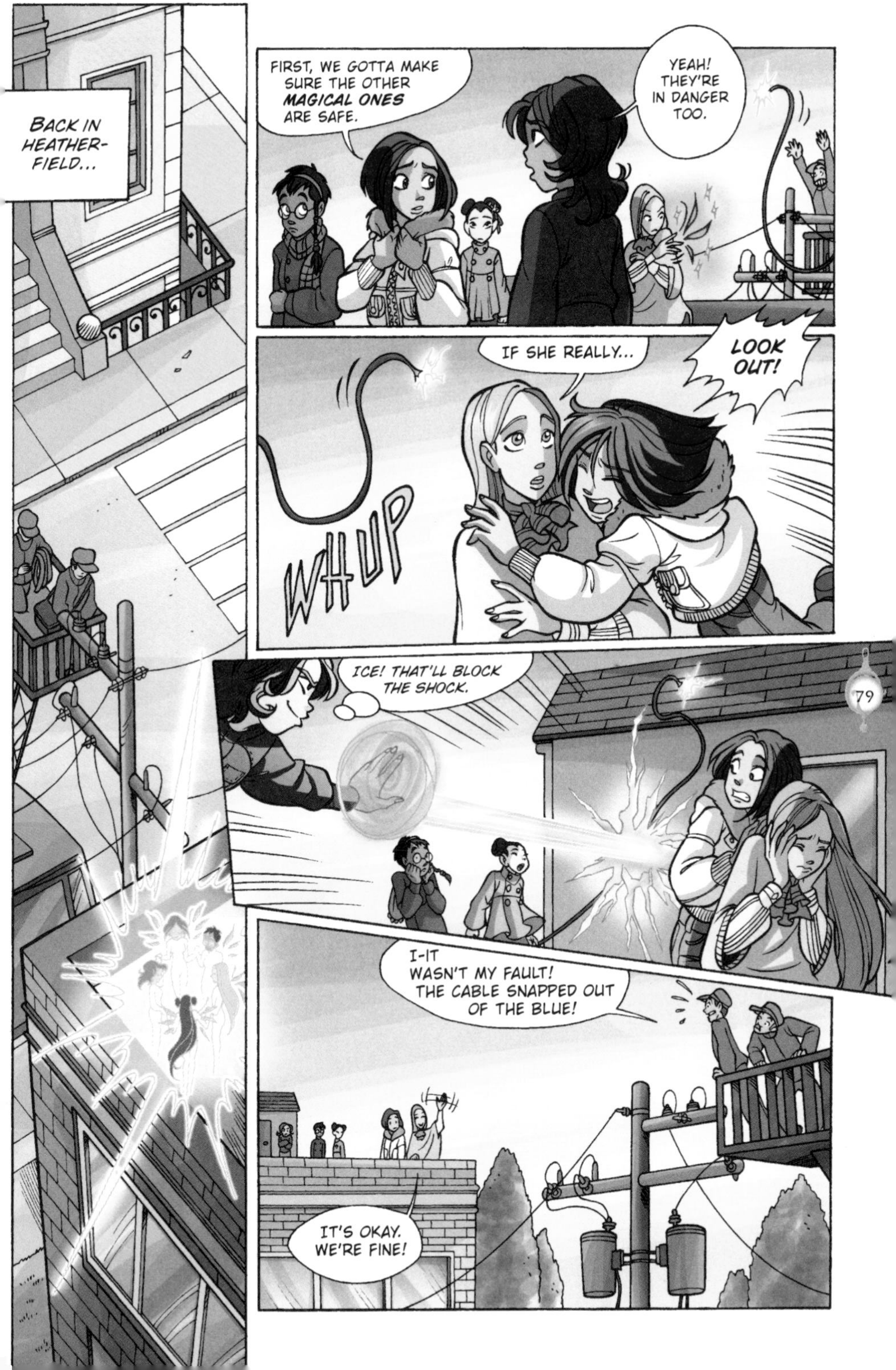
BACK IN HEATHER-FIELD...
FIRST, WE GOTTA MAKE SURE THE OTHER MAGICAL ONES ARE SAFE.
YEAH! THEY'RE IN DANGER TOO.
IF SHE REALLY...
LOOK OUT!
WHUP
ICE! THAT'LL BLOCK THE SHOCK.
I-IT WASN'T MY FAULT! THE CABLE SNAPPED OUT OF THE BLUE!
IT'S OKAY. WE'RE FINE!

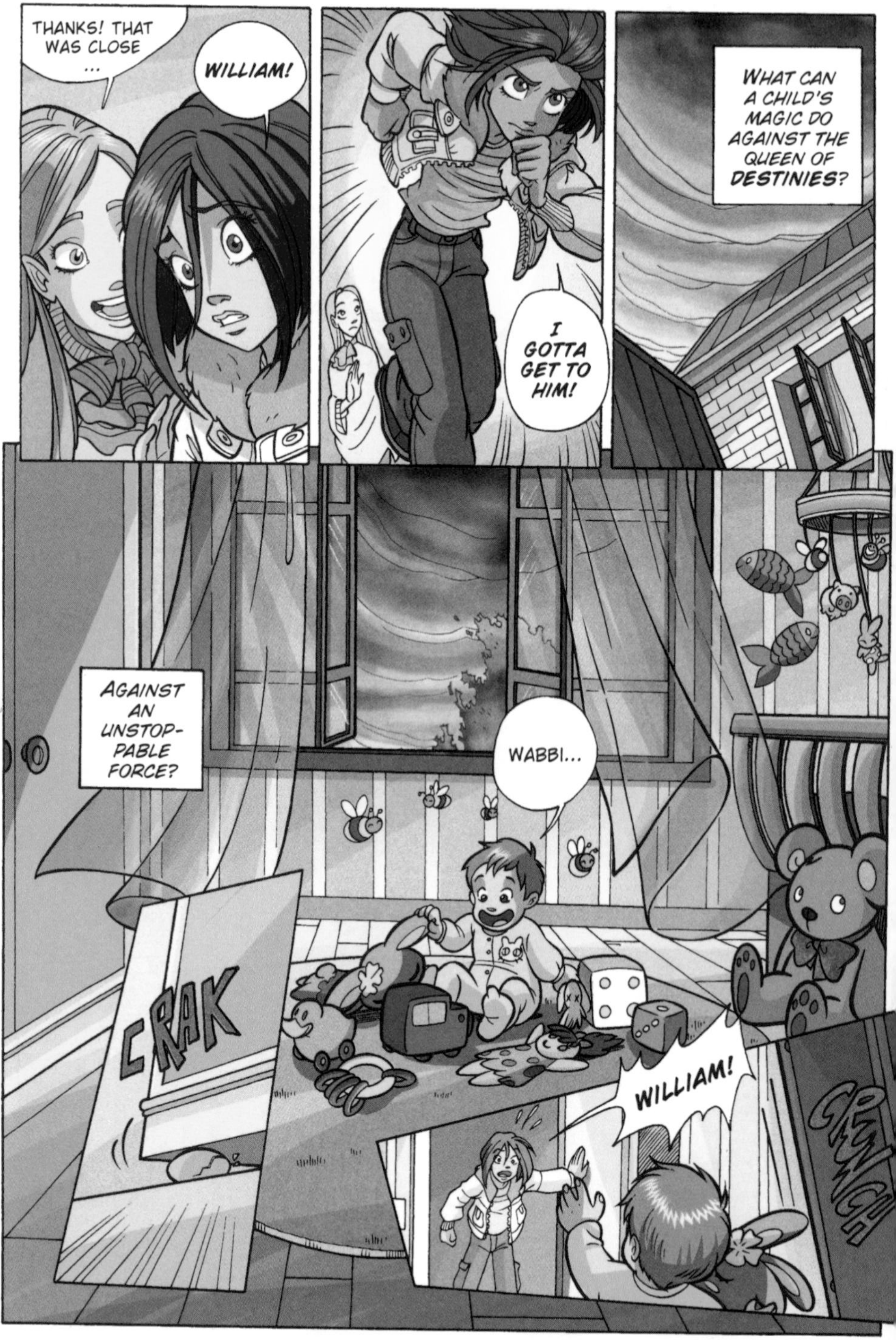
THANKS! THAT WAS CLOSE ...
WILLIAM!
I GOTTA GET TO HIM!
WHAT CAN A CHILD'S MAGIC DO AGAINST THE QUEEN OF DESTINIES?
AGAINST AN UNSTOP-PABLE FORCE?
WABBI...
CRAK
WILLIAM!
CRUNCH

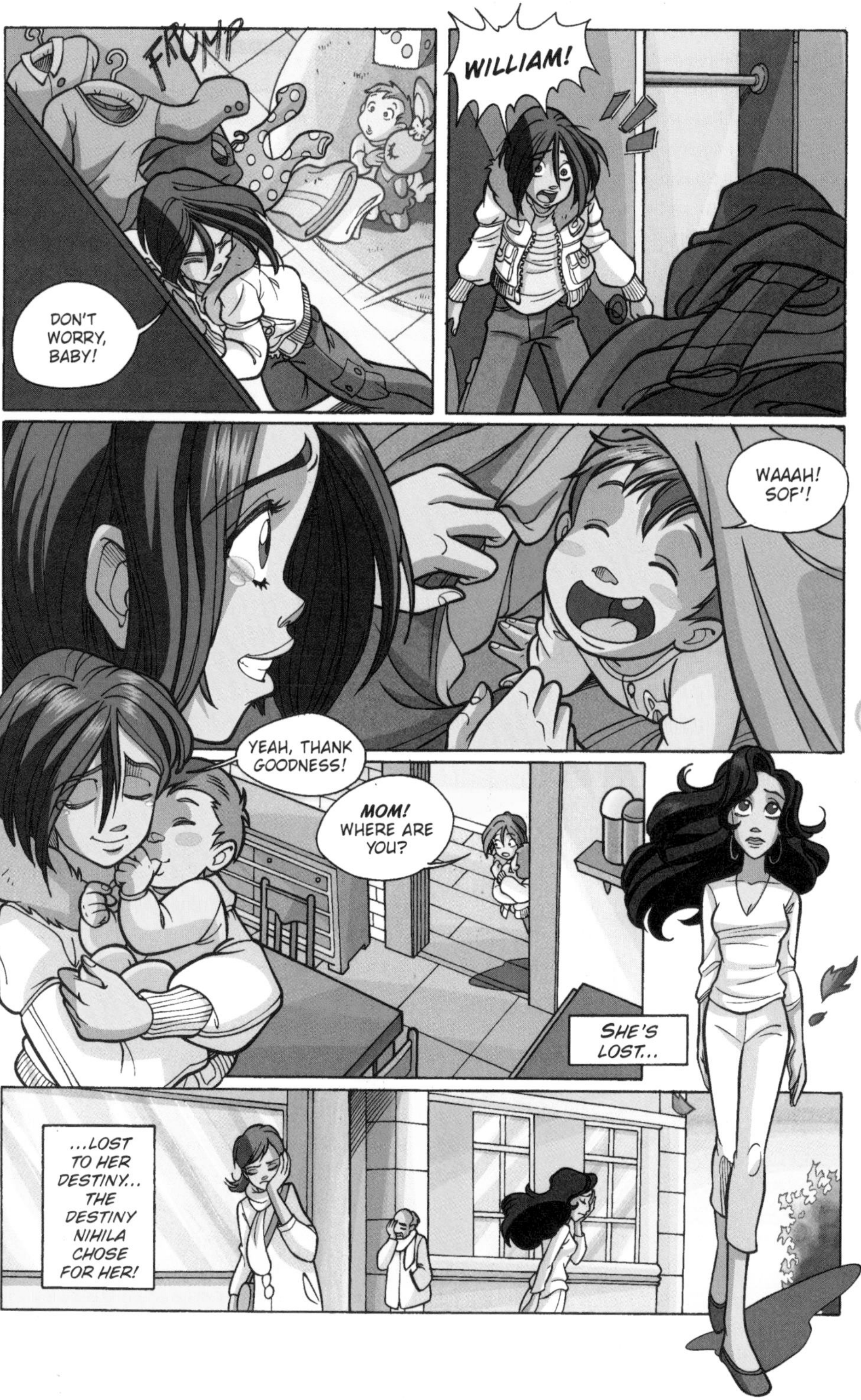
FRUMP
DON'T WORRY, BABY!
WILLIAM!
WAAAH! SOF'!
YEAH, THANK GOODNESS!
MOM! WHERE ARE YOU?
SHE'S LOST...
...LOST TO HER DESTINY... THE DESTINY NIHILA CHOSE FOR HER!

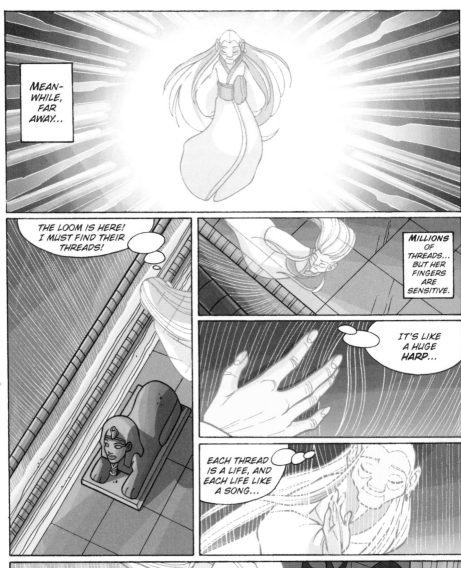

MEAN-
WHILE,
FAR
AWAY...

THE LOOM IS HERE!
I MUST FIND THEIR
THREADS!

MILLIONS
OF
THREADS...
BUT HER
FINGERS
ARE
SENSITIVE.

IT'S LIKE
A HUGE
HARP...

EACH THREAD
IS A LIFE, AND
EACH LIFE LIKE
A SONG...

HERE!
HAY LIN...
WILL...THEIR
FAMILIES...

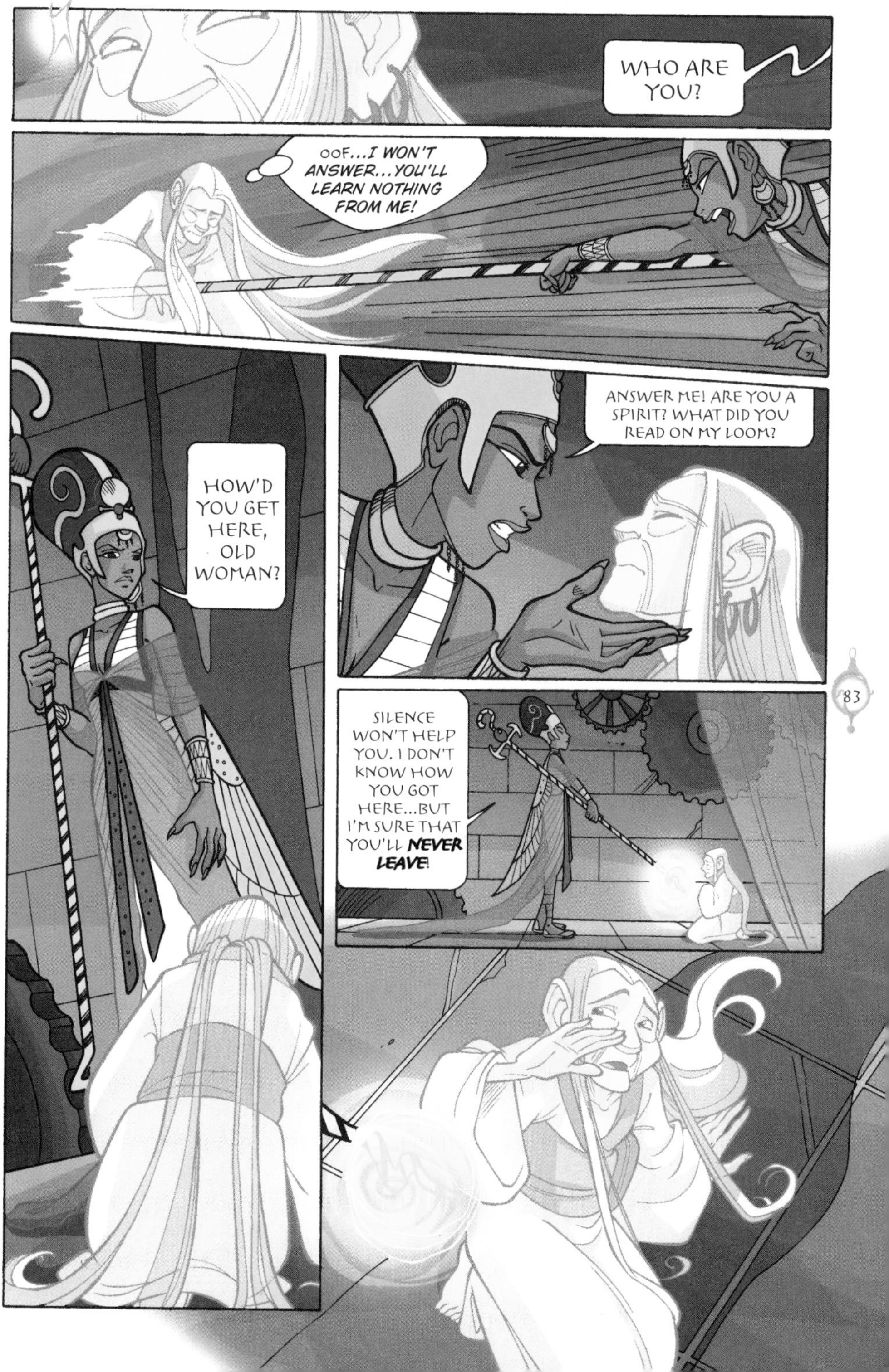
WHO ARE YOU?
OOF...I WON'T ANSWER...YOU'LL LEARN NOTHING FROM ME!
HOW'D YOU GET HERE, OLD WOMAN?
ANSWER ME! ARE YOU A SPIRIT? WHAT DID YOU READ ON MY LOOM?
SILENCE WON'T HELP YOU. I DON'T KNOW HOW YOU GOT HERE...BUT I'M SURE THAT YOU'LL **NEVER LEAVE**!

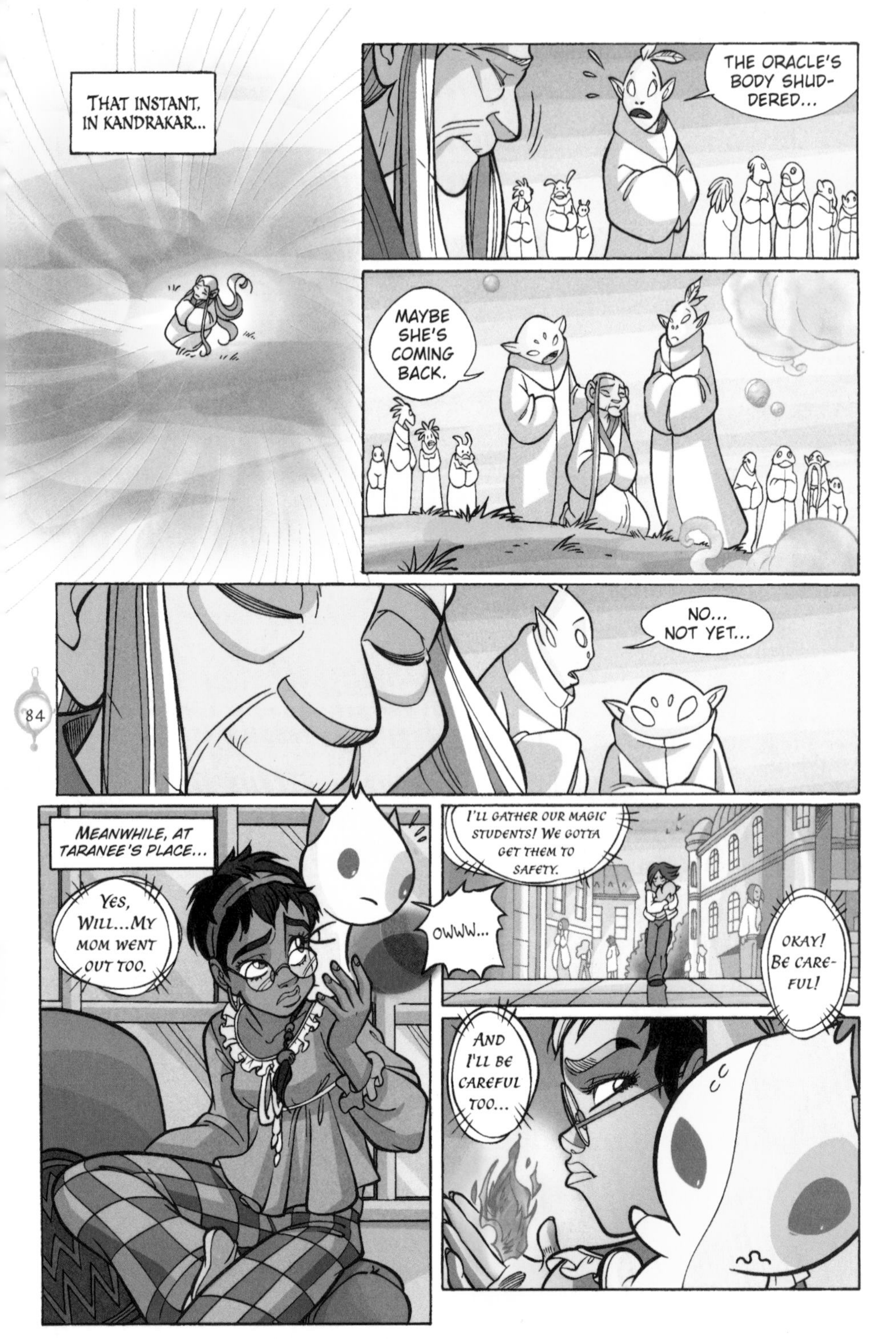
THAT INSTANT, IN KANDRAKAR...
THE ORACLE'S BODY SHUDDERED...
MAYBE SHE'S COMING BACK.
NO... NOT YET...
MEANWHILE, AT TARANEE'S PLACE...
YES, WILL...MY MOM WENT OUT TOO.
OWWW...
I'LL GATHER OUR MAGIC STUDENTS! WE GOTTA GET THEM TO SAFETY.
OKAY! BE CAREFUL!
AND I'LL BE CAREFUL TOO...

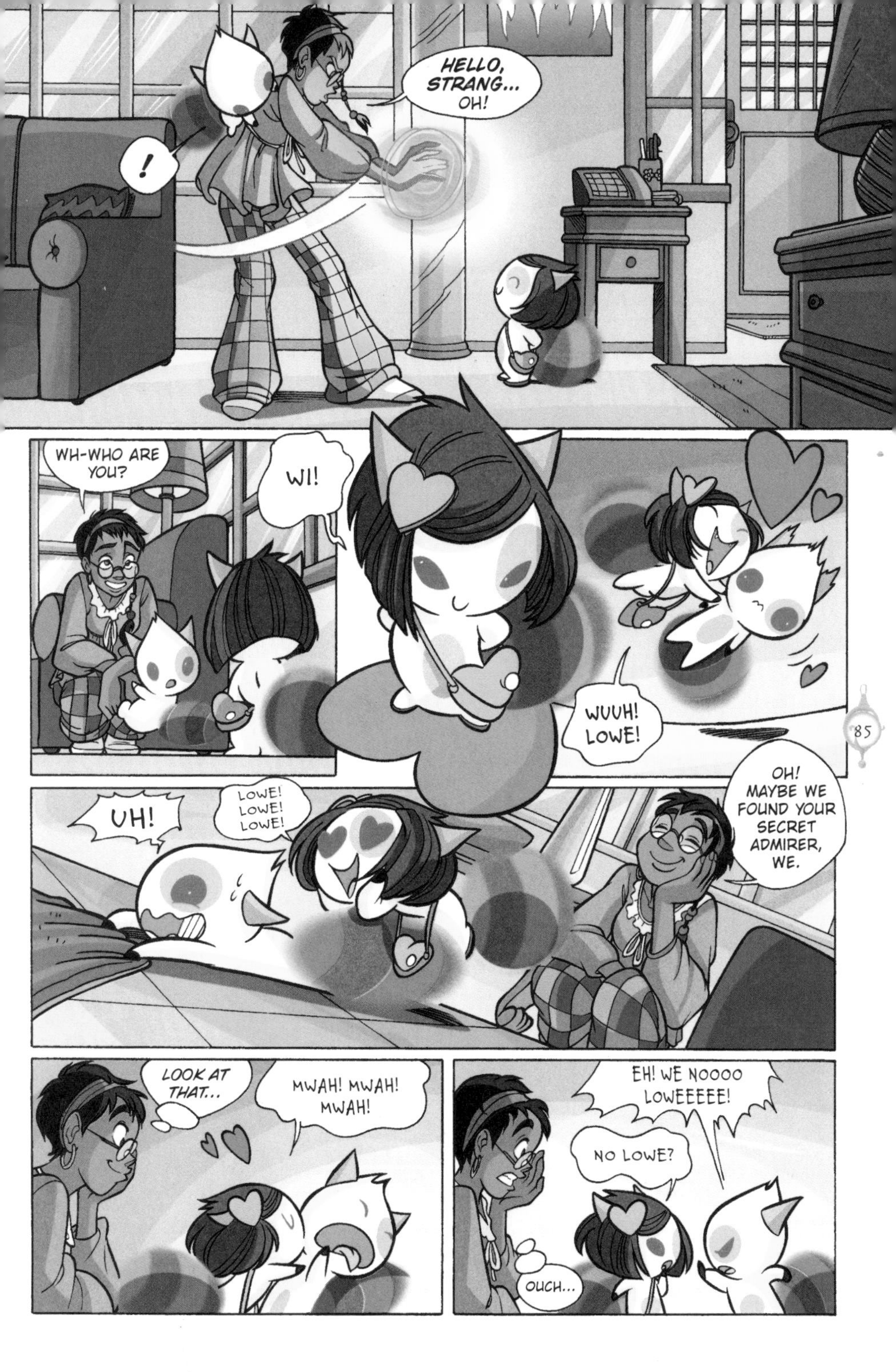
HELLO, STRANG... OH!
!
WH-WHO ARE YOU?
WI!
WUUH! LOWE!
UH!
LOWE! LOWE! LOWE!
OH! MAYBE WE FOUND YOUR SECRET ADMIRER, WE.
LOOK AT THAT...
MWAH! MWAH! MWAH!
EH! WE NOOOO LOWEEEEEE!
NO LOWE?
OUCH...

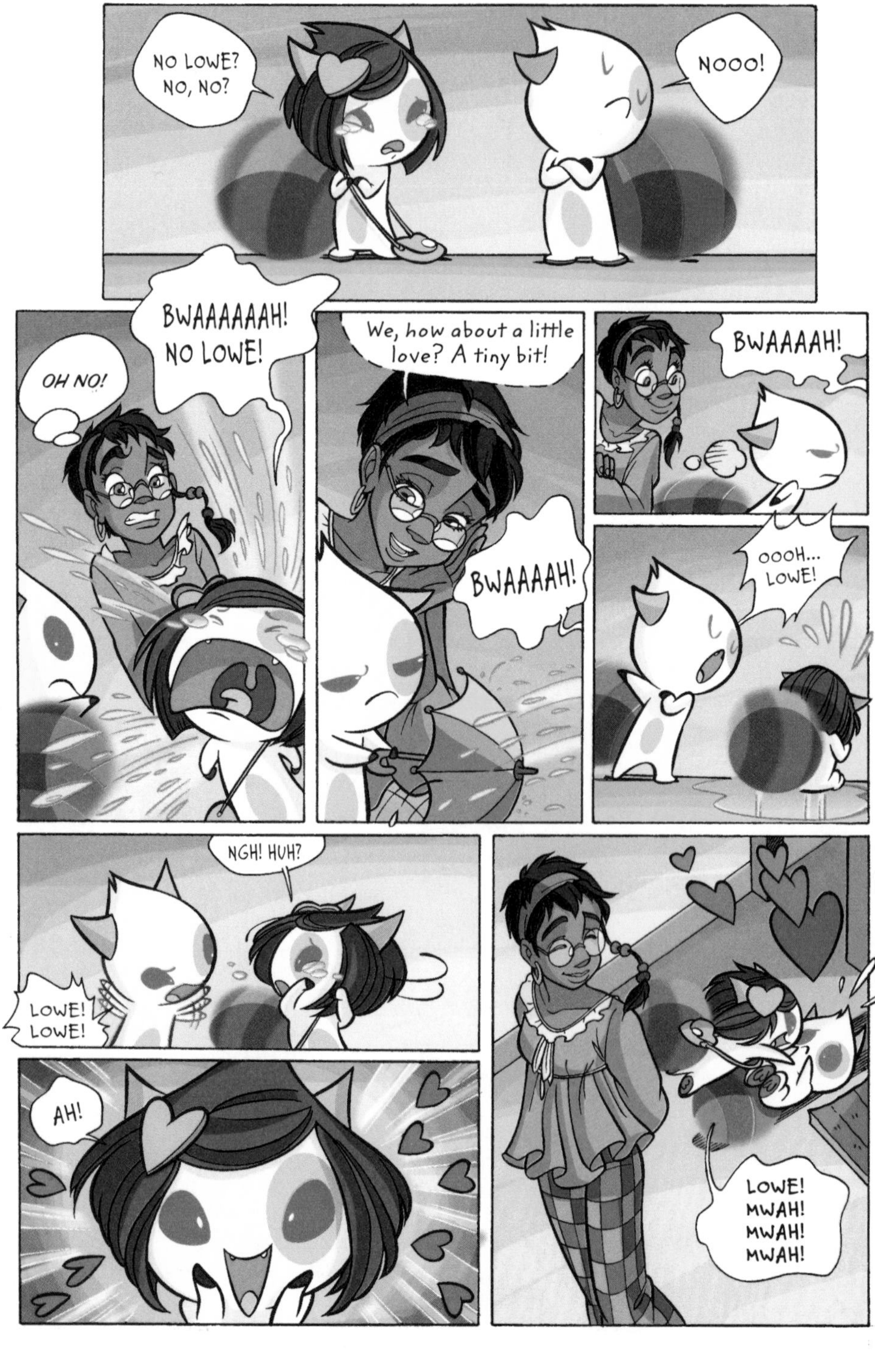
NO LOWE?
NO, NO?
NOOO!
BWAAAAAAH!
NO LOWE!
OH NO!
We, how about a little love? A tiny bit!
BWAAAAH!
BWAAAAH!
OOOH... LOWE!
NGH! HUH?
LOWE! LOWE!
AH!
LOWE! MWAH! MWAH! MWAH!

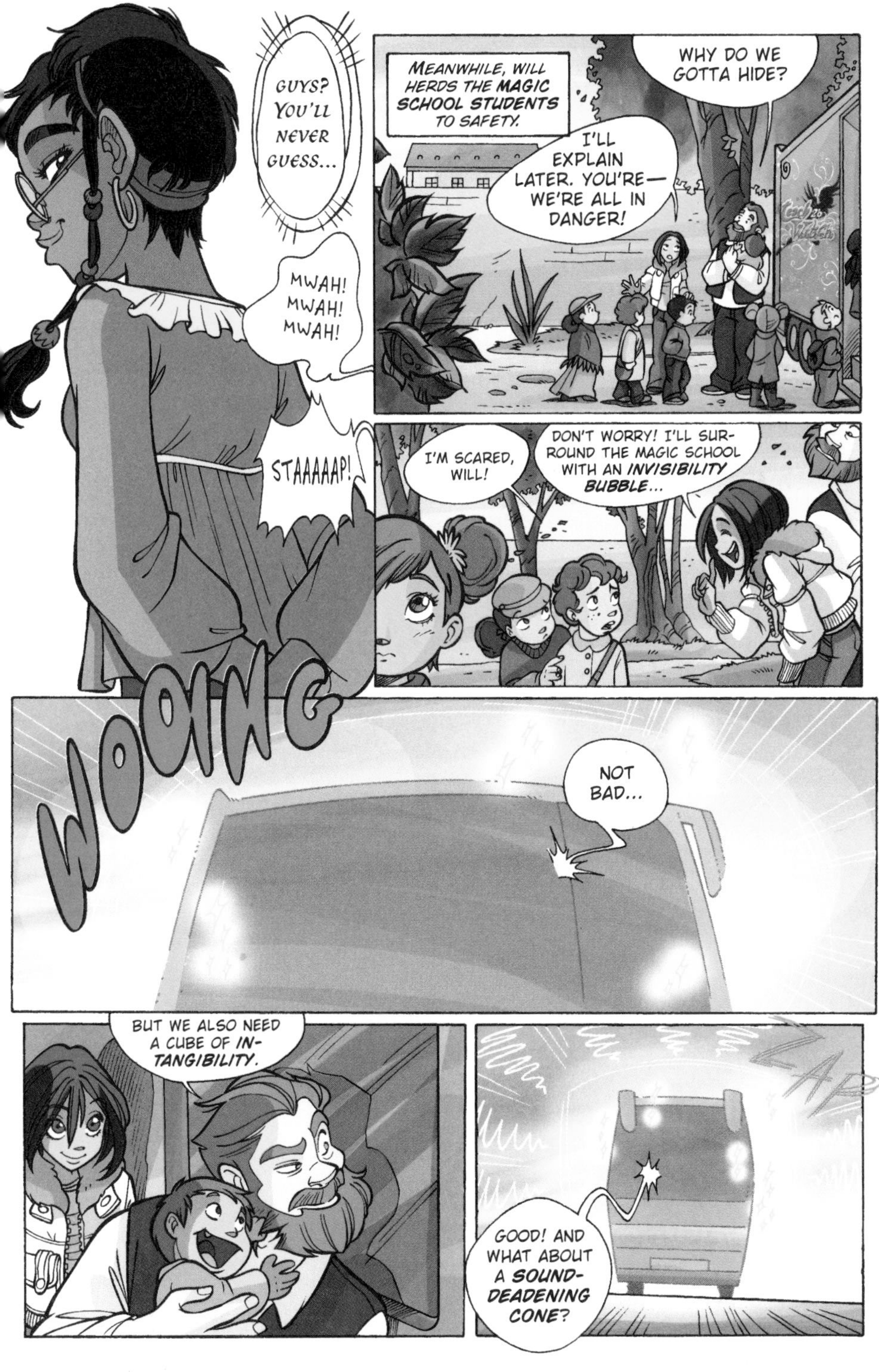
GUYS? YOU'LL NEVER GUESS...
MWAH! MWAH! MWAH!
STAAAAAP!
MEANWHILE, WILL HERDS THE MAGIC SCHOOL STUDENTS TO SAFETY.
WHY DO WE GOTTA HIDE?
I'LL EXPLAIN LATER. YOU'RE— WE'RE ALL IN DANGER!
I'M SCARED, WILL!
DON'T WORRY! I'LL SURROUND THE MAGIC SCHOOL WITH AN INVISIBILITY BUBBLE...
WOOING
NOT BAD...
BUT WE ALSO NEED A CUBE OF INTANGIBILITY.
ZAP
GOOD! AND WHAT ABOUT A SOUND-DEADENING CONE?

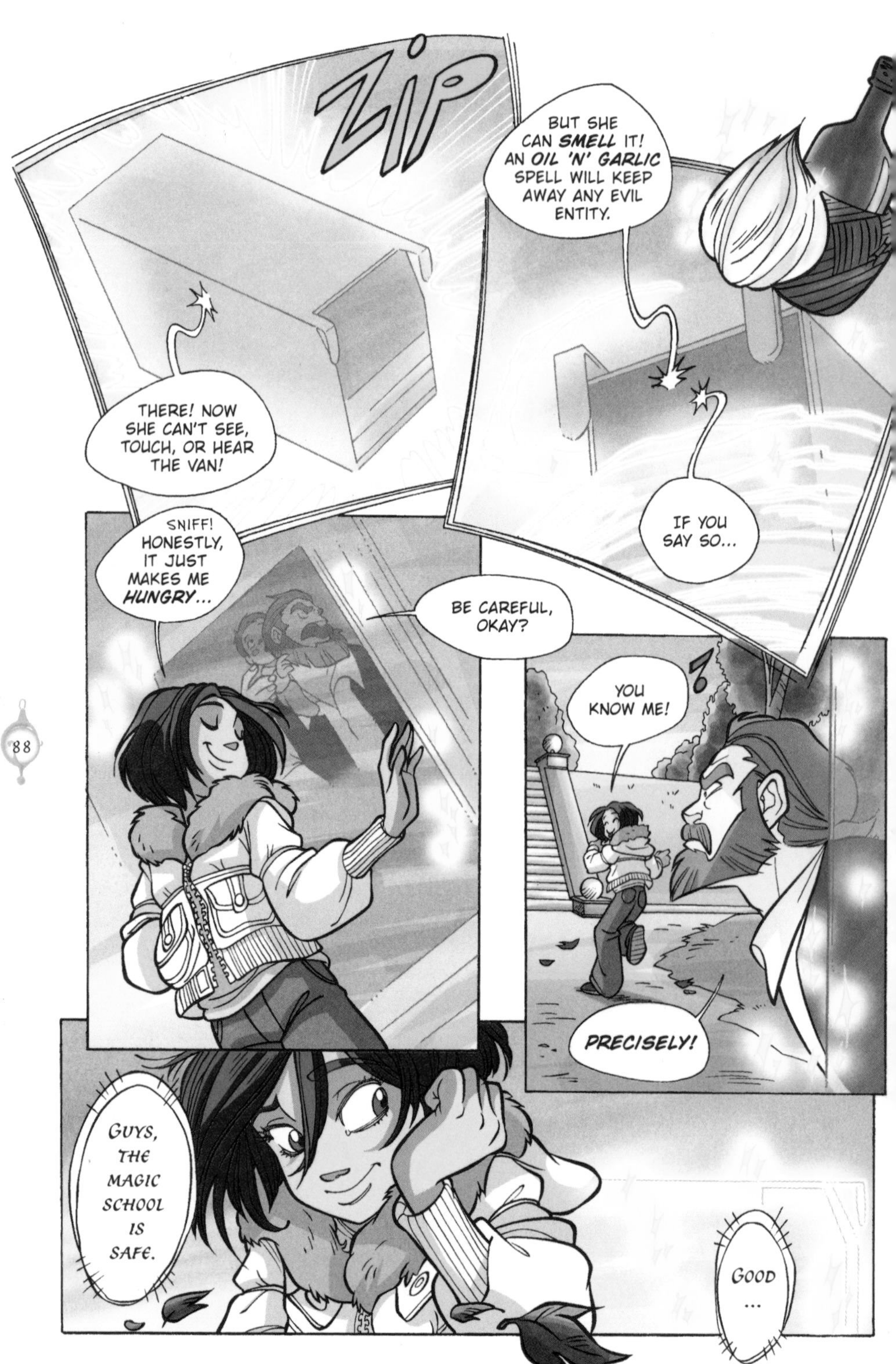
ZIP
THERE! NOW SHE CAN'T SEE, TOUCH, OR HEAR THE VAN!
BUT SHE CAN SMELL IT! AN OIL 'N' GARLIC SPELL WILL KEEP AWAY ANY EVIL ENTITY.
IF YOU SAY SO...
SNIFF! HONESTLY, IT JUST MAKES ME HUNGRY...
BE CAREFUL, OKAY?
YOU KNOW ME!
PRECISELY!
GUYS, THE MAGIC SCHOOL IS SAFE.
GOOD ...

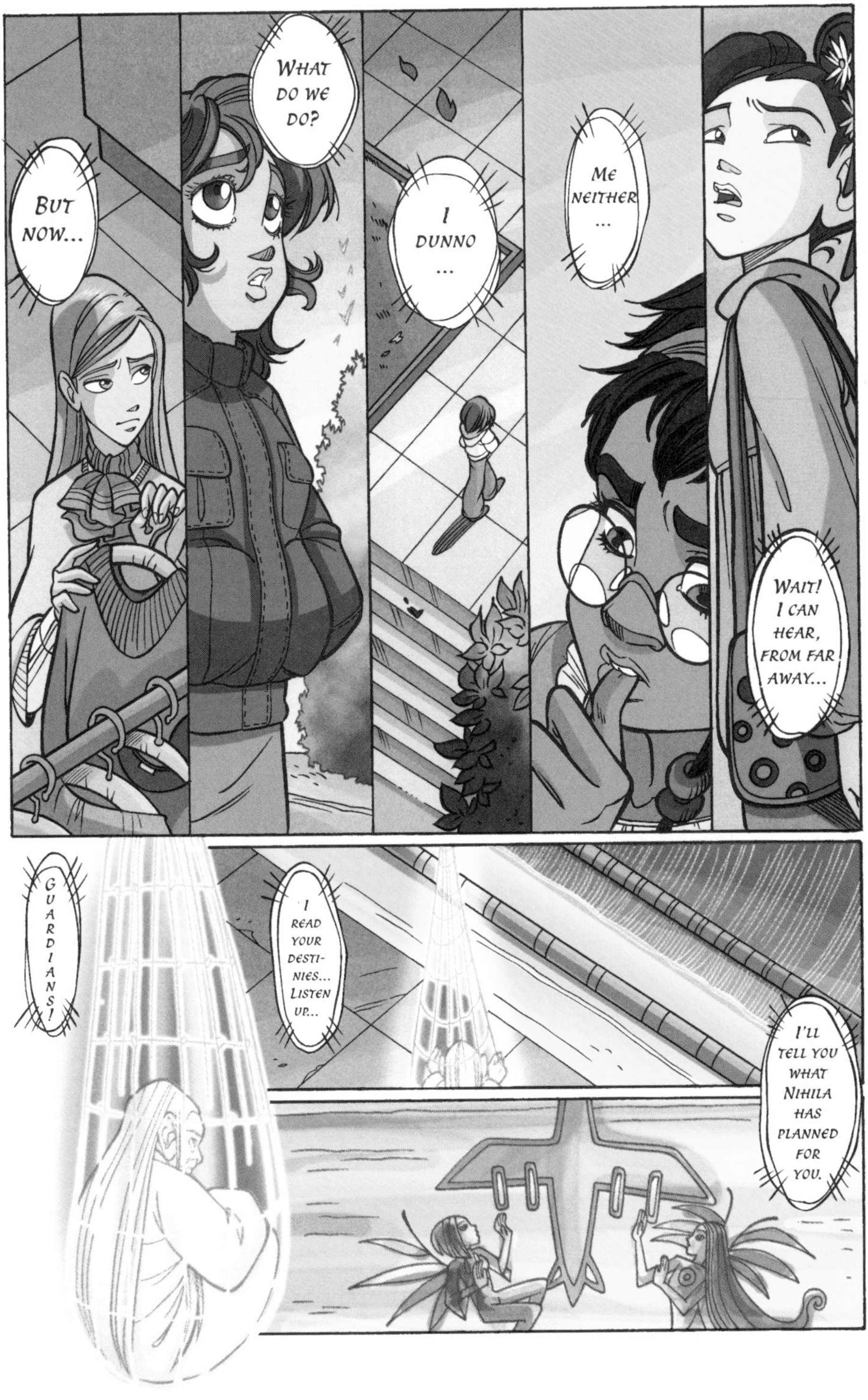
But now...
What do we do?
I dunno ...
Me neither ...
Wait! I can hear, from far away...
Guardians!
I read your desti-nies... Listen up...
I'll tell you what Nihila has planned for you.

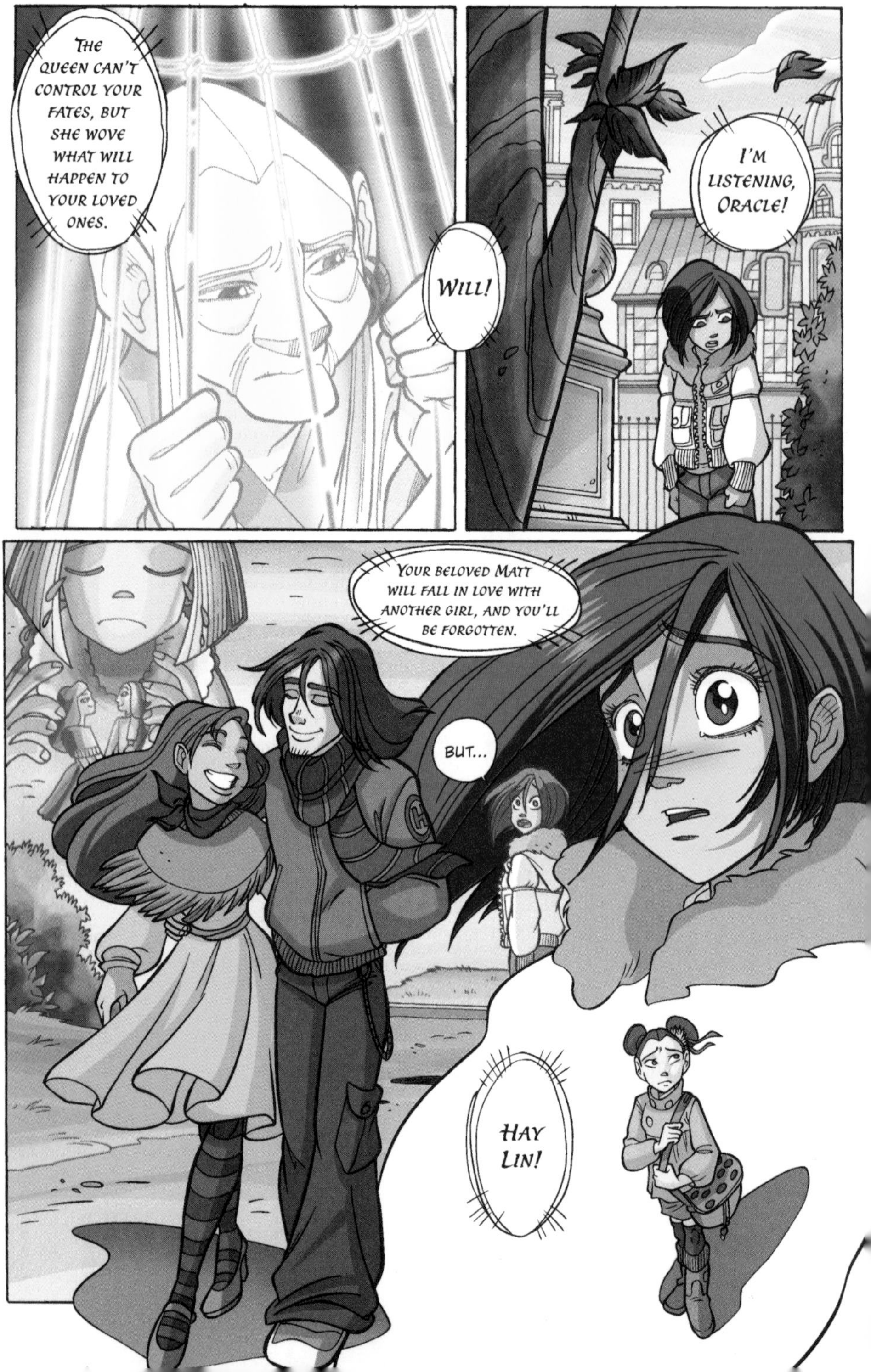
THE QUEEN CAN'T CONTROL YOUR FATES, BUT SHE WOVE WHAT WILL HAPPEN TO YOUR LOVED ONES.
WILL!
I'M LISTENING, ORACLE!
YOUR BELOVED MATT WILL FALL IN LOVE WITH ANOTHER GIRL, AND YOU'LL BE FORGOTTEN.
BUT...
HAY LIN!

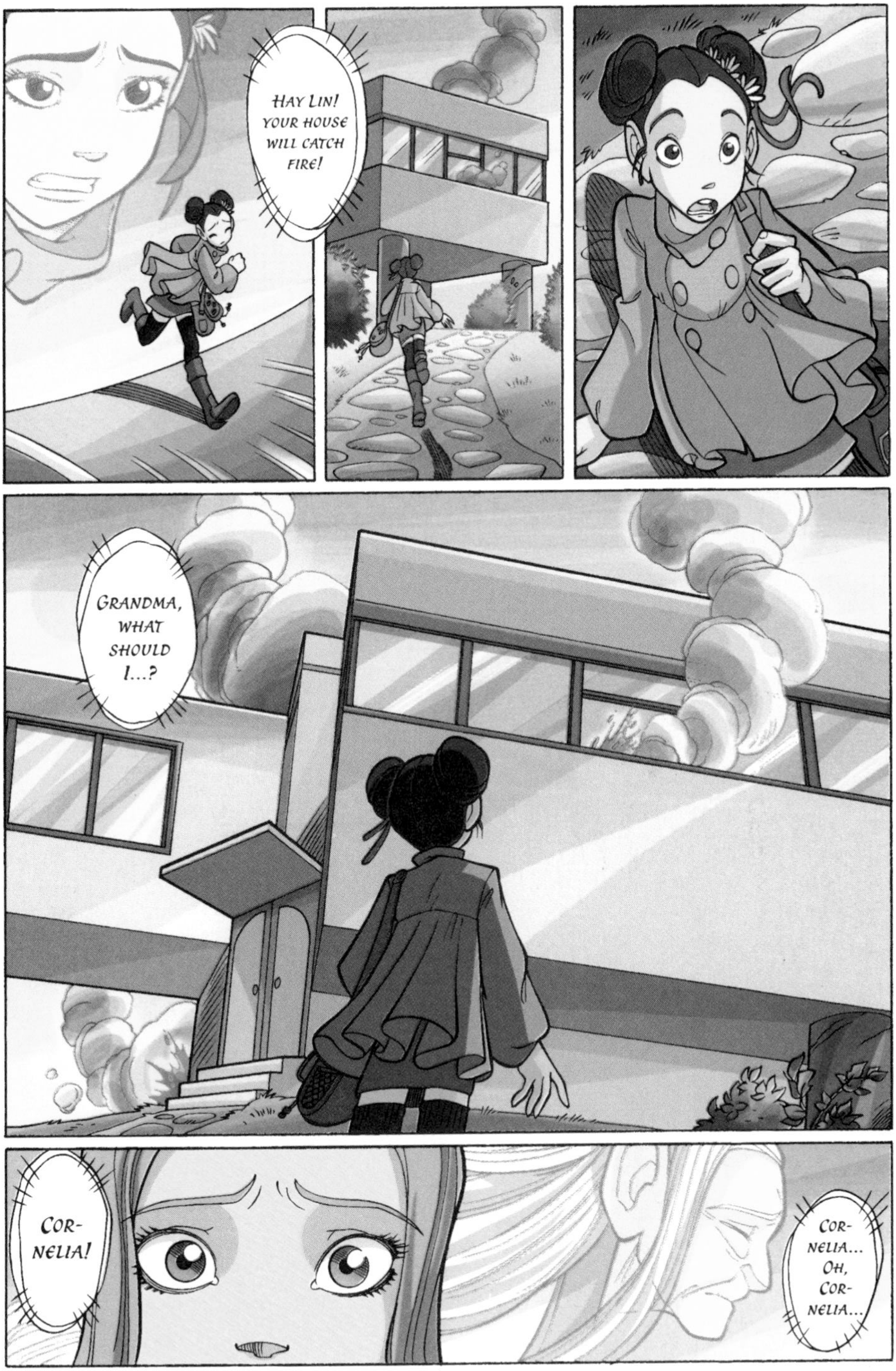
HAY LIN! YOUR HOUSE WILL CATCH FIRE!
GRANDMA, WHAT SHOULD I...?
COR-NELIA!
COR-NELIA... OH, COR-NELIA...

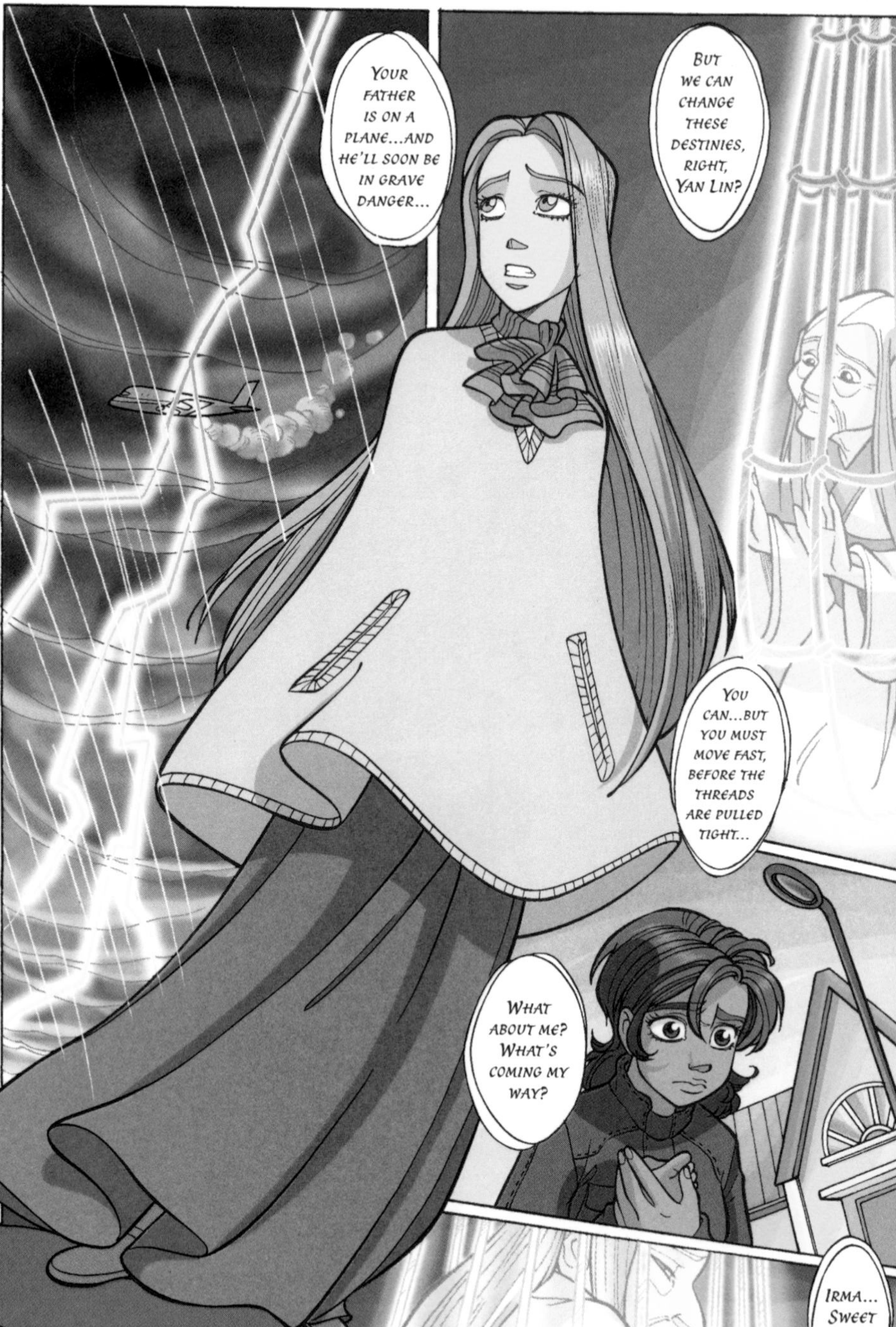
Your father is on a plane...and he'll soon be in grave danger...
But we can change these destinies, right, Yan Lin?
You can...but you must move fast, before the threads are pulled tight...
What about me? What's coming my way?
Irma... Sweet Irma...

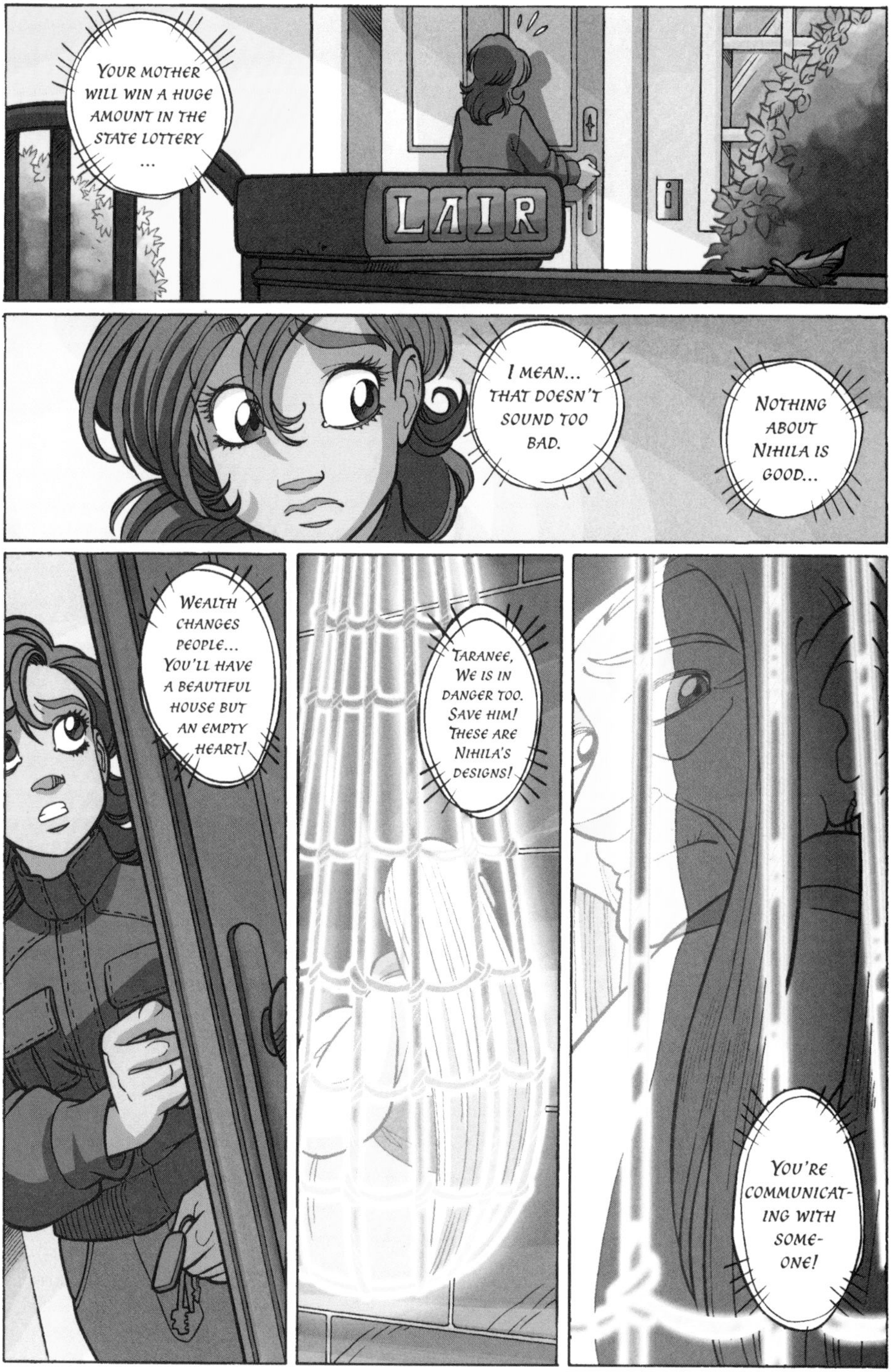
LAIR
YOUR MOTHER WILL WIN A HUGE AMOUNT IN THE STATE LOTTERY ...
I MEAN... THAT DOESN'T SOUND TOO BAD.
NOTHING ABOUT NIHILA IS GOOD...
WEALTH CHANGES PEOPLE... YOU'LL HAVE A BEAUTIFUL HOUSE BUT AN EMPTY HEART!
TARANEE, WE IS IN DANGER TOO. SAVE HIM! THESE ARE NIHILA'S DESIGNS!
YOU'RE COMMUNICAT-ING WITH SOME-ONE!

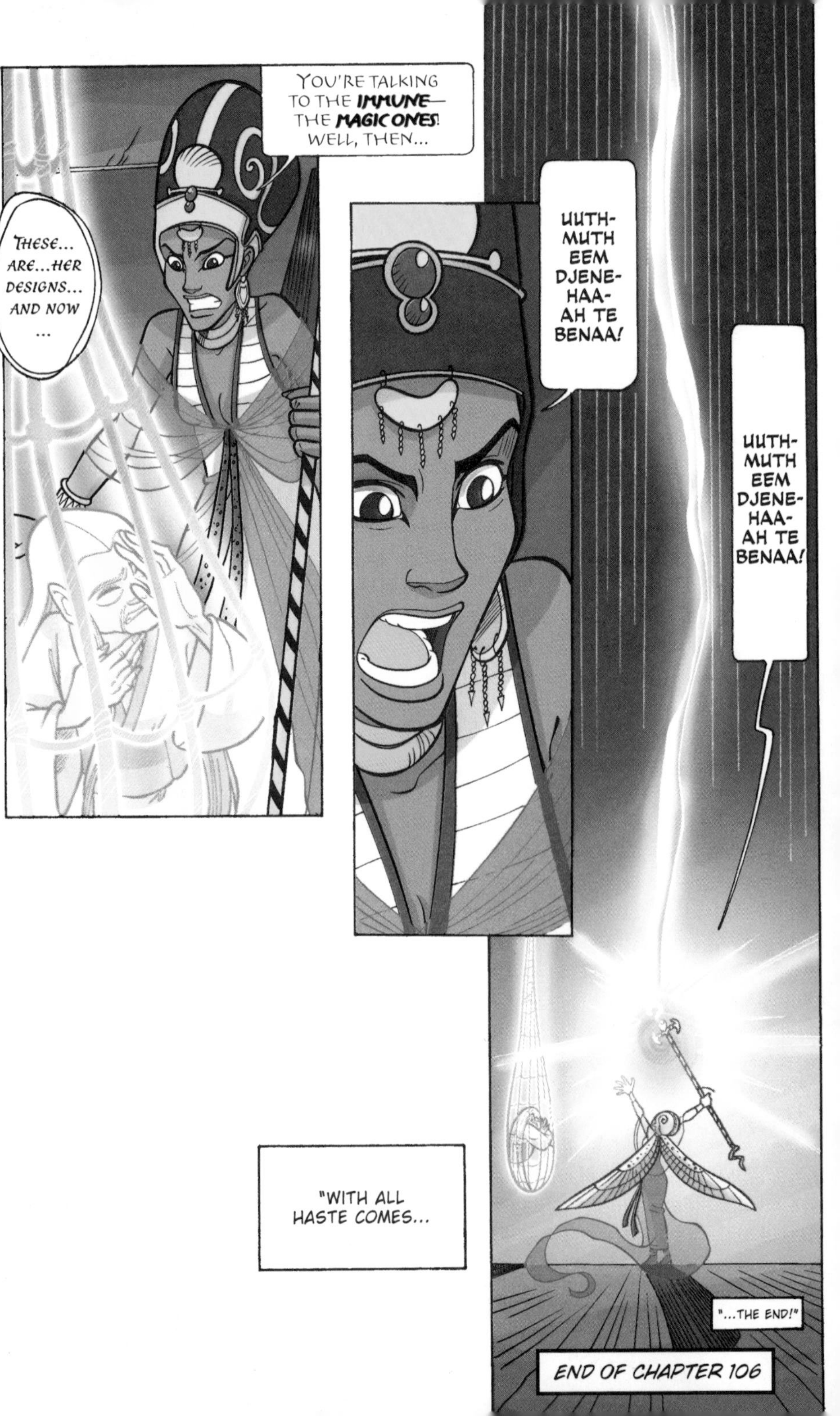

YOU'RE TALKING TO THE IMMUNE— THE MAGIC ONES! WELL, THEN...
THESE... ARE... HER DESIGNS... AND NOW ...
UUTH-MUTH EEM DJENE-HAA-AH TE BENAA!
UUTH-MUTH EEM DJENE-HAA-AH TE BENAA!
"WITH ALL HASTE COMES...
"...THE END!"
END OF CHAPTER 106

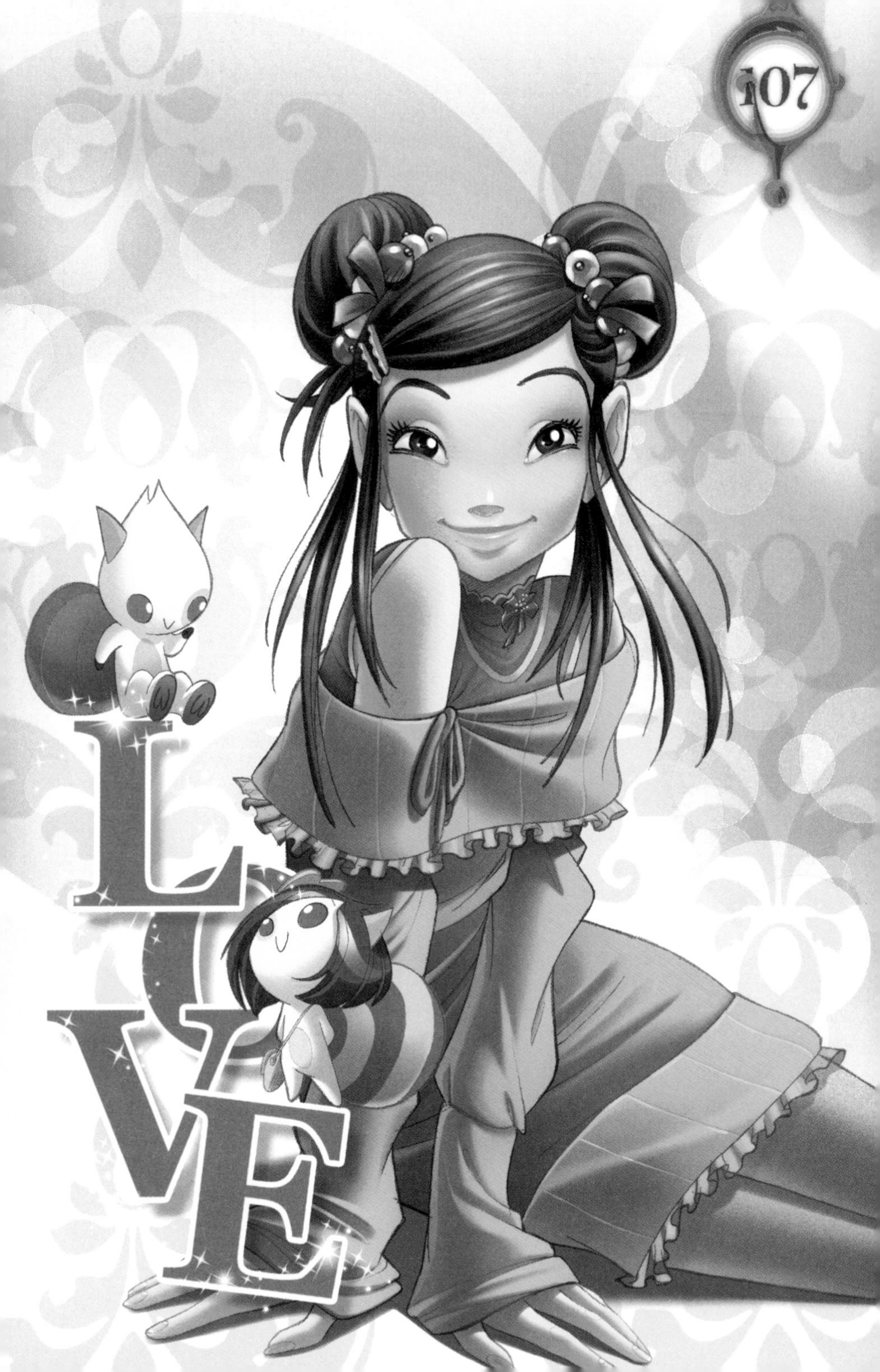
LOVE

W.I.T.C.H.

Will Irma Taranee Cornelia Hay Lin

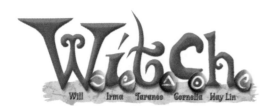

It Was Fate

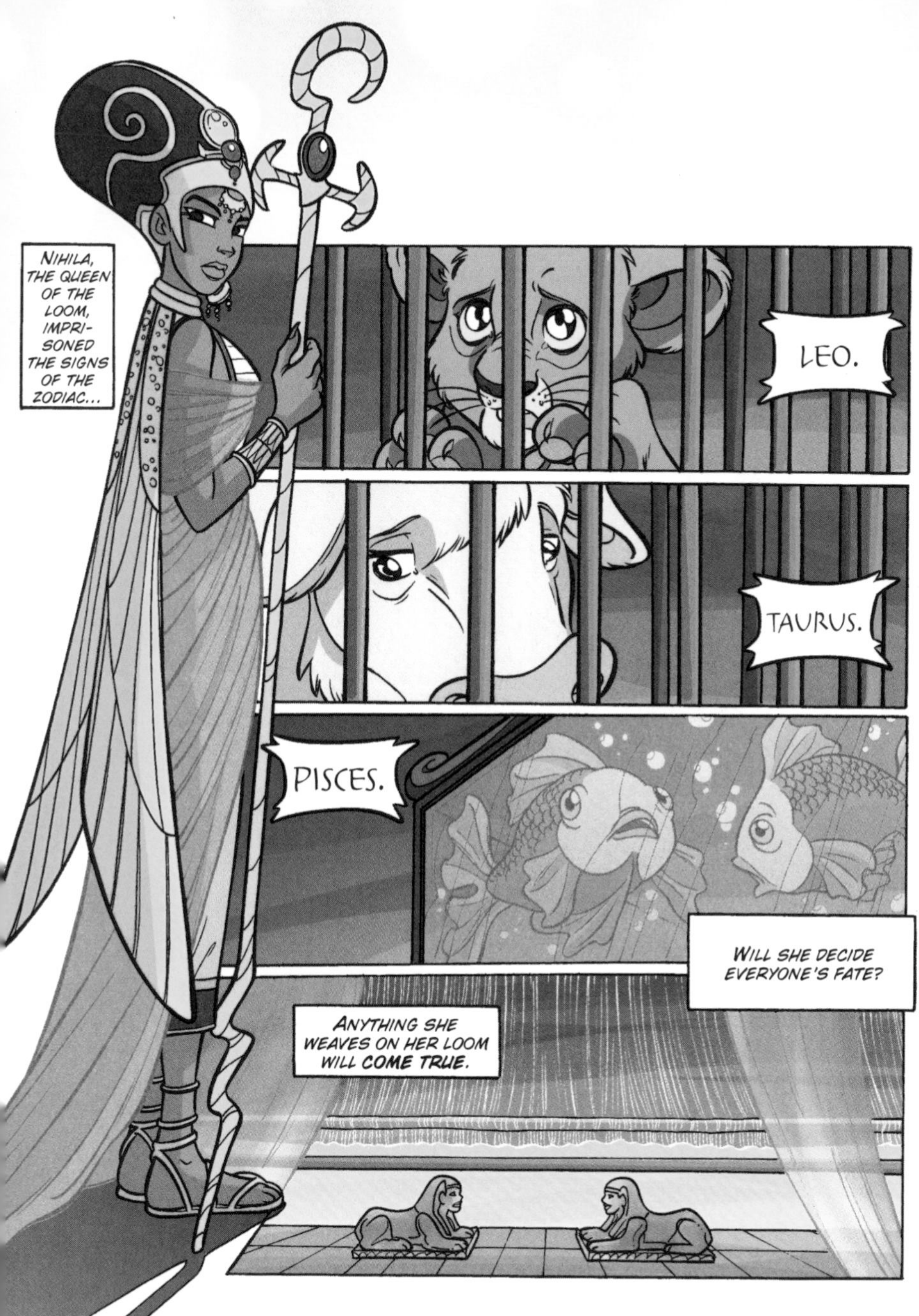

NIHILA, THE QUEEN OF THE LOOM, IMPRISONED THE SIGNS OF THE ZODIAC...
LEO.
TAURUS.
PISCES.
WILL SHE DECIDE EVERYONE'S FATE?
ANYTHING SHE WEAVES ON HER LOOM WILL **COME TRUE**.

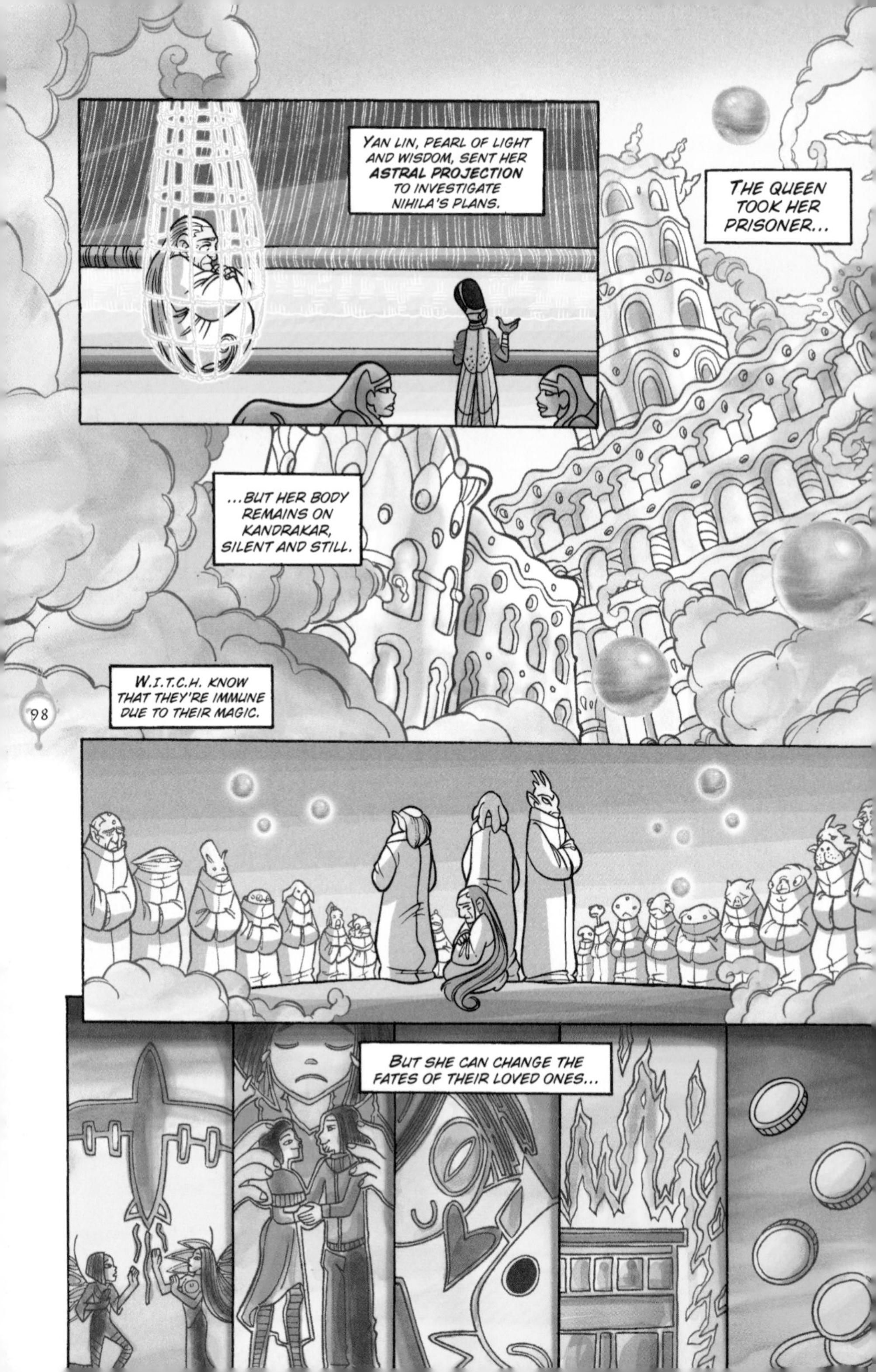
YAN LIN, PEARL OF LIGHT AND WISDOM, SENT HER ASTRAL PROJECTION TO INVESTIGATE NIHILA'S PLANS.
THE QUEEN TOOK HER PRISONER...
...BUT HER BODY REMAINS ON KANDRAKAR, SILENT AND STILL.
W.I.T.C.H. KNOW THAT THEY'RE IMMUNE DUE TO THEIR MAGIC.
BUT SHE CAN CHANGE THE FATES OF THEIR LOVED ONES...

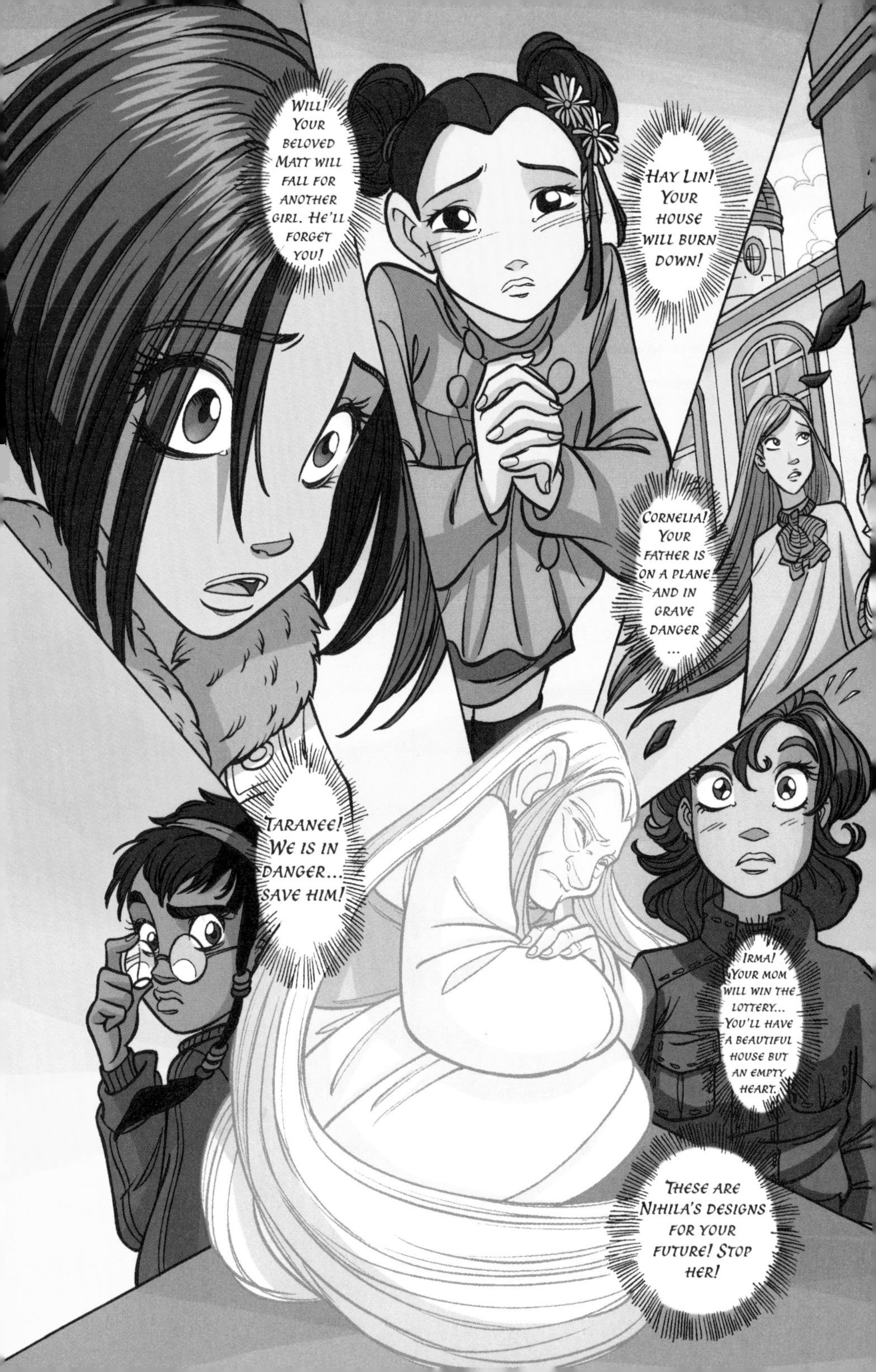
WILL! YOUR BELOVED MATT WILL FALL FOR ANOTHER GIRL. HE'LL FORGET YOU!
HAY LIN! YOUR HOUSE WILL BURN DOWN!
CORNELIA! YOUR FATHER IS ON A PLANE AND IN GRAVE DANGER ...
TARANEE! WE IS IN DANGER... SAVE HIM!
IRMA! YOUR MOM WILL WIN THE LOTTERY... YOU'LL HAVE A BEAUTIFUL HOUSE BUT AN EMPTY HEART.
THESE ARE NIHILA'S DESIGNS FOR YOUR FUTURE! STOP HER!

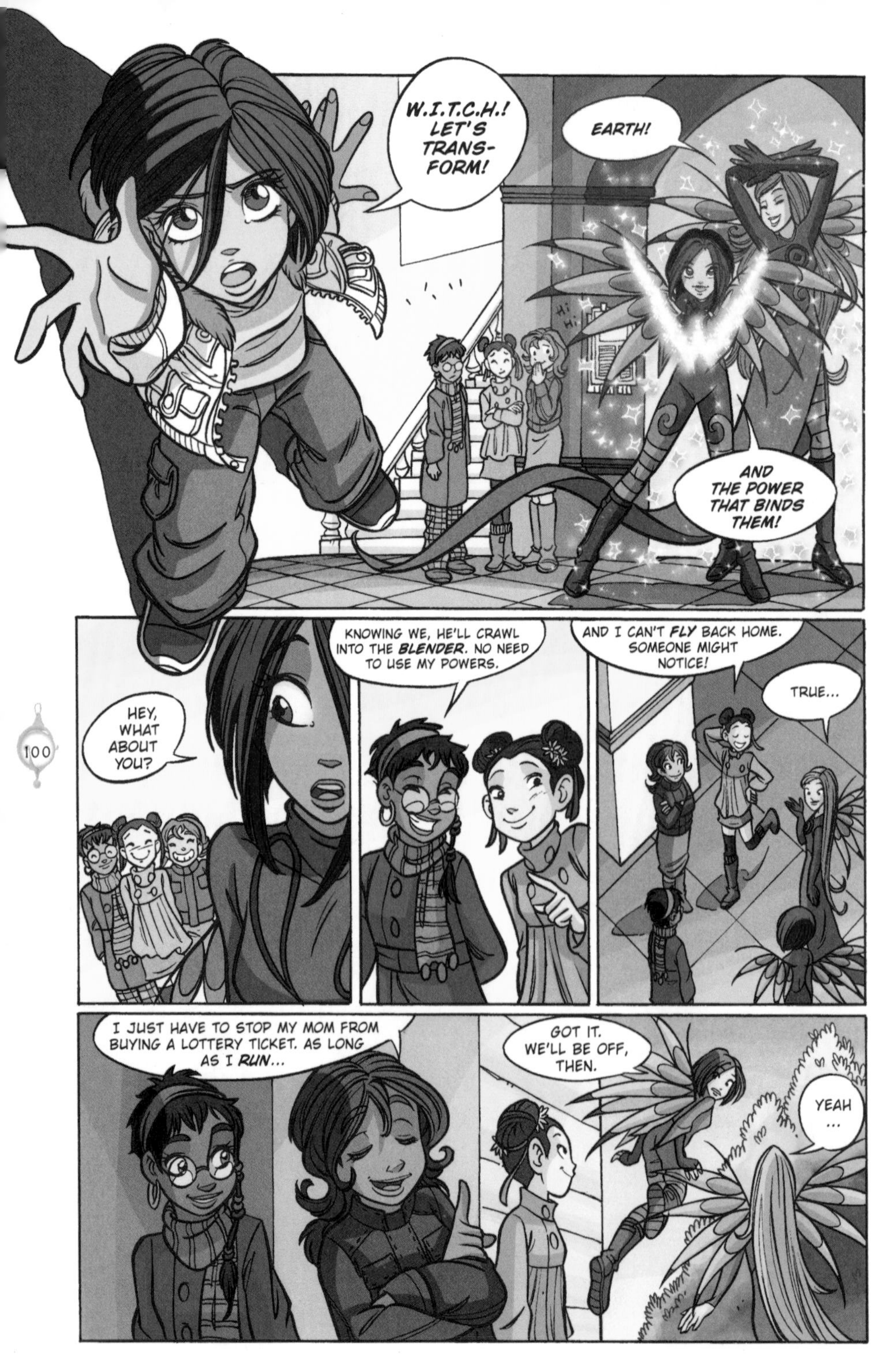

W.I.T.C.H.! LET'S TRANS-FORM!
EARTH!
AND THE POWER THAT BINDS THEM!
HEY, WHAT ABOUT YOU?
KNOWING WE, HE'LL CRAWL INTO THE **BLENDER**. NO NEED TO USE MY POWERS.
AND I CAN'T ***FLY*** BACK HOME. SOMEONE MIGHT NOTICE!
TRUE...
I JUST HAVE TO STOP MY MOM FROM BUYING A LOTTERY TICKET. AS LONG AS I ***RUN***...
GOT IT. WE'LL BE OFF, THEN.
YEAH ...

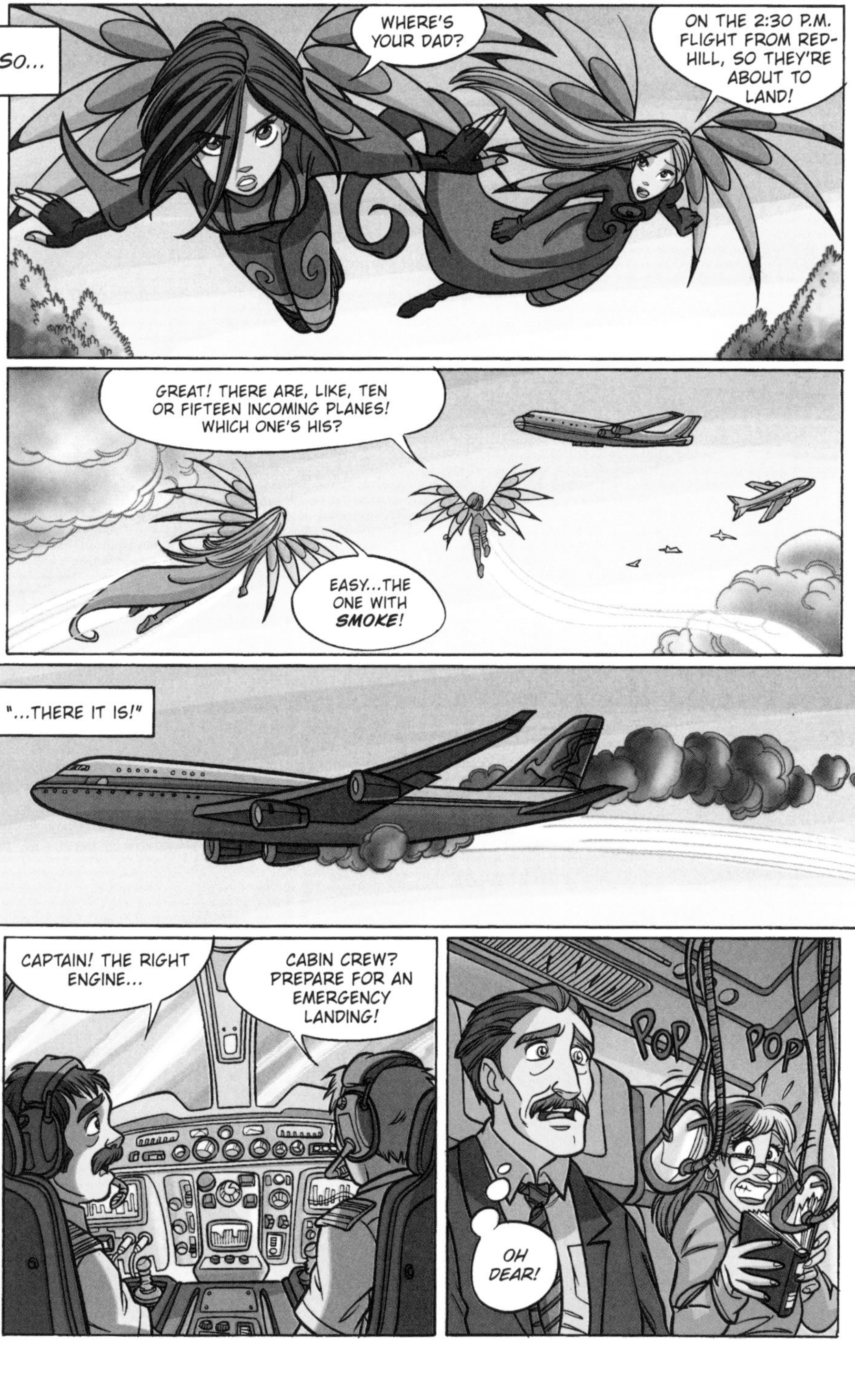
SO...
WHERE'S YOUR DAD?
ON THE 2:30 P.M. FLIGHT FROM RED-HILL, SO THEY'RE ABOUT TO LAND!
GREAT! THERE ARE, LIKE, TEN OR FIFTEEN INCOMING PLANES! WHICH ONE'S HIS?
EASY...THE ONE WITH **SMOKE**!
"...THERE IT IS!"
CAPTAIN! THE RIGHT ENGINE...
CABIN CREW? PREPARE FOR AN EMERGENCY LANDING!
POP
POP
OH DEAR!

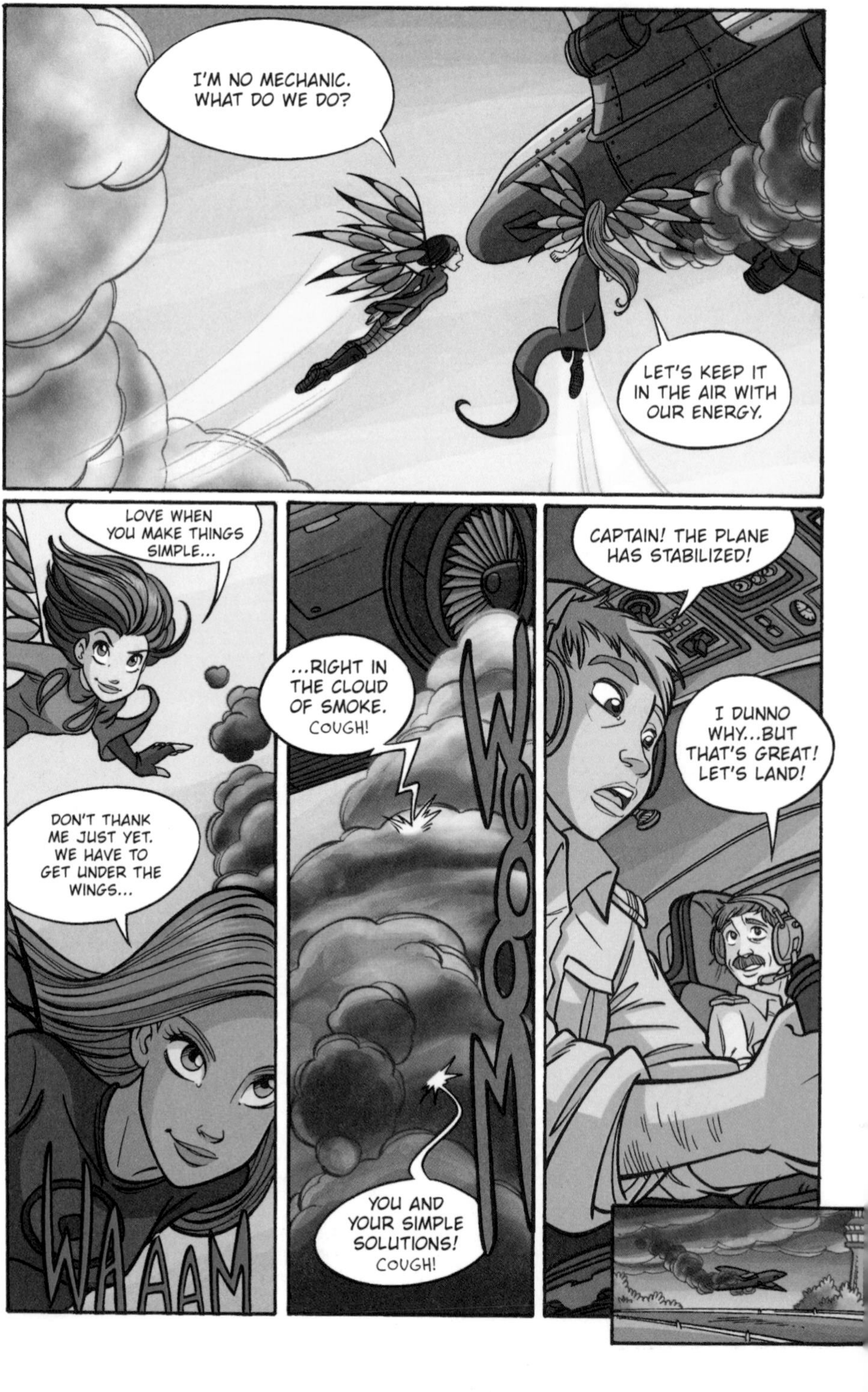
I'M NO MECHANIC. WHAT DO WE DO?
LET'S KEEP IT IN THE AIR WITH OUR ENERGY.
LOVE WHEN YOU MAKE THINGS SIMPLE...
DON'T THANK ME JUST YET. WE HAVE TO GET UNDER THE WINGS...
WAAAM
...RIGHT IN THE CLOUD OF SMOKE. COUGH!
WOOOOM
YOU AND YOUR SIMPLE SOLUTIONS! COUGH!
CAPTAIN! THE PLANE HAS STABILIZED!
I DUNNO WHY...BUT THAT'S GREAT! LET'S LAND!

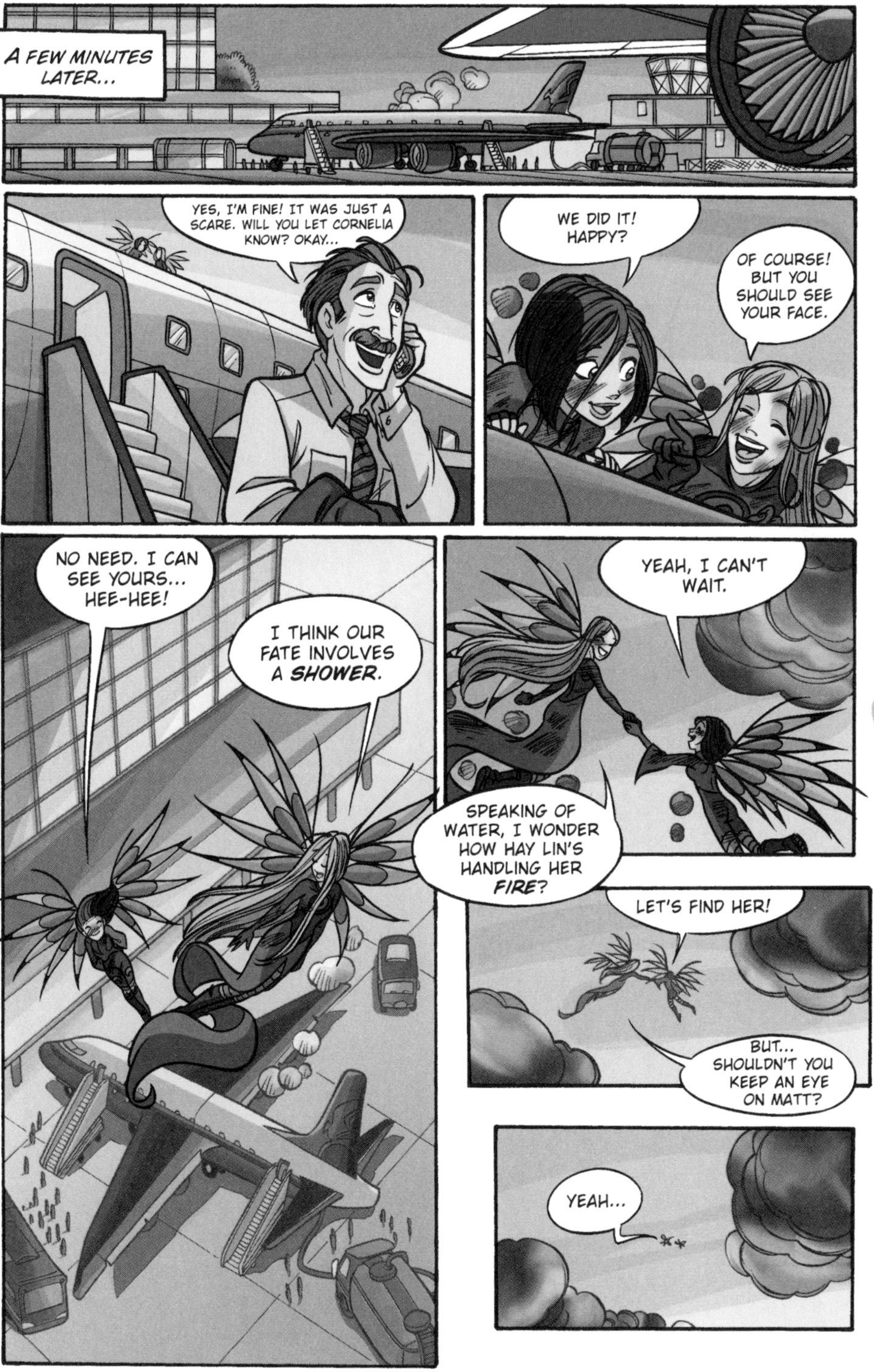
A FEW MINUTES LATER...
YES, I'M FINE! IT WAS JUST A SCARE. WILL YOU LET CORNELIA KNOW? OKAY...
WE DID IT! HAPPY?
OF COURSE! BUT YOU SHOULD SEE YOUR FACE.
NO NEED. I CAN SEE YOURS... HEE-HEE!
I THINK OUR FATE INVOLVES A SHOWER.
YEAH, I CAN'T WAIT.
SPEAKING OF WATER, I WONDER HOW HAY LIN'S HANDLING HER FIRE?
LET'S FIND HER!
BUT... SHOULDN'T YOU KEEP AN EYE ON MATT?
YEAH...

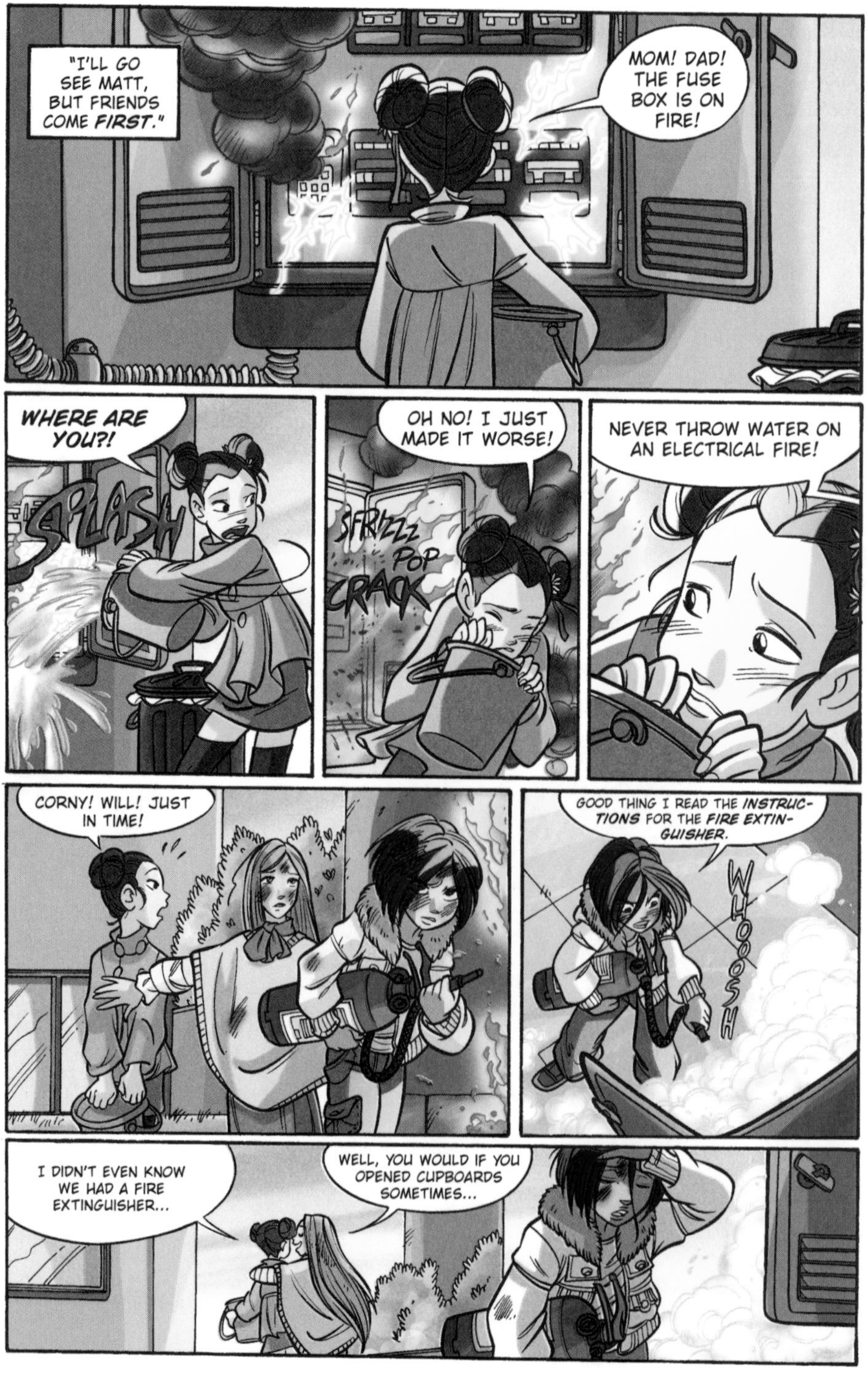
"I'LL GO SEE MATT, BUT FRIENDS COME FIRST."
MOM! DAD! THE FUSE BOX IS ON FIRE!
WHERE ARE YOU?!
SPLASH
OH NO! I JUST MADE IT WORSE!
SFRIZZZ
POP
CRACK
NEVER THROW WATER ON AN ELECTRICAL FIRE!
CORNY! WILL! JUST IN TIME!
GOOD THING I READ THE INSTRUCTIONS FOR THE FIRE EXTINGUISHER.
WHOOOSH
I DIDN'T EVEN KNOW WE HAD A FIRE EXTINGUISHER...
WELL, YOU WOULD IF YOU OPENED CUPBOARDS SOMETIMES...

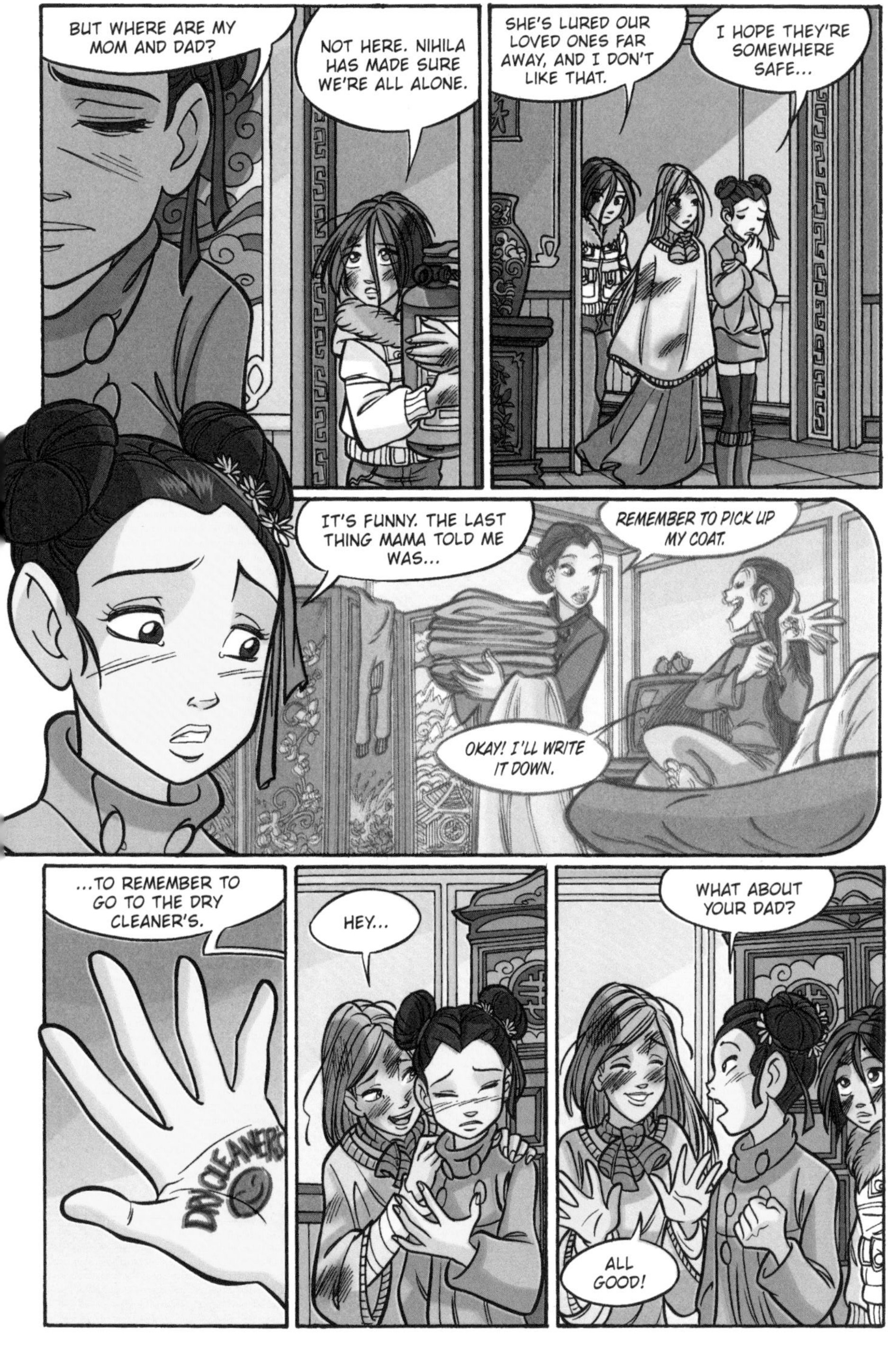
BUT WHERE ARE MY MOM AND DAD?
NOT HERE. NIHILA HAS MADE SURE WE'RE ALL ALONE.
SHE'S LURED OUR LOVED ONES FAR AWAY, AND I DON'T LIKE THAT.
I HOPE THEY'RE SOMEWHERE SAFE...
IT'S FUNNY. THE LAST THING MAMA TOLD ME WAS...
REMEMBER TO PICK UP MY COAT.
OKAY! I'LL WRITE IT DOWN.
...TO REMEMBER TO GO TO THE DRY CLEANER'S.
DRYCLEANERS
HEY...
WHAT ABOUT YOUR DAD?
ALL GOOD!

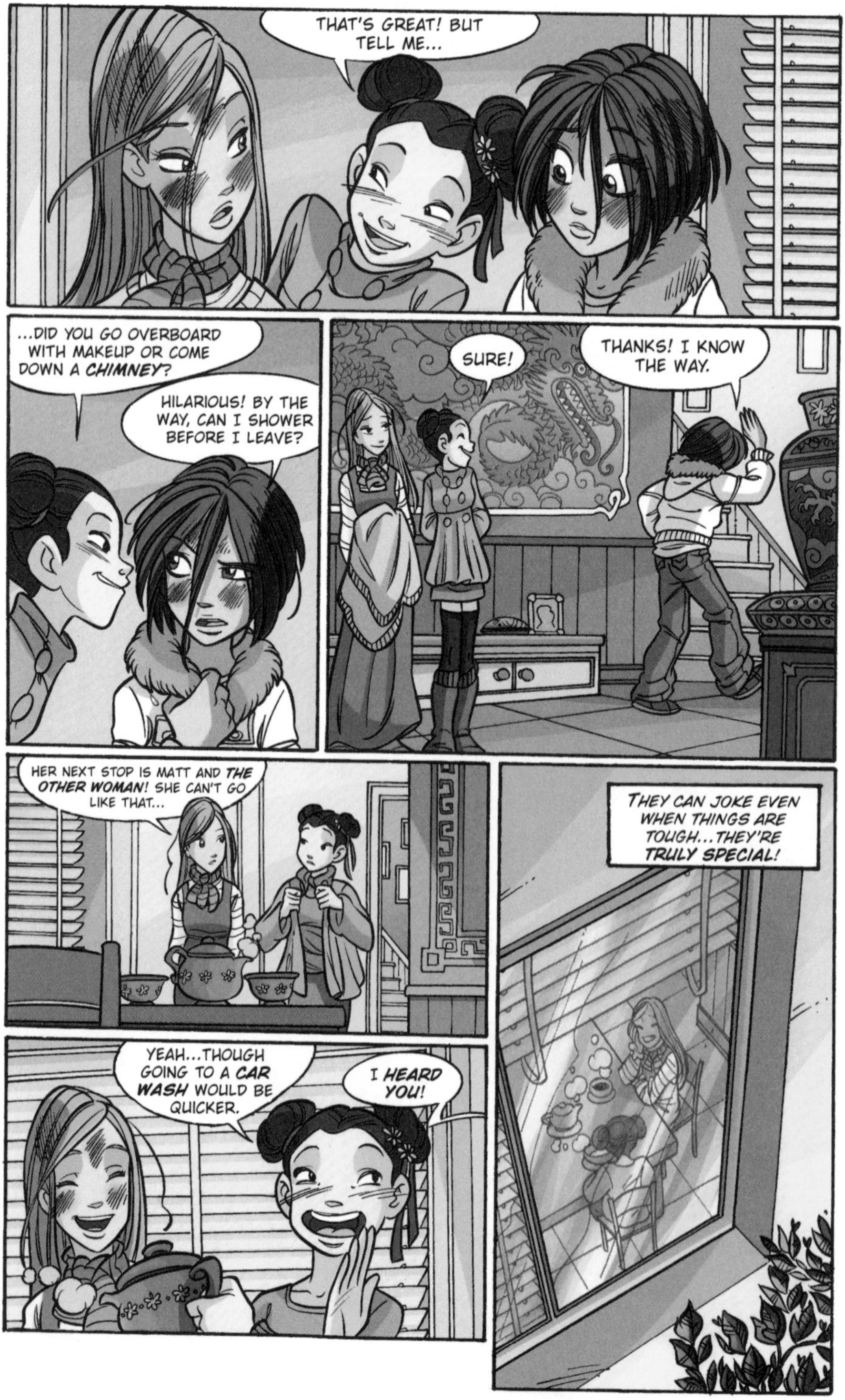
THAT'S GREAT! BUT TELL ME...
...DID YOU GO OVERBOARD WITH MAKEUP OR COME DOWN A *CHIMNEY*?
HILARIOUS! BY THE WAY, CAN I SHOWER BEFORE I LEAVE?
SURE!
THANKS! I KNOW THE WAY.
HER NEXT STOP IS MATT AND *THE OTHER WOMAN*! SHE CAN'T GO LIKE THAT...
YEAH...THOUGH GOING TO A *CAR WASH* WOULD BE QUICKER.
I *HEARD YOU*!
THEY CAN JOKE EVEN WHEN THINGS ARE TOUGH...THEY'RE ***TRULY SPECIAL!***

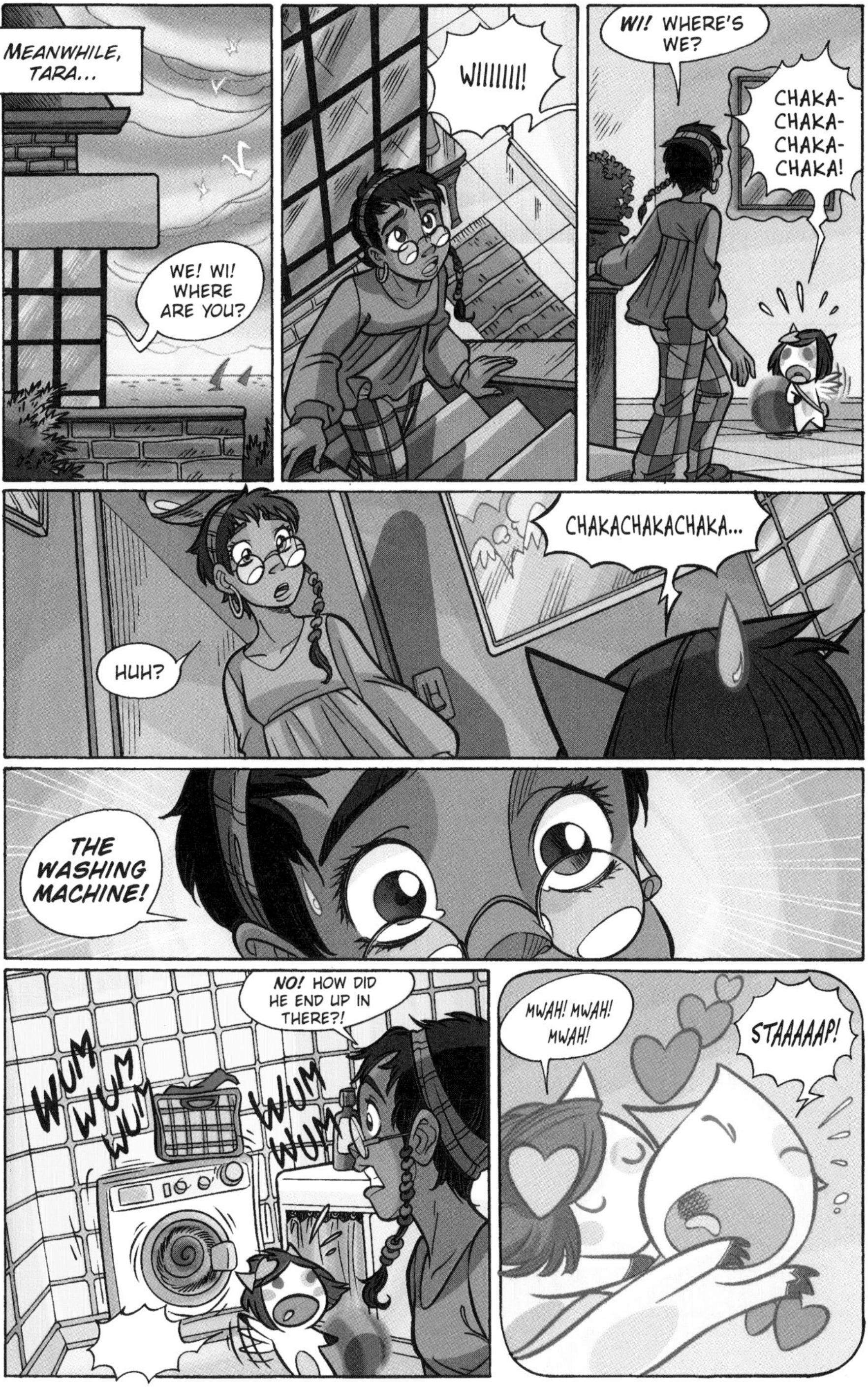
MEANWHILE, TARA...
WE! WI! WHERE ARE YOU?
WIIIIIII!
WI! WHERE'S WE?
CHAKA-CHAKA-CHAKA-CHAKA!
CHAKACHAKACHAKA...
HUH?
THE WASHING MACHINE!
NO! HOW DID HE END UP IN THERE?!
WUM WUM WUM
WUM WUM
MWAH! MWAH! MWAH!
STAAAAAP!

LOWE! LOWE!
HEEEEWP!
LOWE!
CO HEEEWE!
CO HEEEWE!
NO!
LOWE!
WHYYY?
BECAWSE!
NO!
LOWE!
CLUNK
LOWE!
CO HEEEWE!
TUMP
CLIC
UH-OH...

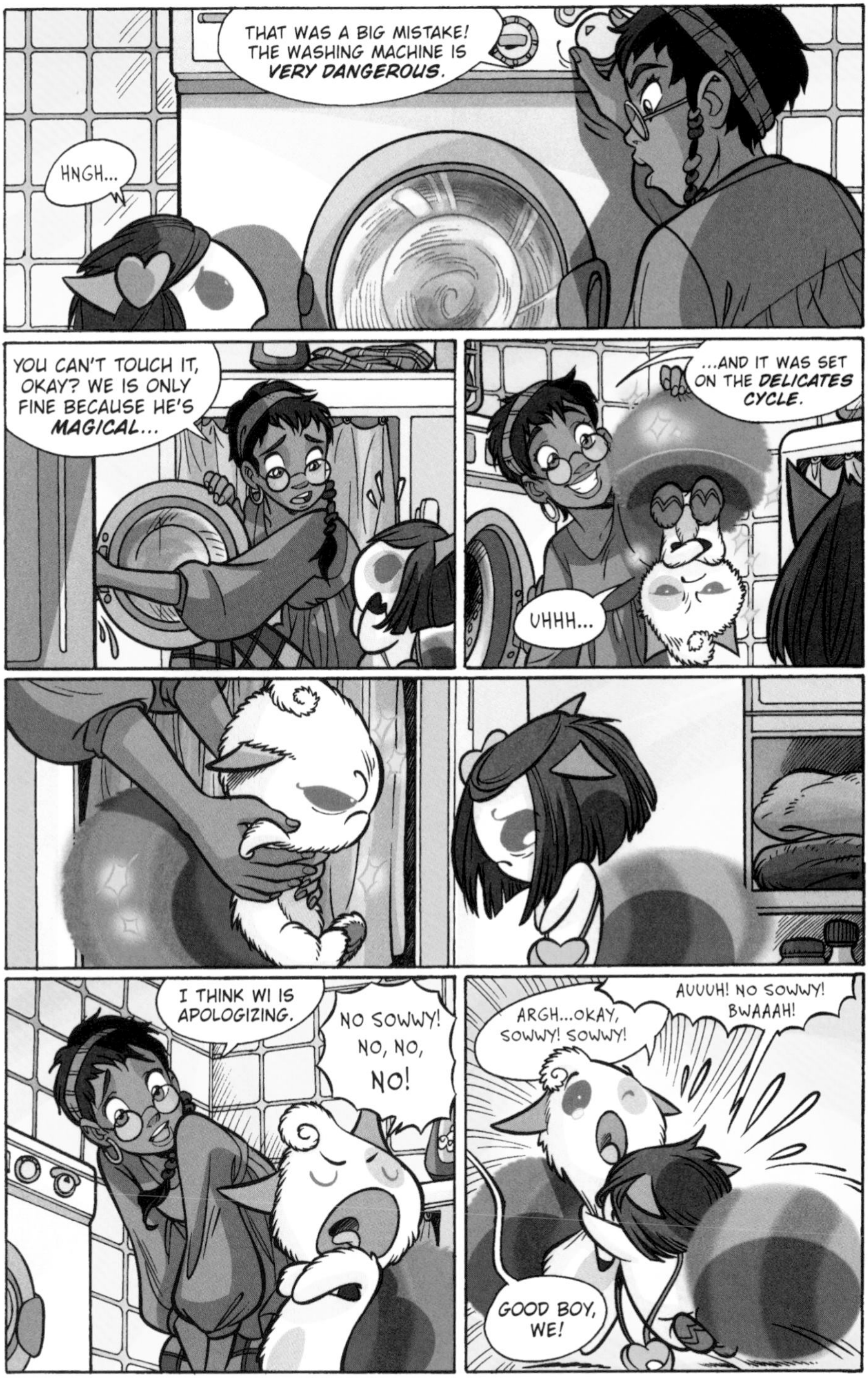

THAT WAS A BIG MISTAKE! THE WASHING MACHINE IS VERY DANGEROUS.
HNGH...
YOU CAN'T TOUCH IT, OKAY? WE IS ONLY FINE BECAUSE HE'S MAGICAL...
...AND IT WAS SET ON THE DELICATES CYCLE.
UHHH...
I THINK WI IS APOLOGIZING.
NO SOWWY! NO, NO, NO!
ARGH...OKAY, SOWWY! SOWWY!
AUUUH! NO SOWWY! BWAAAH!
GOOD BOY, WE!

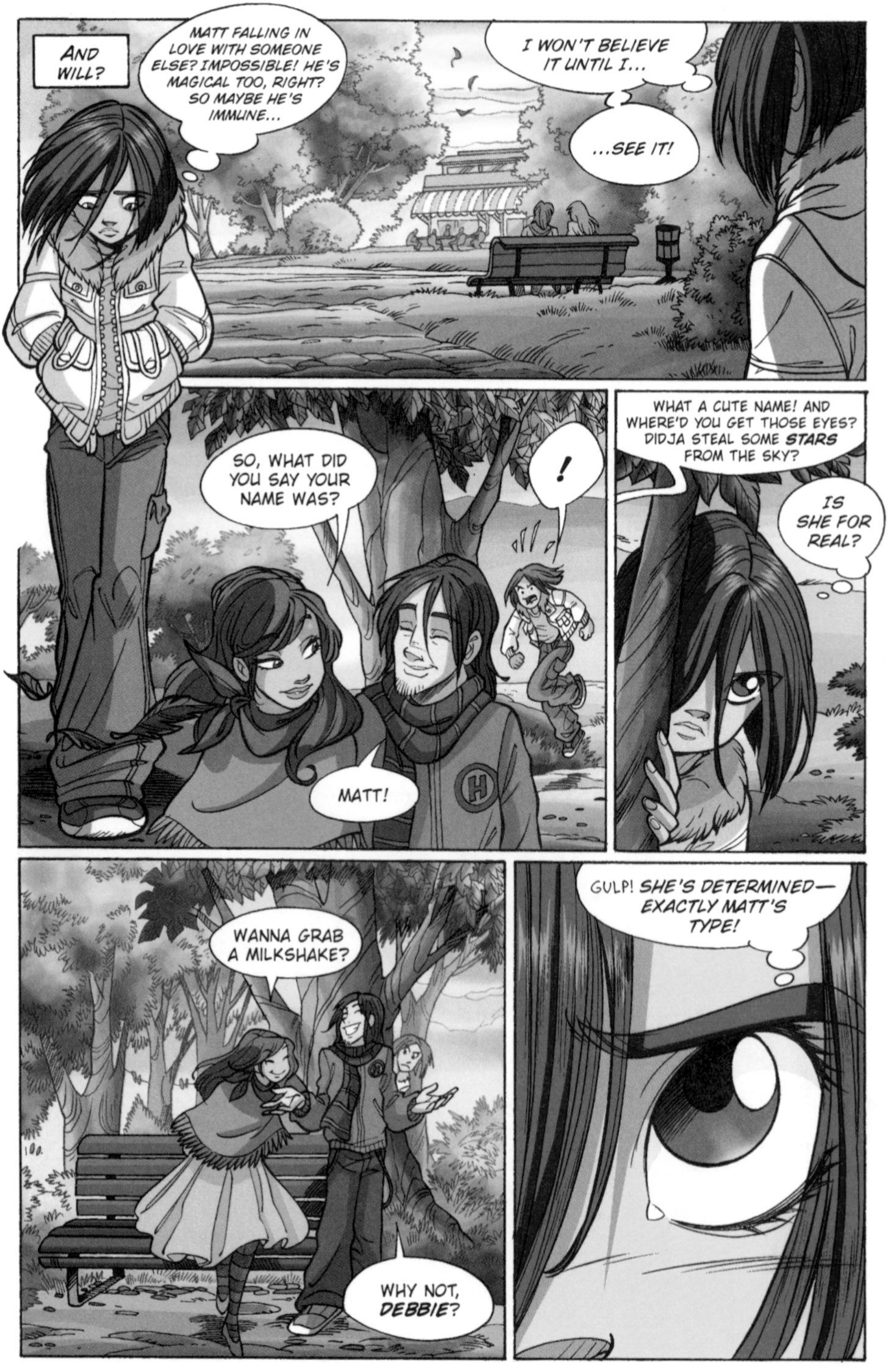
AND WILL?
MATT FALLING IN LOVE WITH SOMEONE ELSE? IMPOSSIBLE! HE'S MAGICAL TOO, RIGHT? SO MAYBE HE'S IMMUNE...
I WON'T BELIEVE IT UNTIL I...
...SEE IT!
SO, WHAT DID YOU SAY YOUR NAME WAS?
!
MATT!
WHAT A CUTE NAME! AND WHERE'D YOU GET THOSE EYES? DIDJA STEAL SOME STARS FROM THE SKY?
IS SHE FOR REAL?
WANNA GRAB A MILKSHAKE?
WHY NOT, DEBBIE?
GULP! SHE'S DETERMINED— EXACTLY MATT'S TYPE!

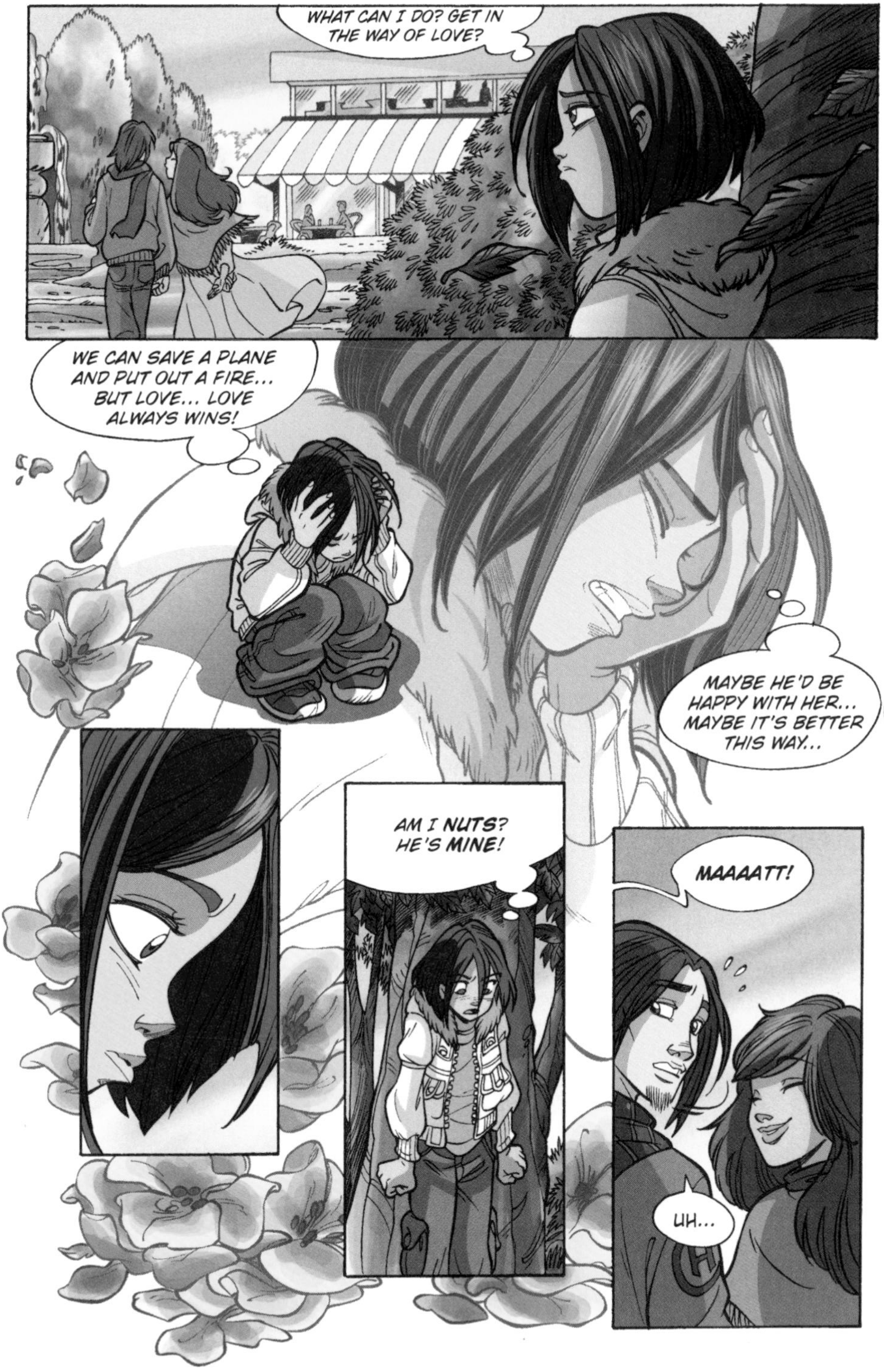
WHAT CAN I DO? GET IN THE WAY OF LOVE?
WE CAN SAVE A PLANE AND PUT OUT A FIRE... BUT LOVE... LOVE ALWAYS WINS!
MAYBE HE'D BE HAPPY WITH HER... MAYBE IT'S BETTER THIS WAY...
AM I NUTS? HE'S MINE!
MAAAATT!
UH...

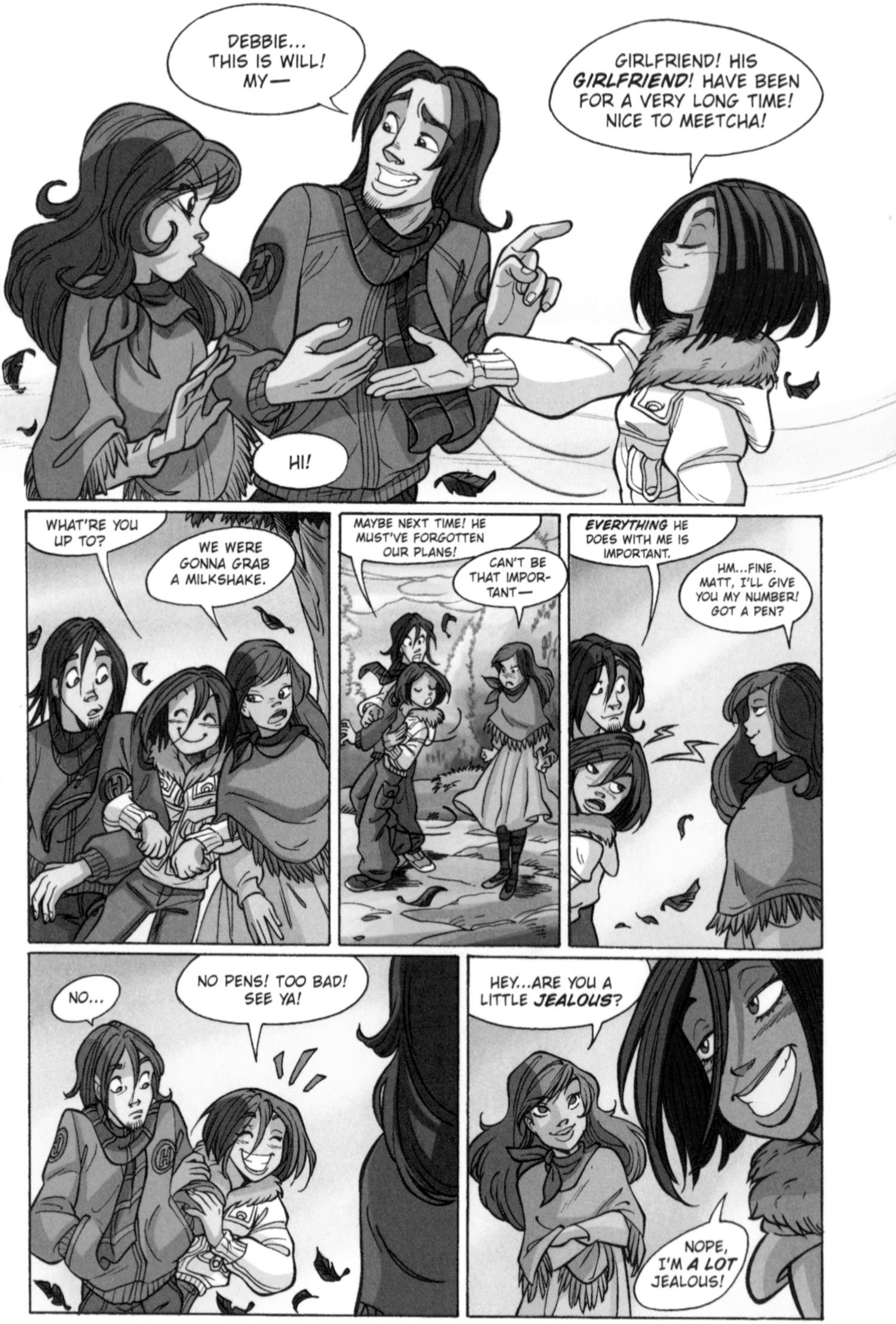
DEBBIE... THIS IS WILL! MY—
GIRLFRIEND! HIS GIRLFRIEND! HAVE BEEN FOR A VERY LONG TIME! NICE TO MEETCHA!
HI!
WHAT'RE YOU UP TO?
WE WERE GONNA GRAB A MILKSHAKE.
MAYBE NEXT TIME! HE MUST'VE FORGOTTEN OUR PLANS!
CAN'T BE THAT IMPOR-TANT—
EVERYTHING HE DOES WITH ME IS IMPORTANT.
HM...FINE. MATT, I'LL GIVE YOU MY NUMBER! GOT A PEN?
NO...
NO PENS! TOO BAD! SEE YA!
HEY...ARE YOU A LITTLE JEALOUS?
NOPE, I'M A LOT JEALOUS!

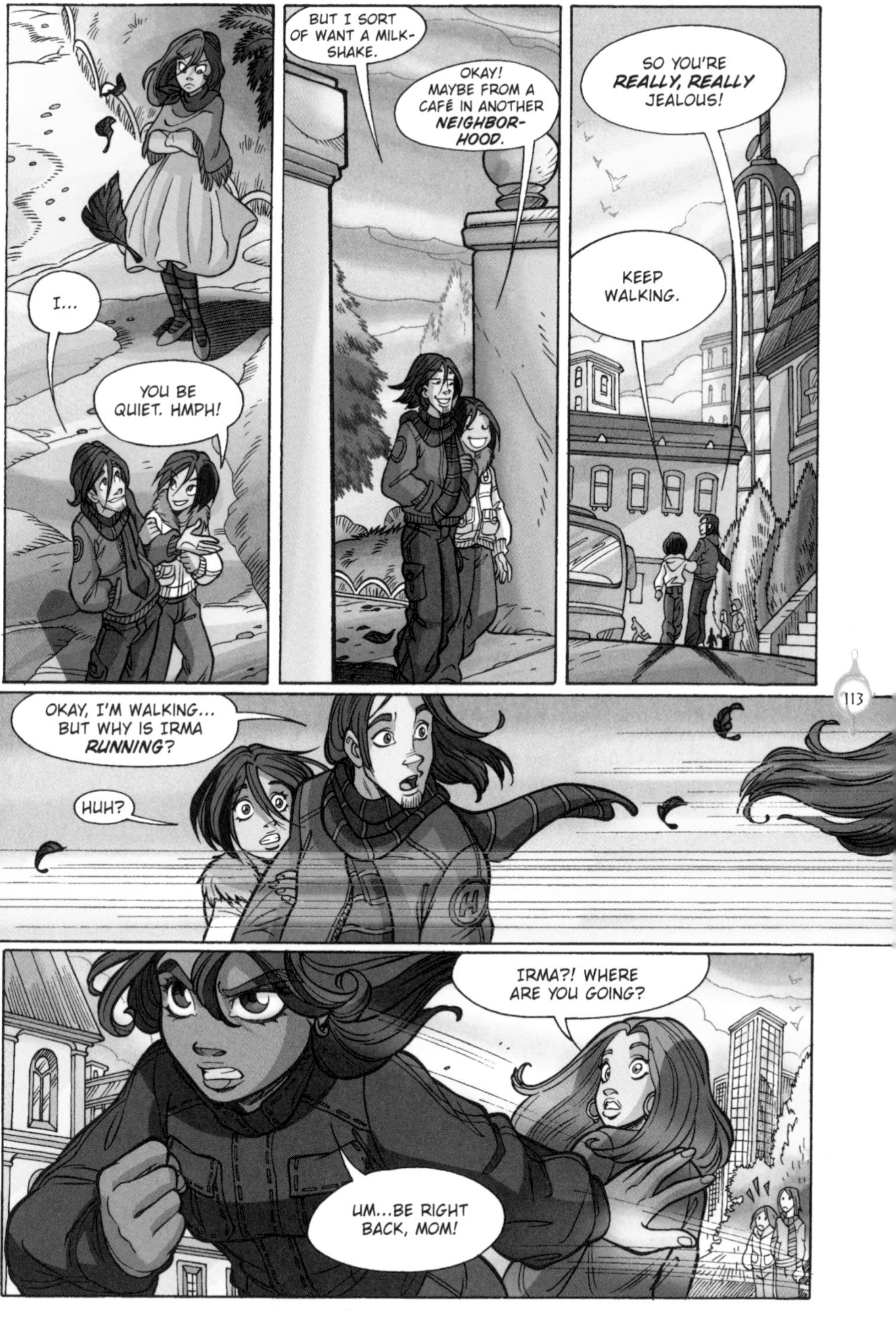
I...
YOU BE QUIET. HMPH!
BUT I SORT OF WANT A MILK-SHAKE.
OKAY! MAYBE FROM A CAFÉ IN ANOTHER NEIGHBOR-HOOD.
SO YOU'RE REALLY, REALLY JEALOUS!
KEEP WALKING.
OKAY, I'M WALKING... BUT WHY IS IRMA RUNNING?
HUH?
IRMA?! WHERE ARE YOU GOING?
UM...BE RIGHT BACK, MOM!

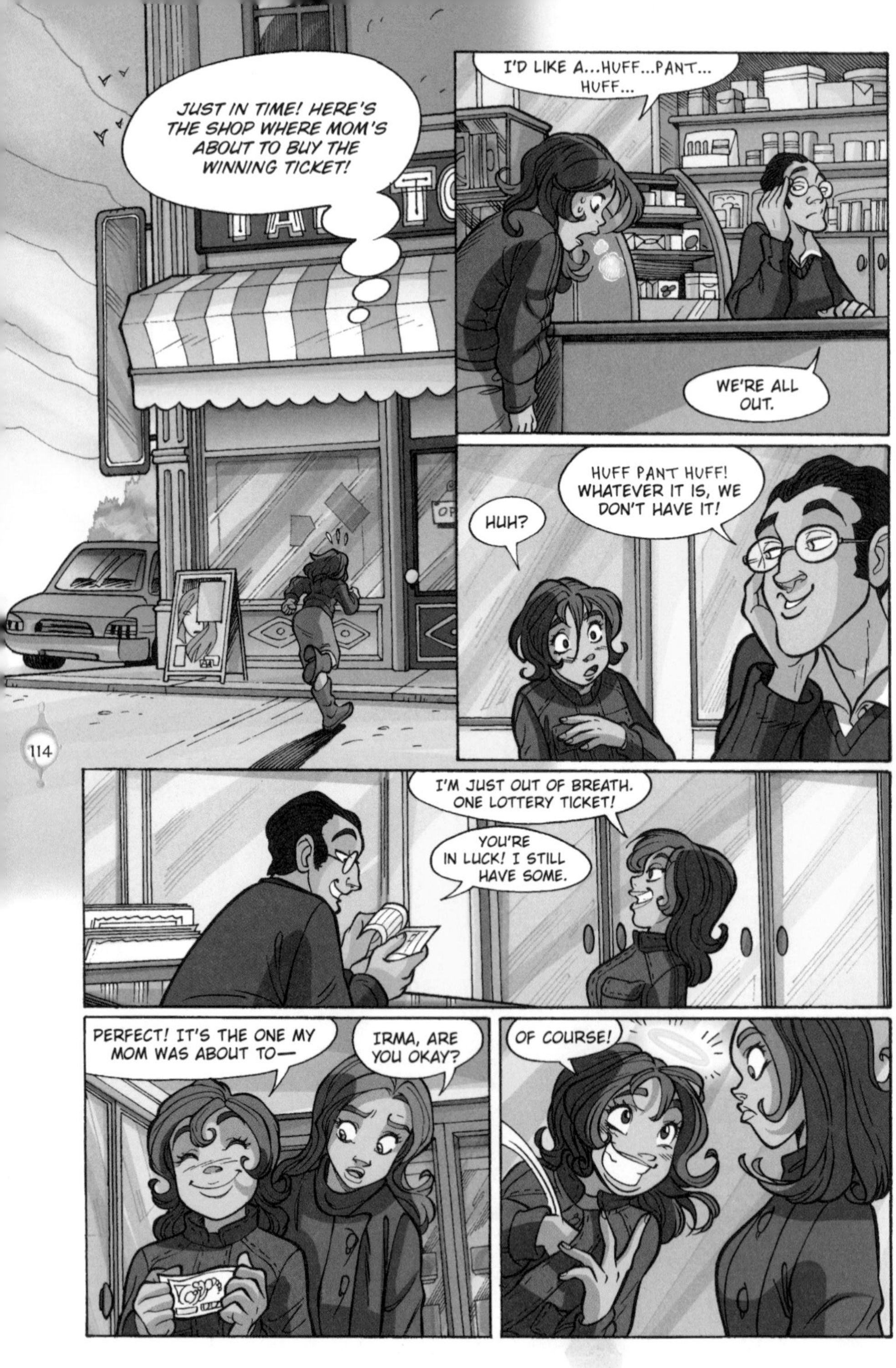

JUST IN TIME! HERE'S THE SHOP WHERE MOM'S ABOUT TO BUY THE WINNING TICKET!
I'D LIKE A...HUFF...PANT... HUFF...
WE'RE ALL OUT.
HUFF PANT HUFF! WHATEVER IT IS, WE DON'T HAVE IT!
HUH?
I'M JUST OUT OF BREATH. ONE LOTTERY TICKET!
YOU'RE IN LUCK! I STILL HAVE SOME.
PERFECT! IT'S THE ONE MY MOM WAS ABOUT TO—
IRMA, ARE YOU OKAY?
OF COURSE!

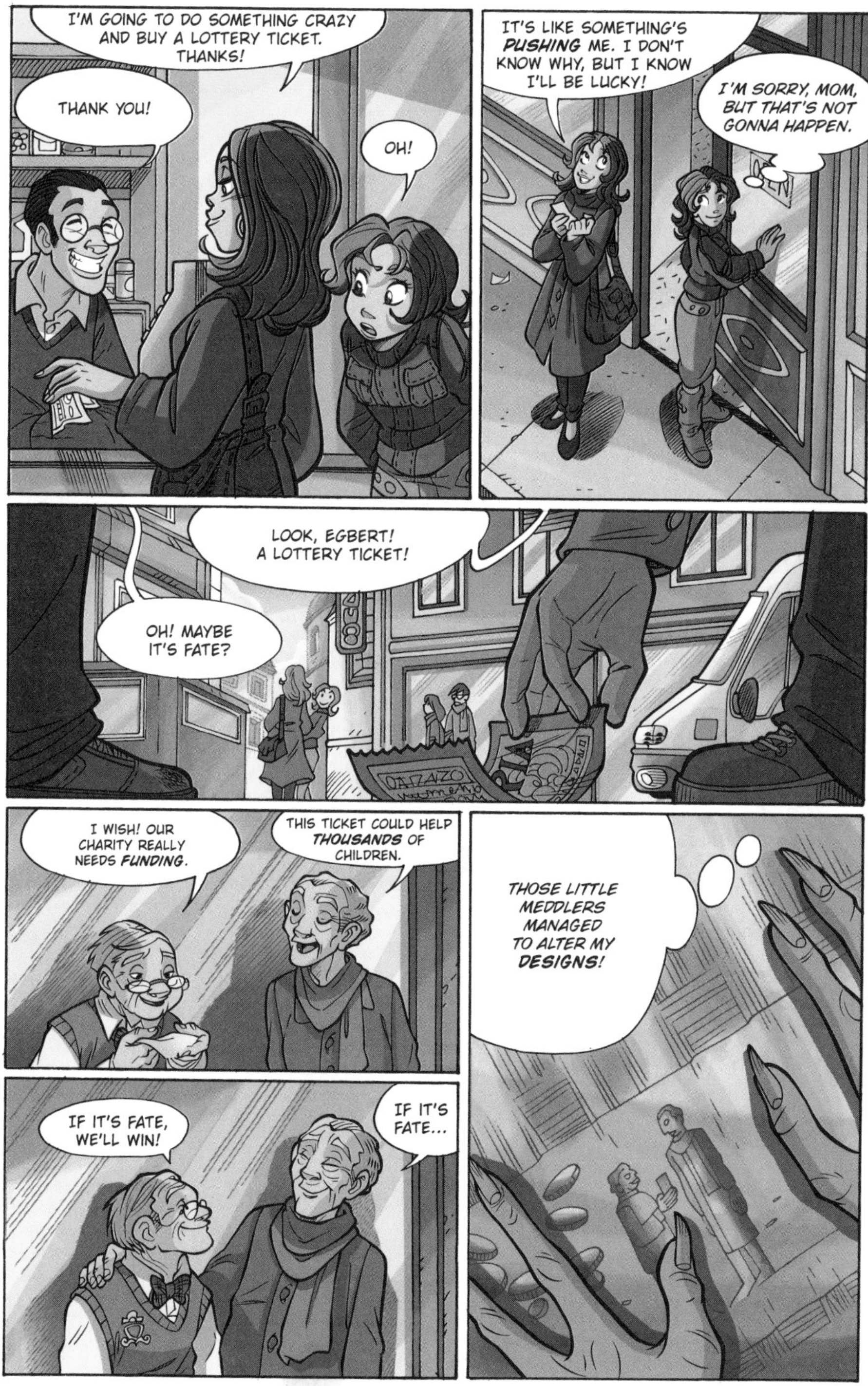
I'M GOING TO DO SOMETHING CRAZY AND BUY A LOTTERY TICKET. THANKS!
THANK YOU!
OH!
IT'S LIKE SOMETHING'S PUSHING ME. I DON'T KNOW WHY, BUT I KNOW I'LL BE LUCKY!
I'M SORRY, MOM, BUT THAT'S NOT GONNA HAPPEN.
LOOK, EGBERT! A LOTTERY TICKET!
OH! MAYBE IT'S FATE?
I WISH! OUR CHARITY REALLY NEEDS FUNDING.
THIS TICKET COULD HELP THOUSANDS OF CHILDREN.
THOSE LITTLE MEDDLERS MANAGED TO ALTER MY DESIGNS!
IF IT'S FATE, WE'LL WIN!
IF IT'S FATE...

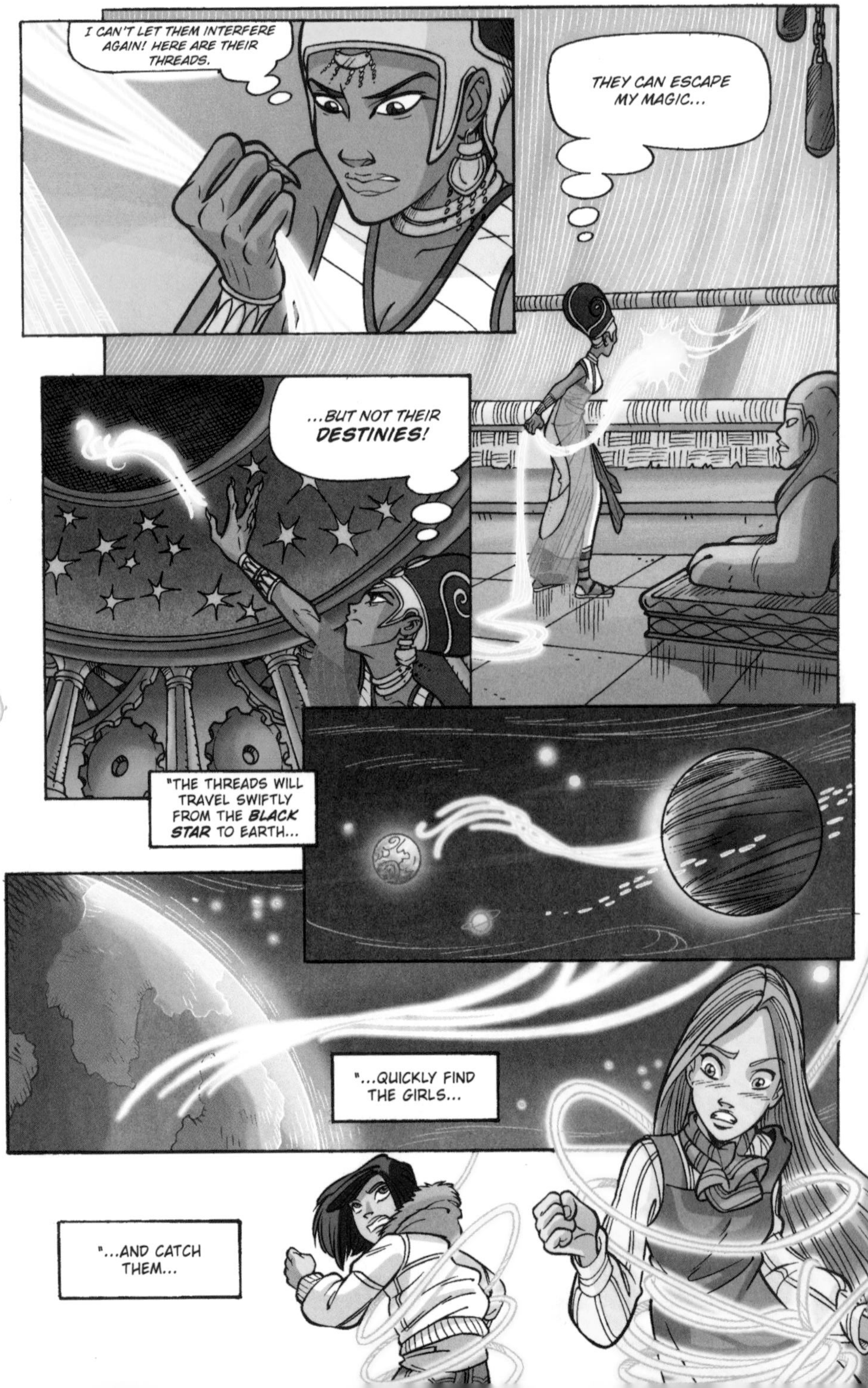
I CAN'T LET THEM INTERFERE AGAIN! HERE ARE THEIR THREADS.
THEY CAN ESCAPE MY MAGIC...
...BUT NOT THEIR DESTINIES!
"THE THREADS WILL TRAVEL SWIFTLY FROM THE BLACK STAR TO EARTH...
"...QUICKLY FIND THE GIRLS...
"...AND CATCH THEM...

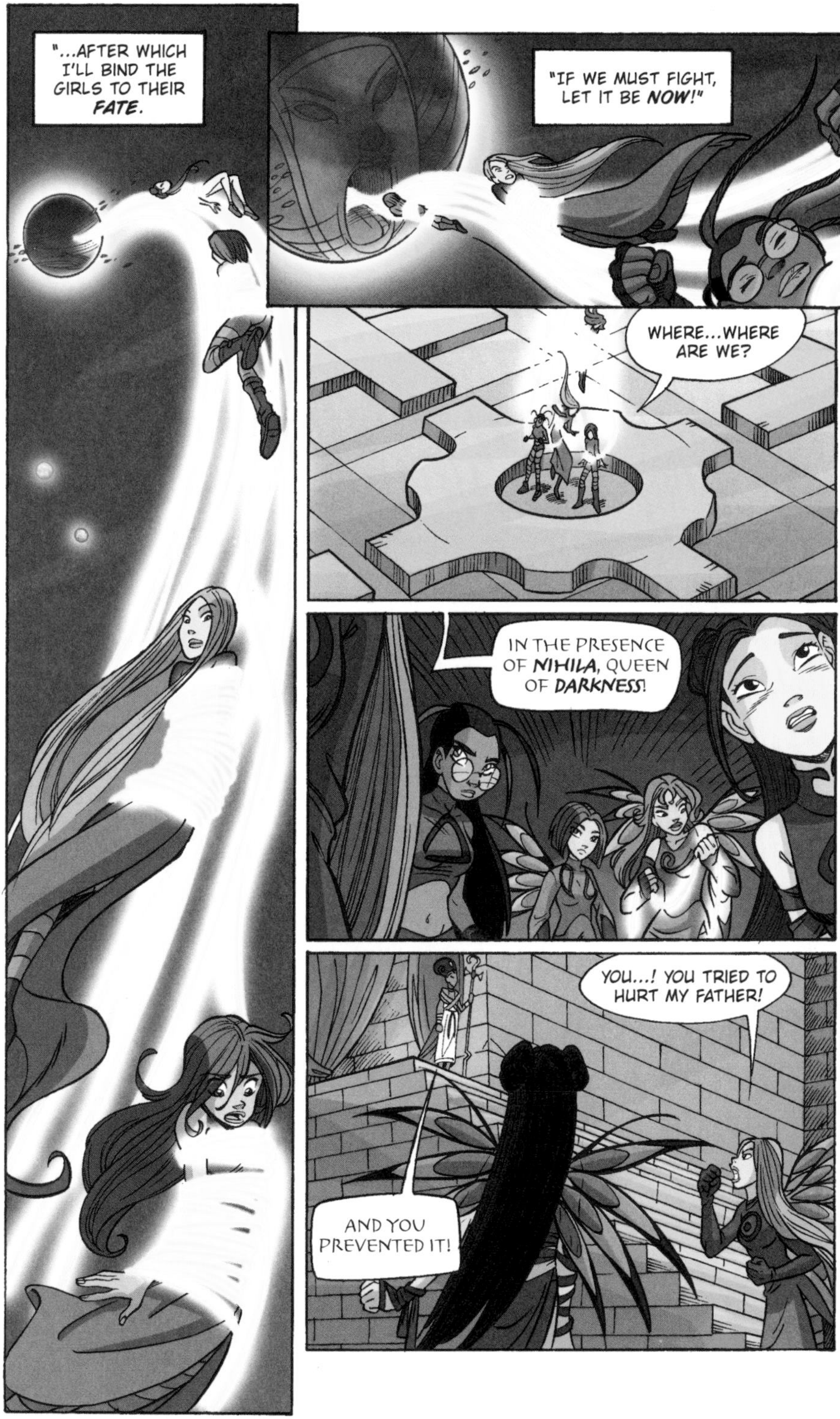
"...AFTER WHICH I'LL BIND THE GIRLS TO THEIR FATE.
"IF WE MUST FIGHT, LET IT BE NOW!"
WHERE...WHERE ARE WE?
IN THE PRESENCE OF NIHILA, QUEEN OF DARKNESS!
YOU...! YOU TRIED TO HURT MY FATHER!
AND YOU PREVENTED IT!

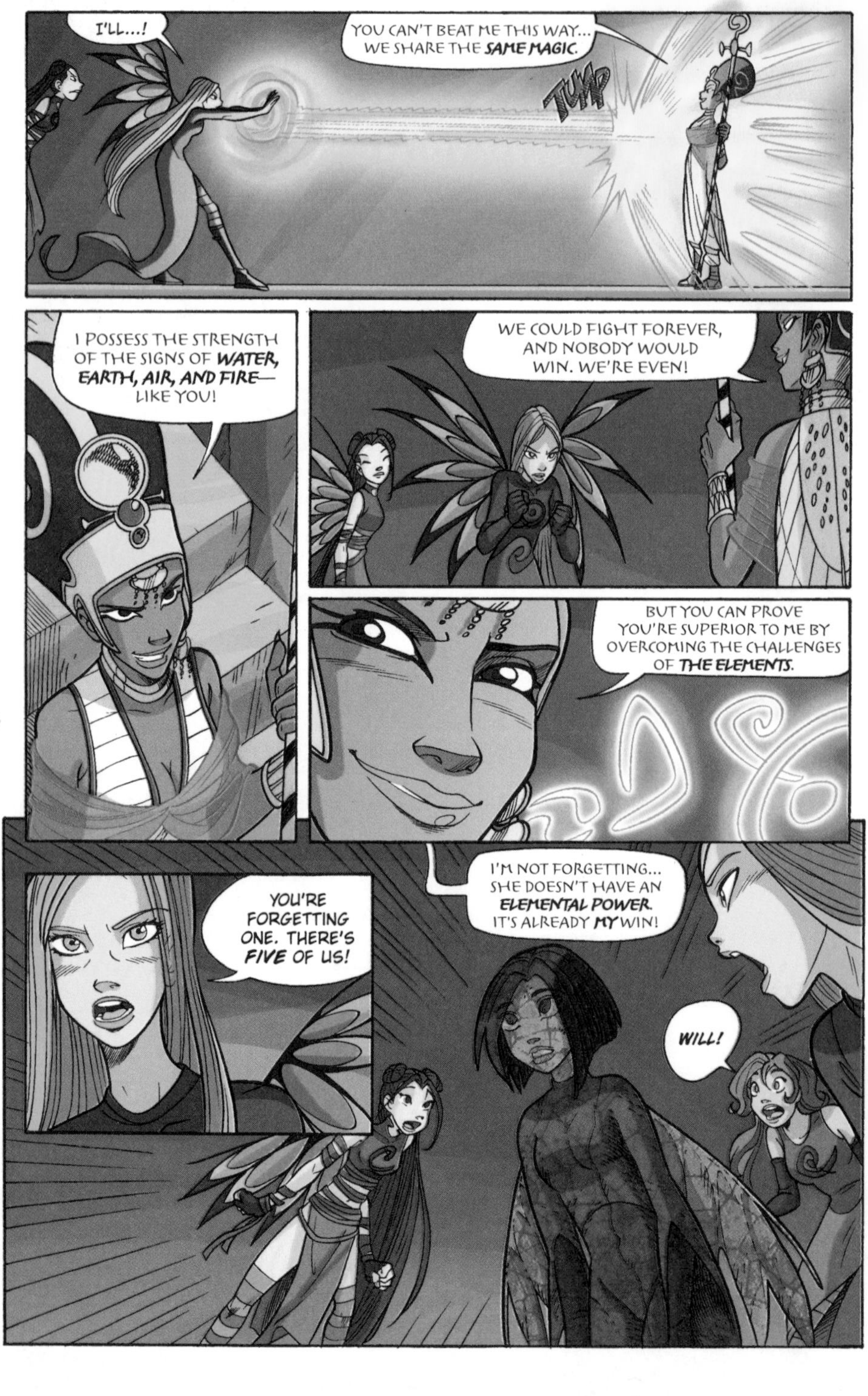
I'LL...!
YOU CAN'T BEAT ME THIS WAY... WE SHARE THE SAME MAGIC.
TUMP
I POSSESS THE STRENGTH OF THE SIGNS OF WATER, EARTH, AIR, AND FIRE— LIKE YOU!
WE COULD FIGHT FOREVER, AND NOBODY WOULD WIN. WE'RE EVEN!
BUT YOU CAN PROVE YOU'RE SUPERIOR TO ME BY OVERCOMING THE CHALLENGES OF THE ELEMENTS.
YOU'RE FORGETTING ONE. THERE'S FIVE OF US!
I'M NOT FORGETTING... SHE DOESN'T HAVE AN ELEMENTAL POWER. IT'S ALREADY MY WIN!
WILL!

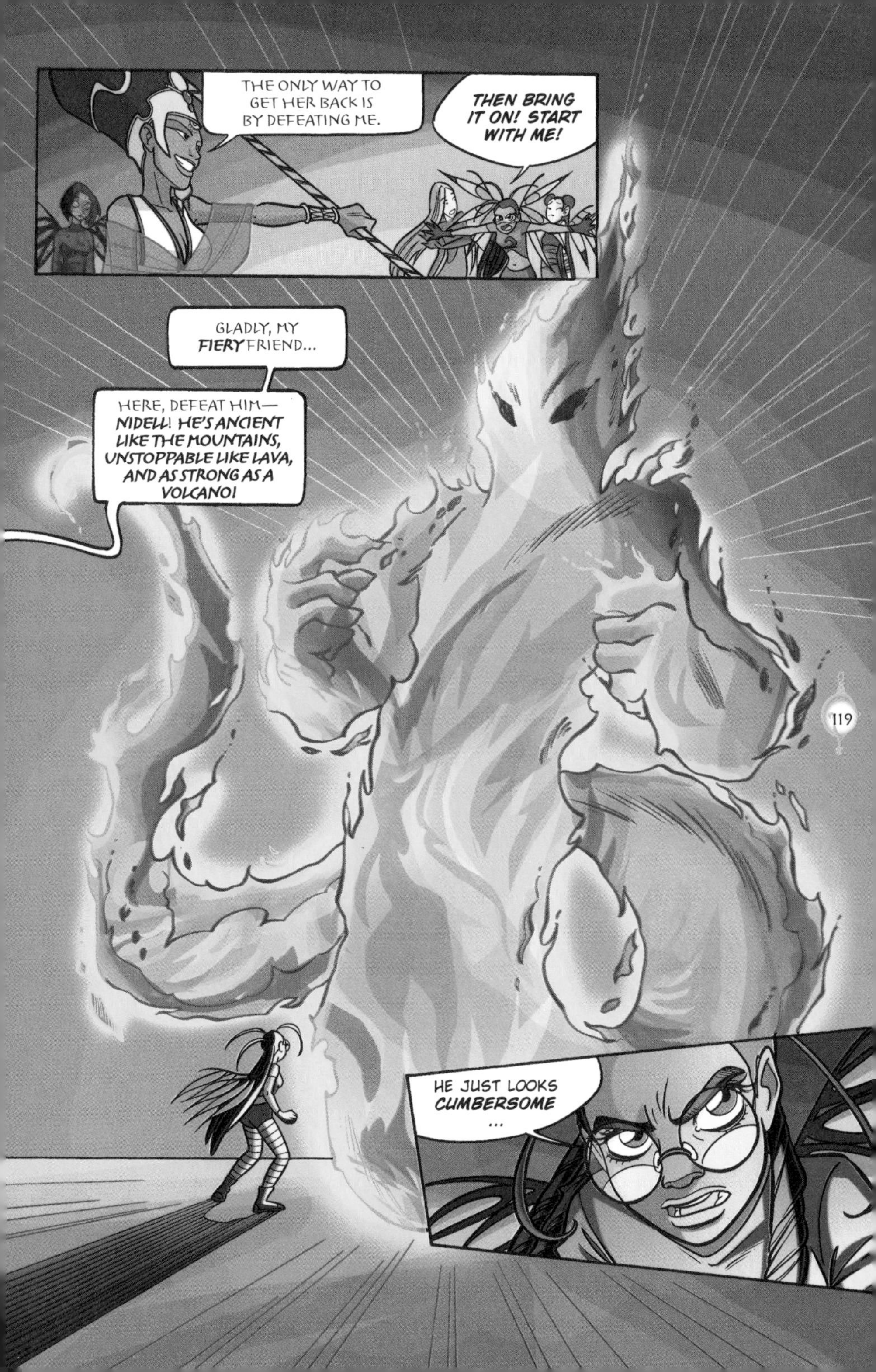
THE ONLY WAY TO GET HER BACK IS BY DEFEATING ME.
THEN BRING IT ON! START WITH ME!
GLADLY, MY FIERY FRIEND...
HERE, DEFEAT HIM— NIDELL! HE'S ANCIENT LIKE THE MOUNTAINS, UNSTOPPABLE LIKE LAVA, AND AS STRONG AS A VOLCANO!
HE JUST LOOKS CUMBERSOME ...

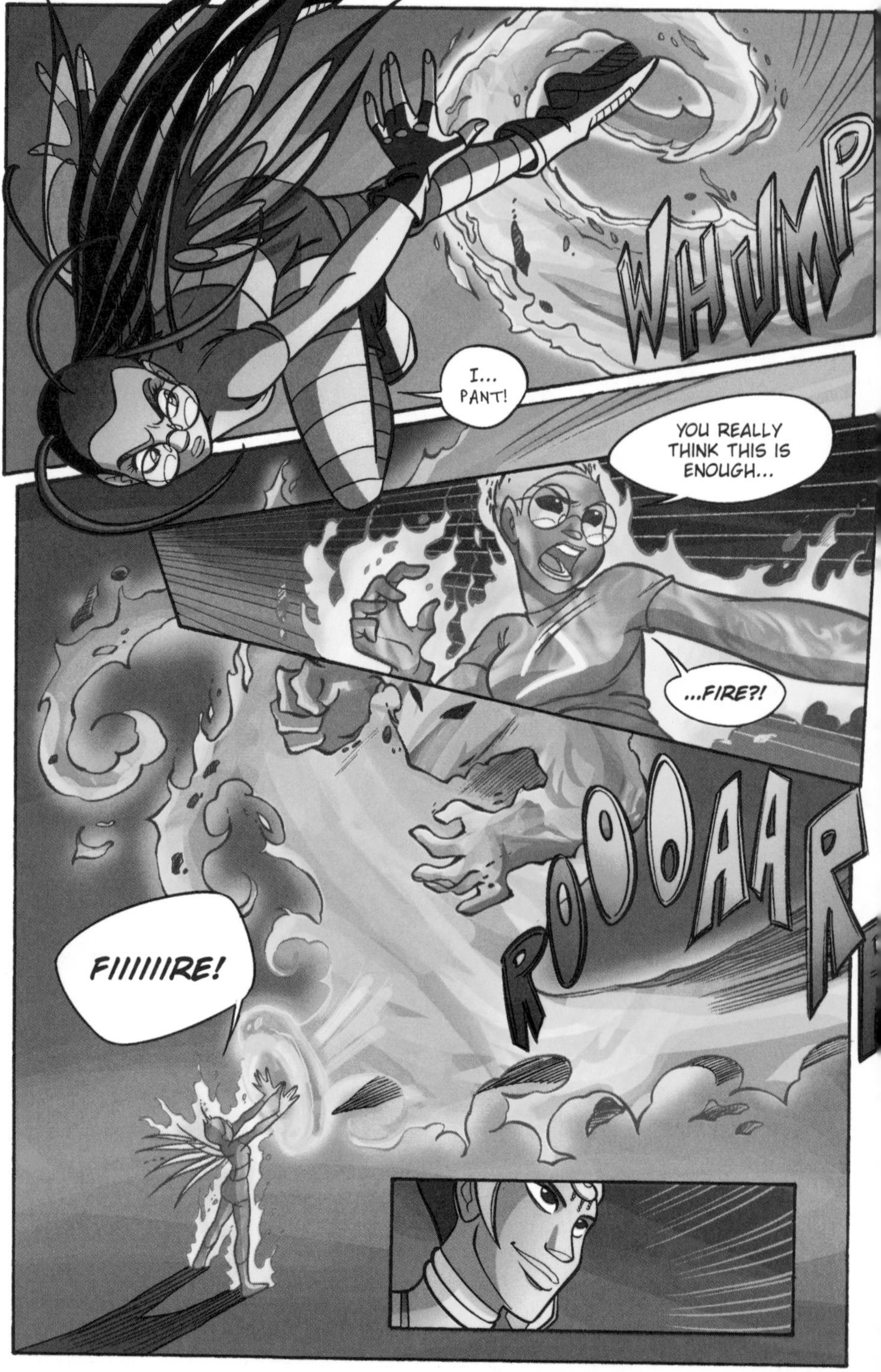
WHUMP
I... PANT!
YOU REALLY THINK THIS IS ENOUGH...
...FIRE?!
ROOOAAR
FIIIIIRE!

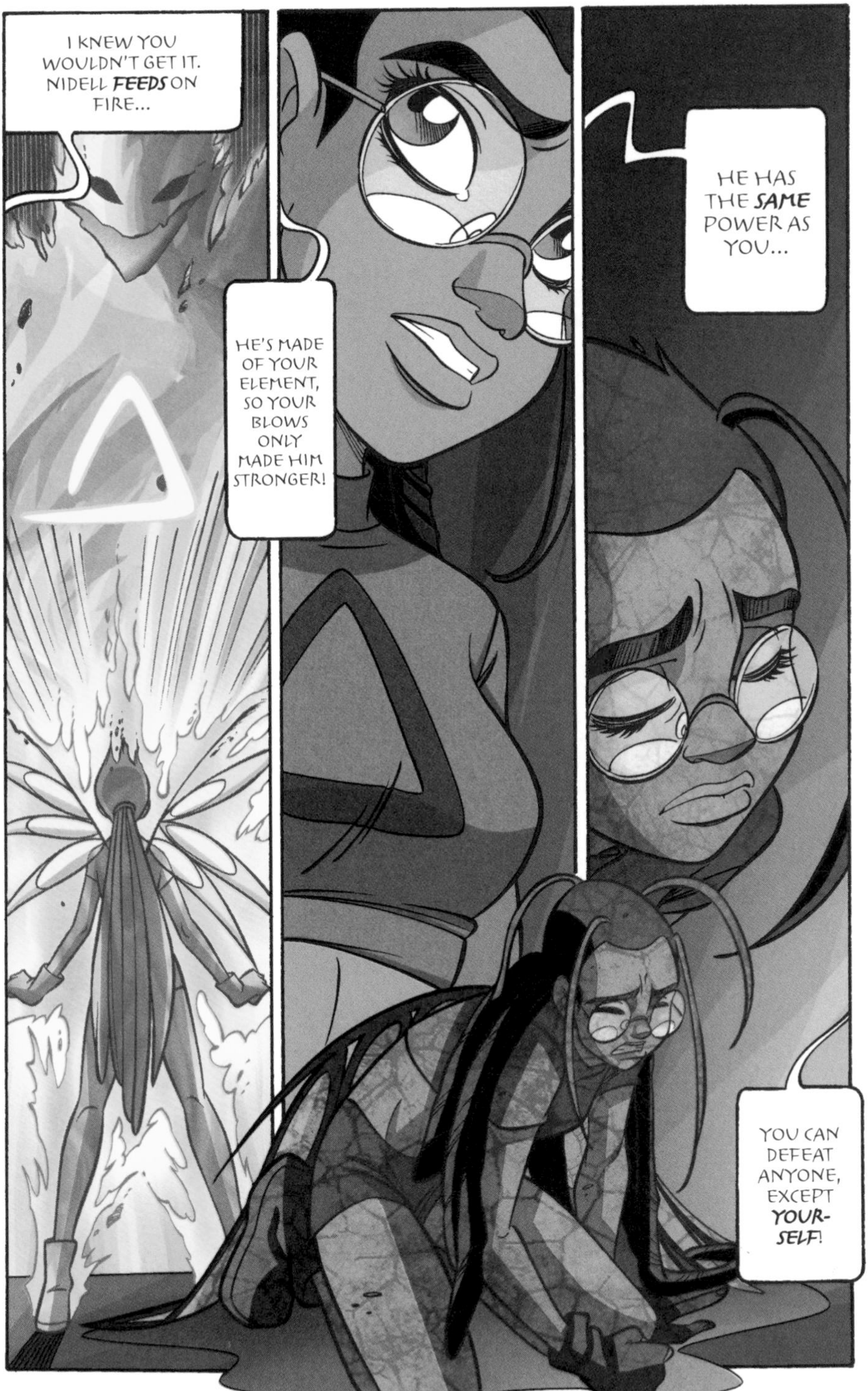
I KNEW YOU WOULDN'T GET IT. NIDELL **FEEDS** ON FIRE...
HE'S MADE OF YOUR ELEMENT, SO YOUR BLOWS ONLY MADE HIM STRONGER!
HE HAS THE **SAME** POWER AS YOU...
YOU CAN DEFEAT ANYONE, EXCEPT **YOURSELF**!

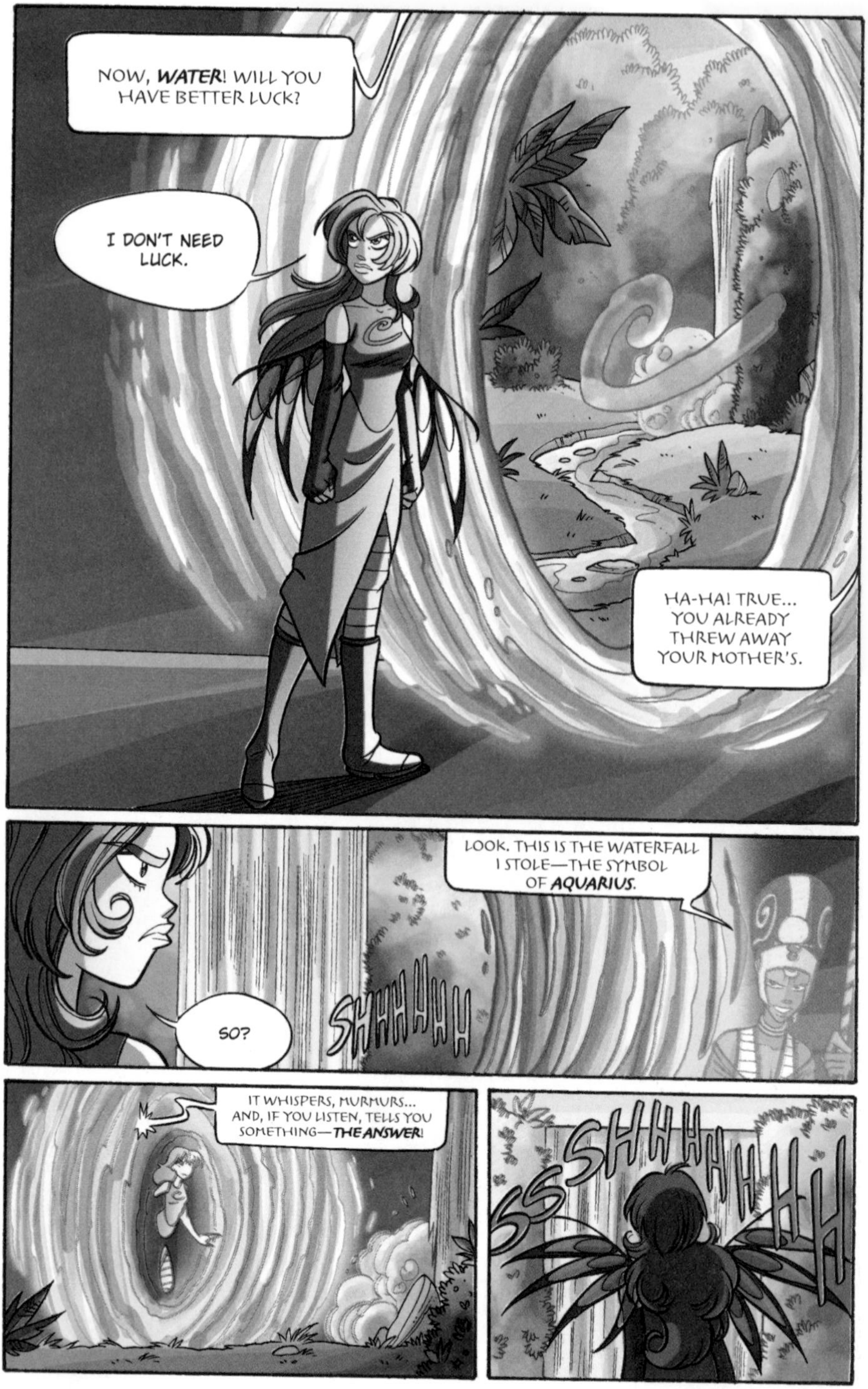
NOW, **WATER**! WILL YOU HAVE BETTER LUCK?
I DON'T NEED LUCK.
HA-HA! TRUE... YOU ALREADY THREW AWAY YOUR MOTHER'S.
LOOK. THIS IS THE WATERFALL I STOLE—THE SYMBOL OF **AQUARIUS**.
SHHHHHH
SO?
IT WHISPERS, MURMURS... AND, IF YOU LISTEN, TELLS YOU SOMETHING—**THE ANSWER**!
SSSHHHHHHHH

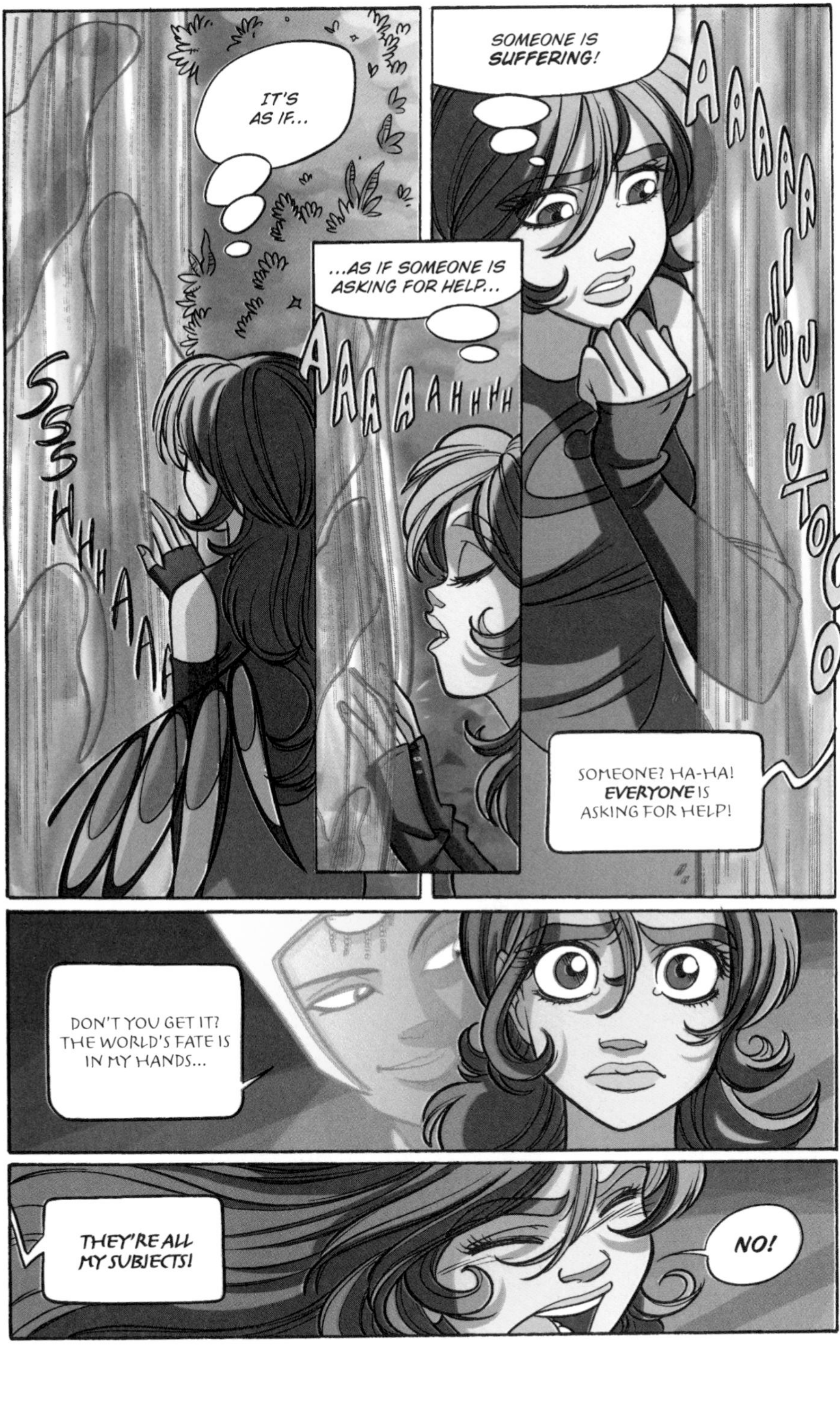
IT'S AS IF...
SSSHHHHAAAA
SOMEONE IS SUFFERING!
AAAAAAAAAIIIIUUUUUUUOOOOO
...AS IF SOMEONE IS ASKING FOR HELP...
AAAAAAHHHHH
SOMEONE? HA-HA! EVERYONE IS ASKING FOR HELP!
DON'T YOU GET IT? THE WORLD'S FATE IS IN MY HANDS...
THEY'RE ALL MY SUBJECTS!
NO!

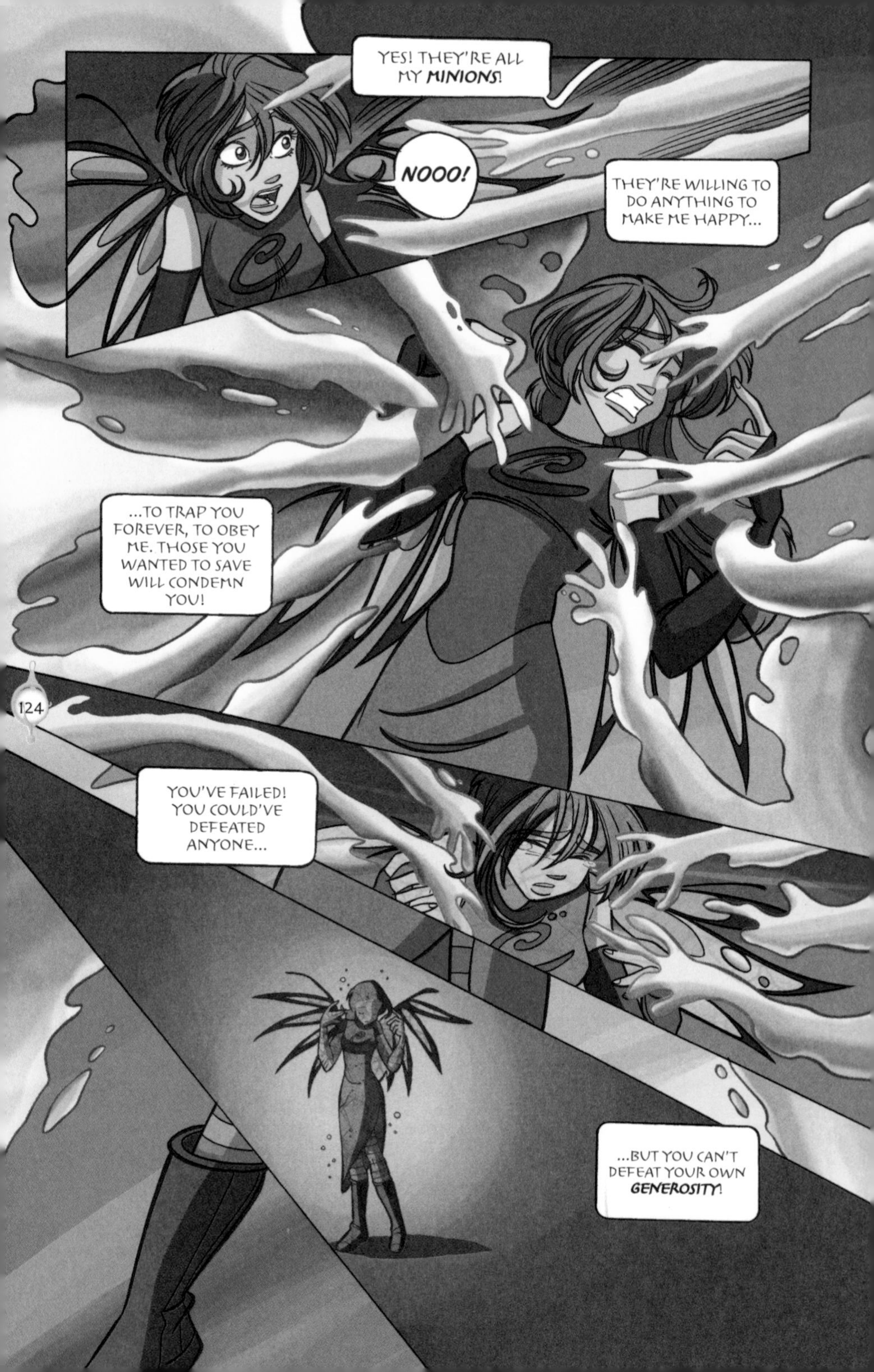

YES! THEY'RE ALL MY **MINIONS**!
NOOO!
THEY'RE WILLING TO DO ANYTHING TO MAKE ME HAPPY...
...TO TRAP YOU FOREVER, TO OBEY ME. THOSE YOU WANTED TO SAVE WILL CONDEMN YOU!
YOU'VE FAILED! YOU COULD'VE DEFEATED ANYONE...
...BUT YOU CAN'T DEFEAT YOUR OWN **GENEROSITY**!

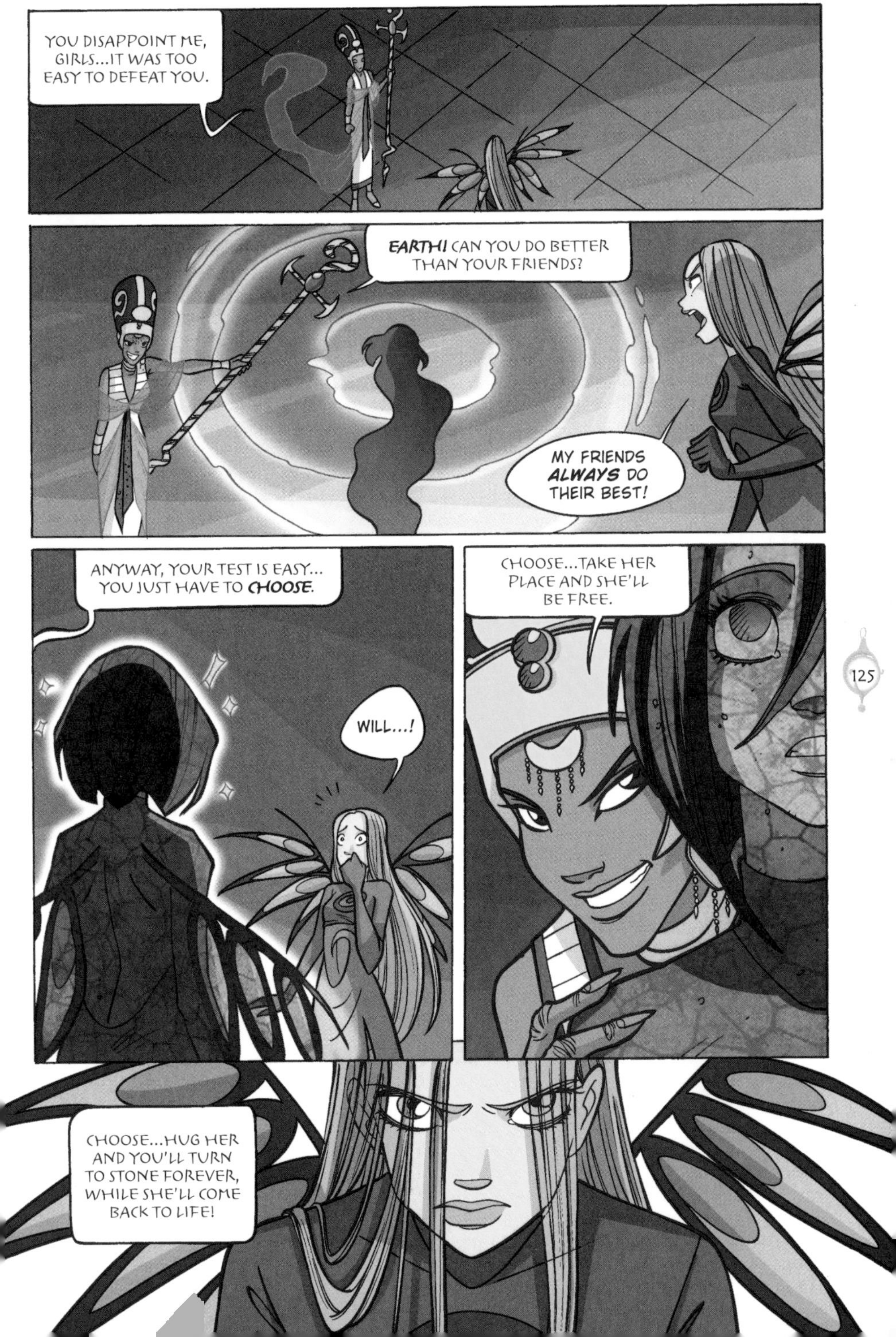
YOU DISAPPOINT ME, GIRLS...IT WAS TOO EASY TO DEFEAT YOU.
EARTH! CAN YOU DO BETTER THAN YOUR FRIENDS?
MY FRIENDS ALWAYS DO THEIR BEST!
ANYWAY, YOUR TEST IS EASY... YOU JUST HAVE TO CHOOSE.
WILL...!
CHOOSE...TAKE HER PLACE AND SHE'LL BE FREE.
CHOOSE...HUG HER AND YOU'LL TURN TO STONE FOREVER, WHILE SHE'LL COME BACK TO LIFE!

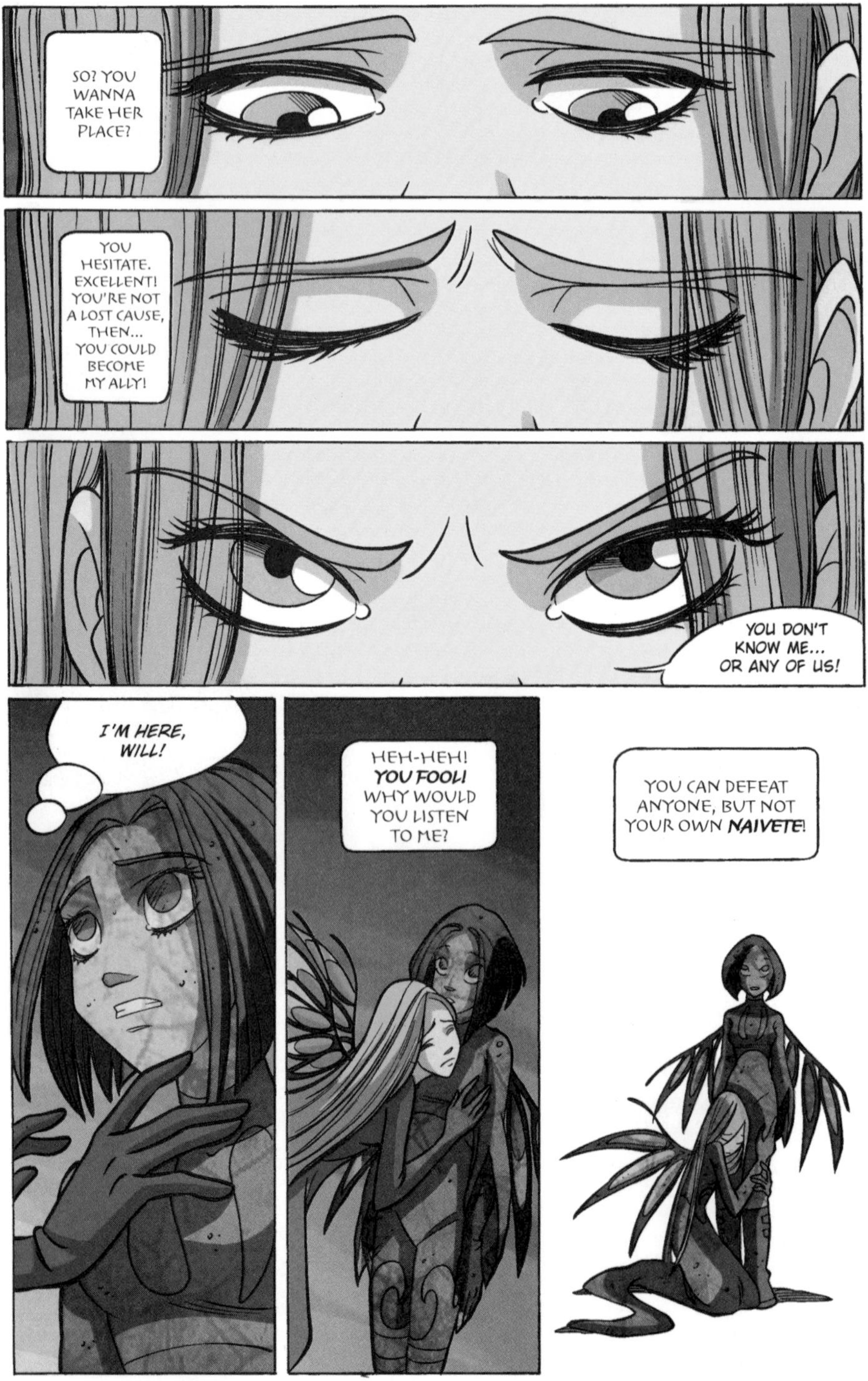
SO? YOU WANNA TAKE HER PLACE?
YOU HESITATE. EXCELLENT! YOU'RE NOT A LOST CAUSE, THEN... YOU COULD BECOME MY ALLY!
YOU DON'T KNOW ME... OR ANY OF US!
I'M HERE, WILL!
HEH-HEH! YOU FOOL! WHY WOULD YOU LISTEN TO ME?
YOU CAN DEFEAT ANYONE, BUT NOT YOUR OWN NAIVETE!

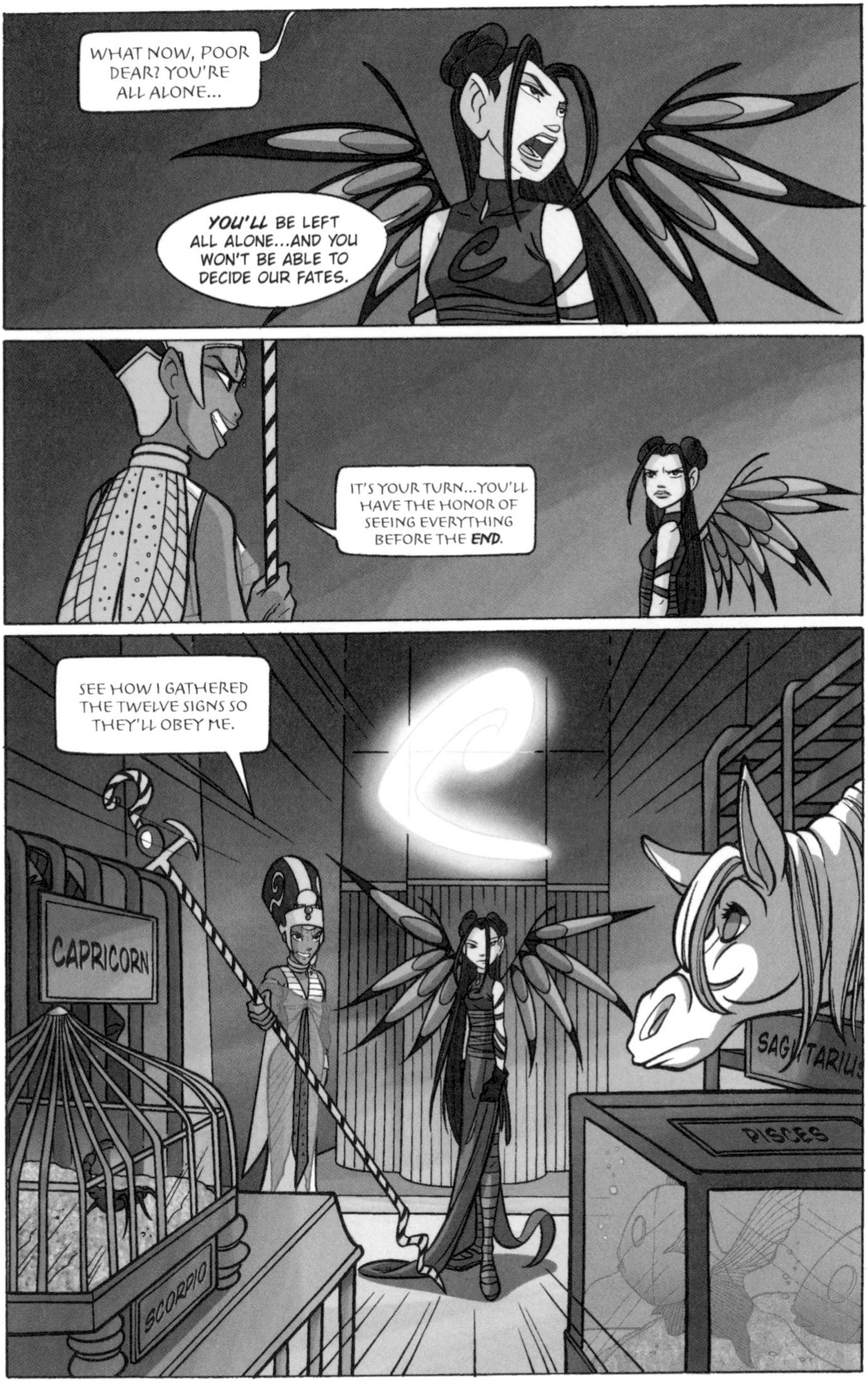
WHAT NOW, POOR DEAR? YOU'RE ALL ALONE...
YOU'LL BE LEFT ALL ALONE...AND YOU WON'T BE ABLE TO DECIDE OUR FATES.
IT'S YOUR TURN...YOU'LL HAVE THE HONOR OF SEEING EVERYTHING BEFORE THE **END**.
SEE HOW I GATHERED THE TWELVE SIGNS SO THEY'LL OBEY ME.
CAPRICORN
SAGITTARIUS
PISCES
SCORPIO

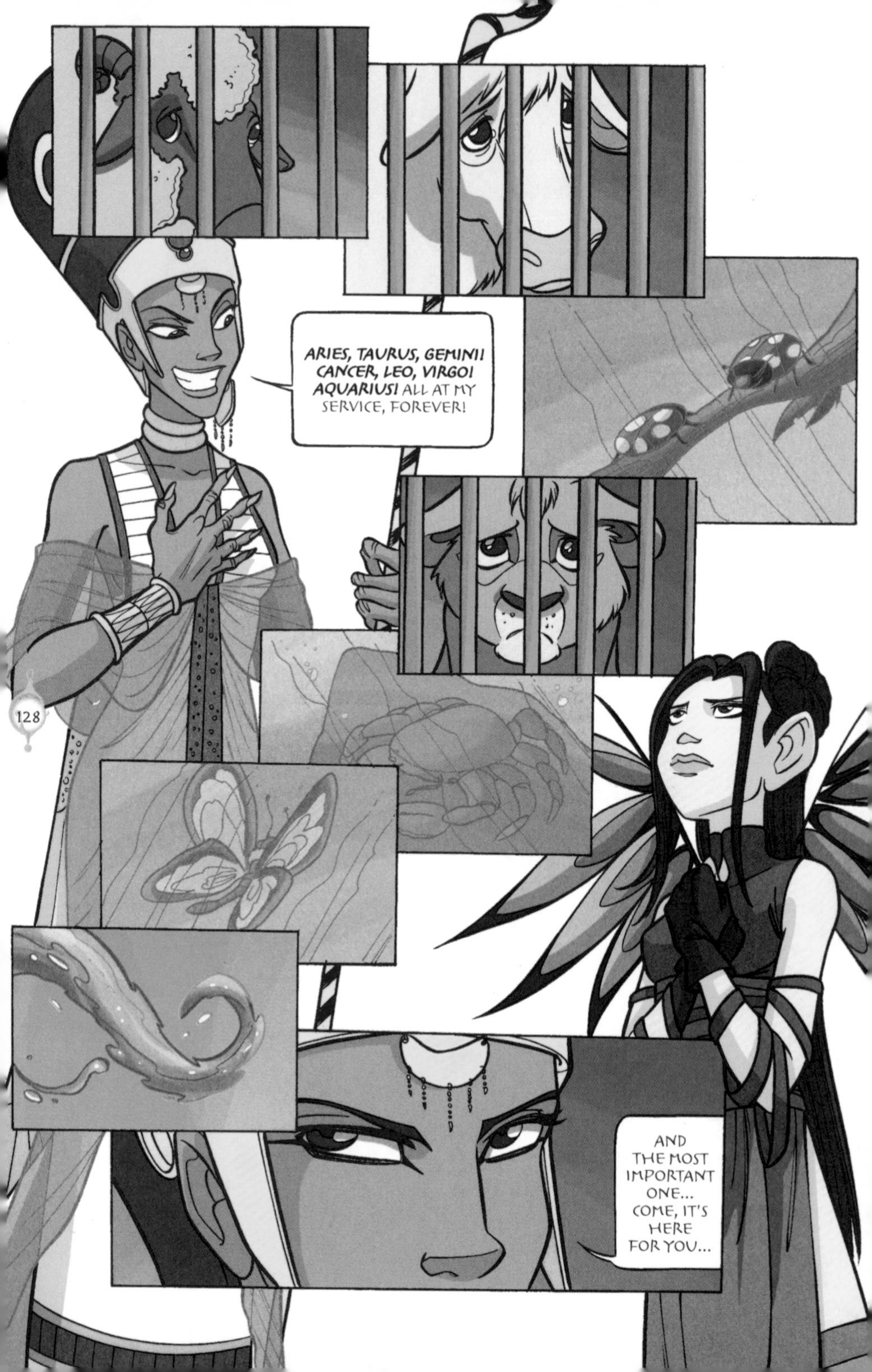
ARIES, TAURUS, GEMINI! CANCER, LEO, VIRGO! AQUARIUS! ALL AT MY SERVICE, FOREVER!
AND THE MOST IMPORTANT ONE... COME, IT'S HERE FOR YOU...

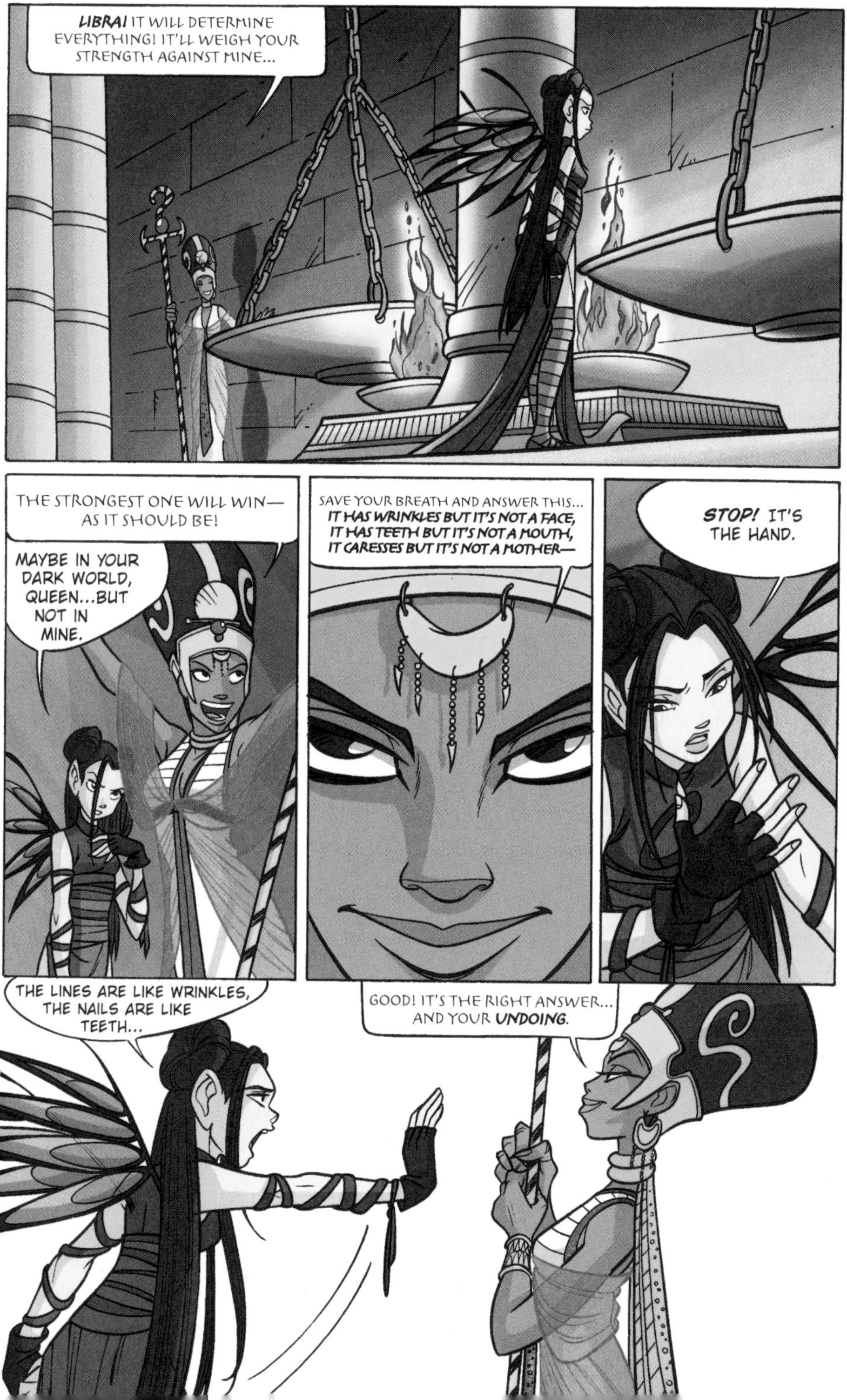
LIBRA! IT WILL DETERMINE EVERYTHING! IT'LL WEIGH YOUR STRENGTH AGAINST MINE...
THE STRONGEST ONE WILL WIN— AS IT SHOULD BE!
MAYBE IN YOUR DARK WORLD, QUEEN...BUT NOT IN MINE.
SAVE YOUR BREATH AND ANSWER THIS... IT HAS WRINKLES BUT IT'S NOT A FACE, IT HAS TEETH BUT IT'S NOT A MOUTH, IT CARESSES BUT IT'S NOT A MOTHER—
STOP! IT'S THE HAND.
THE LINES ARE LIKE WRINKLES, THE NAILS ARE LIKE TEETH...
GOOD! IT'S THE RIGHT ANSWER... AND YOUR UNDOING.

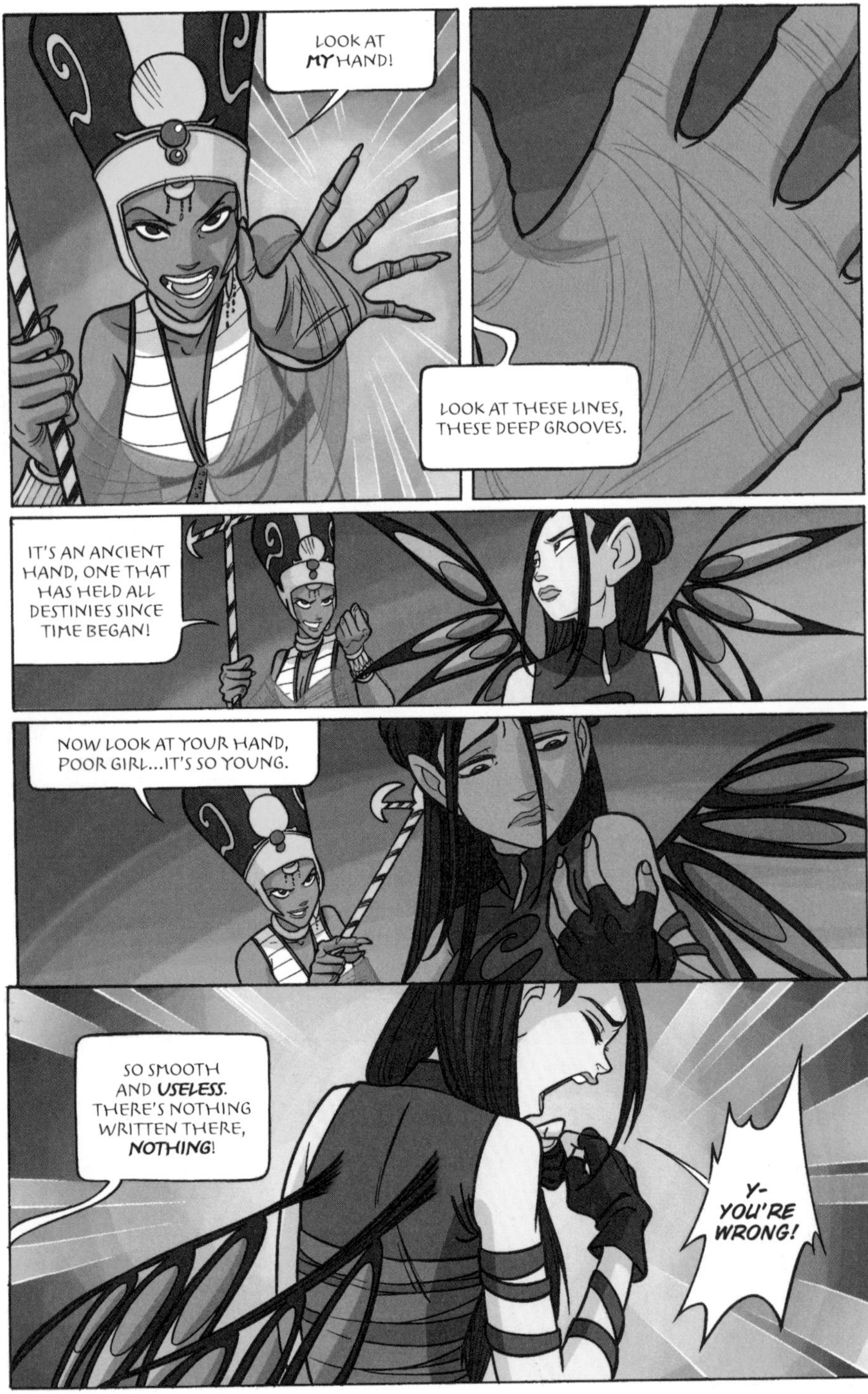
LOOK AT MY HAND!
LOOK AT THESE LINES, THESE DEEP GROOVES.
IT'S AN ANCIENT HAND, ONE THAT HAS HELD ALL DESTINIES SINCE TIME BEGAN!
NOW LOOK AT YOUR HAND, POOR GIRL...IT'S SO YOUNG.
SO SMOOTH AND USELESS. THERE'S NOTHING WRITTEN THERE, NOTHING!
Y-YOU'RE WRONG!

PLACE YOUR HAND ON THE SCALES, CHILD! LET'S SEE WHICH WEIGHS MORE...MY MILLENNIA OR YOUR FEW YEARS...

I... I DUNNO...

YOU'RE WRONG! MY HAND IS YOUNG AND STILL NEEDS TO BE WRITTEN ON... BUT I...

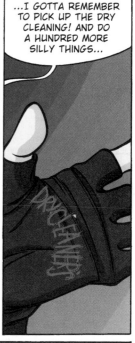

...I GOTTA REMEMBER TO PICK UP THE DRY CLEANING! AND DO A HUNDRED MORE SILLY THINGS...

...I GOTTA GO TO SCHOOL...LAUGH WITH MY FRIENDS...

...DECIDE WHAT I WANNA DO WITH MY LIFE...I STILL HAVE TO CHOOSE...

I HAVE TO... I HAVE TO...

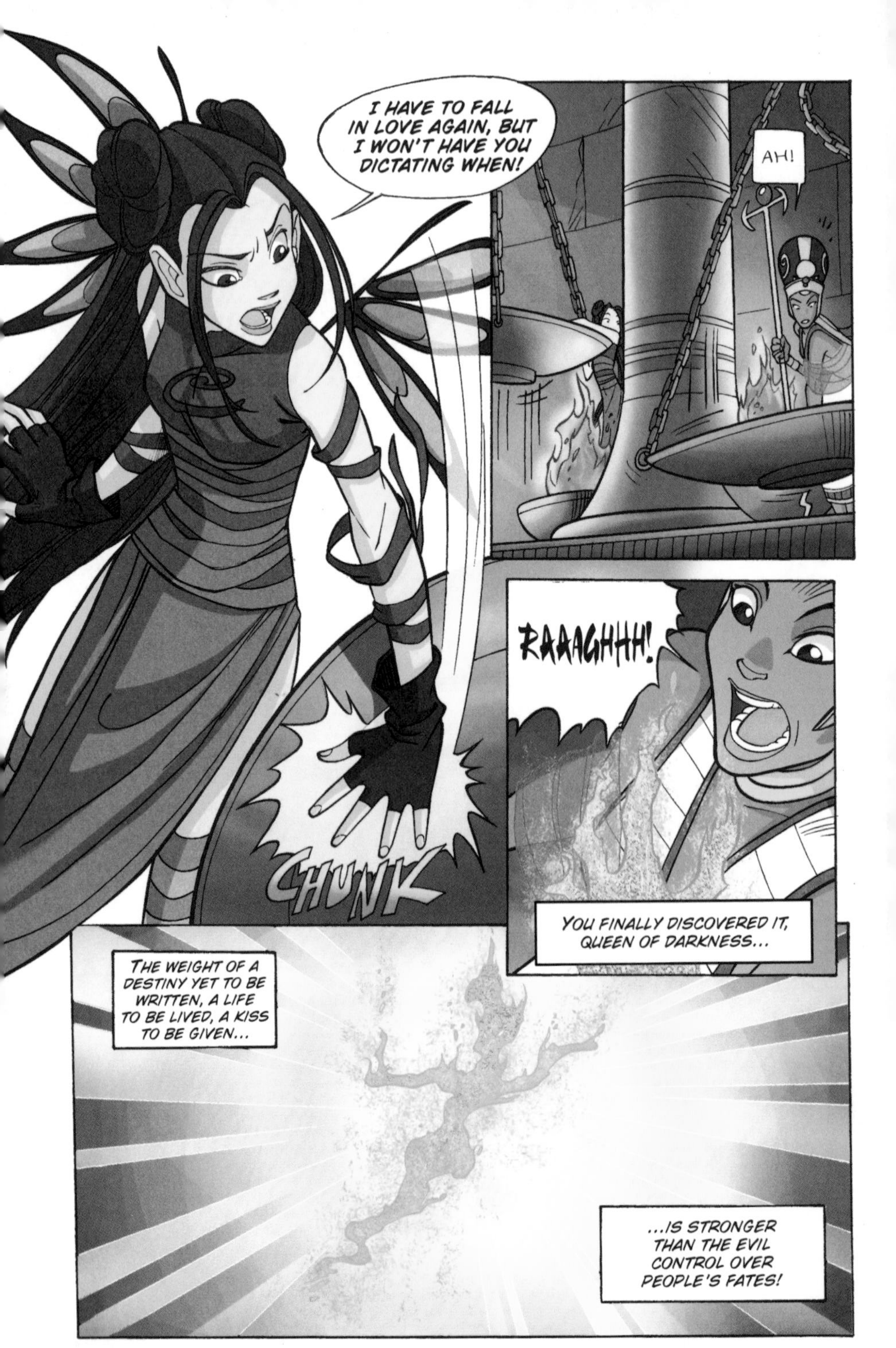
I HAVE TO FALL IN LOVE AGAIN, BUT I WON'T HAVE YOU DICTATING WHEN!
AH!
CHUNK
RAAAGHHH!
YOU FINALLY DISCOVERED IT, QUEEN OF DARKNESS...
THE WEIGHT OF A DESTINY YET TO BE WRITTEN, A LIFE TO BE LIVED, A KISS TO BE GIVEN...
...IS STRONGER THAN THE EVIL CONTROL OVER PEOPLE'S FATES!

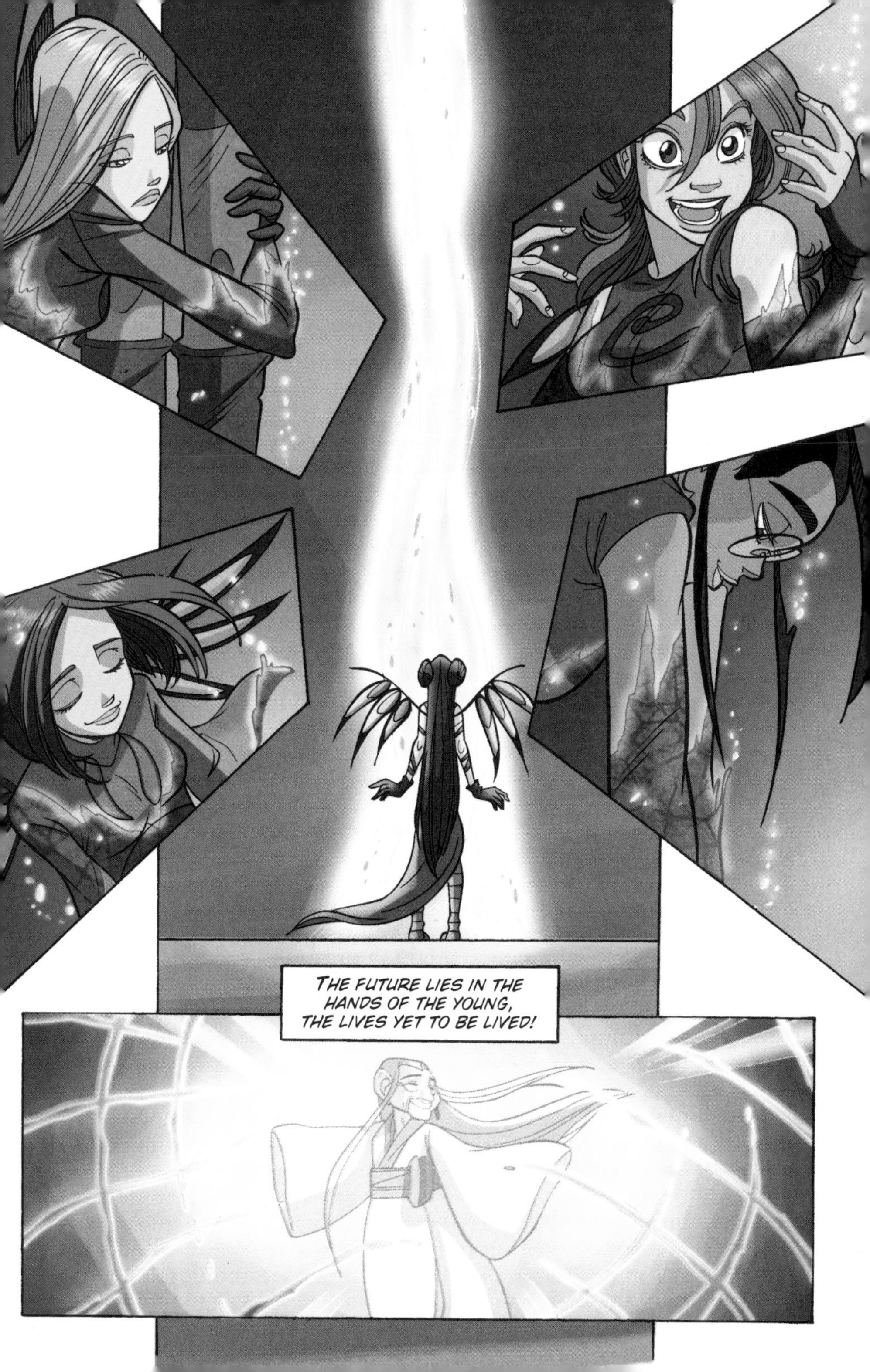
THE FUTURE LIES IN THE HANDS OF THE YOUNG, THE LIVES YET TO BE LIVED!

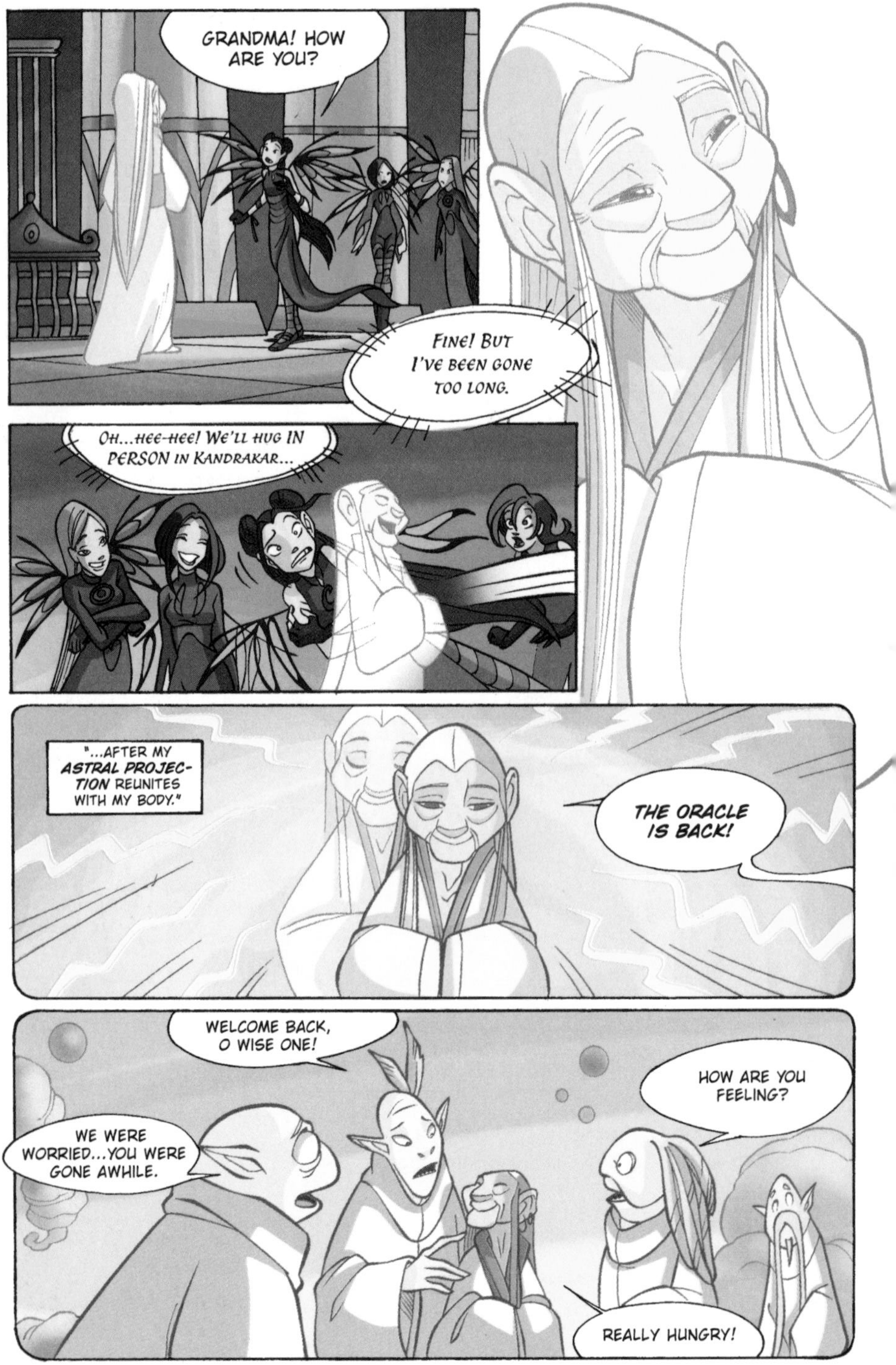
GRANDMA! HOW ARE YOU?
FINE! BUT I'VE BEEN GONE TOO LONG.
OH...HEE-HEE! WE'LL HUG IN PERSON IN KANDRAKAR...
"...AFTER MY ASTRAL PROJECTION REUNITES WITH MY BODY."
THE ORACLE IS BACK!
WELCOME BACK, O WISE ONE!
WE WERE WORRIED...YOU WERE GONE AWHILE.
HOW ARE YOU FEELING?
REALLY HUNGRY!

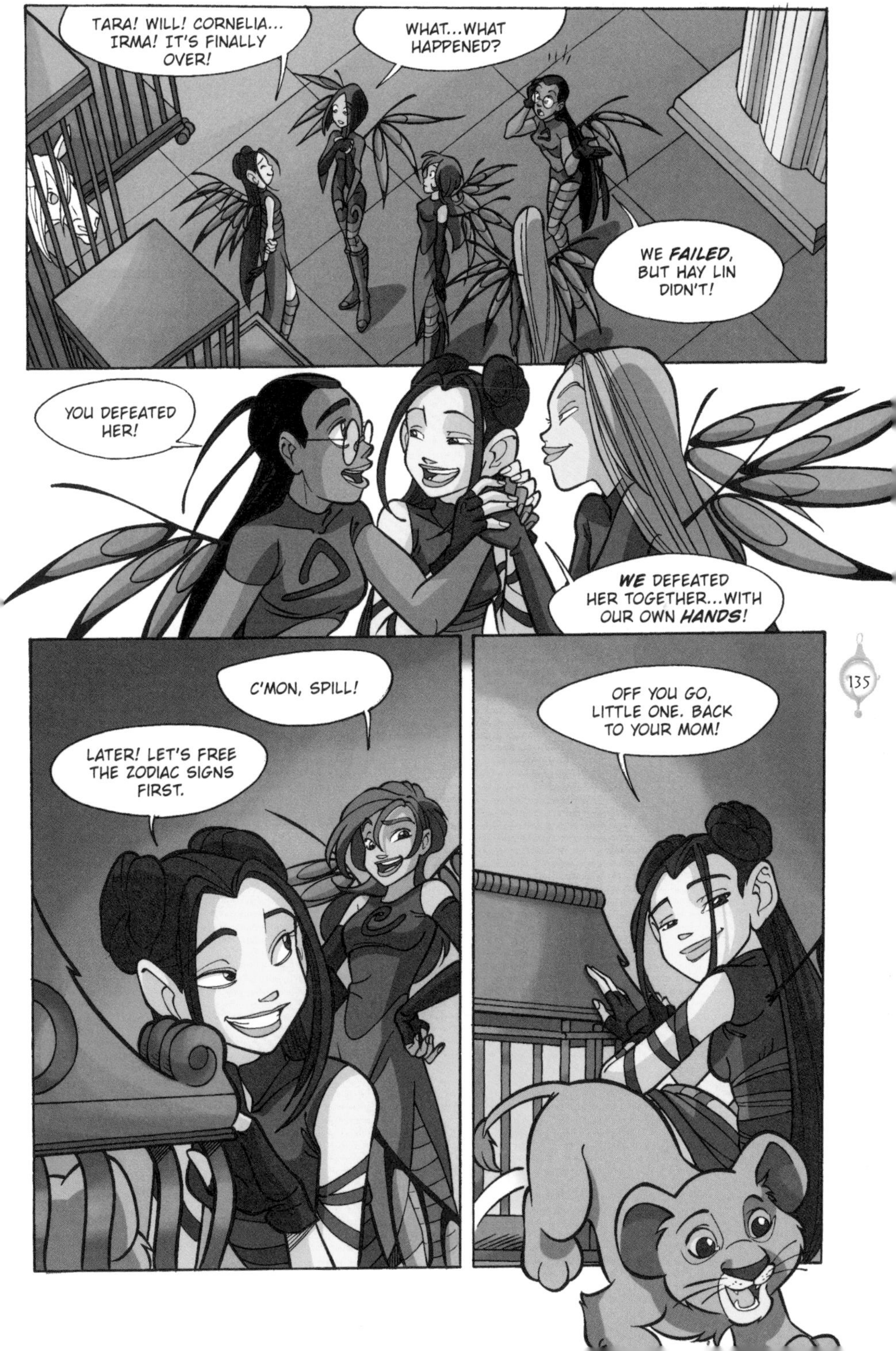
TARA! WILL! CORNELIA... IRMA! IT'S FINALLY OVER!
WHAT...WHAT HAPPENED?
WE FAILED, BUT HAY LIN DIDN'T!
YOU DEFEATED HER!
WE DEFEATED HER TOGETHER...WITH OUR OWN HANDS!
C'MON, SPILL!
LATER! LET'S FREE THE ZODIAC SIGNS FIRST.
OFF YOU GO, LITTLE ONE. BACK TO YOUR MOM!

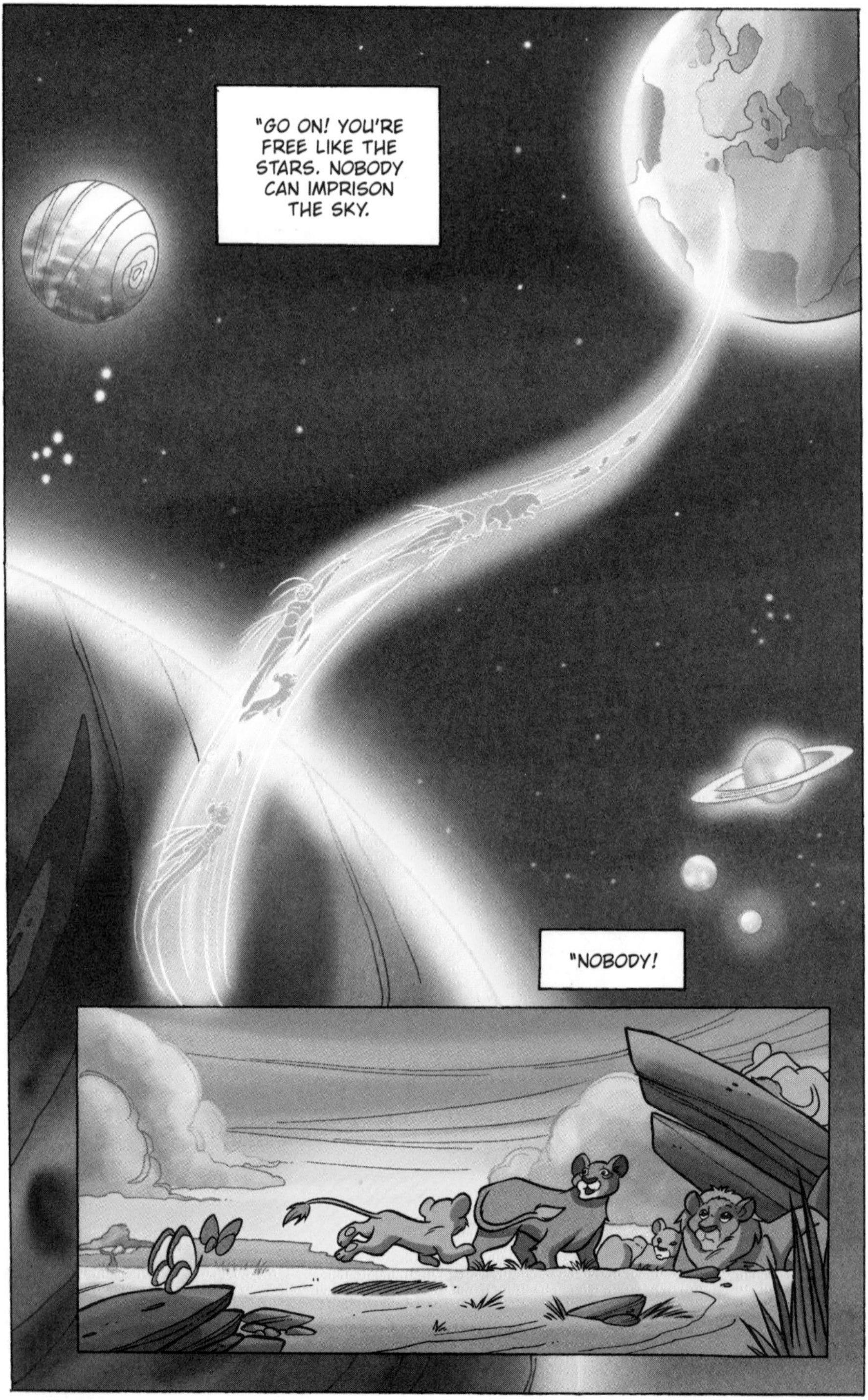
"GO ON! YOU'RE FREE LIKE THE STARS. NOBODY CAN IMPRISON THE SKY.
"NOBODY!

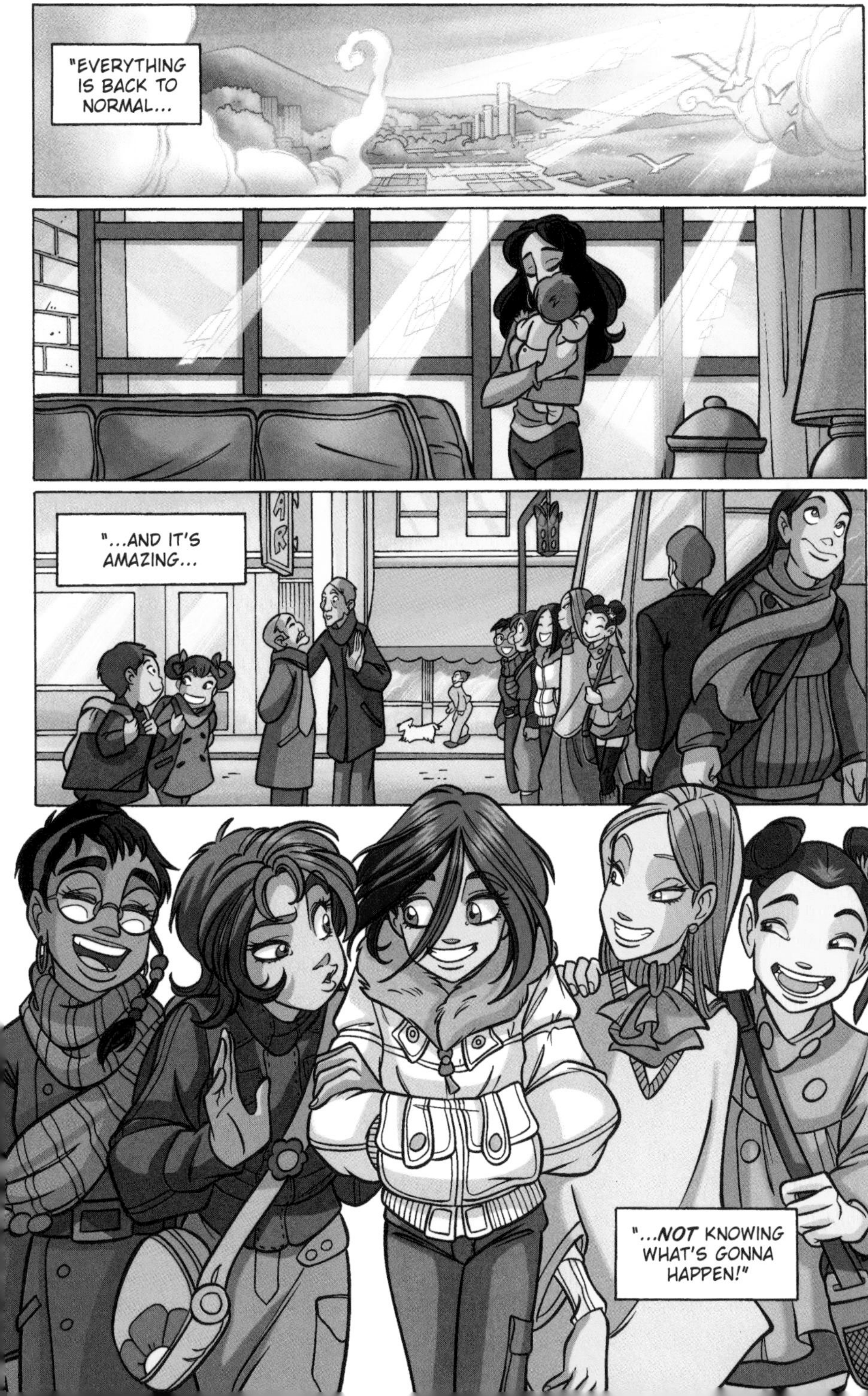
"EVERYTHING IS BACK TO NORMAL...
"...AND IT'S AMAZING...
"...NOT KNOWING WHAT'S GONNA HAPPEN!"

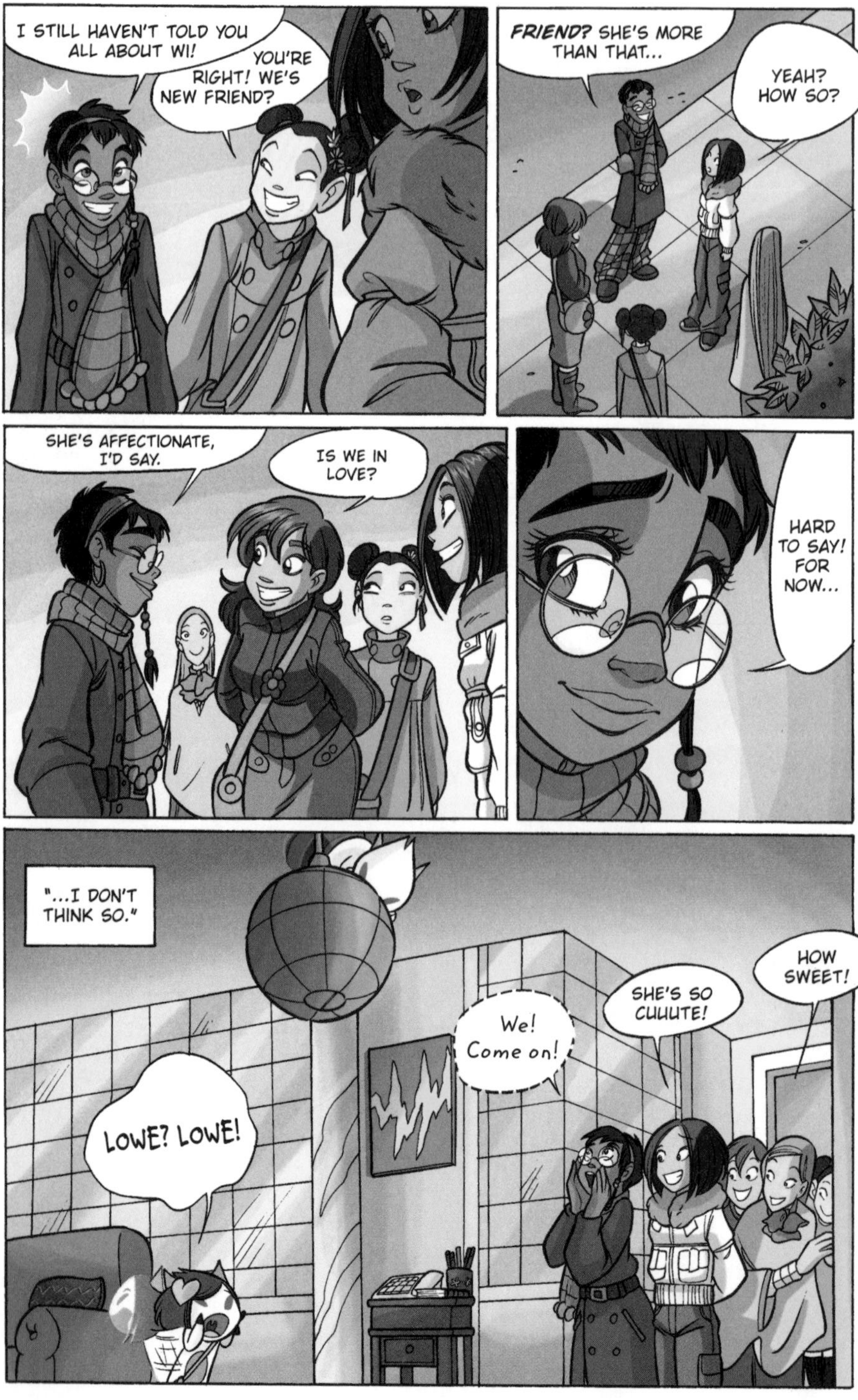
I STILL HAVEN'T TOLD YOU ALL ABOUT WI!
YOU'RE RIGHT! WE'S NEW FRIEND?
FRIEND? SHE'S MORE THAN THAT...
YEAH? HOW SO?
SHE'S AFFECTIONATE, I'D SAY.
IS WE IN LOVE?
HARD TO SAY! FOR NOW...
"...I DON'T THINK SO."
LOWE? LOWE!
We! Come on!
SHE'S SO CUUUTE!
HOW SWEET!

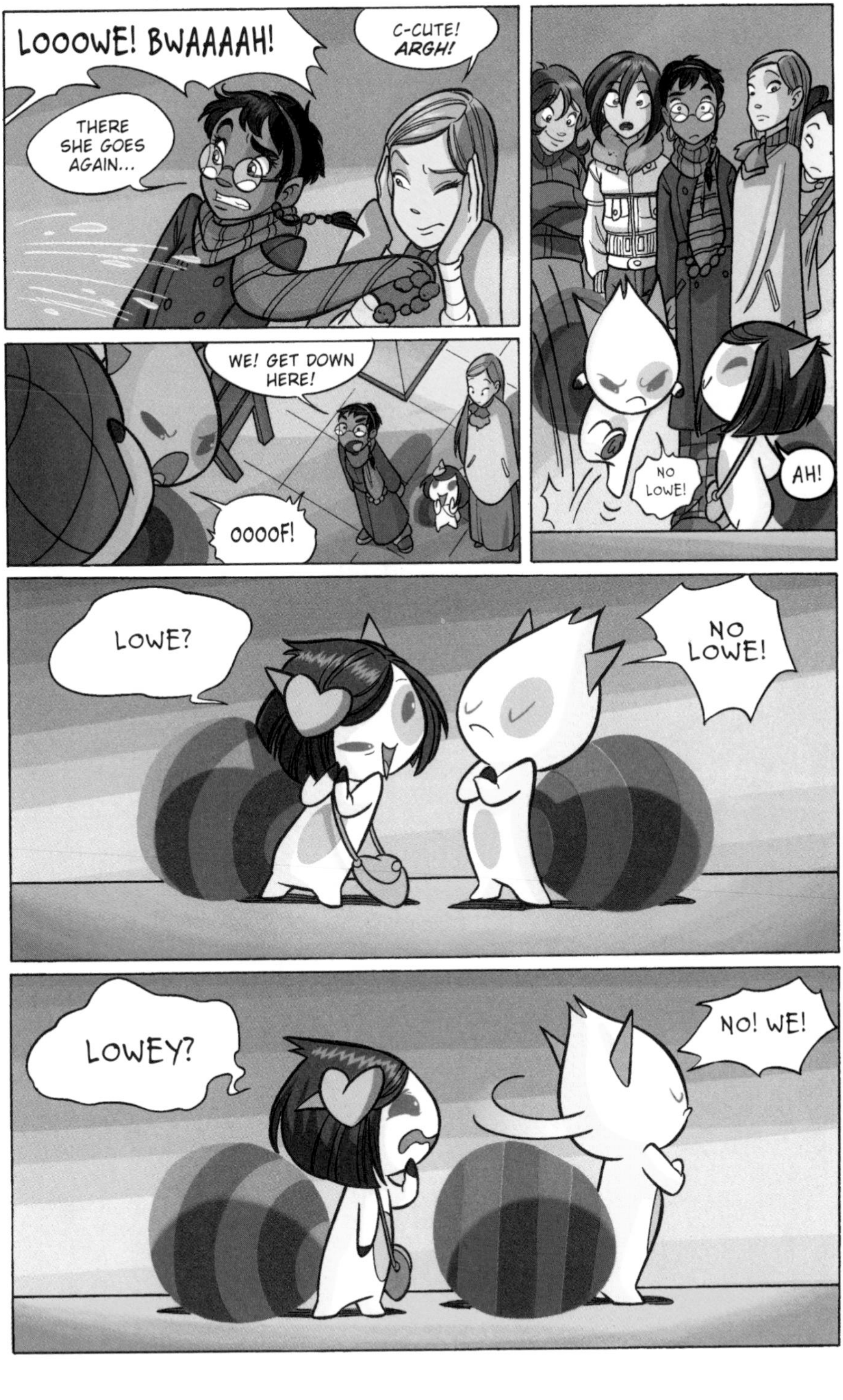
LOOOWE! BWAAAAH!
C-CUTE! ARGH!
THERE SHE GOES AGAIN...
WE! GET DOWN HERE!
OOOOF!
NO LOWE!
AH!
LOWE?
NO LOWE!
LOWEY?
NO! WE!

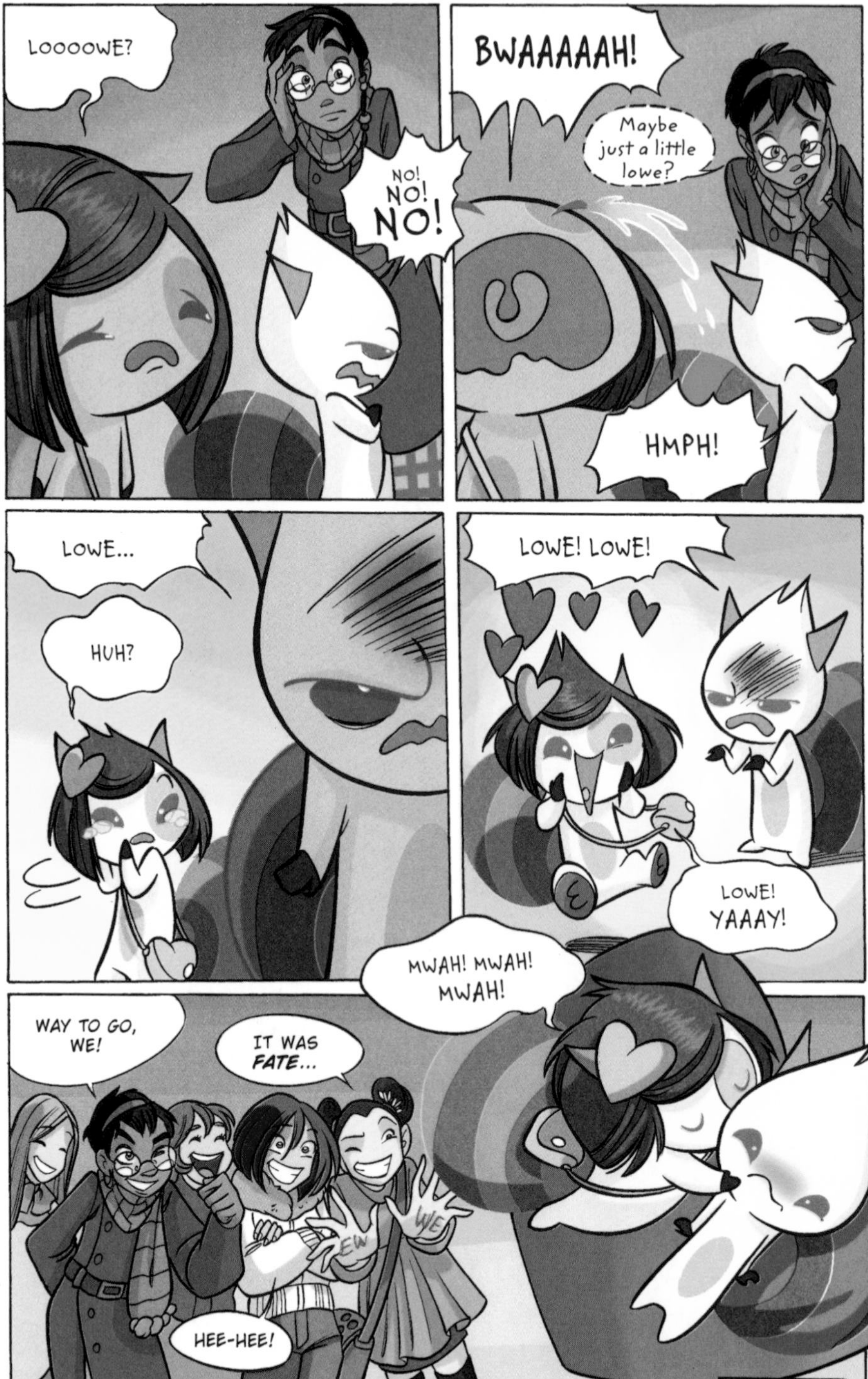

LOOOOWE?
NO! NO! NO!
BWAAAAAH!
Maybe just a little lowe?
HMPH!
LOWE...
HUH?
LOWE! LOWE!
LOWE! YAAAY!
MWAH! MWAH! MWAH!
WAY TO GO, WE!
IT WAS FATE...
HEE-HEE!
END OF CHAPTER 107

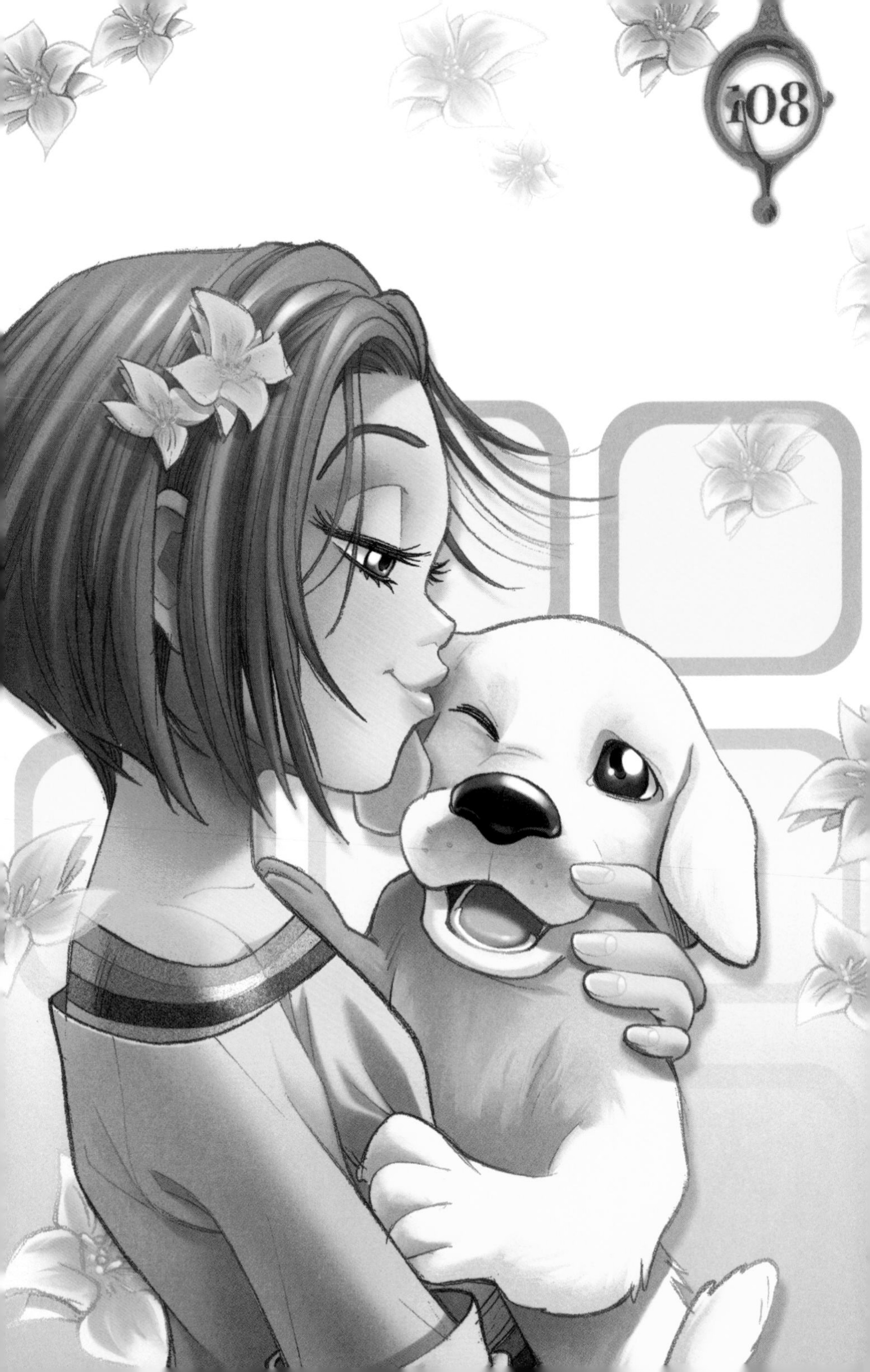

W.i.t.c.h.

Will Irma Taranee Cornelia Hay Lin

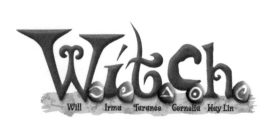

A Father's Heart

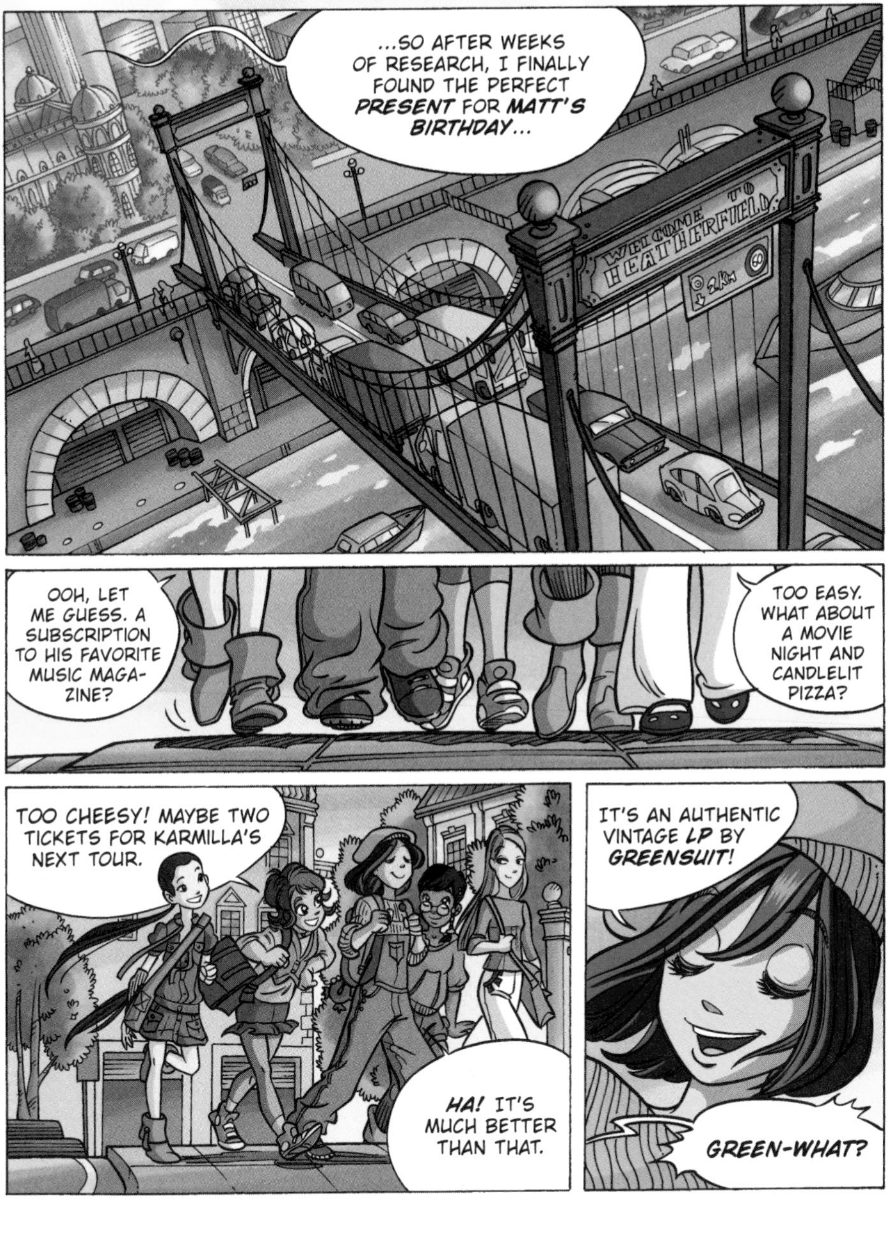

...SO AFTER WEEKS OF RESEARCH, I FINALLY FOUND THE PERFECT PRESENT FOR MATT'S BIRTHDAY...
WELCOME TO HEATHERFIELD
OOH, LET ME GUESS. A SUBSCRIPTION TO HIS FAVORITE MUSIC MAGAZINE?
TOO EASY. WHAT ABOUT A MOVIE NIGHT AND CANDLELIT PIZZA?
TOO CHEESY! MAYBE TWO TICKETS FOR KARMILLA'S NEXT TOUR.
HA! IT'S MUCH BETTER THAN THAT.
IT'S AN AUTHENTIC VINTAGE LP BY GREENSUIT!
GREEN-WHAT?

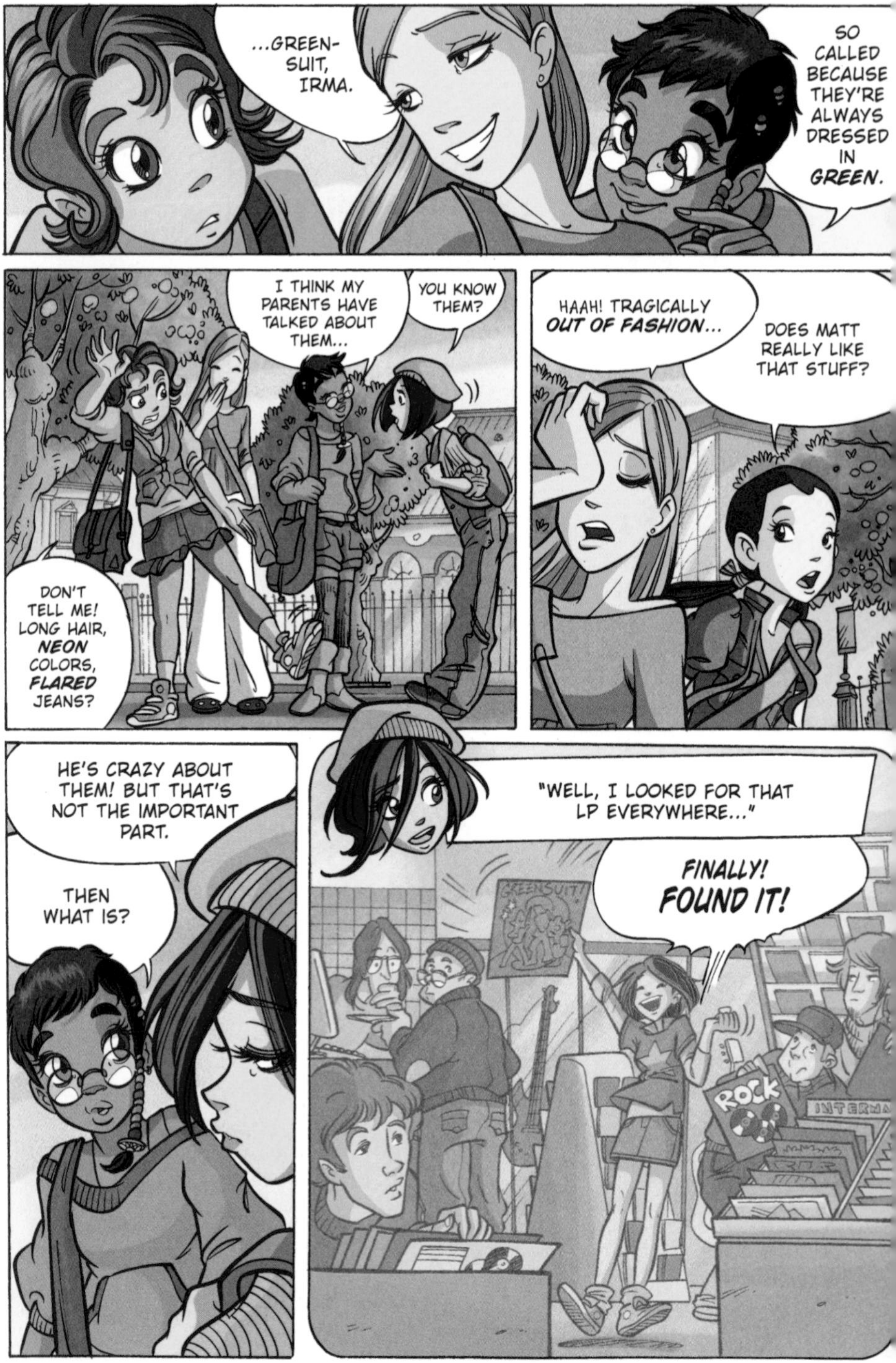
...GREEN-SUIT, IRMA.
SO CALLED BECAUSE THEY'RE ALWAYS DRESSED IN GREEN.
I THINK MY PARENTS HAVE TALKED ABOUT THEM...
YOU KNOW THEM?
DON'T TELL ME! LONG HAIR, NEON COLORS, FLARED JEANS?
HAAH! TRAGICALLY OUT OF FASHION...
DOES MATT REALLY LIKE THAT STUFF?
HE'S CRAZY ABOUT THEM! BUT THAT'S NOT THE IMPORTANT PART.
THEN WHAT IS?
"WELL, I LOOKED FOR THAT LP EVERYWHERE..."
FINALLY! FOUND IT!
GREENSUIT!
ROCK

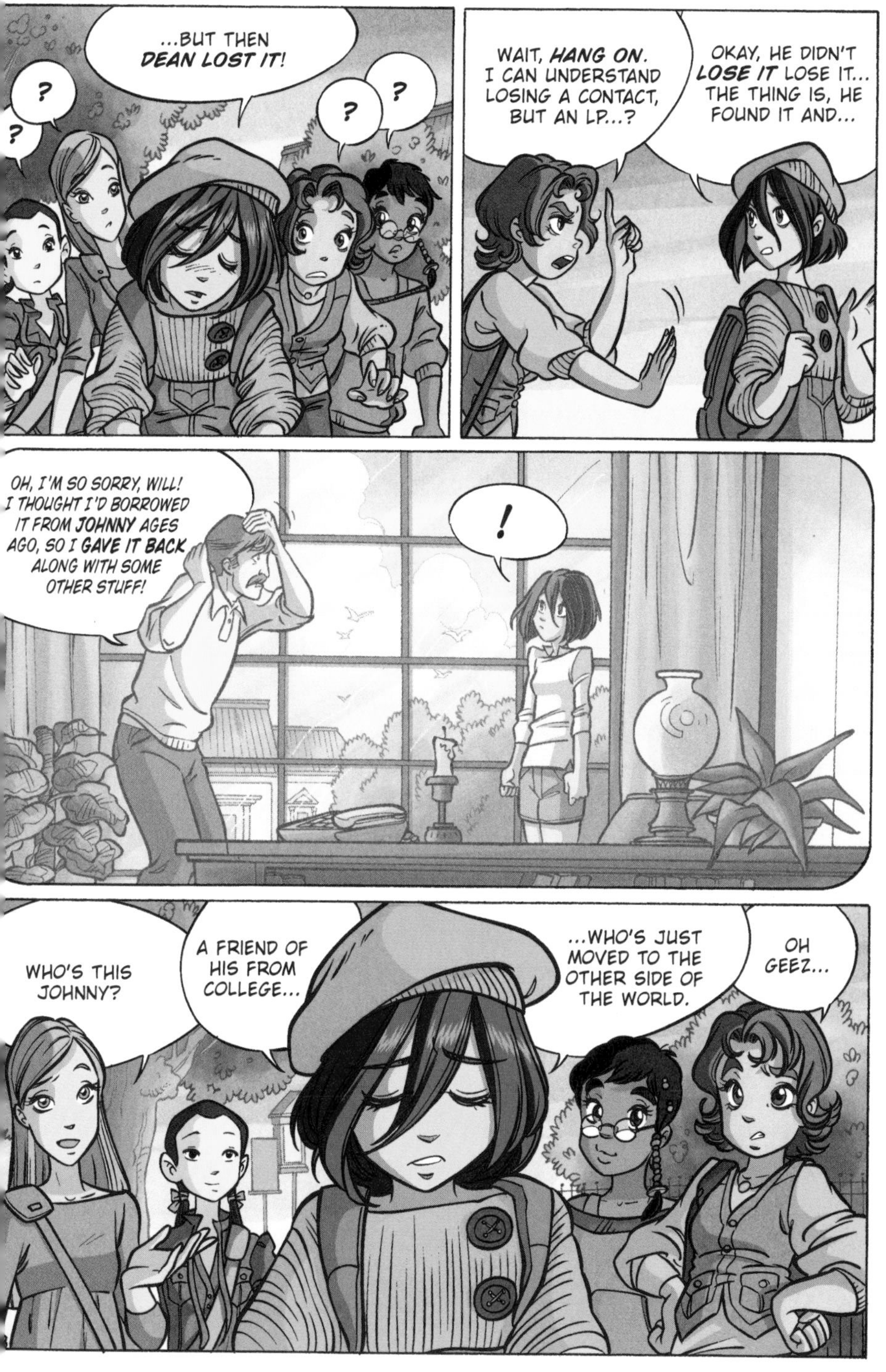
...BUT THEN DEAN LOST IT!
?
?
?
?
WAIT, HANG ON. I CAN UNDERSTAND LOSING A CONTACT, BUT AN LP...?
OKAY, HE DIDN'T LOSE IT LOSE IT... THE THING IS, HE FOUND IT AND...
OH, I'M SO SORRY, WILL! I THOUGHT I'D BORROWED IT FROM JOHNNY AGES AGO, SO I GAVE IT BACK ALONG WITH SOME OTHER STUFF!
!
WHO'S THIS JOHNNY?
A FRIEND OF HIS FROM COLLEGE...
...WHO'S JUST MOVED TO THE OTHER SIDE OF THE WORLD.
OH GEEZ...

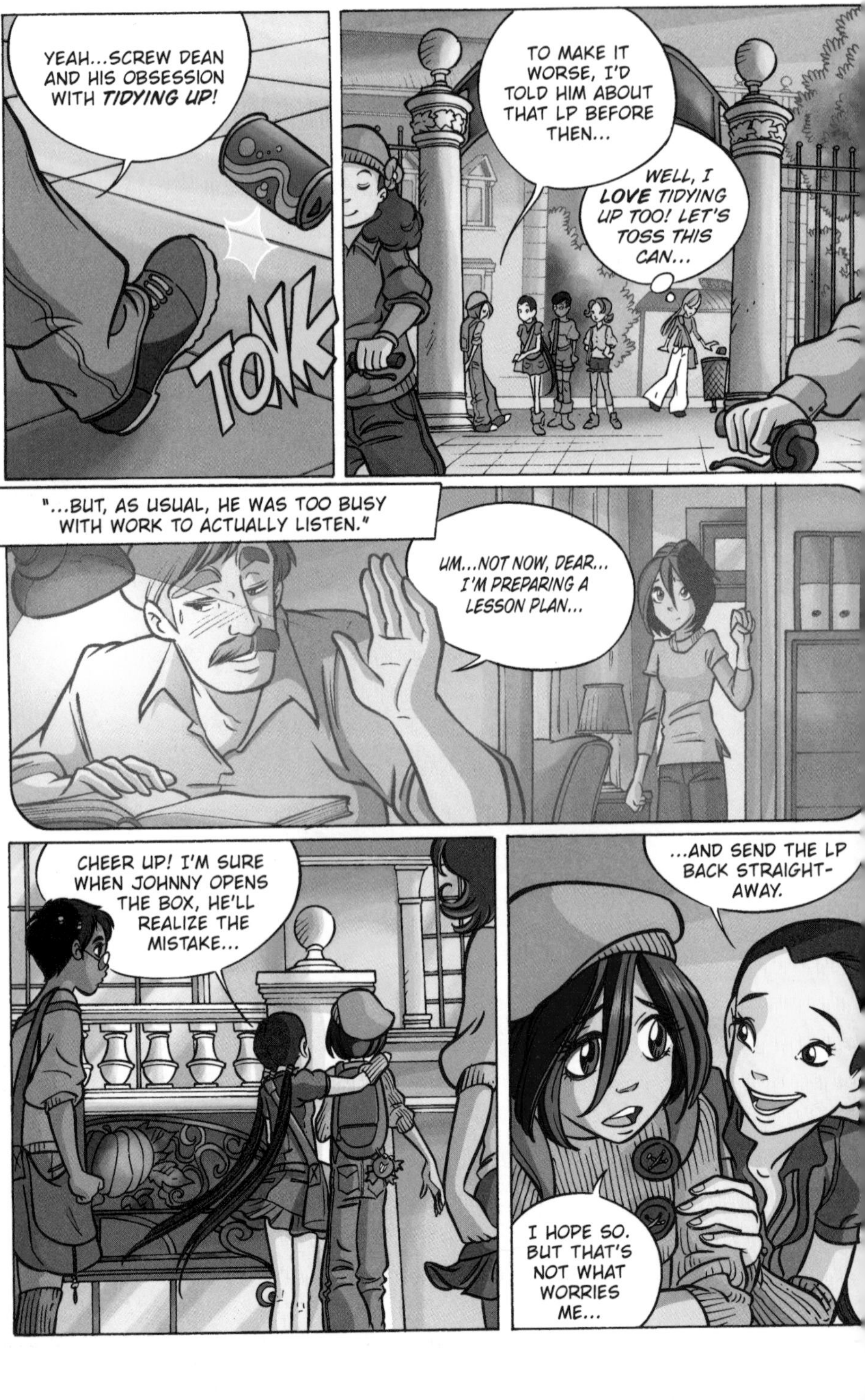
YEAH...SCREW DEAN AND HIS OBSESSION WITH *TIDYING UP*!
TONK
TO MAKE IT WORSE, I'D TOLD HIM ABOUT THAT LP BEFORE THEN...
WELL, I **LOVE** TIDYING UP TOO! LET'S TOSS THIS CAN...
"...BUT, AS USUAL, HE WAS TOO BUSY WITH WORK TO ACTUALLY LISTEN."
UM...NOT NOW, DEAR... I'M PREPARING A LESSON PLAN...
CHEER UP! I'M SURE WHEN JOHNNY OPENS THE BOX, HE'LL REALIZE THE MISTAKE...
...AND SEND THE LP BACK STRAIGHT-AWAY.
I HOPE SO. BUT THAT'S NOT WHAT WORRIES ME...

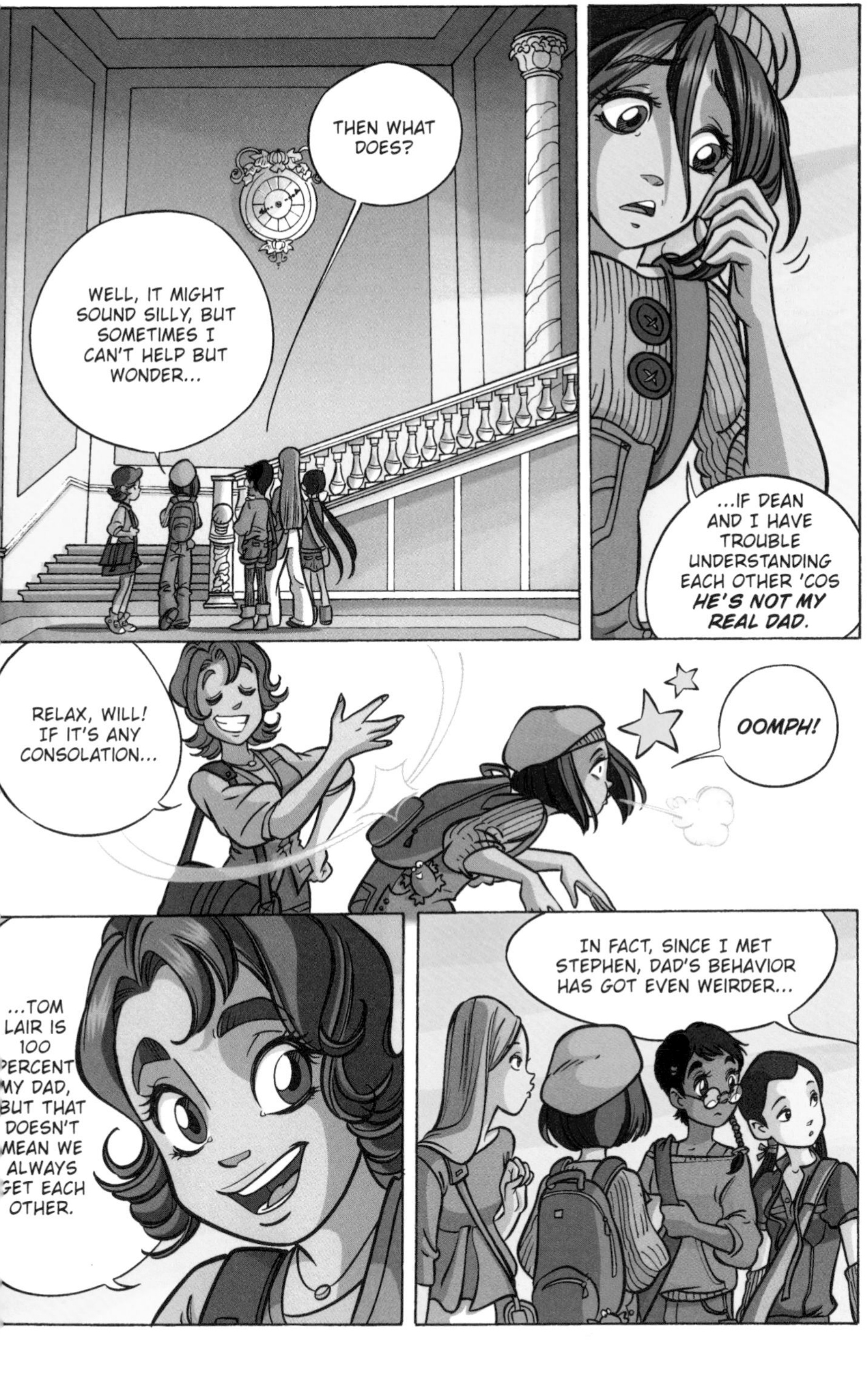
THEN WHAT DOES?
WELL, IT MIGHT SOUND SILLY, BUT SOMETIMES I CAN'T HELP BUT WONDER...
...IF DEAN AND I HAVE TROUBLE UNDERSTANDING EACH OTHER 'COS ***HE'S NOT MY REAL DAD.***
RELAX, WILL! IF IT'S ANY CONSOLATION...
OOMPH!
...TOM LAIR IS 100 PERCENT MY DAD, BUT THAT DOESN'T MEAN WE ALWAYS GET EACH OTHER.
IN FACT, SINCE I MET STEPHEN, DAD'S BEHAVIOR HAS GOT EVEN WEIRDER...

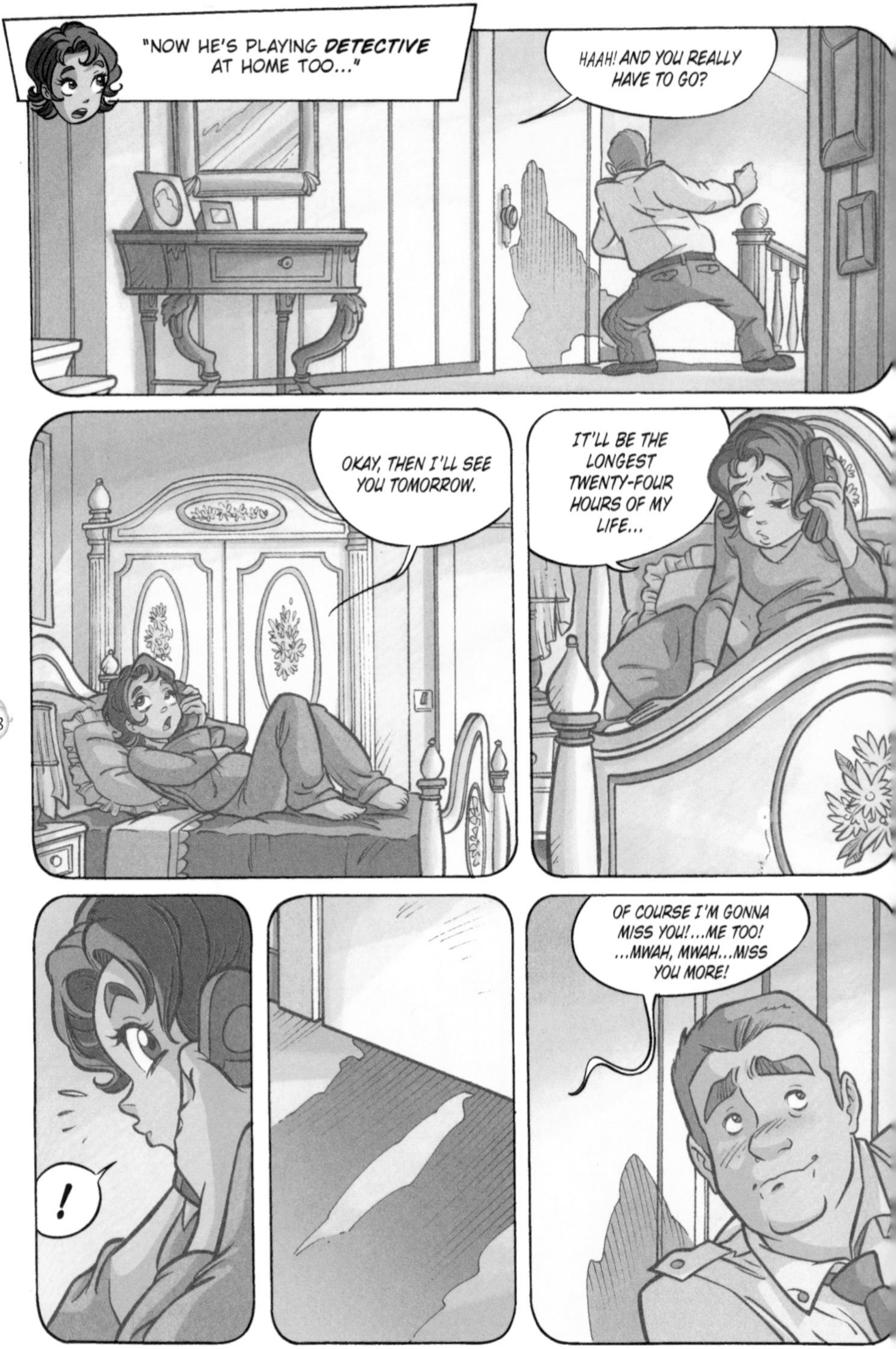
"NOW HE'S PLAYING **DETECTIVE** AT HOME TOO..."
HAAH! AND YOU REALLY HAVE TO GO?
OKAY, THEN I'LL SEE YOU TOMORROW.
IT'LL BE THE LONGEST TWENTY-FOUR HOURS OF MY LIFE...
!
OF COURSE I'M GONNA MISS YOU!...ME TOO! ...MWAH, MWAH...MISS YOU MORE!

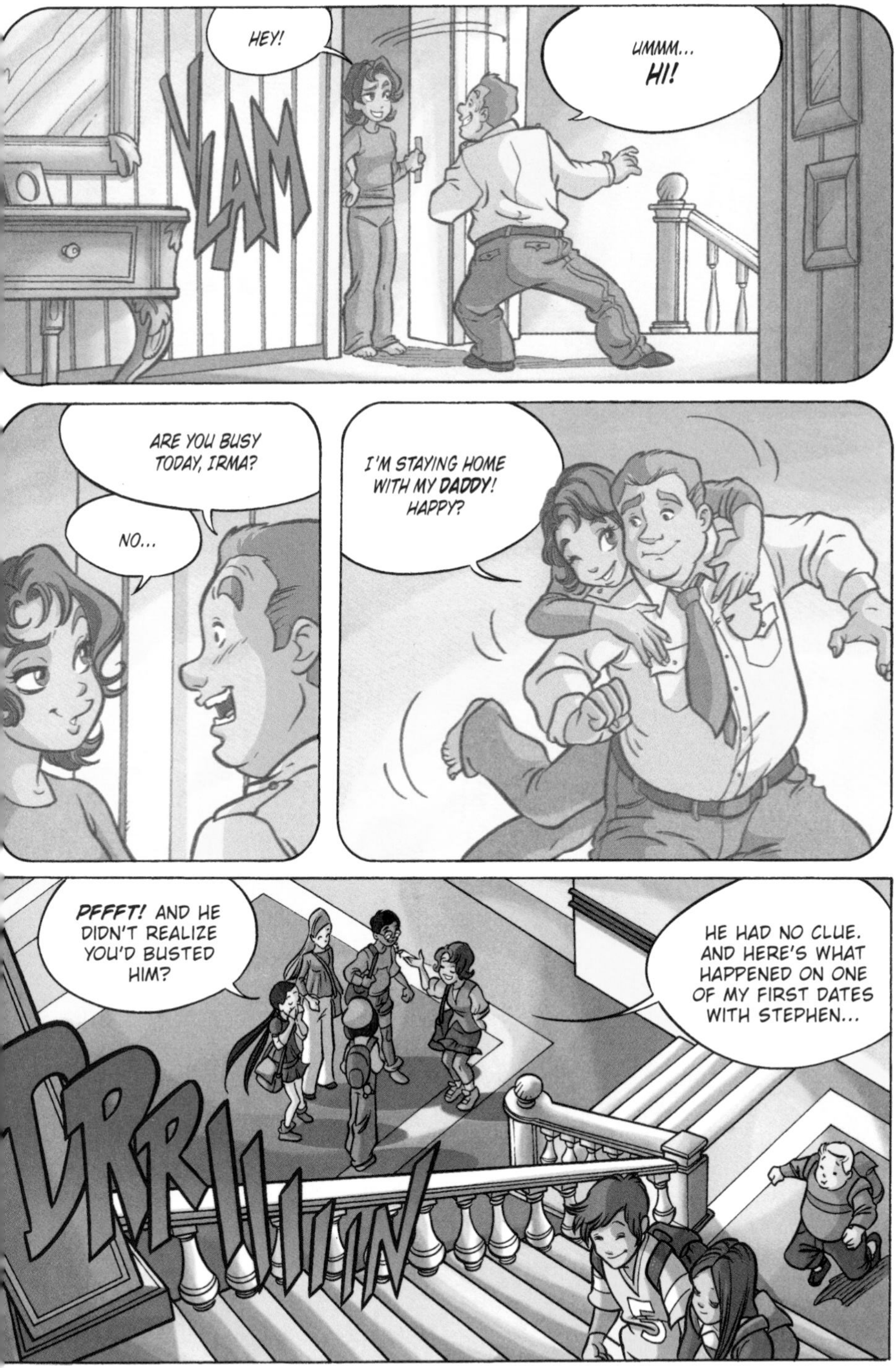
HEY!
VLAM
UMMM... HI!
ARE YOU BUSY TODAY, IRMA?
NO...
I'M STAYING HOME WITH MY DADDY! HAPPY?
PFFFT! AND HE DIDN'T REALIZE YOU'D BUSTED HIM?
HE HAD NO CLUE. AND HERE'S WHAT HAPPENED ON ONE OF MY FIRST DATES WITH STEPHEN...
DRRIIIIIN

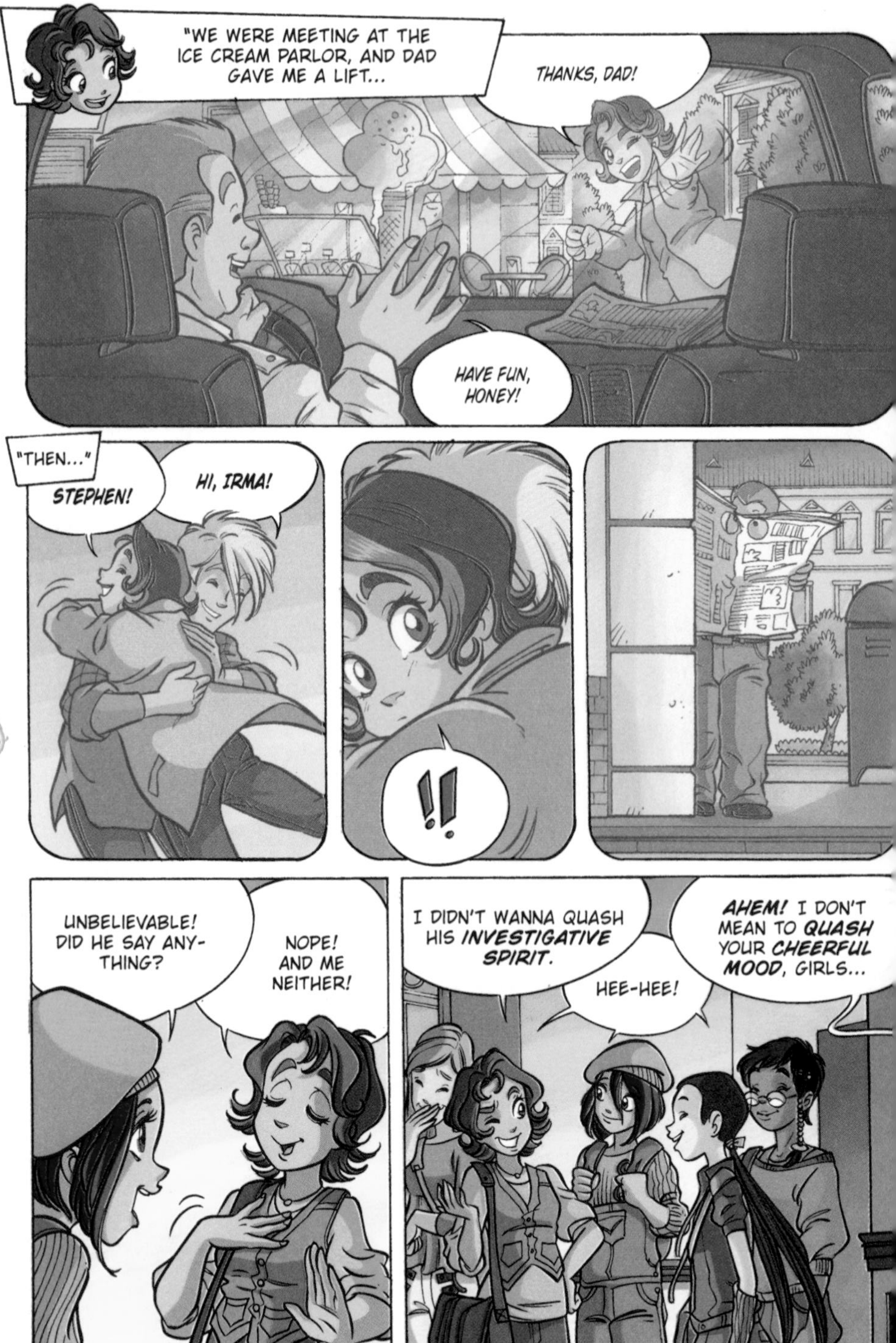

"WE WERE MEETING AT THE ICE CREAM PARLOR, AND DAD GAVE ME A LIFT...
THANKS, DAD!
HAVE FUN, HONEY!
"THEN..."
STEPHEN!
HI, IRMA!
!!
UNBELIEVABLE! DID HE SAY ANY-THING?
NOPE! AND ME NEITHER!
I DIDN'T WANNA QUASH HIS INVESTIGATIVE SPIRIT.
HEE-HEE!
AHEM! I DON'T MEAN TO QUASH YOUR CHEERFUL MOOD, GIRLS...

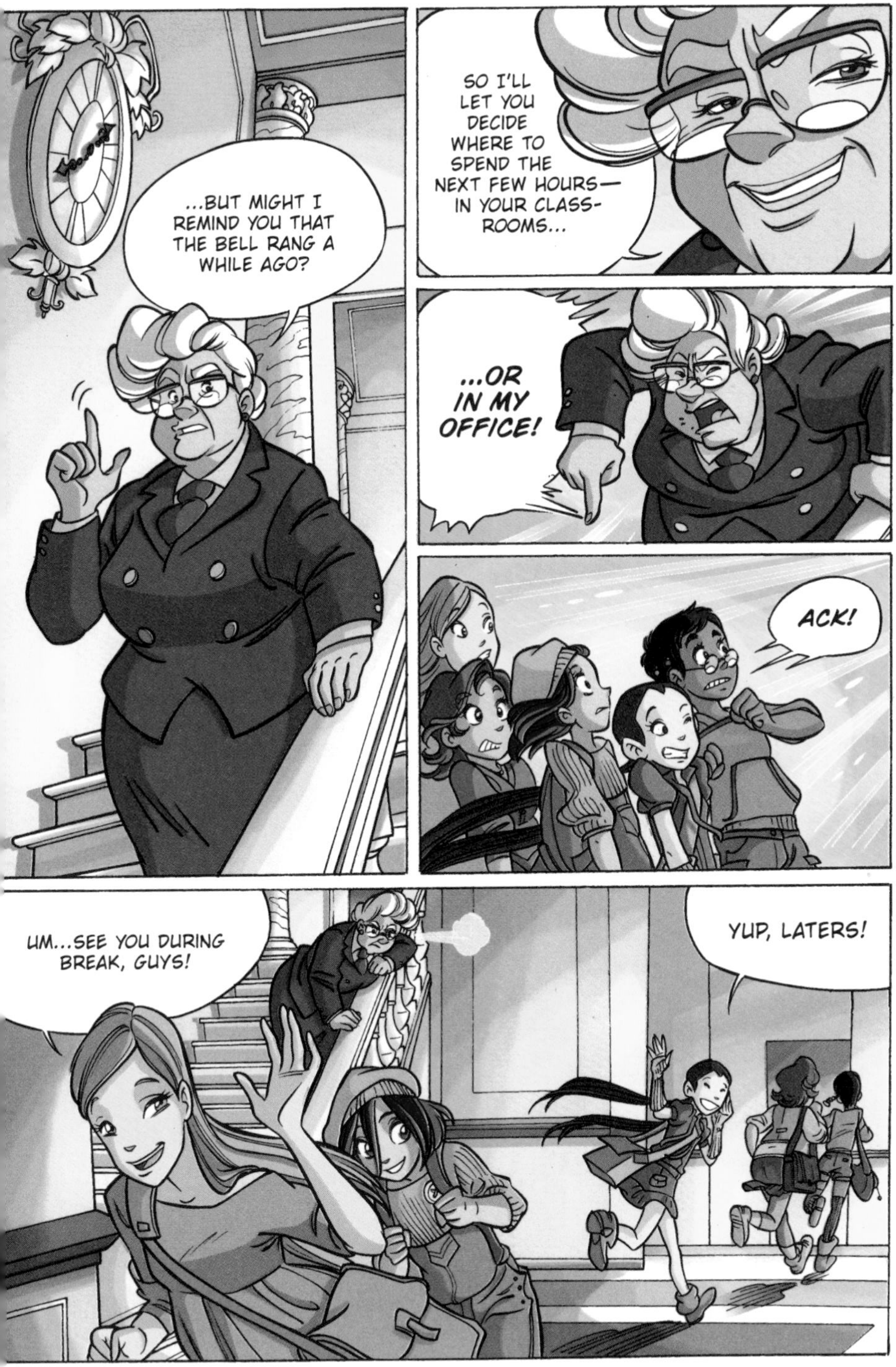
...BUT MIGHT I REMIND YOU THAT THE BELL RANG A WHILE AGO?
SO I'LL LET YOU DECIDE WHERE TO SPEND THE NEXT FEW HOURS— IN YOUR CLASS-ROOMS...
...OR IN MY OFFICE!
ACK!
UM...SEE YOU DURING BREAK, GUYS!
YUP, LATERS!

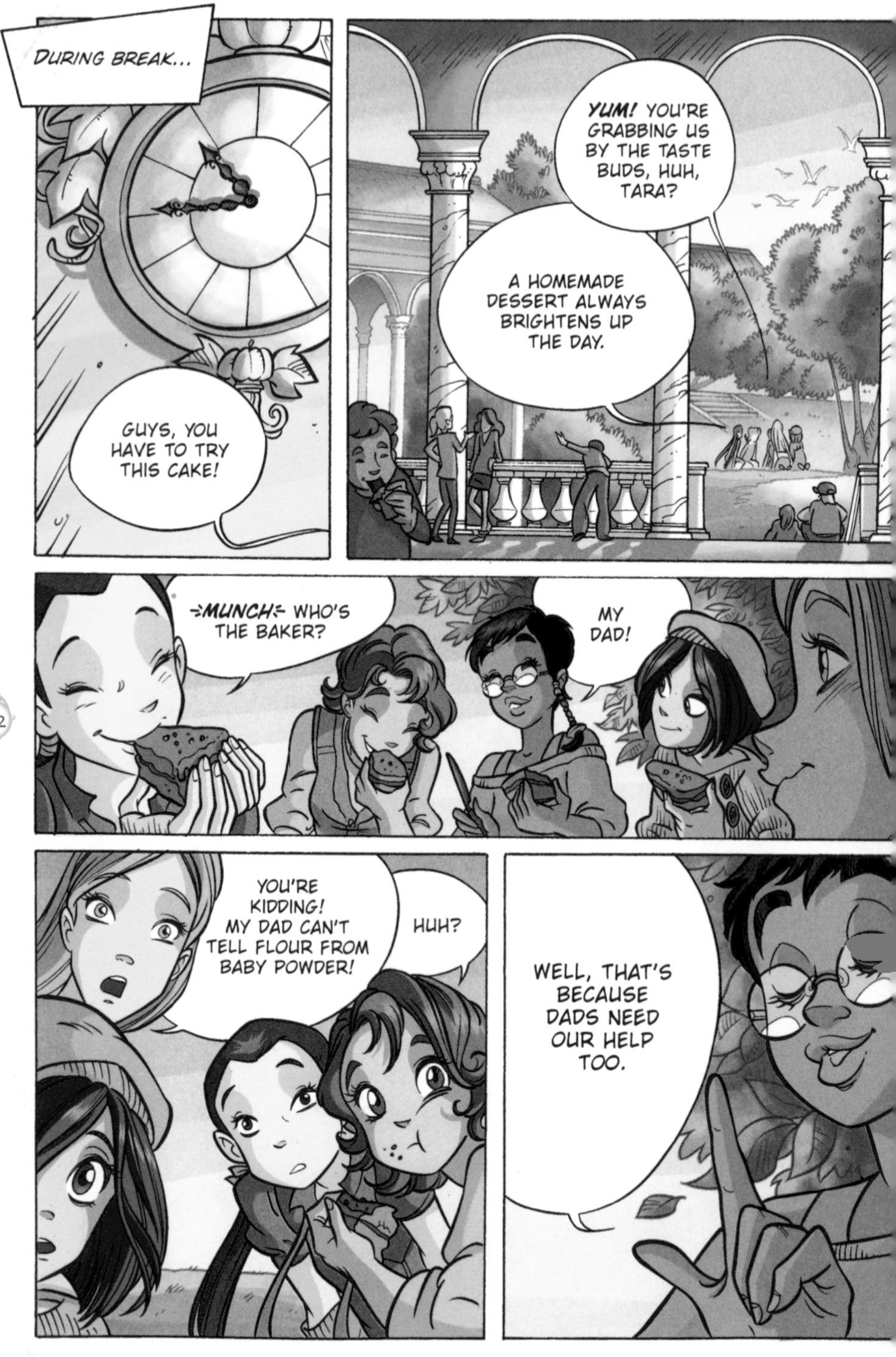
DURING BREAK...
GUYS, YOU HAVE TO TRY THIS CAKE!
YUM! YOU'RE GRABBING US BY THE TASTE BUDS, HUH, TARA?
A HOMEMADE DESSERT ALWAYS BRIGHTENS UP THE DAY.
-MUNCH- WHO'S THE BAKER?
MY DAD!
YOU'RE KIDDING! MY DAD CAN'T TELL FLOUR FROM BABY POWDER!
HUH?
WELL, THAT'S BECAUSE DADS NEED OUR HELP TOO.

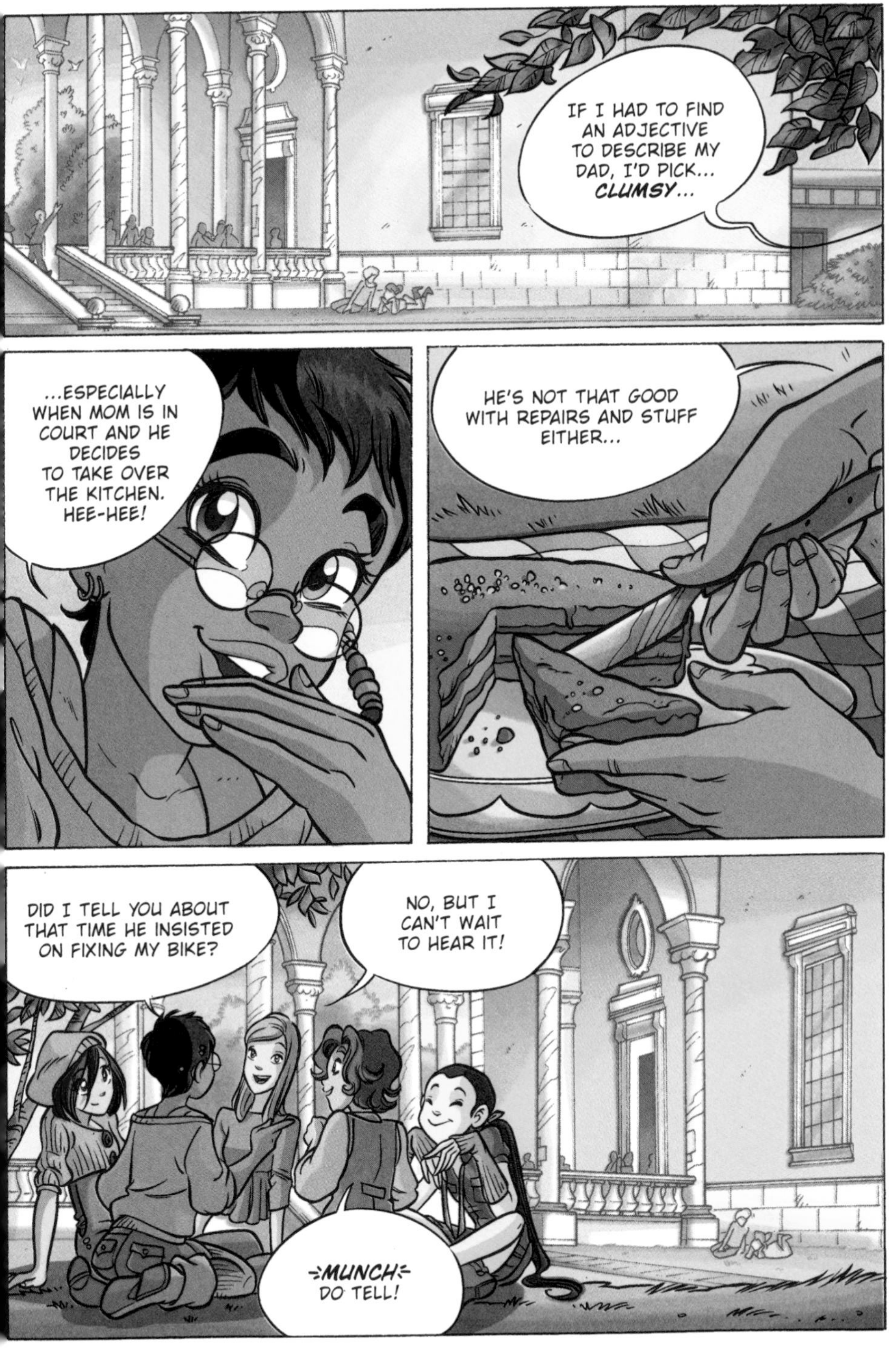
IF I HAD TO FIND AN ADJECTIVE TO DESCRIBE MY DAD, I'D PICK... **CLUMSY**...
...ESPECIALLY WHEN MOM IS IN COURT AND HE DECIDES TO TAKE OVER THE KITCHEN. HEE-HEE!
HE'S NOT THAT GOOD WITH REPAIRS AND STUFF EITHER...
DID I TELL YOU ABOUT THAT TIME HE INSISTED ON FIXING MY BIKE?
NO, BUT I CAN'T WAIT TO HEAR IT!
MUNCH
DO TELL!

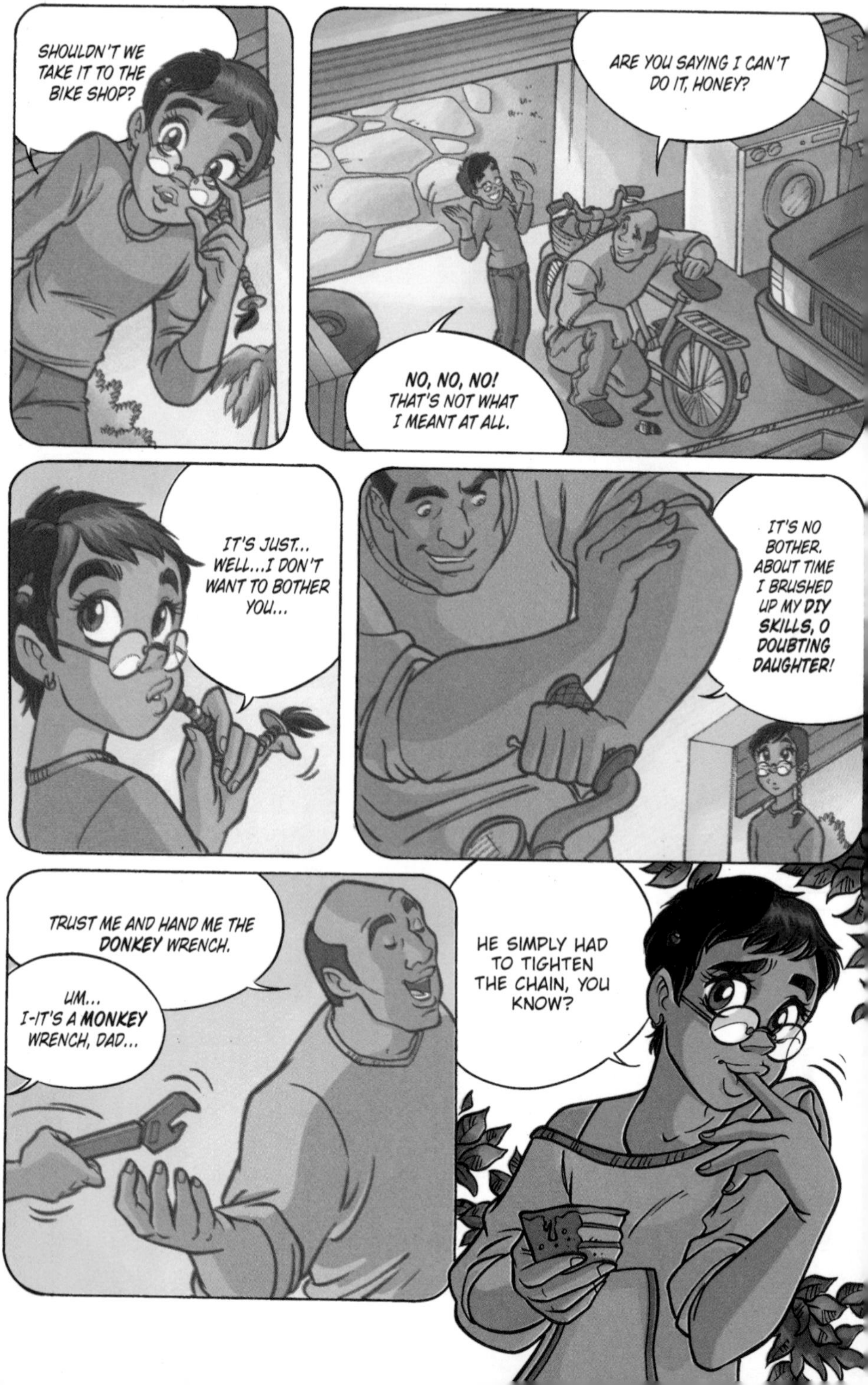
SHOULDN'T WE TAKE IT TO THE BIKE SHOP?
ARE YOU SAYING I CAN'T DO IT, HONEY?
NO, NO, NO! THAT'S NOT WHAT I MEANT AT ALL.
IT'S JUST... WELL...I DON'T WANT TO BOTHER YOU...
IT'S NO BOTHER. ABOUT TIME I BRUSHED UP MY DIY SKILLS, O DOUBTING DAUGHTER!
TRUST ME AND HAND ME THE DONKEY WRENCH.
UM... I-IT'S A MONKEY WRENCH, DAD...
HE SIMPLY HAD TO TIGHTEN THE CHAIN, YOU KNOW?

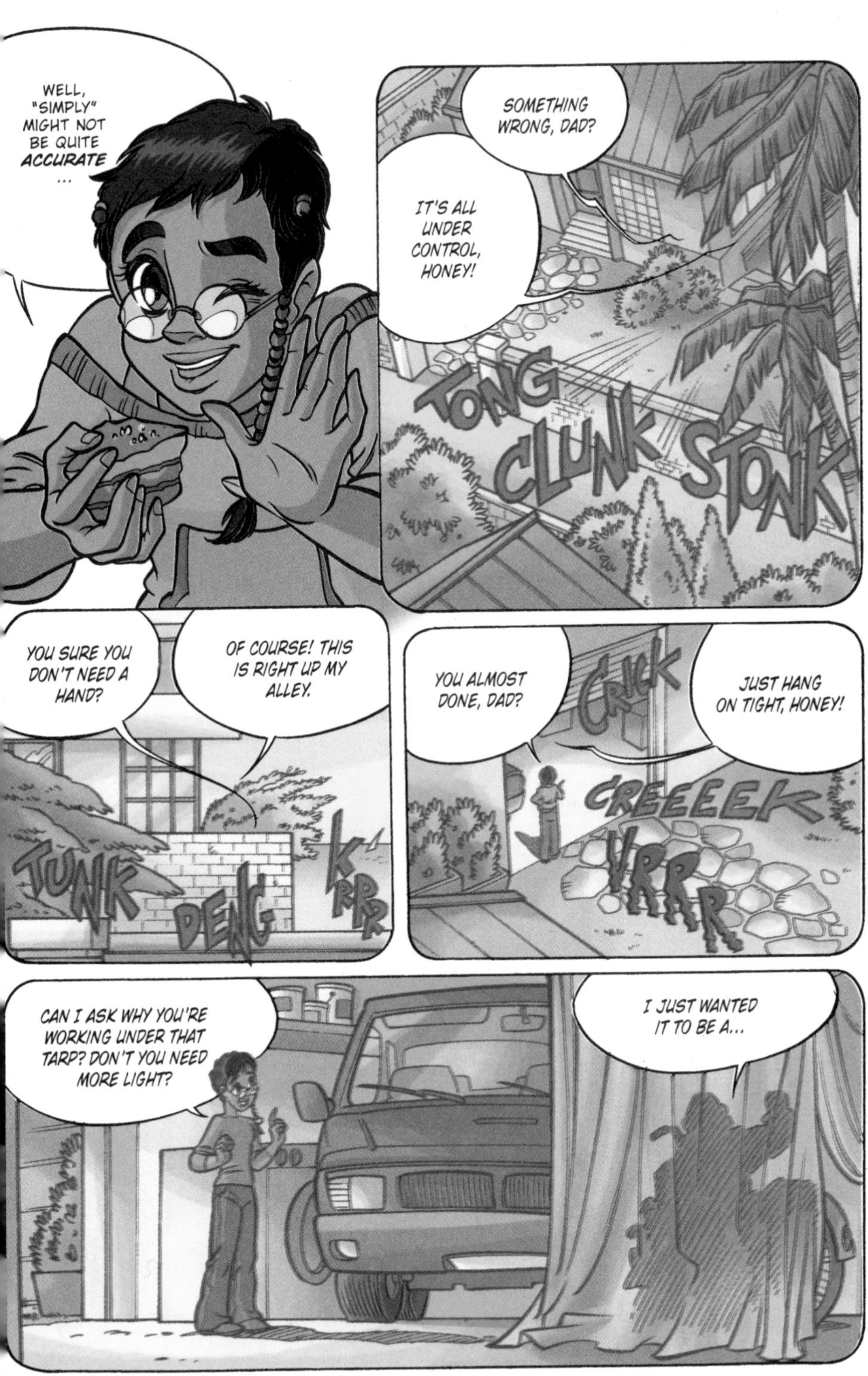
WELL, "SIMPLY" MIGHT NOT BE QUITE ACCURATE ...
SOMETHING WRONG, DAD?
IT'S ALL UNDER CONTROL, HONEY!
TONG
CLUNK
STONK
YOU SURE YOU DON'T NEED A HAND?
OF COURSE! THIS IS RIGHT UP MY ALLEY.
TUNK
DENG
KRRRR
YOU ALMOST DONE, DAD?
CRICK
JUST HANG ON TIGHT, HONEY!
CREEEEK
VRRRR
CAN I ASK WHY YOU'RE WORKING UNDER THAT TARP? DON'T YOU NEED MORE LIGHT?
I JUST WANTED IT TO BE A...

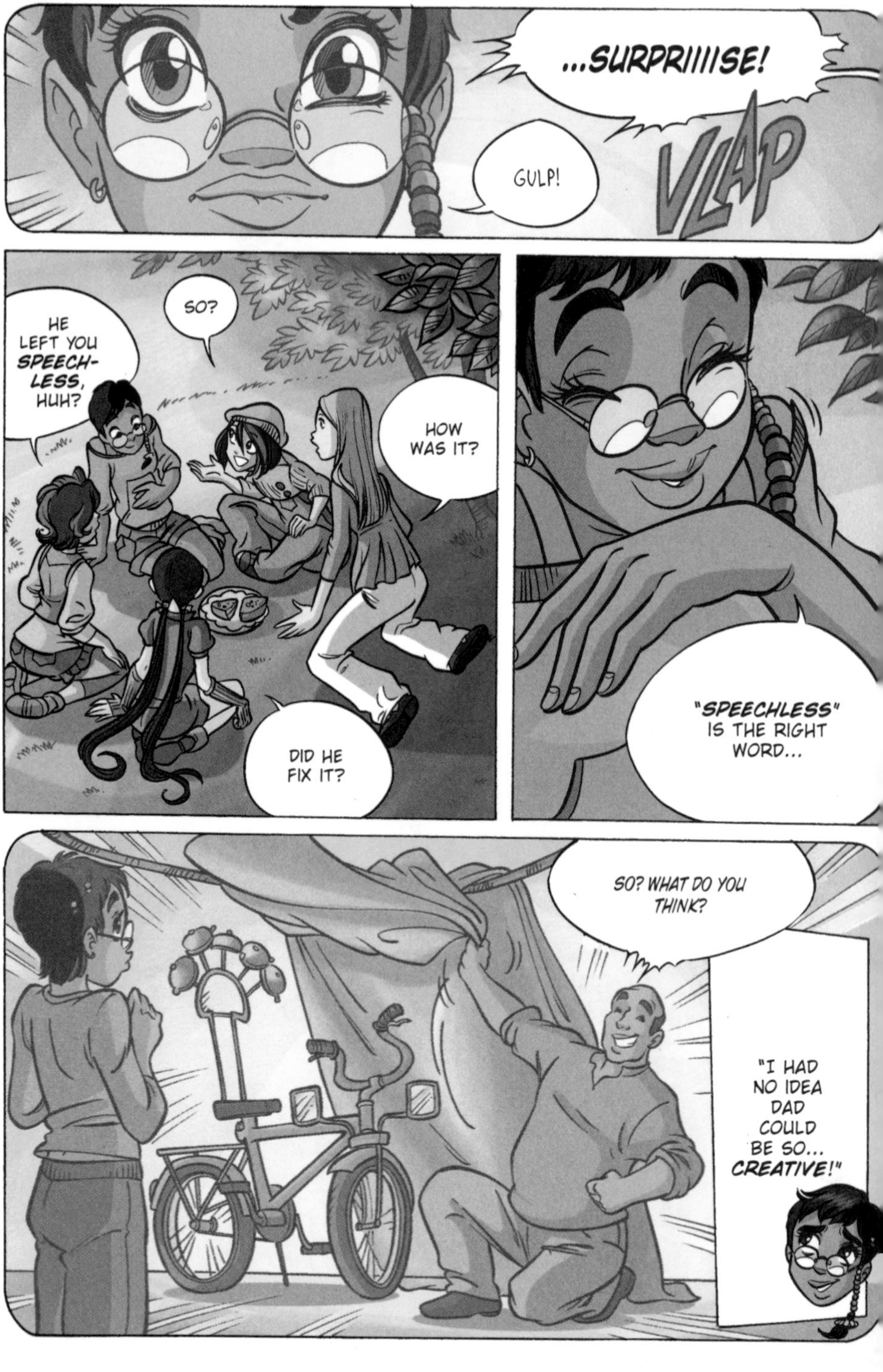
...SURPRIIIISE!
GULP!
VLAP
HE LEFT YOU SPEECH-LESS, HUH?
SO?
HOW WAS IT?
DID HE FIX IT?
"SPEECHLESS" IS THE RIGHT WORD...
SO? WHAT DO YOU THINK?
"I HAD NO IDEA DAD COULD BE SO... CREATIVE!"

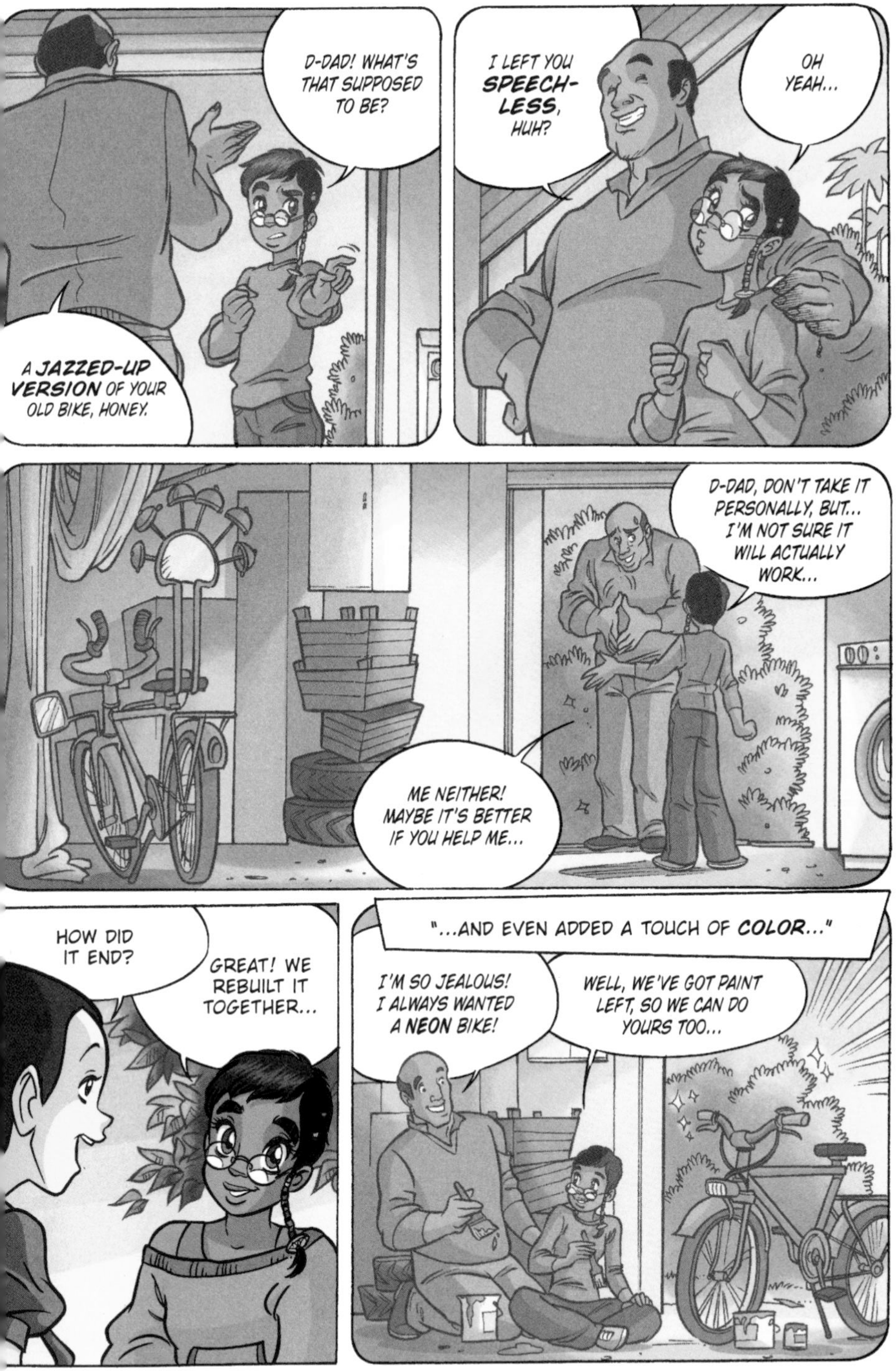
D-DAD! WHAT'S THAT SUPPOSED TO BE?
A JAZZED-UP VERSION OF YOUR OLD BIKE, HONEY.
I LEFT YOU SPEECH-LESS, HUH?
OH YEAH...
D-DAD, DON'T TAKE IT PERSONALLY, BUT... I'M NOT SURE IT WILL ACTUALLY WORK...
ME NEITHER! MAYBE IT'S BETTER IF YOU HELP ME...
HOW DID IT END?
GREAT! WE REBUILT IT TOGETHER...
"...AND EVEN ADDED A TOUCH OF COLOR..."
I'M SO JEALOUS! I ALWAYS WANTED A NEON BIKE!
WELL, WE'VE GOT PAINT LEFT, SO WE CAN DO YOURS TOO...

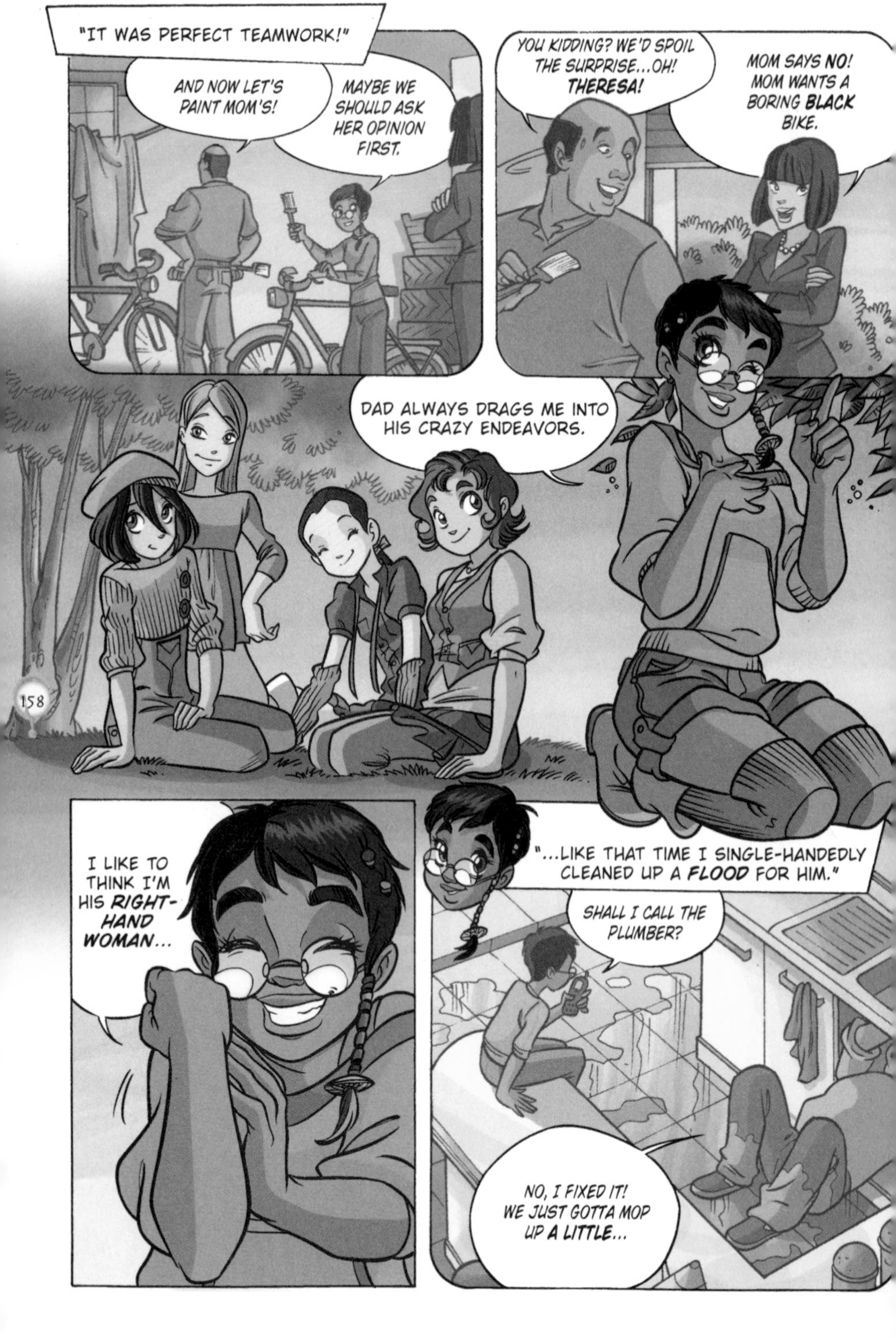
"IT WAS PERFECT TEAMWORK!"
AND NOW LET'S PAINT MOM'S!
MAYBE WE SHOULD ASK HER OPINION FIRST.
YOU KIDDING? WE'D SPOIL THE SURPRISE...OH! THERESA!
MOM SAYS NO! MOM WANTS A BORING BLACK BIKE.
DAD ALWAYS DRAGS ME INTO HIS CRAZY ENDEAVORS.
I LIKE TO THINK I'M HIS RIGHT-HAND WOMAN...
"...LIKE THAT TIME I SINGLE-HANDEDLY CLEANED UP A FLOOD FOR HIM."
SHALL I CALL THE PLUMBER?
NO, I FIXED IT! WE JUST GOTTA MOP UP A LITTLE...

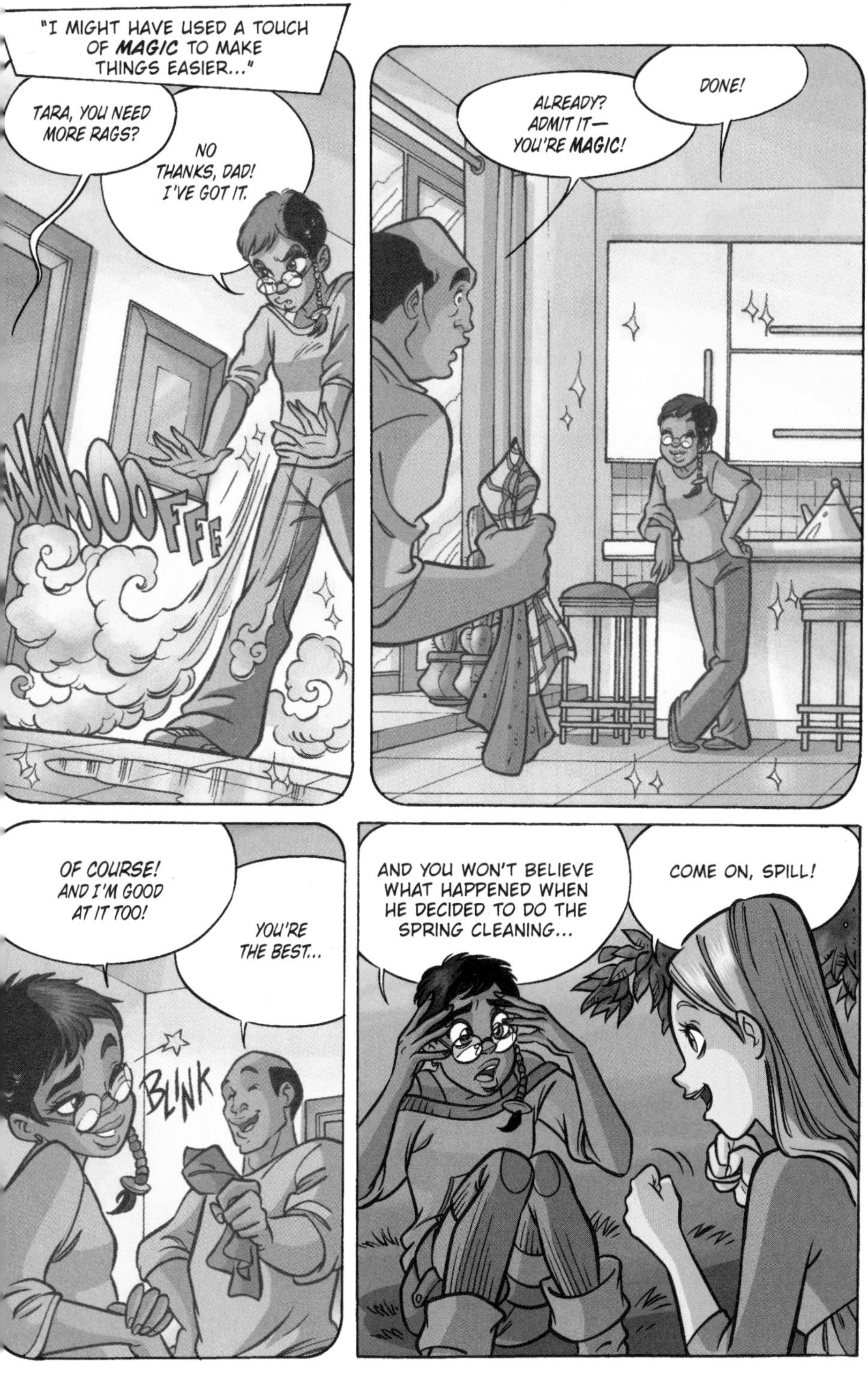
"I MIGHT HAVE USED A TOUCH OF MAGIC TO MAKE THINGS EASIER..."
TARA, YOU NEED MORE RAGS?
NO THANKS, DAD! I'VE GOT IT.
FWHOOOFFFF
ALREADY? ADMIT IT— YOU'RE MAGIC!
DONE!
OF COURSE! AND I'M GOOD AT IT TOO!
YOU'RE THE BEST...
BLINK
AND YOU WON'T BELIEVE WHAT HAPPENED WHEN HE DECIDED TO DO THE SPRING CLEANING...
COME ON, SPILL!

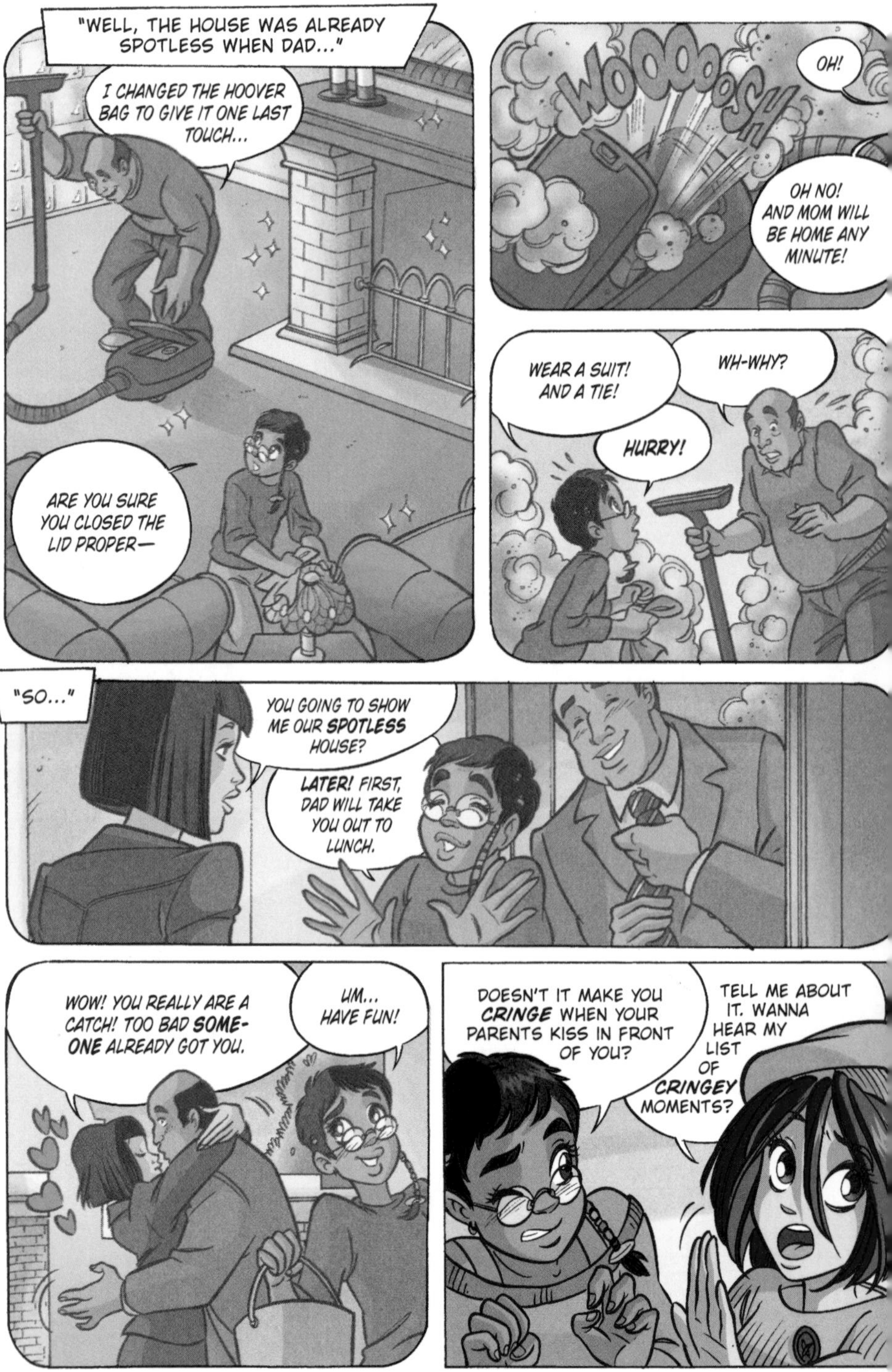
"WELL, THE HOUSE WAS ALREADY SPOTLESS WHEN DAD..."
I CHANGED THE HOOVER BAG TO GIVE IT ONE LAST TOUCH...
ARE YOU SURE YOU CLOSED THE LID PROPER—
WOOOOOSH
OH!
OH NO! AND MOM WILL BE HOME ANY MINUTE!
WEAR A SUIT! AND A TIE!
WH-WHY?
HURRY!
"SO..."
YOU GOING TO SHOW ME OUR SPOTLESS HOUSE?
LATER! FIRST, DAD WILL TAKE YOU OUT TO LUNCH.
WOW! YOU REALLY ARE A CATCH! TOO BAD SOME-ONE ALREADY GOT YOU.
UM... HAVE FUN!
DOESN'T IT MAKE YOU CRINGE WHEN YOUR PARENTS KISS IN FRONT OF YOU?
TELL ME ABOUT IT. WANNA HEAR MY LIST OF CRINGEY MOMENTS?

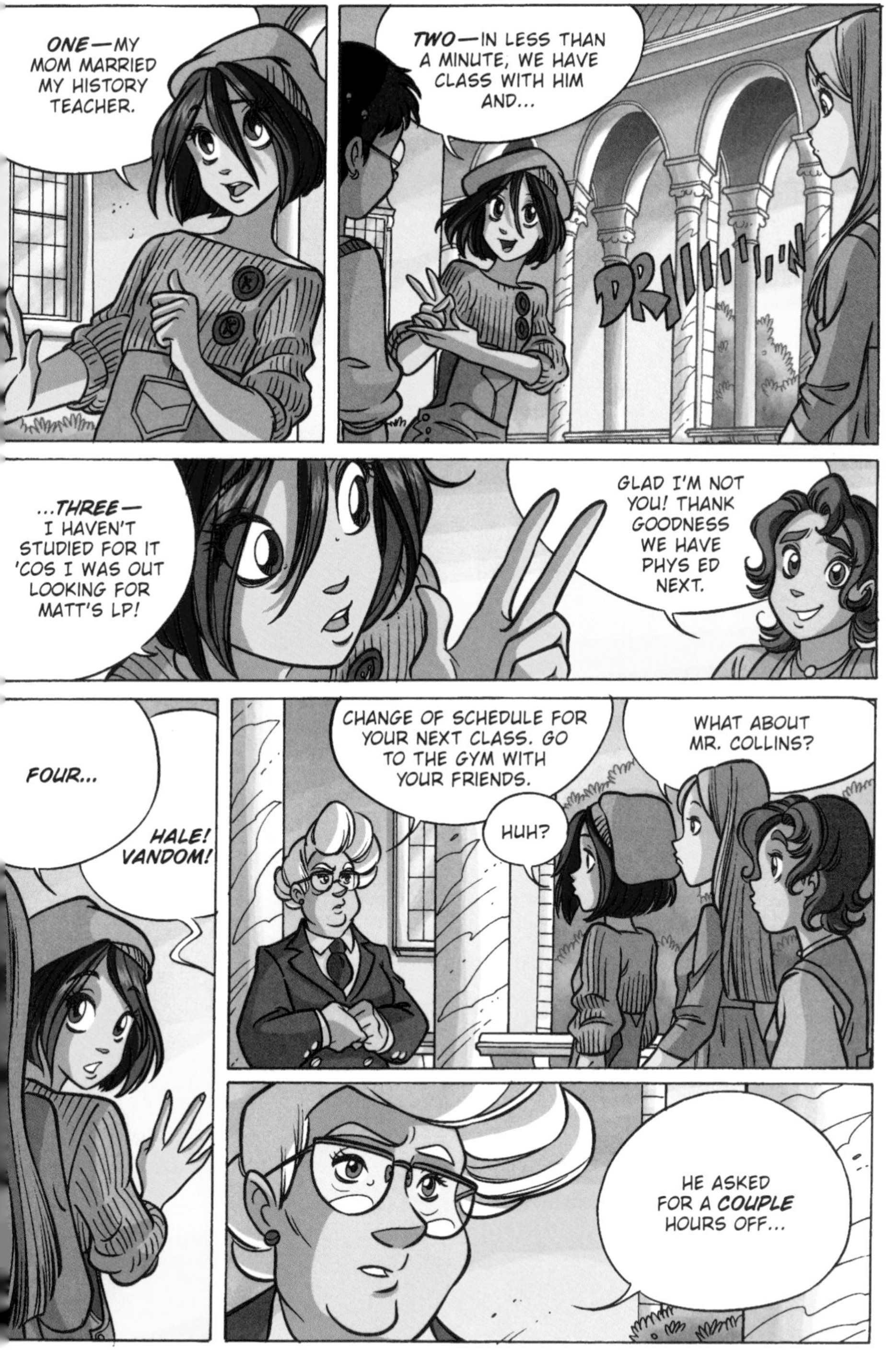
ONE—MY MOM MARRIED MY HISTORY TEACHER.
TWO—IN LESS THAN A MINUTE, WE HAVE CLASS WITH HIM AND...
DRIIIIIIIN
...THREE—I HAVEN'T STUDIED FOR IT 'COS I WAS OUT LOOKING FOR MATT'S LP!
GLAD I'M NOT YOU! THANK GOODNESS WE HAVE PHYS ED NEXT.
FOUR...
HALE! VANDOM!
CHANGE OF SCHEDULE FOR YOUR NEXT CLASS. GO TO THE GYM WITH YOUR FRIENDS.
HUH?
WHAT ABOUT MR. COLLINS?
HE ASKED FOR A COUPLE HOURS OFF...

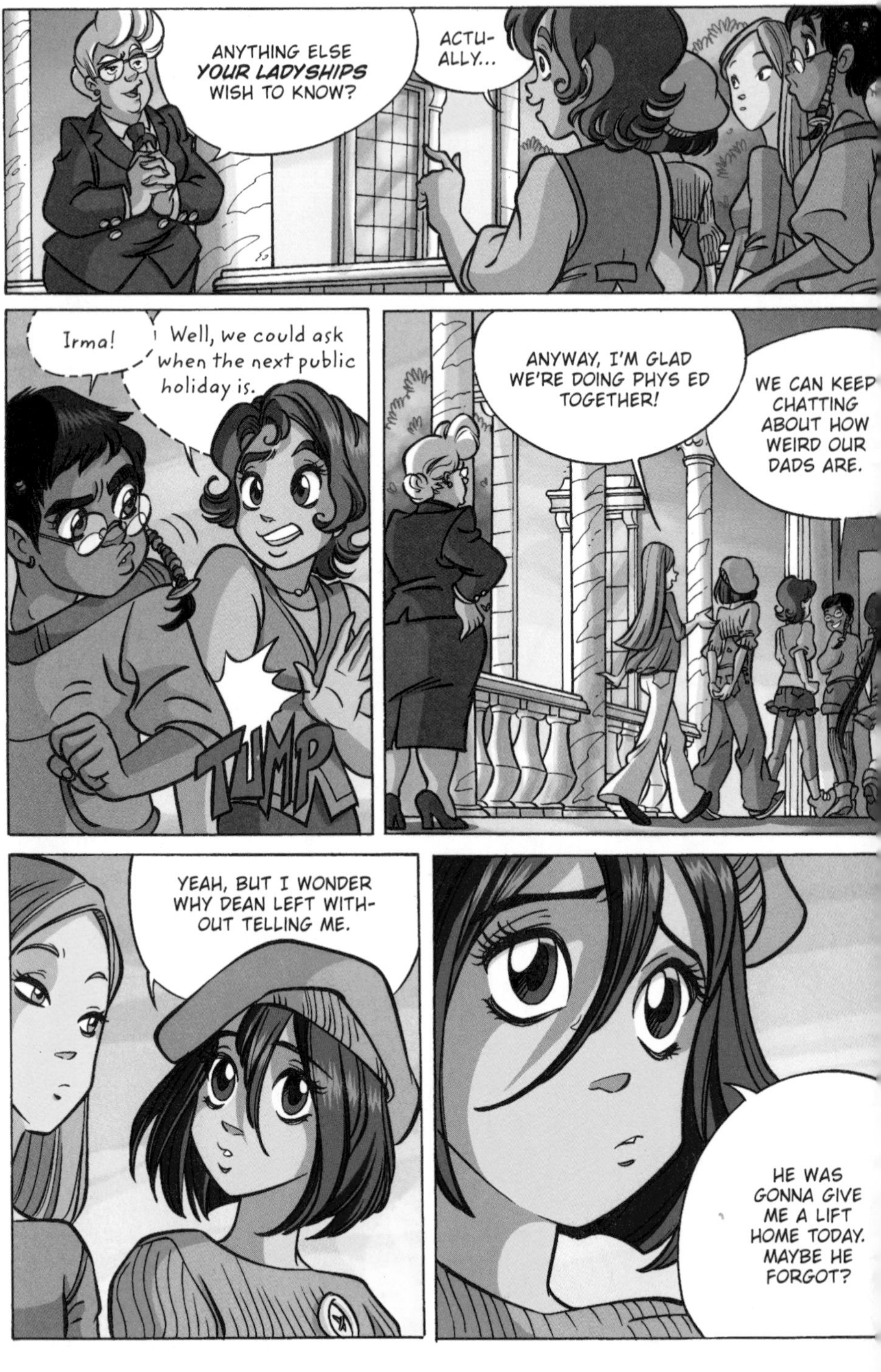
ANYTHING ELSE ***YOUR LADYSHIPS*** WISH TO KNOW?
ACTU- ALLY...
Irma!
Well, we could ask when the next public holiday is.
TUMP
ANYWAY, I'M GLAD WE'RE DOING PHYS ED TOGETHER!
WE CAN KEEP CHATTING ABOUT HOW WEIRD OUR DADS ARE.
YEAH, BUT I WONDER WHY DEAN LEFT WITH- OUT TELLING ME.
HE WAS GONNA GIVE ME A LIFT HOME TODAY. MAYBE HE FORGOT?

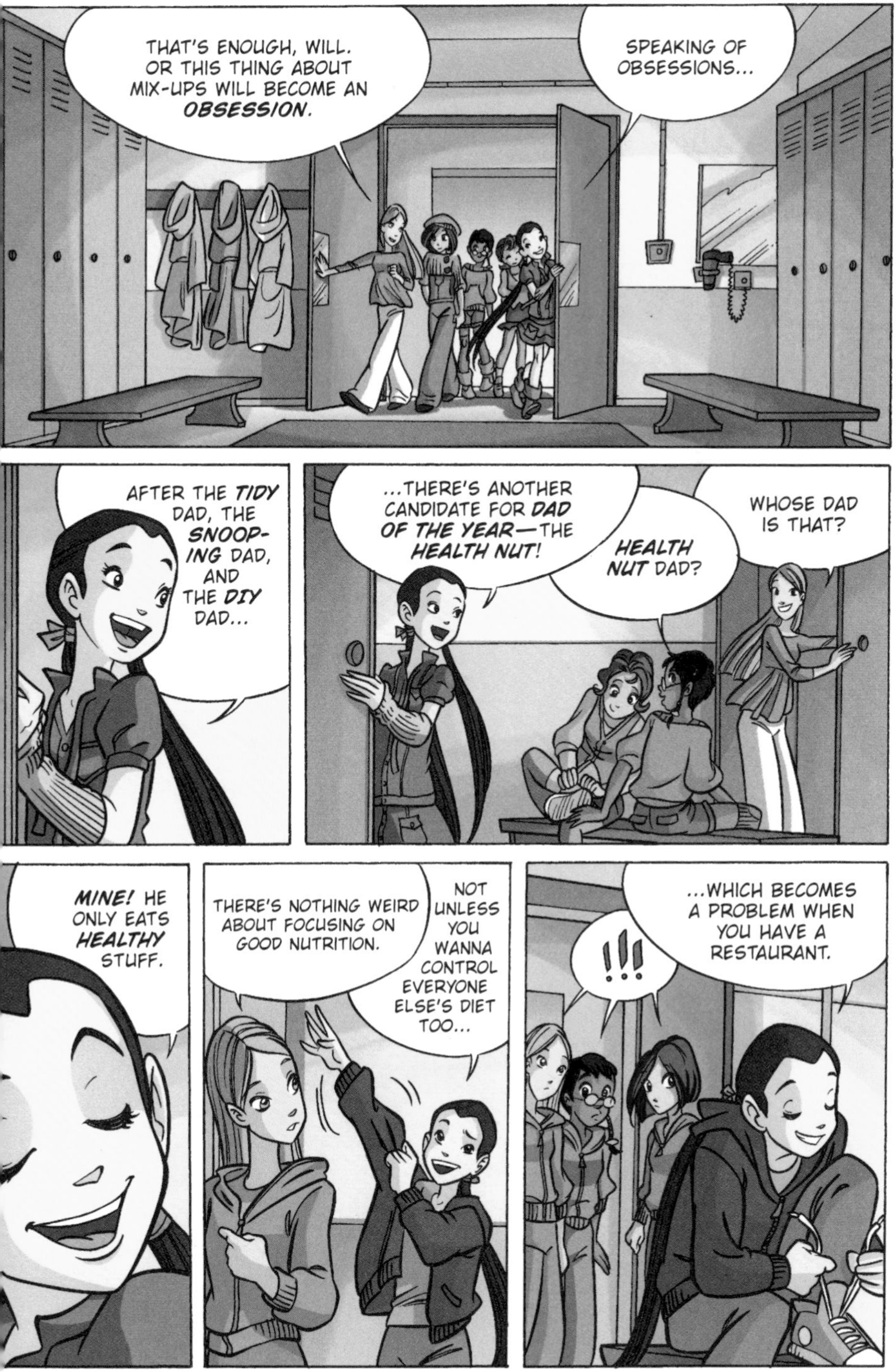
THAT'S ENOUGH, WILL. OR THIS THING ABOUT MIX-UPS WILL BECOME AN **OBSESSION**.
SPEAKING OF OBSESSIONS...
AFTER THE ***TIDY*** DAD, THE ***SNOOP-ING*** DAD, AND THE ***DIY*** DAD...
...THERE'S ANOTHER CANDIDATE FOR ***DAD OF THE YEAR***—THE ***HEALTH NUT***!
HEALTH NUT DAD?
WHOSE DAD IS THAT?
MINE! HE ONLY EATS ***HEALTHY*** STUFF.
THERE'S NOTHING WEIRD ABOUT FOCUSING ON GOOD NUTRITION.
NOT UNLESS YOU WANNA CONTROL EVERYONE ELSE'S DIET TOO...
!!!
...WHICH BECOMES A PROBLEM WHEN YOU HAVE A RESTAURANT.

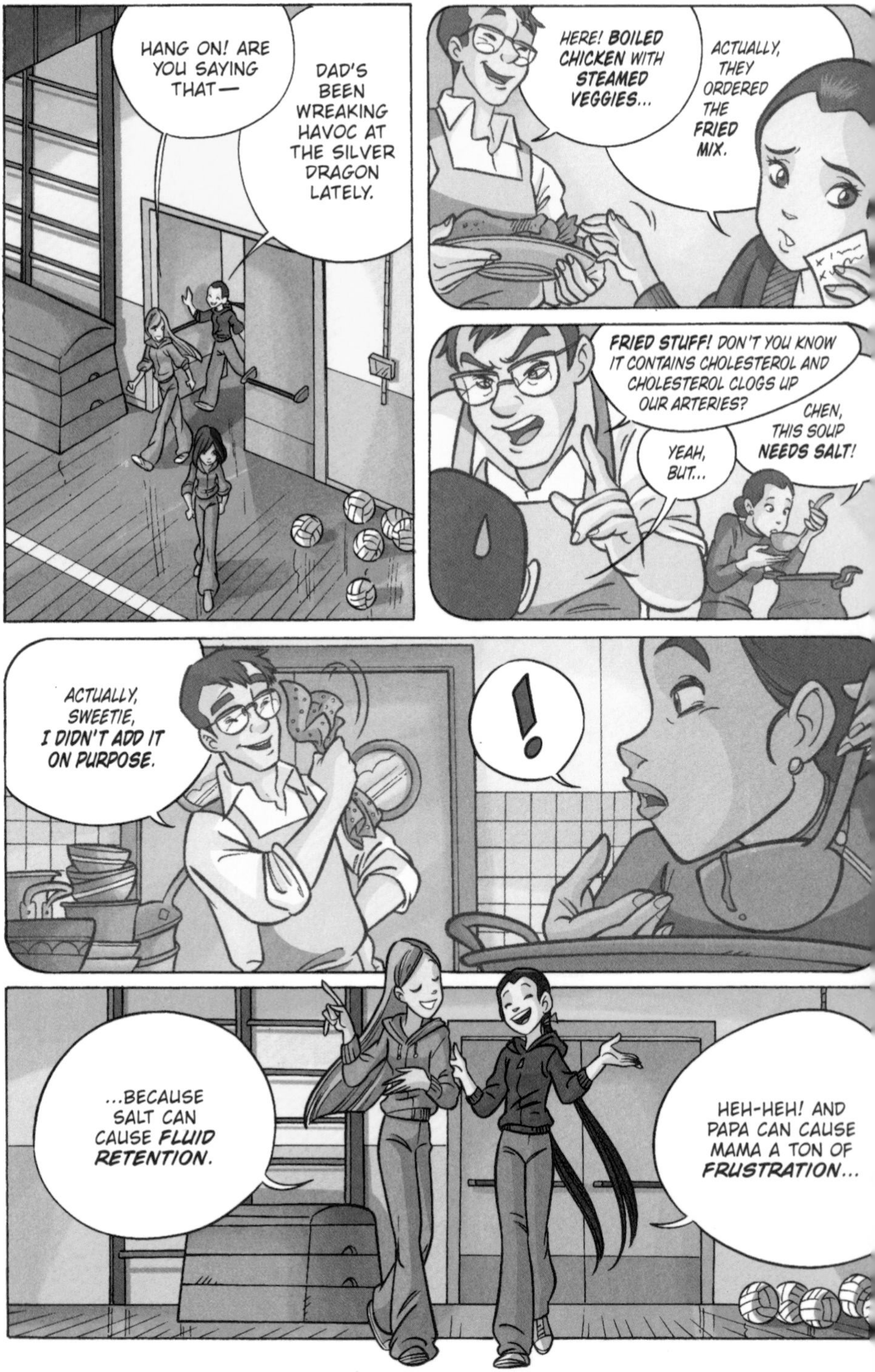
HANG ON! ARE YOU SAYING THAT—
DAD'S BEEN WREAKING HAVOC AT THE SILVER DRAGON LATELY.
HERE! **BOILED CHICKEN** WITH **STEAMED VEGGIES**...
ACTUALLY, THEY ORDERED THE **FRIED MIX**.
FRIED STUFF! DON'T YOU KNOW IT CONTAINS CHOLESTEROL AND CHOLESTEROL CLOGS UP OUR ARTERIES?
YEAH, BUT...
CHEN, THIS SOUP **NEEDS SALT**!
ACTUALLY, SWEETIE, **I DIDN'T ADD IT ON PURPOSE**.
!
...BECAUSE SALT CAN CAUSE **FLUID RETENTION**.
HEH-HEH! AND PAPA CAN CAUSE MAMA A TON OF **FRUSTRATION**...

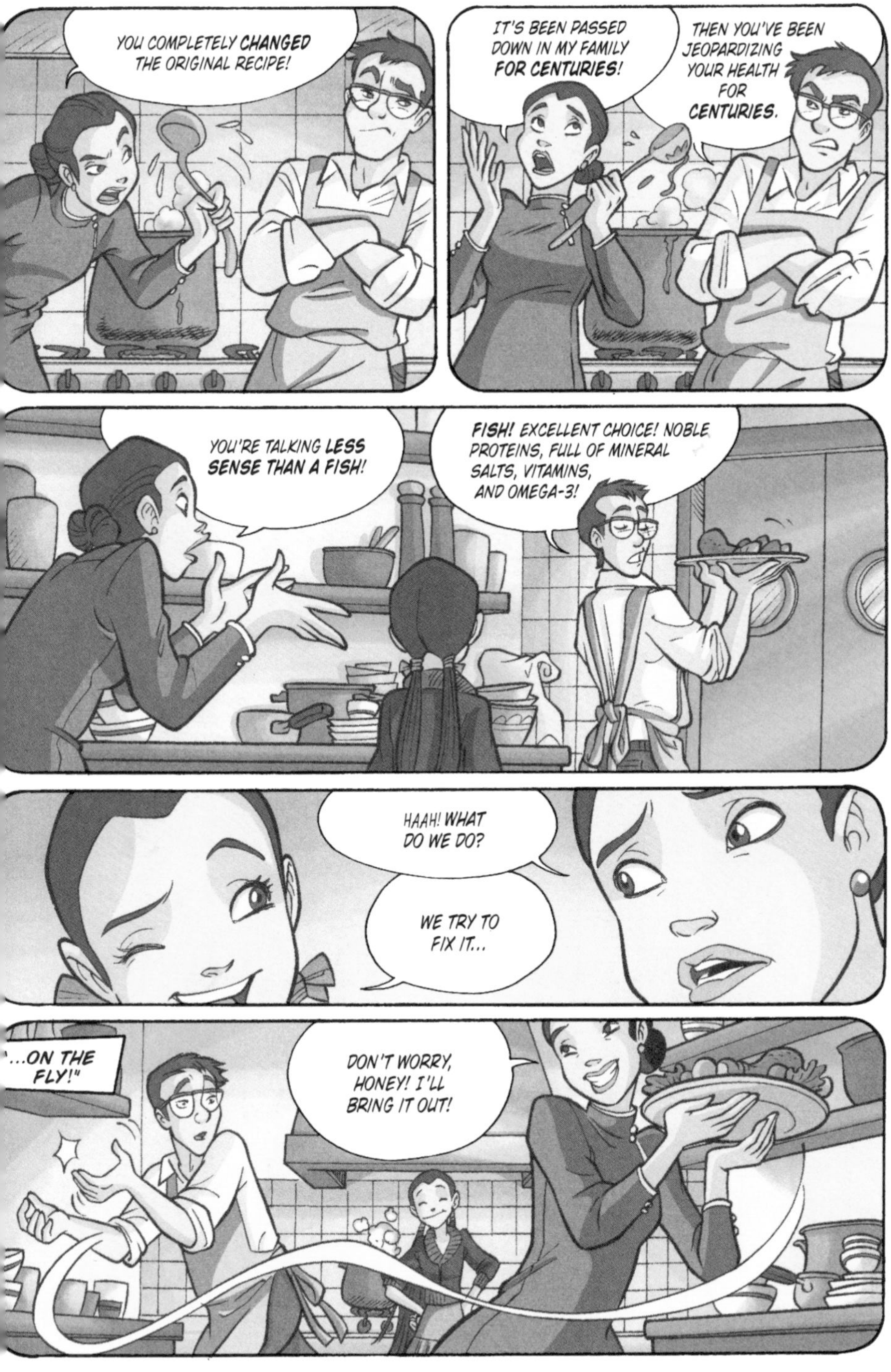
YOU COMPLETELY CHANGED THE ORIGINAL RECIPE!
IT'S BEEN PASSED DOWN IN MY FAMILY FOR CENTURIES!
THEN YOU'VE BEEN JEOPARDIZING YOUR HEALTH FOR CENTURIES.
YOU'RE TALKING LESS SENSE THAN A FISH!
FISH! EXCELLENT CHOICE! NOBLE PROTEINS, FULL OF MINERAL SALTS, VITAMINS, AND OMEGA-3!
HAAH! WHAT DO WE DO?
WE TRY TO FIX IT...
"...ON THE FLY!"
DON'T WORRY, HONEY! I'LL BRING IT OUT!

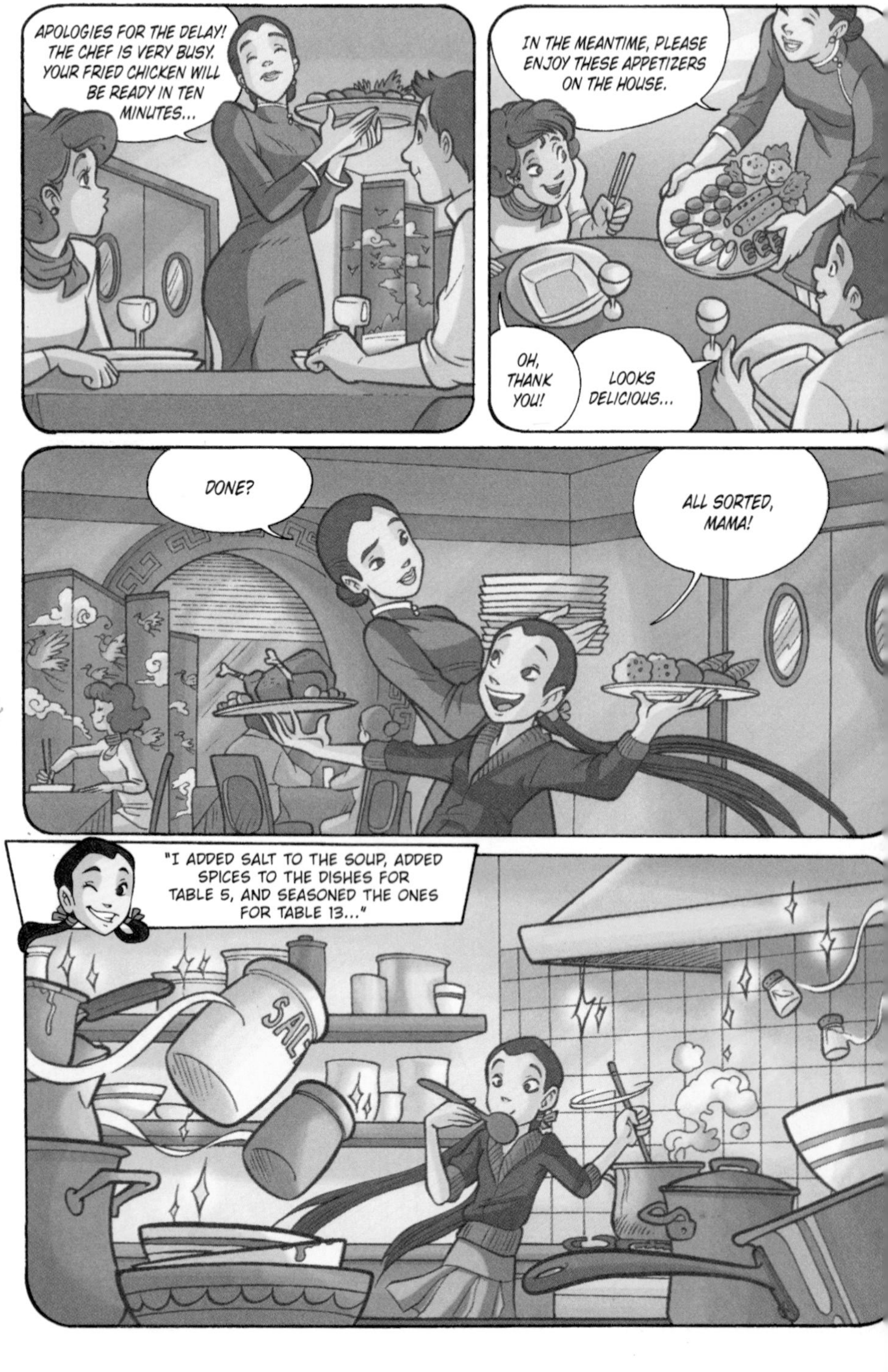
APOLOGIES FOR THE DELAY! THE CHEF IS VERY BUSY. YOUR FRIED CHICKEN WILL BE READY IN TEN MINUTES...
IN THE MEANTIME, PLEASE ENJOY THESE APPETIZERS ON THE HOUSE.
OH, THANK YOU!
LOOKS DELICIOUS...
DONE?
ALL SORTED, MAMA!
"I ADDED SALT TO THE SOUP, ADDED SPICES TO THE DISHES FOR TABLE 5, AND SEASONED THE ONES FOR TABLE 13..."
SALT

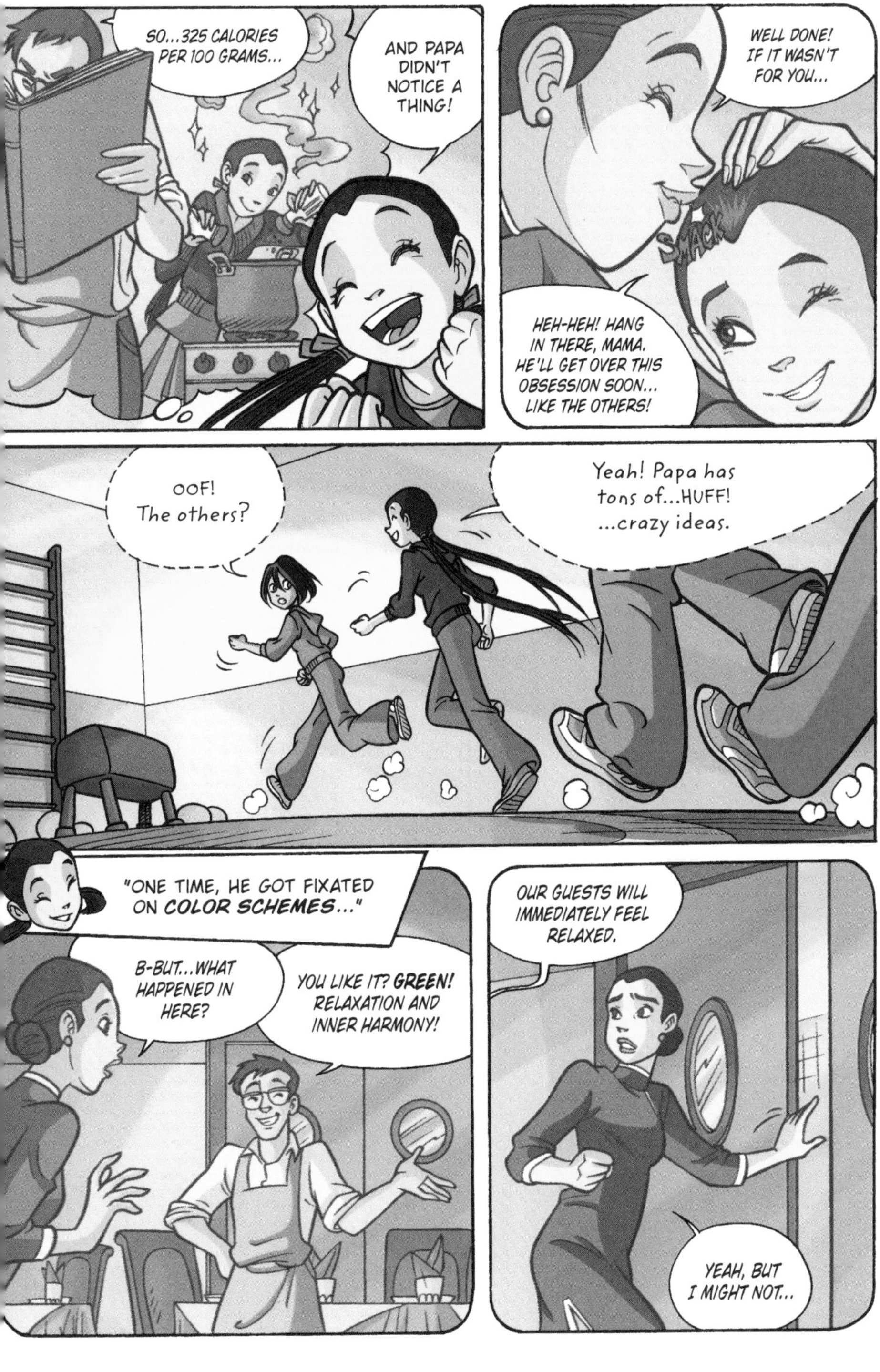
SO...325 CALORIES PER 100 GRAMS...
AND PAPA DIDN'T NOTICE A THING!
WELL DONE! IF IT WASN'T FOR YOU...
SMACK
HEH-HEH! HANG IN THERE, MAMA. HE'LL GET OVER THIS OBSESSION SOON... LIKE THE OTHERS!
OOF! The others?
Yeah! Papa has tons of...HUFF! ...crazy ideas.
"ONE TIME, HE GOT FIXATED ON COLOR SCHEMES..."
B-BUT...WHAT HAPPENED IN HERE?
YOU LIKE IT? GREEN! RELAXATION AND INNER HARMONY!
OUR GUESTS WILL IMMEDIATELY FEEL RELAXED.
YEAH, BUT I MIGHT NOT...

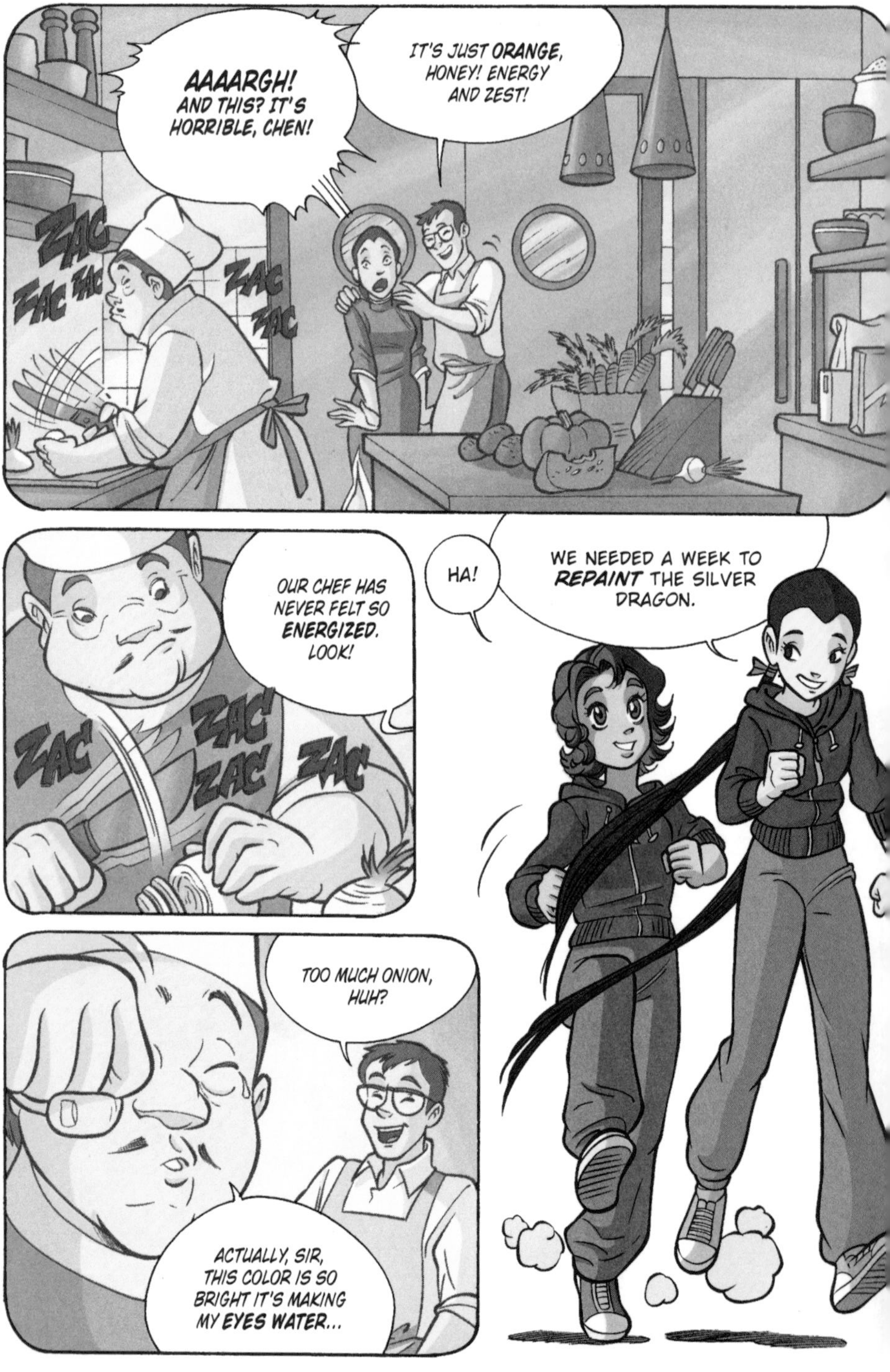
AAAARGH! AND THIS? IT'S HORRIBLE, CHEN!
IT'S JUST ORANGE, HONEY! ENERGY AND ZEST!
ZAC ZAC TAC
ZAC ZAC
OUR CHEF HAS NEVER FELT SO ENERGIZED. LOOK!
ZAC ZAC ZAC ZAC
TOO MUCH ONION, HUH?
ACTUALLY, SIR, THIS COLOR IS SO BRIGHT IT'S MAKING MY EYES WATER...
HA!
WE NEEDED A WEEK TO REPAINT THE SILVER DRAGON.

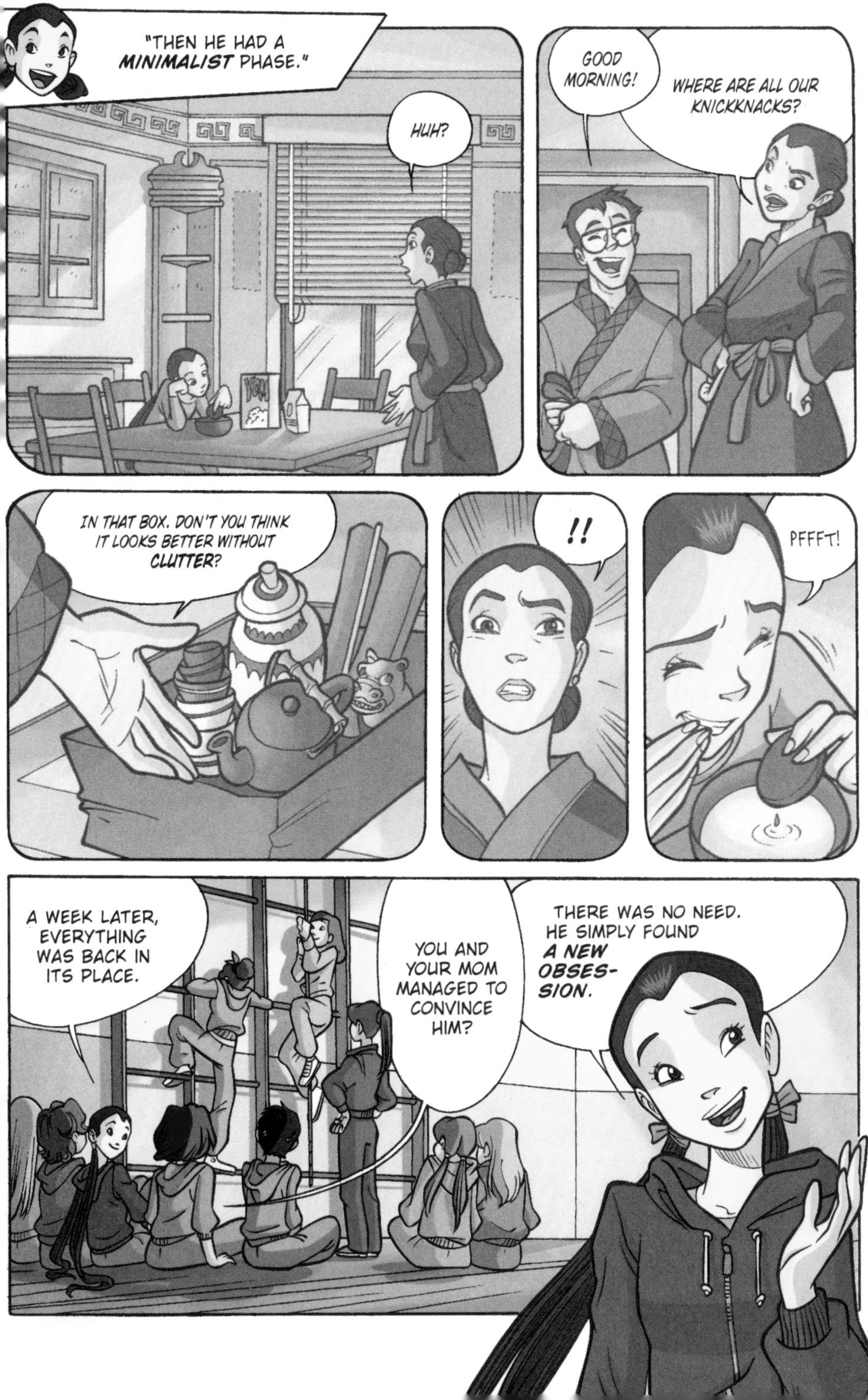
"THEN HE HAD A MINIMALIST PHASE."
HUH?
GOOD MORNING!
WHERE ARE ALL OUR KNICKKNACKS?
IN THAT BOX. DON'T YOU THINK IT LOOKS BETTER WITHOUT CLUTTER?
!!
PFFFT!
A WEEK LATER, EVERYTHING WAS BACK IN ITS PLACE.
YOU AND YOUR MOM MANAGED TO CONVINCE HIM?
THERE WAS NO NEED. HE SIMPLY FOUND A NEW OBSESSION.

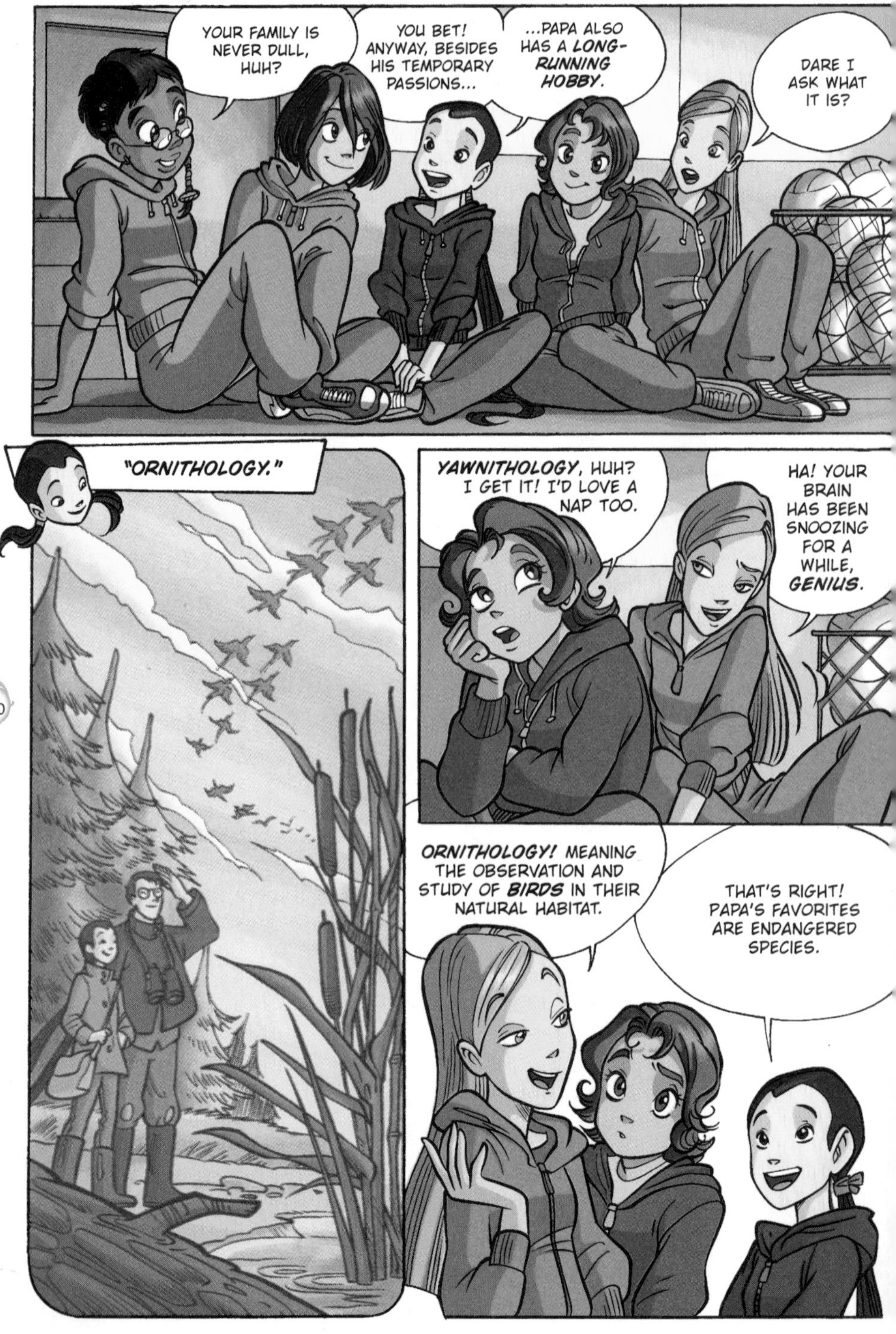
YOUR FAMILY IS NEVER DULL, HUH?
YOU BET! ANYWAY, BESIDES HIS TEMPORARY PASSIONS...
...PAPA ALSO HAS A LONG-RUNNING HOBBY.
DARE I ASK WHAT IT IS?
"ORNITHOLOGY."
YAWNITHOLOGY, HUH? I GET IT! I'D LOVE A NAP TOO.
HA! YOUR BRAIN HAS BEEN SNOOZING FOR A WHILE, GENIUS.
ORNITHOLOGY! MEANING THE OBSERVATION AND STUDY OF BIRDS IN THEIR NATURAL HABITAT.
THAT'S RIGHT! PAPA'S FAVORITES ARE ENDANGERED SPECIES.

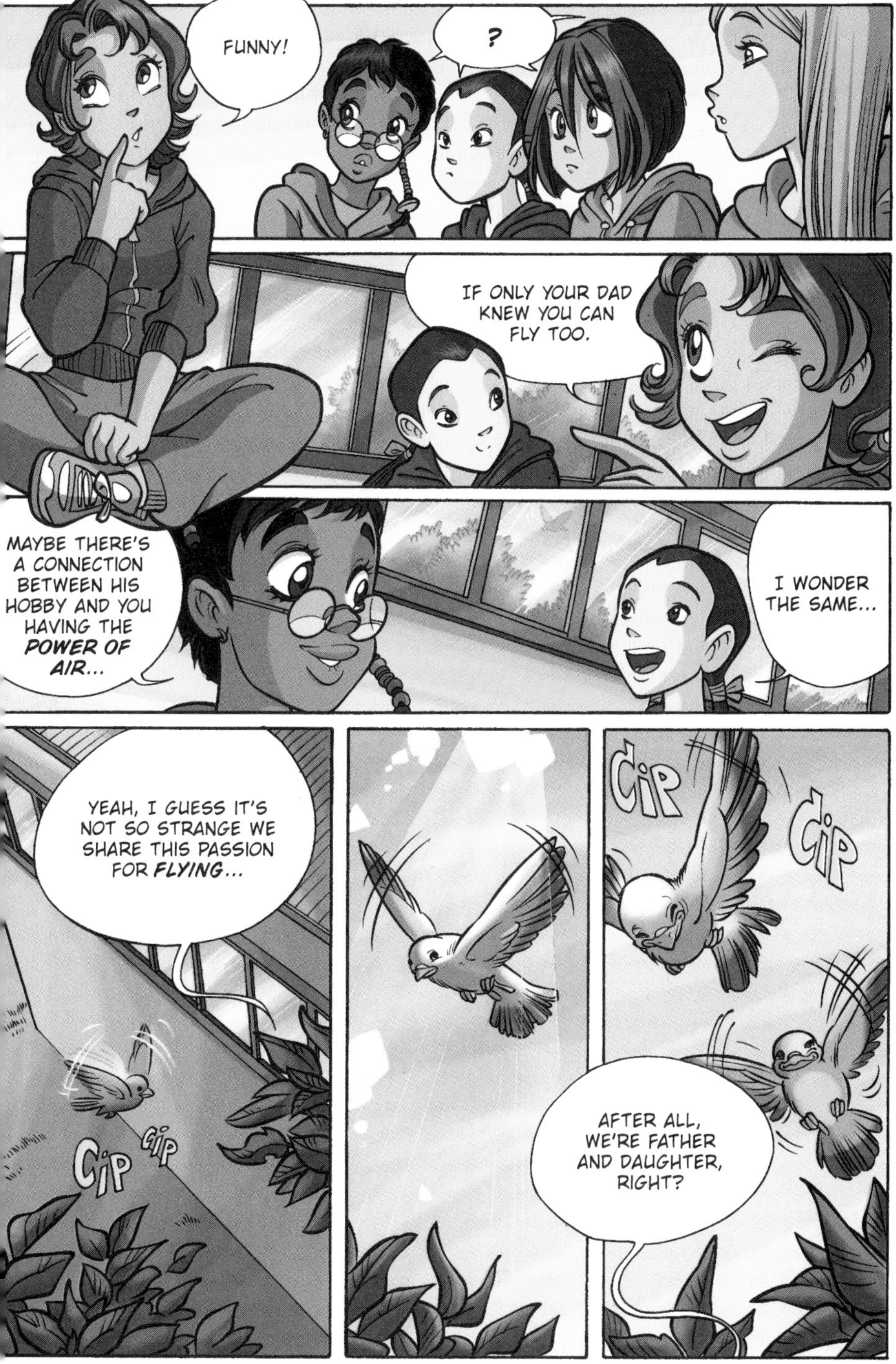
FUNNY!
?
IF ONLY YOUR DAD KNEW YOU CAN FLY TOO.
MAYBE THERE'S A CONNECTION BETWEEN HIS HOBBY AND YOU HAVING THE ***POWER OF AIR***...
I WONDER THE SAME...
YEAH, I GUESS IT'S NOT SO STRANGE WE SHARE THIS PASSION FOR ***FLYING***...
CIP
CIP
CIP
CIP
AFTER ALL, WE'RE FATHER AND DAUGHTER, RIGHT?

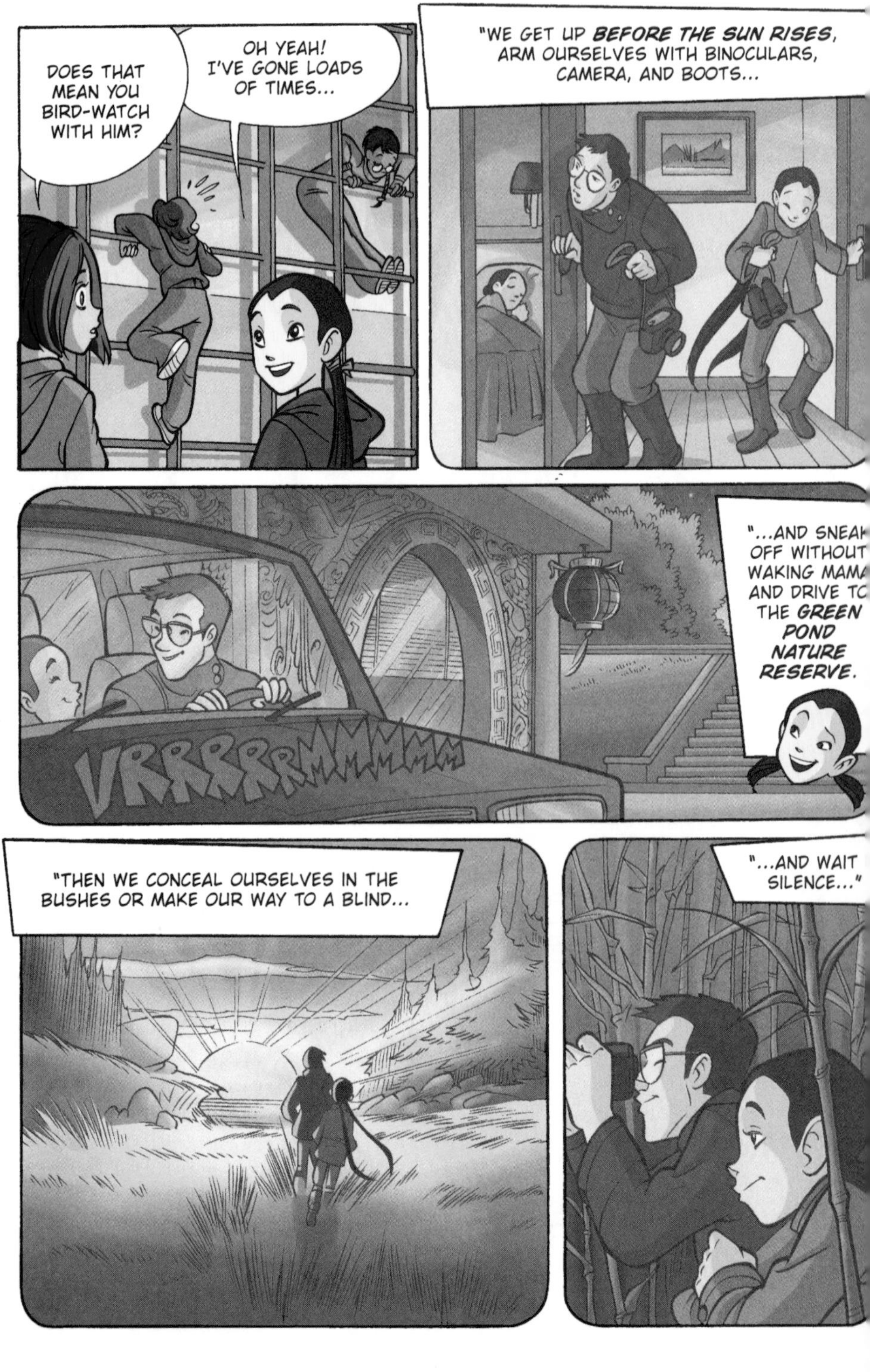
DOES THAT MEAN YOU BIRD-WATCH WITH HIM?
OH YEAH! I'VE GONE LOADS OF TIMES...
"WE GET UP BEFORE THE SUN RISES, ARM OURSELVES WITH BINOCULARS, CAMERA, AND BOOTS...
"...AND SNEAK OFF WITHOUT WAKING MAMA AND DRIVE TO THE GREEN POND NATURE RESERVE.
VRRRRRMMMMMM
"THEN WE CONCEAL OURSELVES IN THE BUSHES OR MAKE OUR WAY TO A BLIND...
"...AND WAIT SILENCE..."

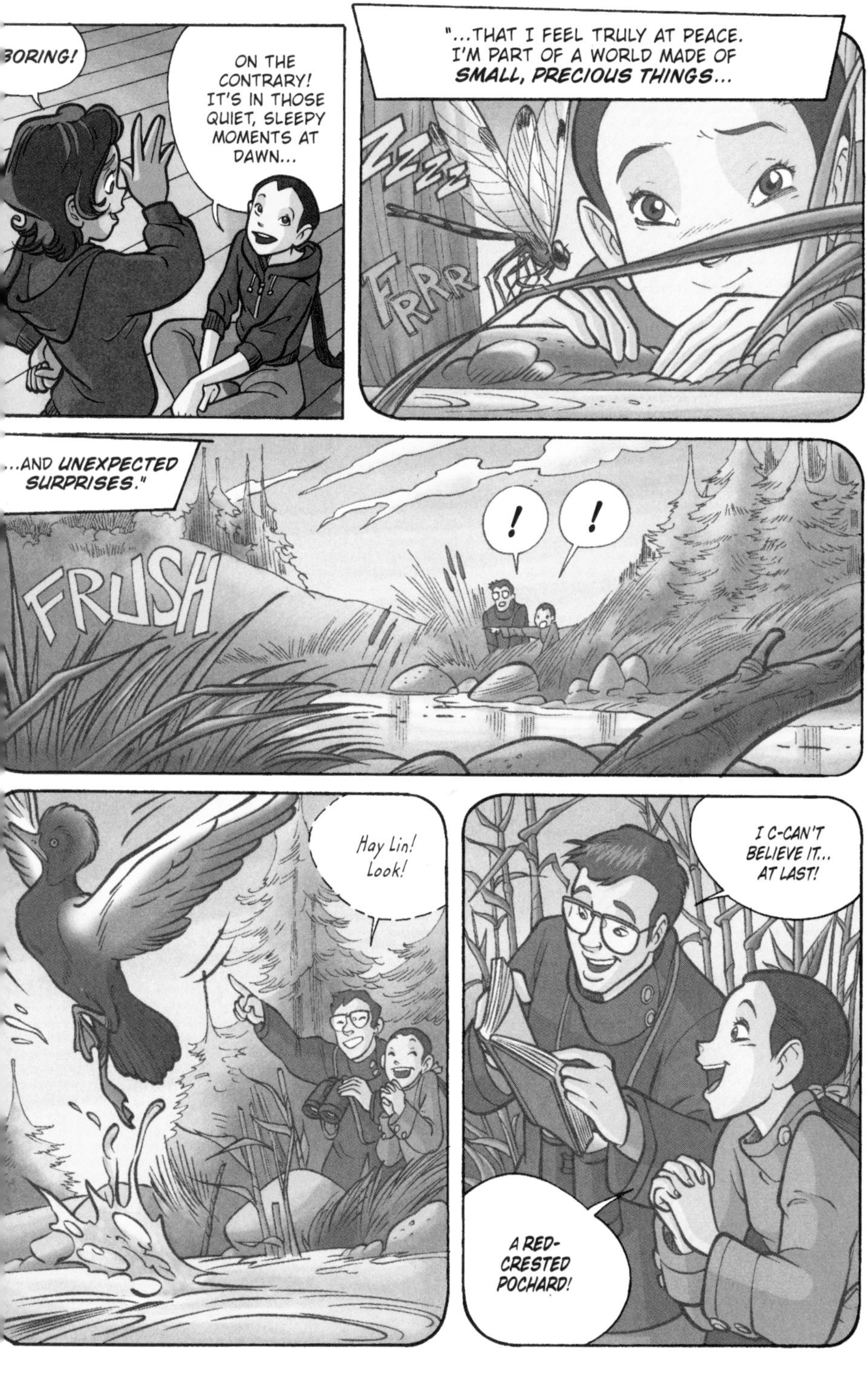
BORING!
ON THE CONTRARY! IT'S IN THOSE QUIET, SLEEPY MOMENTS AT DAWN...
"...THAT I FEEL TRULY AT PEACE. I'M PART OF A WORLD MADE OF SMALL, PRECIOUS THINGS...
ZZZZ
FRRR
...AND UNEXPECTED SURPRISES."
FRUSH
!
!
Hay Lin! Look!
I C-CAN'T BELIEVE IT... AT LAST!
A RED-CRESTED POCHARD!

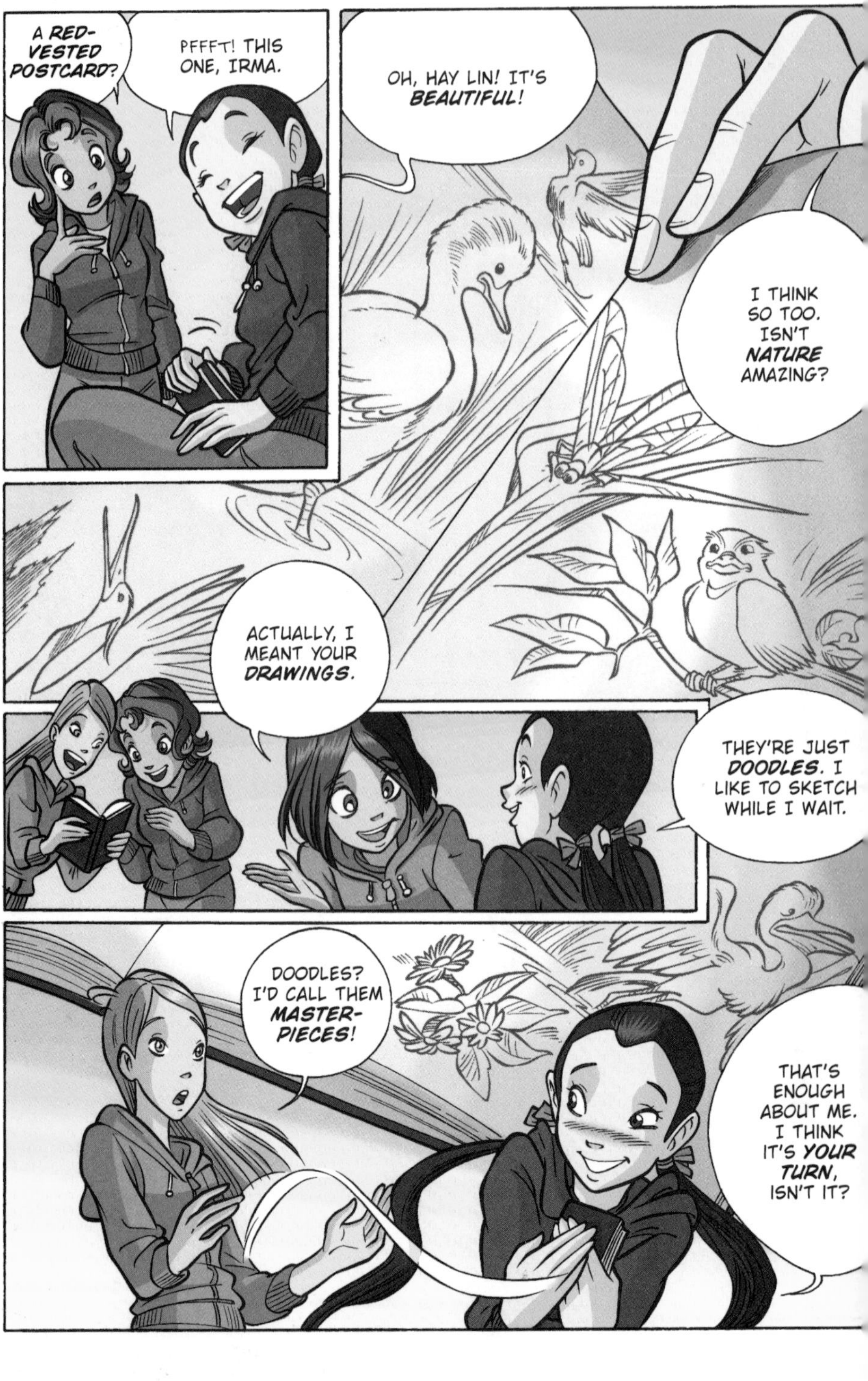
A RED-VESTED POSTCARD?
PFFFT! THIS ONE, IRMA.
OH, HAY LIN! IT'S BEAUTIFUL!
I THINK SO TOO. ISN'T NATURE AMAZING?
ACTUALLY, I MEANT YOUR DRAWINGS.
THEY'RE JUST DOODLES. I LIKE TO SKETCH WHILE I WAIT.
DOODLES? I'D CALL THEM MASTER-PIECES!
THAT'S ENOUGH ABOUT ME. I THINK IT'S YOUR TURN, ISN'T IT?

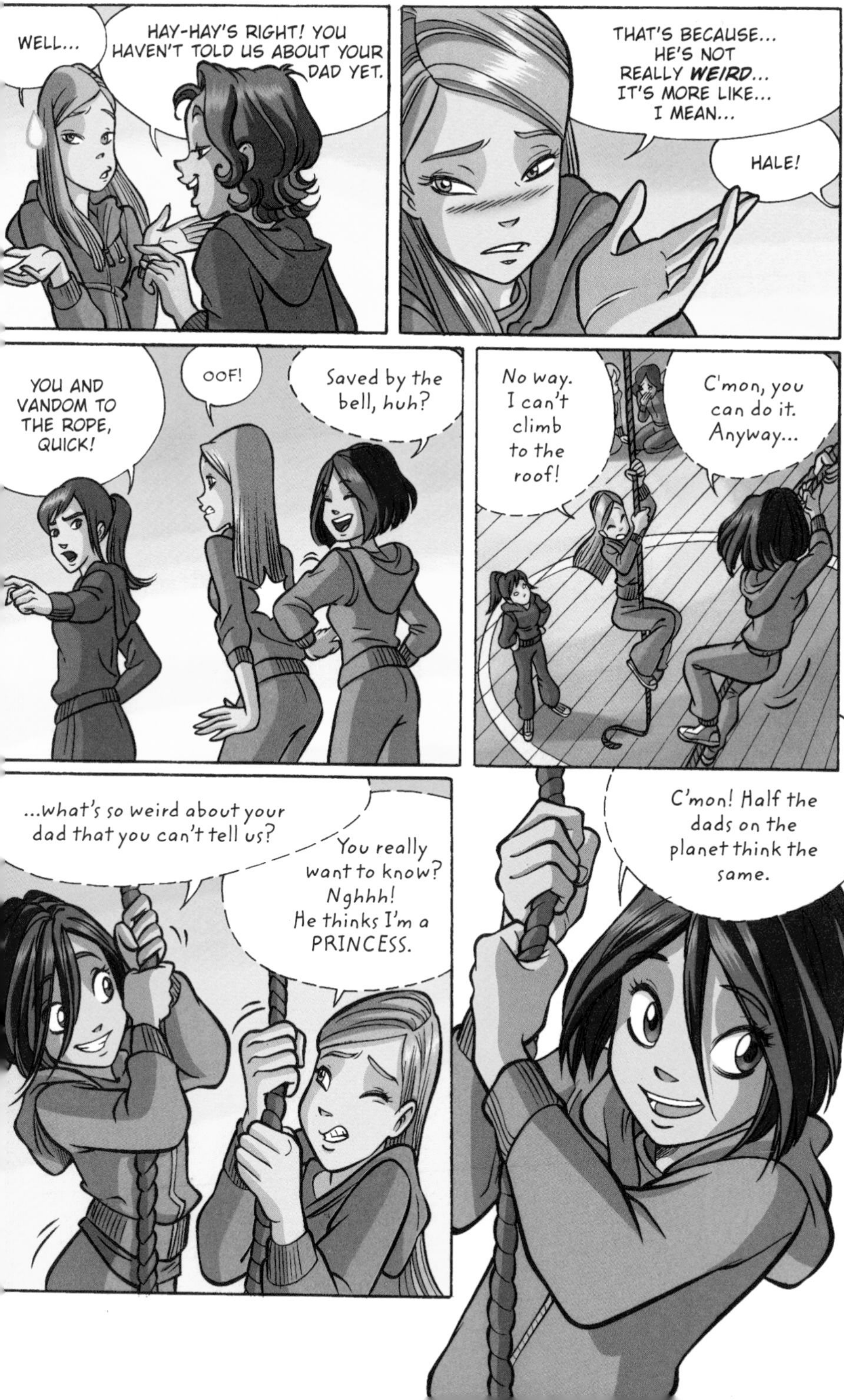
WELL...
HAY-HAY'S RIGHT! YOU HAVEN'T TOLD US ABOUT YOUR DAD YET.
THAT'S BECAUSE... HE'S NOT REALLY ***WEIRD***... IT'S MORE LIKE... I MEAN...
HALE!
YOU AND VANDOM TO THE ROPE, QUICK!
OOF!
Saved by the bell, huh?
No way. I can't climb to the roof!
C'mon, you can do it. Anyway...
...what's so weird about your dad that you can't tell us?
You really want to know? Nghhh! He thinks I'm a PRINCESS.
C'mon! Half the dads on the planet think the same.

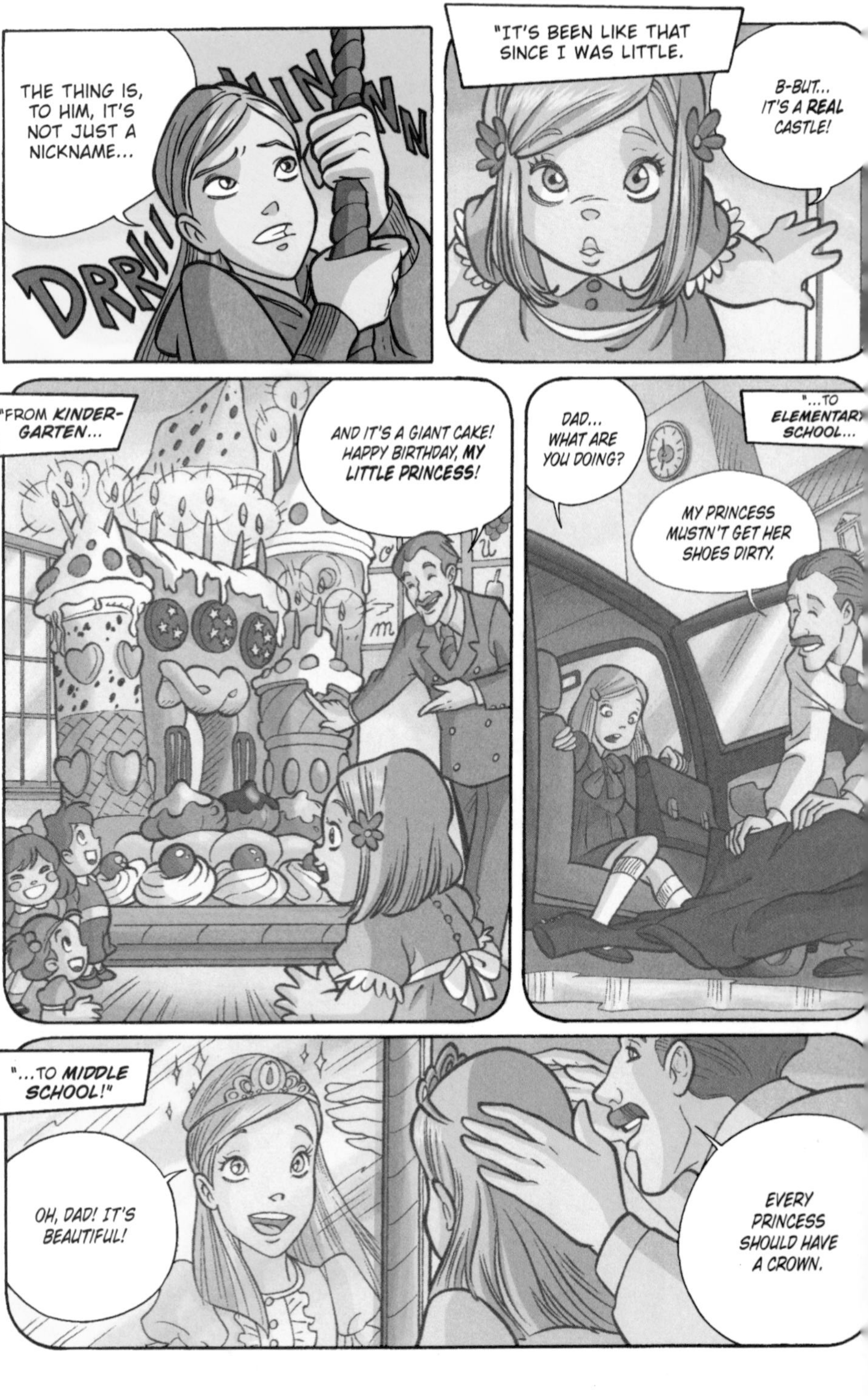
THE THING IS, TO HIM, IT'S NOT JUST A NICKNAME...
DRRIIINNNN
"IT'S BEEN LIKE THAT SINCE I WAS LITTLE.
B-BUT... IT'S A REAL CASTLE!
"FROM KINDER-GARTEN...
AND IT'S A GIANT CAKE! HAPPY BIRTHDAY, MY LITTLE PRINCESS!
DAD... WHAT ARE YOU DOING?
"...TO ELEMENTARY SCHOOL...
MY PRINCESS MUSTN'T GET HER SHOES DIRTY.
"...TO MIDDLE SCHOOL!"
OH, DAD! IT'S BEAUTIFUL!
EVERY PRINCESS SHOULD HAVE A CROWN.

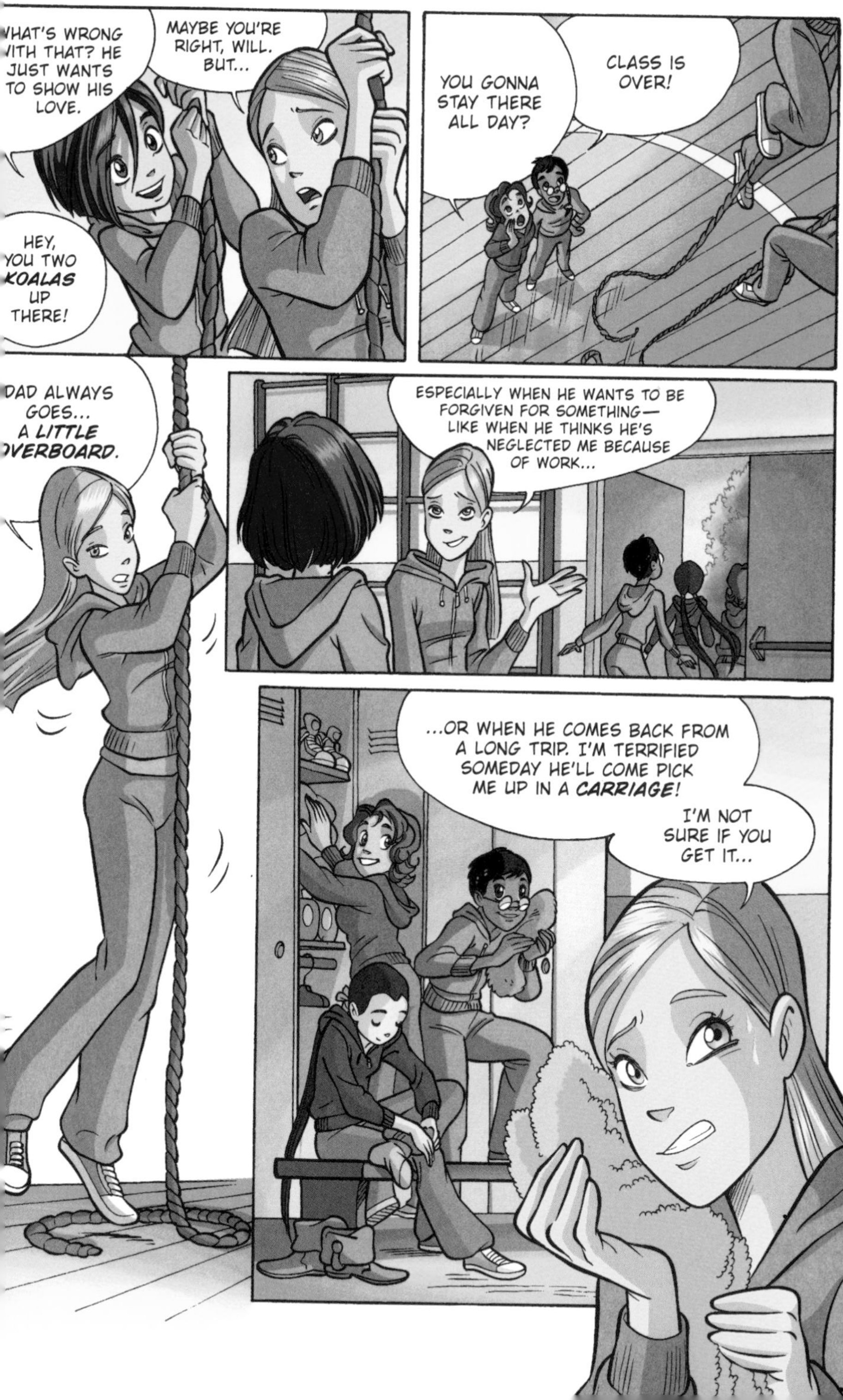
WHAT'S WRONG WITH THAT? HE JUST WANTS TO SHOW HIS LOVE.
MAYBE YOU'RE RIGHT, WILL. BUT...
HEY, YOU TWO KOALAS UP THERE!
YOU GONNA STAY THERE ALL DAY?
CLASS IS OVER!
DAD ALWAYS GOES... A LITTLE OVERBOARD.
ESPECIALLY WHEN HE WANTS TO BE FORGIVEN FOR SOMETHING— LIKE WHEN HE THINKS HE'S NEGLECTED ME BECAUSE OF WORK...
...OR WHEN HE COMES BACK FROM A LONG TRIP. I'M TERRIFIED SOMEDAY HE'LL COME PICK ME UP IN A CARRIAGE!
I'M NOT SURE IF YOU GET IT...

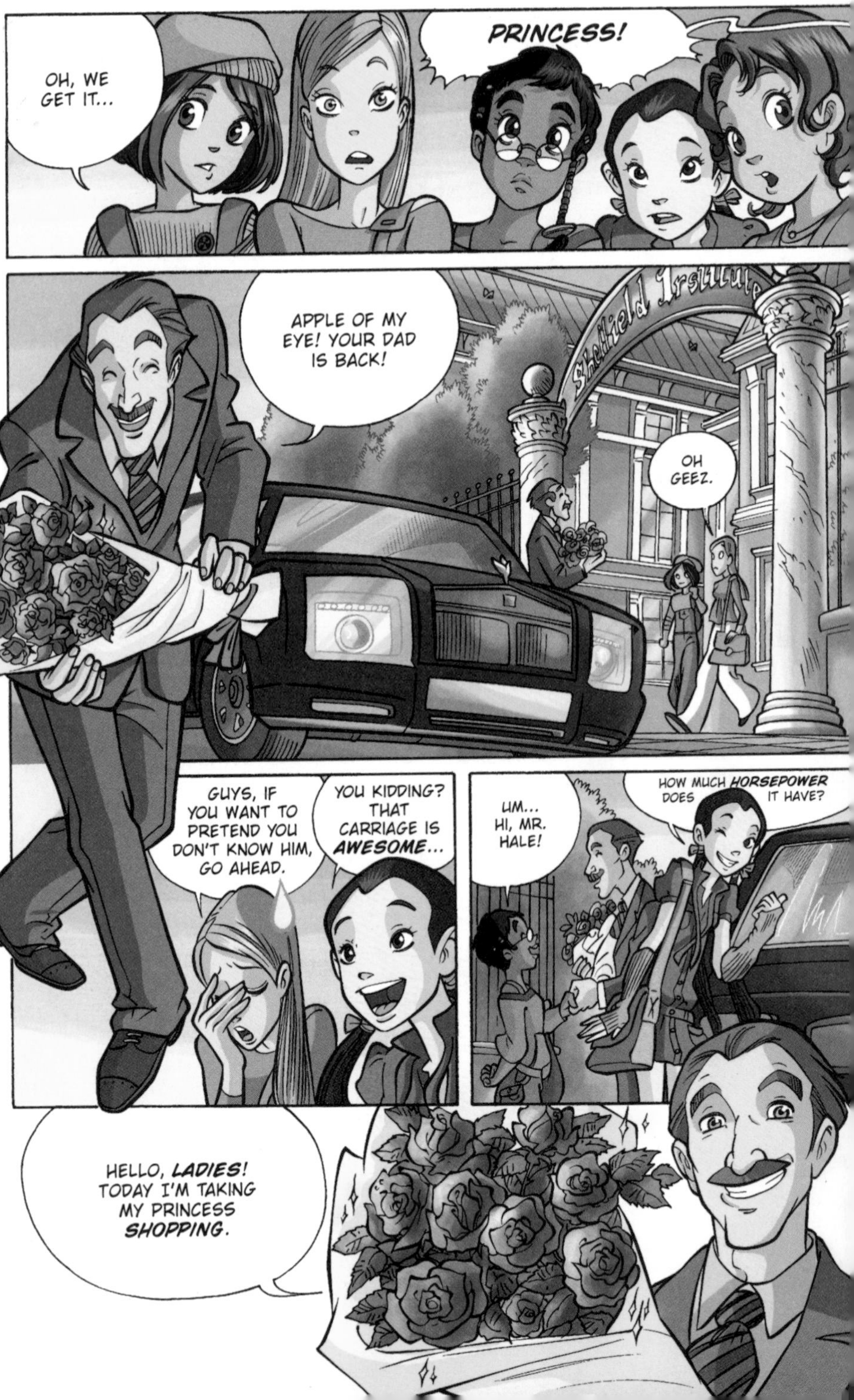
OH, WE GET IT...
PRINCESS!
APPLE OF MY EYE! YOUR DAD IS BACK!
OH GEEZ.
Sheffield Institute
GUYS, IF YOU WANT TO PRETEND YOU DON'T KNOW HIM, GO AHEAD.
YOU KIDDING? THAT CARRIAGE IS AWESOME...
UM... HI, MR. HALE!
HOW MUCH HORSEPOWER DOES IT HAVE?
HELLO, LADIES! TODAY I'M TAKING MY PRINCESS SHOPPING.

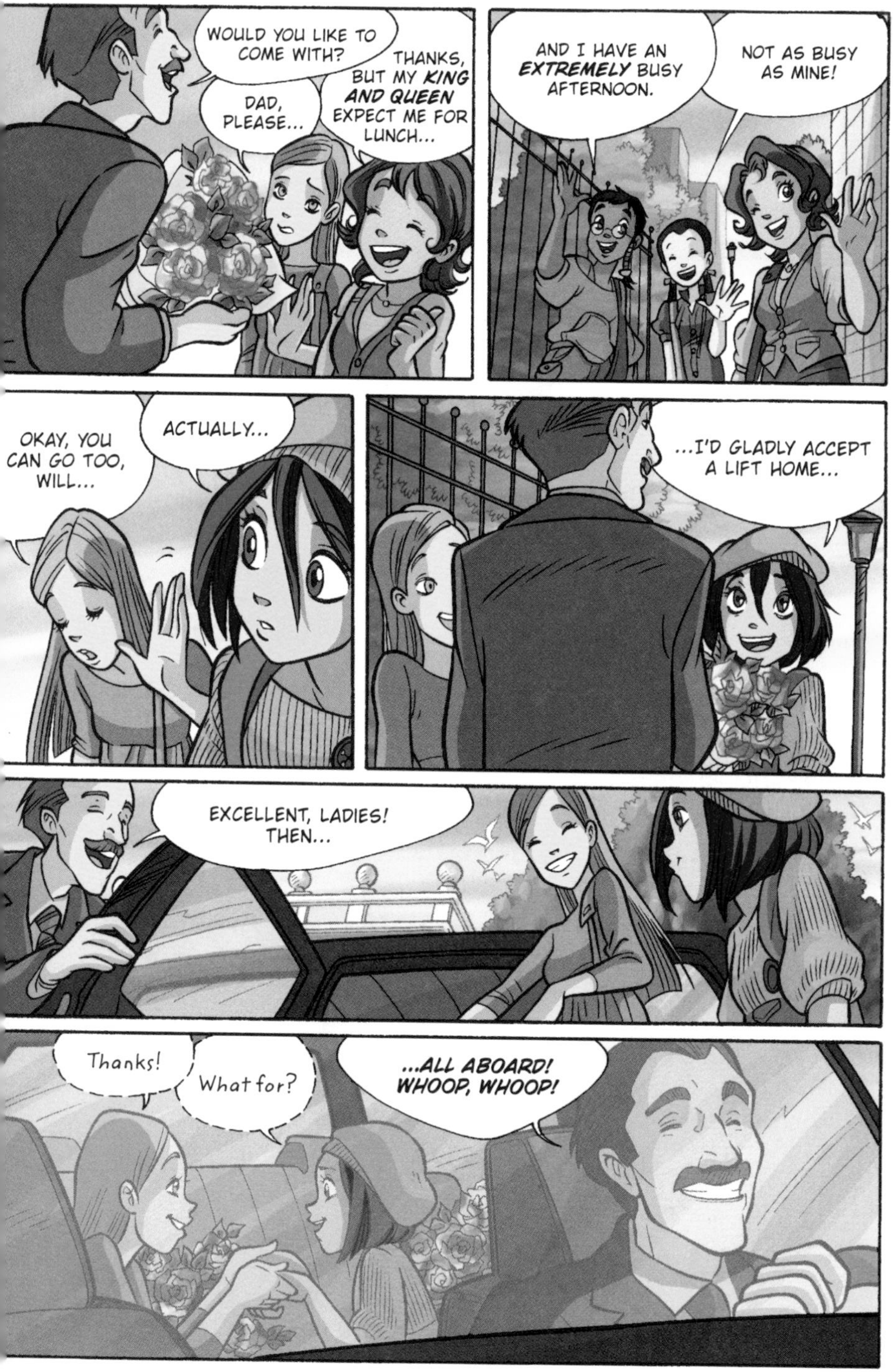
WOULD YOU LIKE TO COME WITH?
DAD, PLEASE...
THANKS, BUT MY KING AND QUEEN EXPECT ME FOR LUNCH...
AND I HAVE AN EXTREMELY BUSY AFTERNOON.
NOT AS BUSY AS MINE!
OKAY, YOU CAN GO TOO, WILL...
ACTUALLY...
...I'D GLADLY ACCEPT A LIFT HOME...
EXCELLENT, LADIES! THEN...
Thanks!
What for?
...ALL ABOARD! WHOOP, WHOOP!

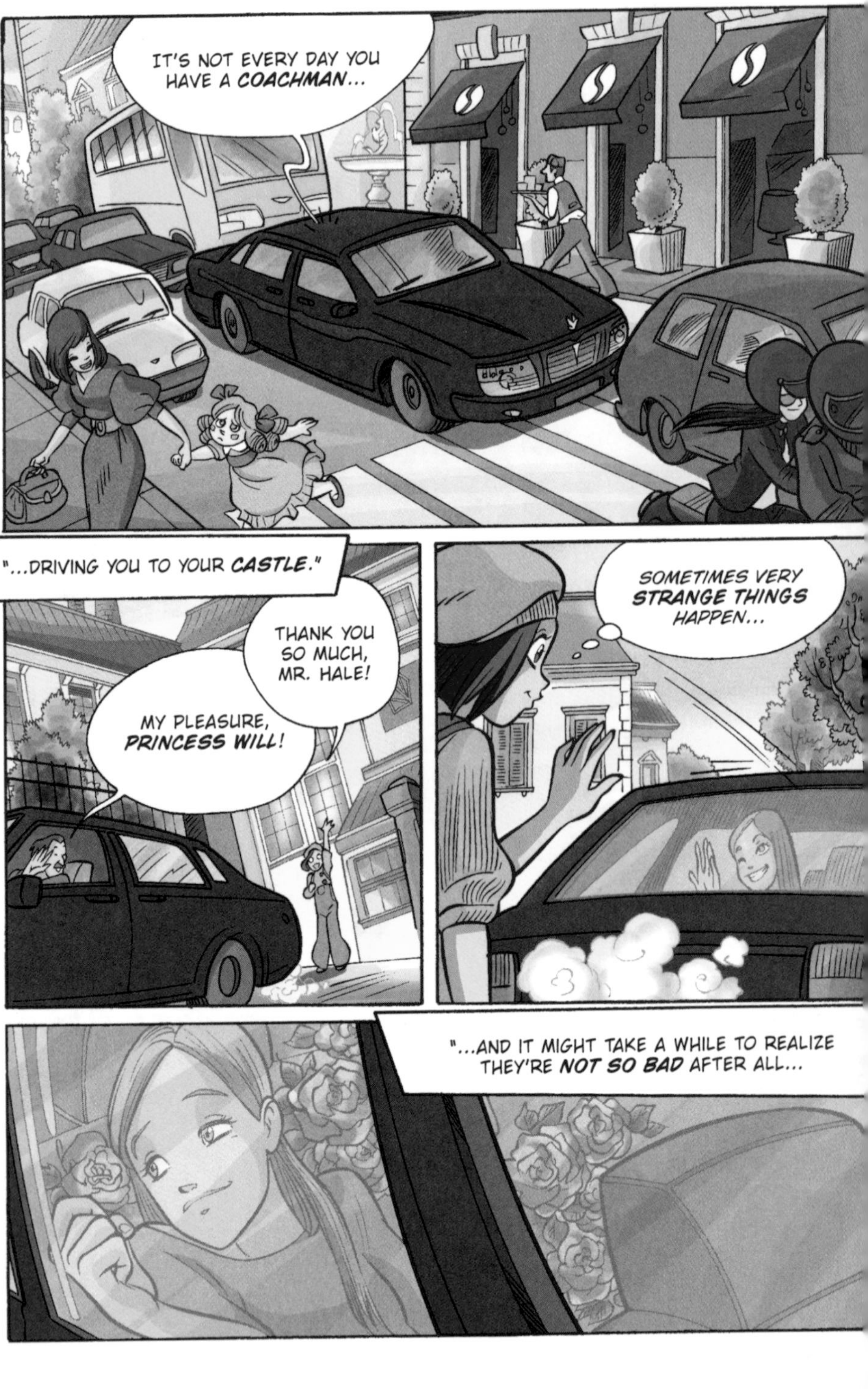
IT'S NOT EVERY DAY YOU HAVE A COACHMAN...
"...DRIVING YOU TO YOUR CASTLE."
THANK YOU SO MUCH, MR. HALE!
MY PLEASURE, PRINCESS WILL!
SOMETIMES VERY STRANGE THINGS HAPPEN...
"...AND IT MIGHT TAKE A WHILE TO REALIZE THEY'RE NOT SO BAD AFTER ALL...

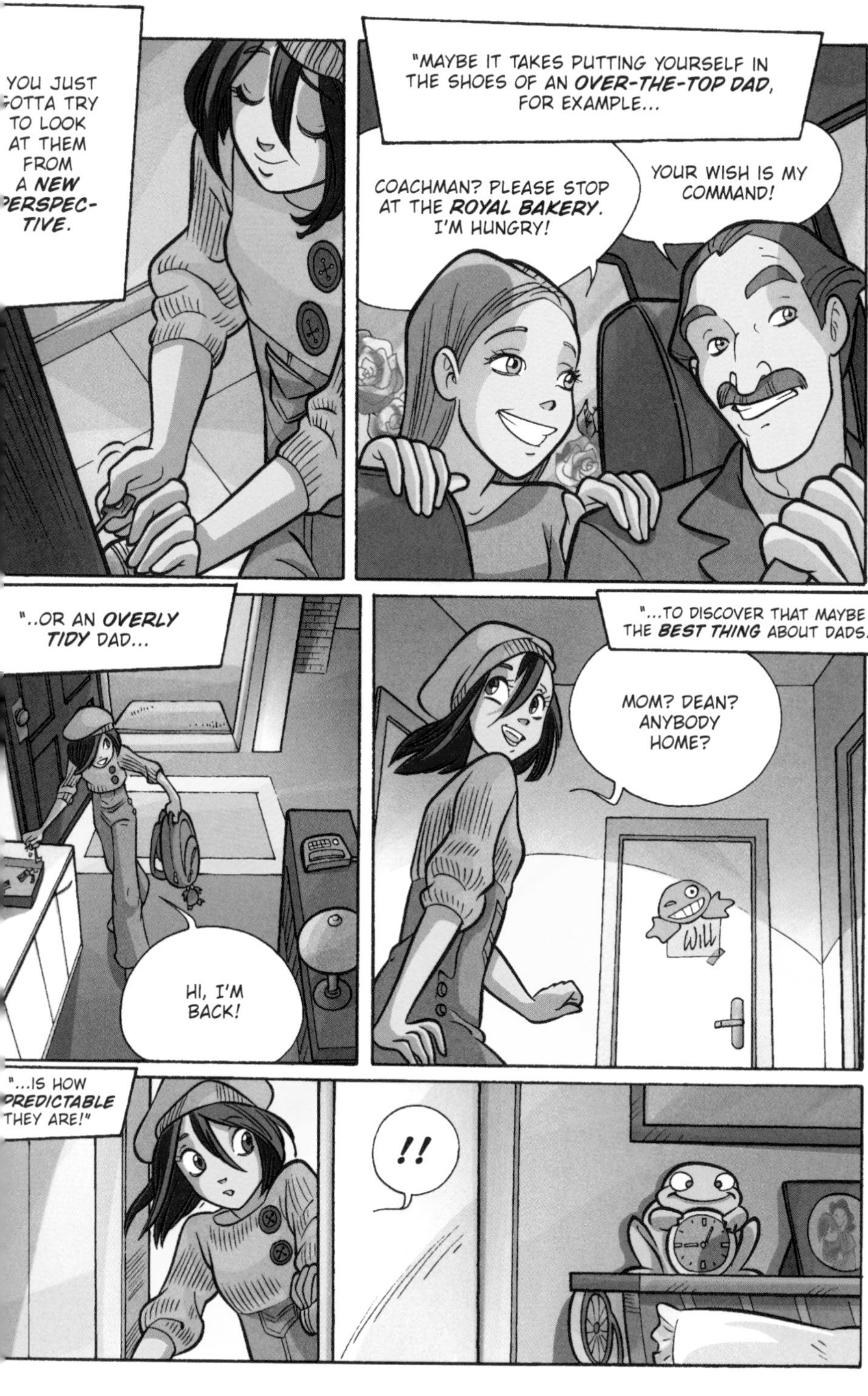
YOU JUST GOTTA TRY TO LOOK AT THEM FROM A NEW PERSPECTIVE.
"MAYBE IT TAKES PUTTING YOURSELF IN THE SHOES OF AN OVER-THE-TOP DAD, FOR EXAMPLE...
COACHMAN? PLEASE STOP AT THE ROYAL BAKERY. I'M HUNGRY!
YOUR WISH IS MY COMMAND!
"..OR AN OVERLY TIDY DAD...
HI, I'M BACK!
"...TO DISCOVER THAT MAYBE THE BEST THING ABOUT DADS...
MOM? DEAN? ANYBODY HOME?
WILL
"...IS HOW PREDICTABLE THEY ARE!"
!!

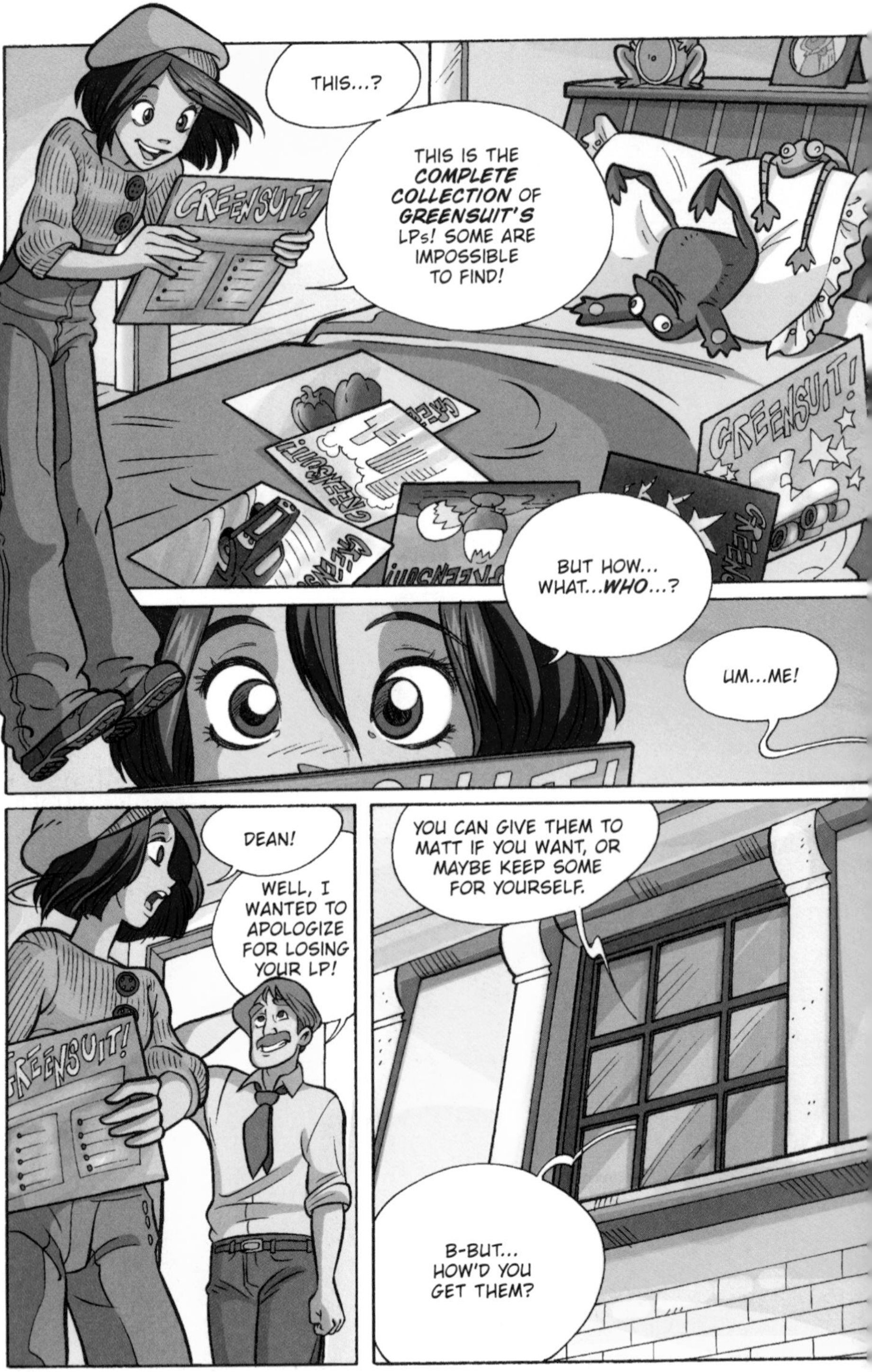
THIS...?
THIS IS THE COMPLETE COLLECTION OF GREENSUIT'S LPs! SOME ARE IMPOSSIBLE TO FIND!
GREENSUIT!
BUT HOW... WHAT...WHO...?
UM...ME!
DEAN!
WELL, I WANTED TO APOLOGIZE FOR LOSING YOUR LP!
GREENSUIT!
YOU CAN GIVE THEM TO MATT IF YOU WANT, OR MAYBE KEEP SOME FOR YOURSELF.
B-BUT... HOW'D YOU GET THEM?

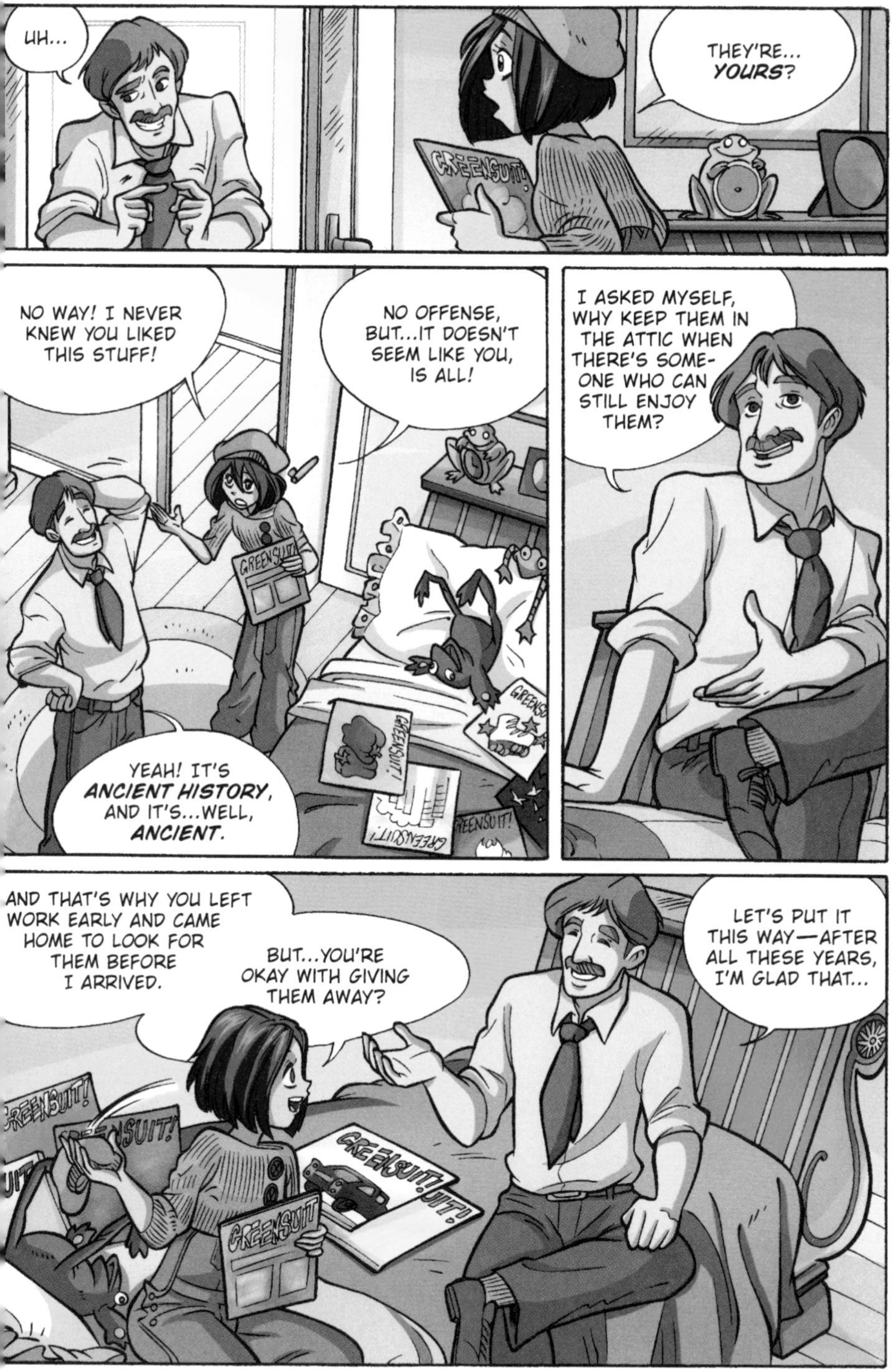
UH...
THEY'RE... *YOURS*?
NO WAY! I NEVER KNEW YOU LIKED THIS STUFF!
NO OFFENSE, BUT...IT DOESN'T SEEM LIKE YOU, IS ALL!
YEAH! IT'S *ANCIENT HISTORY*, AND IT'S...WELL, *ANCIENT*.
GREENSUIT!
I ASKED MYSELF, WHY KEEP THEM IN THE ATTIC WHEN THERE'S SOME-ONE WHO CAN STILL ENJOY THEM?
AND THAT'S WHY YOU LEFT WORK EARLY AND CAME HOME TO LOOK FOR THEM BEFORE I ARRIVED.
BUT...YOU'RE OKAY WITH GIVING THEM AWAY?
LET'S PUT IT THIS WAY—AFTER ALL THESE YEARS, I'M GLAD THAT...
GREENSUIT!

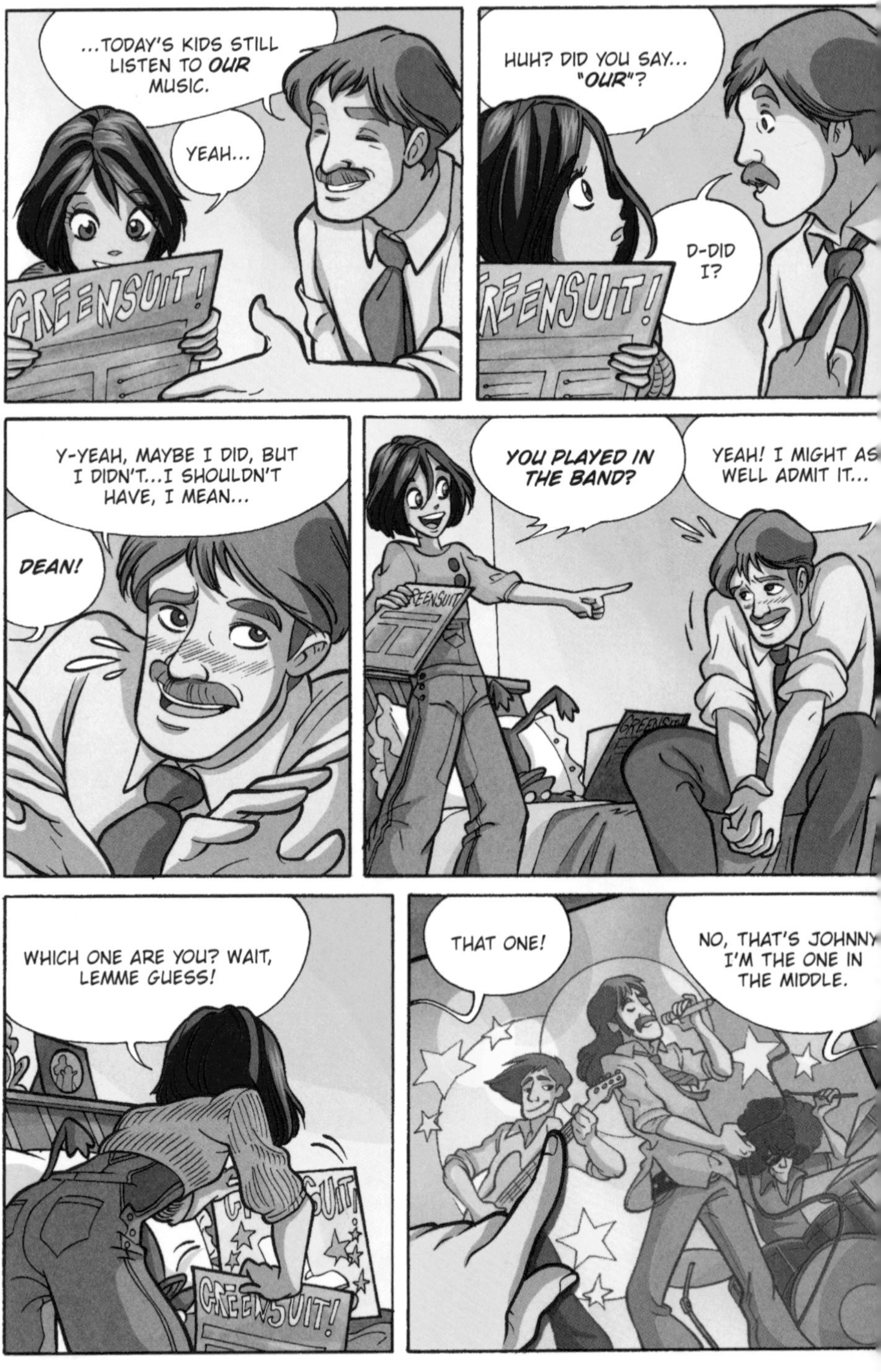
...TODAY'S KIDS STILL LISTEN TO OUR MUSIC.
YEAH...
GREENSUIT!
HUH? DID YOU SAY... "OUR"?
D-DID I?
GREENSUIT!
Y-YEAH, MAYBE I DID, BUT I DIDN'T...I SHOULDN'T HAVE, I MEAN...
DEAN!
YOU PLAYED IN THE BAND?
YEAH! I MIGHT AS WELL ADMIT IT...
WHICH ONE ARE YOU? WAIT, LEMME GUESS!
GREENSUIT!
THAT ONE!
NO, THAT'S JOHNNY I'M THE ONE IN THE MIDDLE.

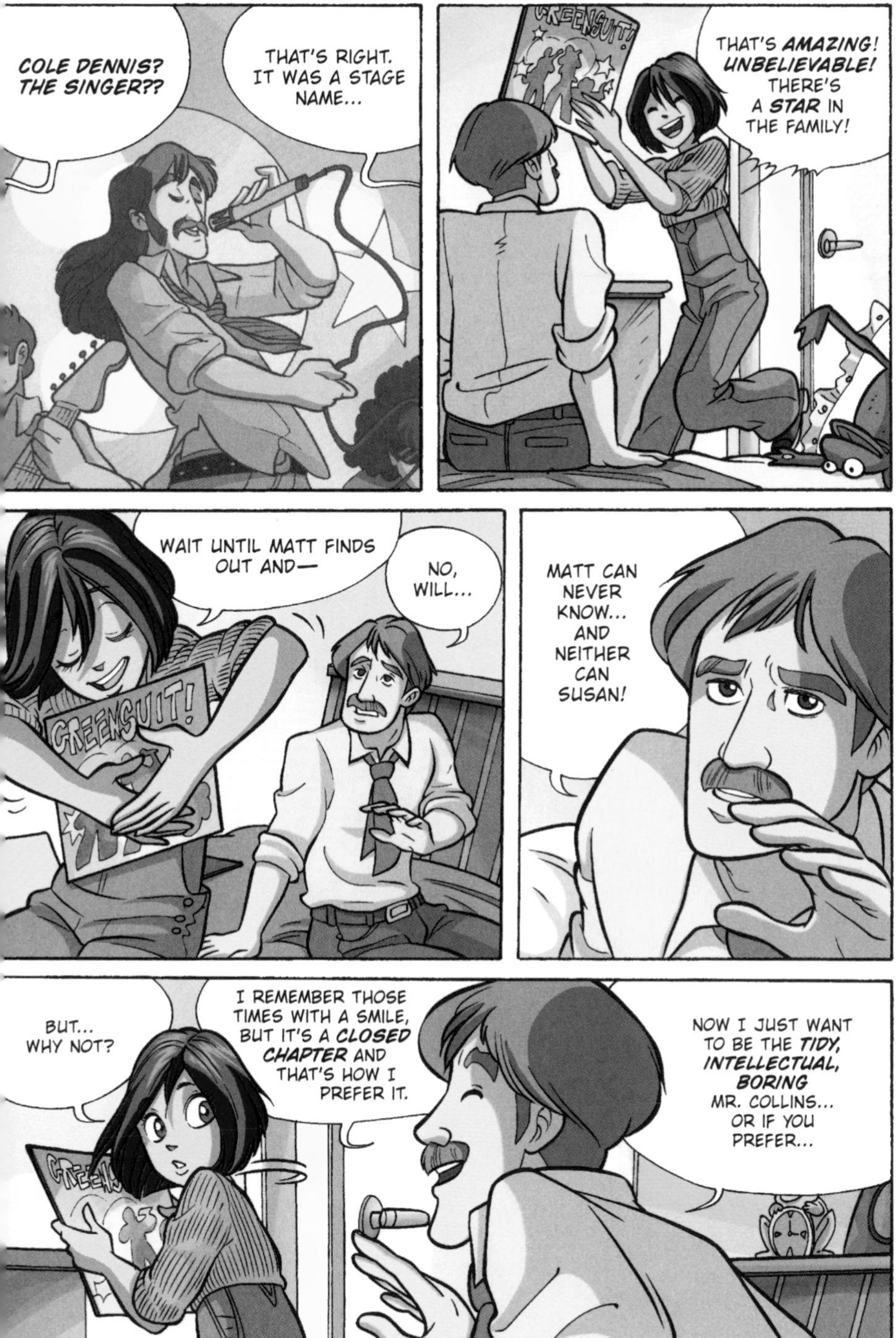
COLE DENNIS? THE SINGER??
THAT'S RIGHT. IT WAS A STAGE NAME...
GREENSUIT!
THAT'S AMAZING! UNBELIEVABLE! THERE'S A STAR IN THE FAMILY!
WAIT UNTIL MATT FINDS OUT AND—
NO, WILL...
GREENSUIT!
MATT CAN NEVER KNOW... AND NEITHER CAN SUSAN!
BUT... WHY NOT?
I REMEMBER THOSE TIMES WITH A SMILE, BUT IT'S A CLOSED CHAPTER AND THAT'S HOW I PREFER IT.
NOW I JUST WANT TO BE THE TIDY, INTELLECTUAL, BORING MR. COLLINS... OR IF YOU PREFER...

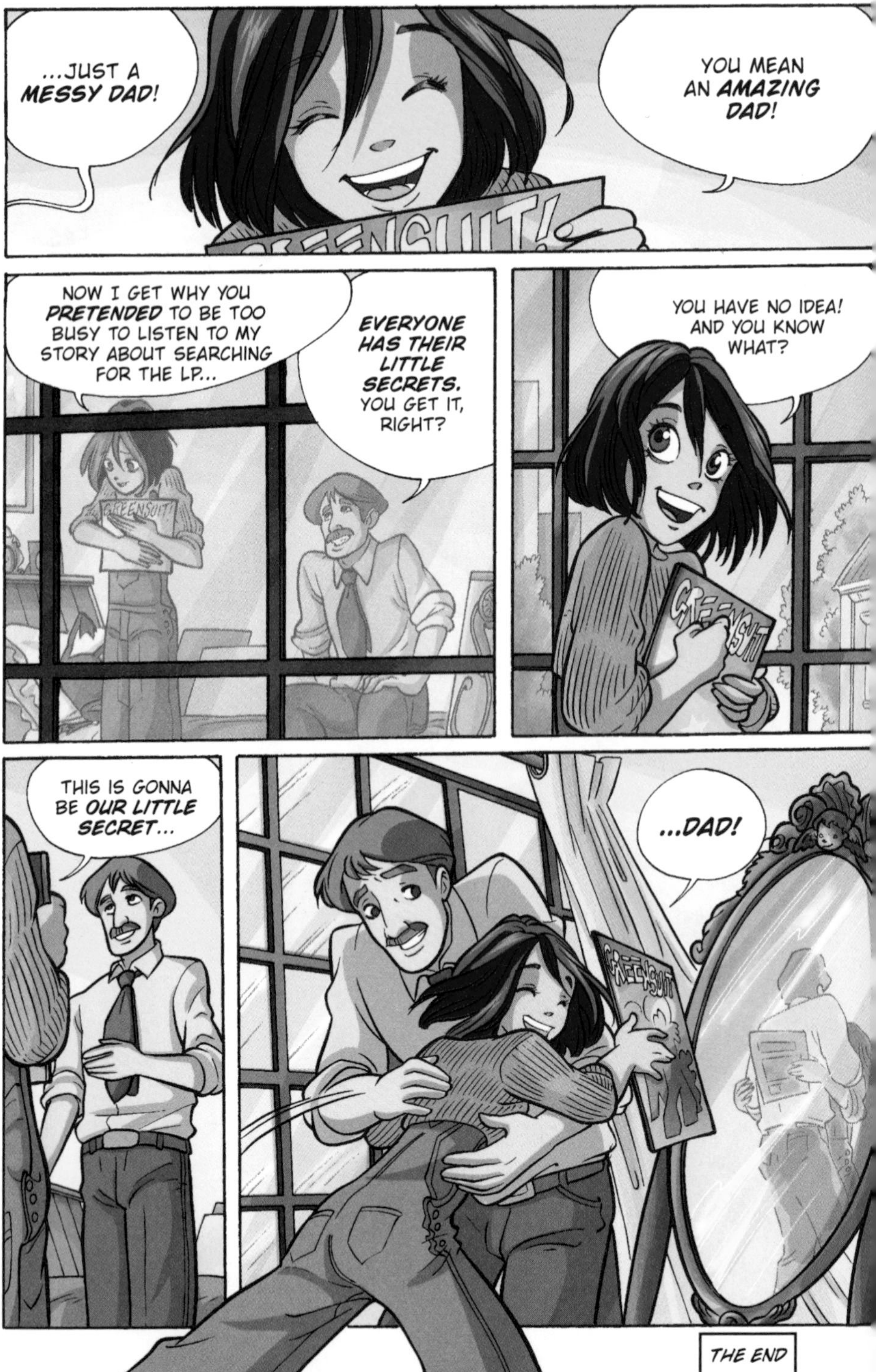
...JUST A MESSY DAD!
YOU MEAN AN AMAZING DAD!
GREENSUIT!
NOW I GET WHY YOU PRETENDED TO BE TOO BUSY TO LISTEN TO MY STORY ABOUT SEARCHING FOR THE LP...
EVERYONE HAS THEIR LITTLE SECRETS. YOU GET IT, RIGHT?
YOU HAVE NO IDEA! AND YOU KNOW WHAT?
THIS IS GONNA BE OUR LITTLE SECRET...
...DAD!
THE END

W.i.t.c.h.

Will Irma Taranee Cornelia Hay Lin

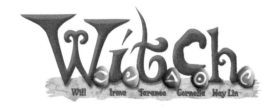

W.i.t.c.h.

Will Irma Taranee Cornelia Hay Lin

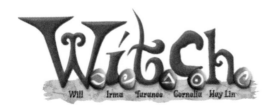

A Tricky Trade

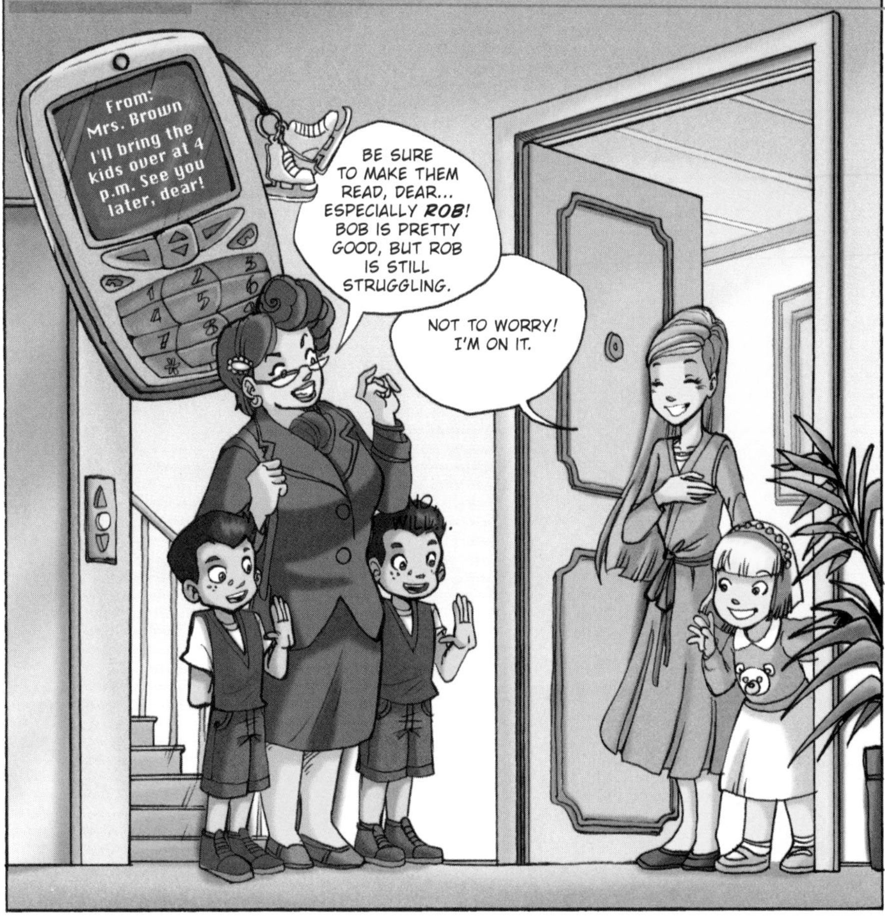
From:
Mrs. Brown
I'll bring the kids over at 4 p.m. See you later, dear!
BE SURE TO MAKE THEM READ, DEAR... ESPECIALLY ROB! BOB IS PRETTY GOOD, BUT ROB IS STILL STRUGGLING.
NOT TO WORRY! I'M ON IT.

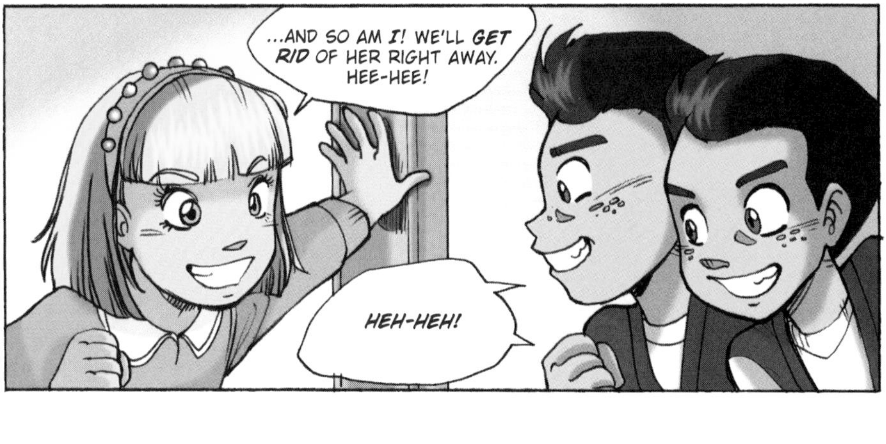
...AND SO AM I! WE'LL GET RID OF HER RIGHT AWAY. HEE-HEE!
HEH-HEH!

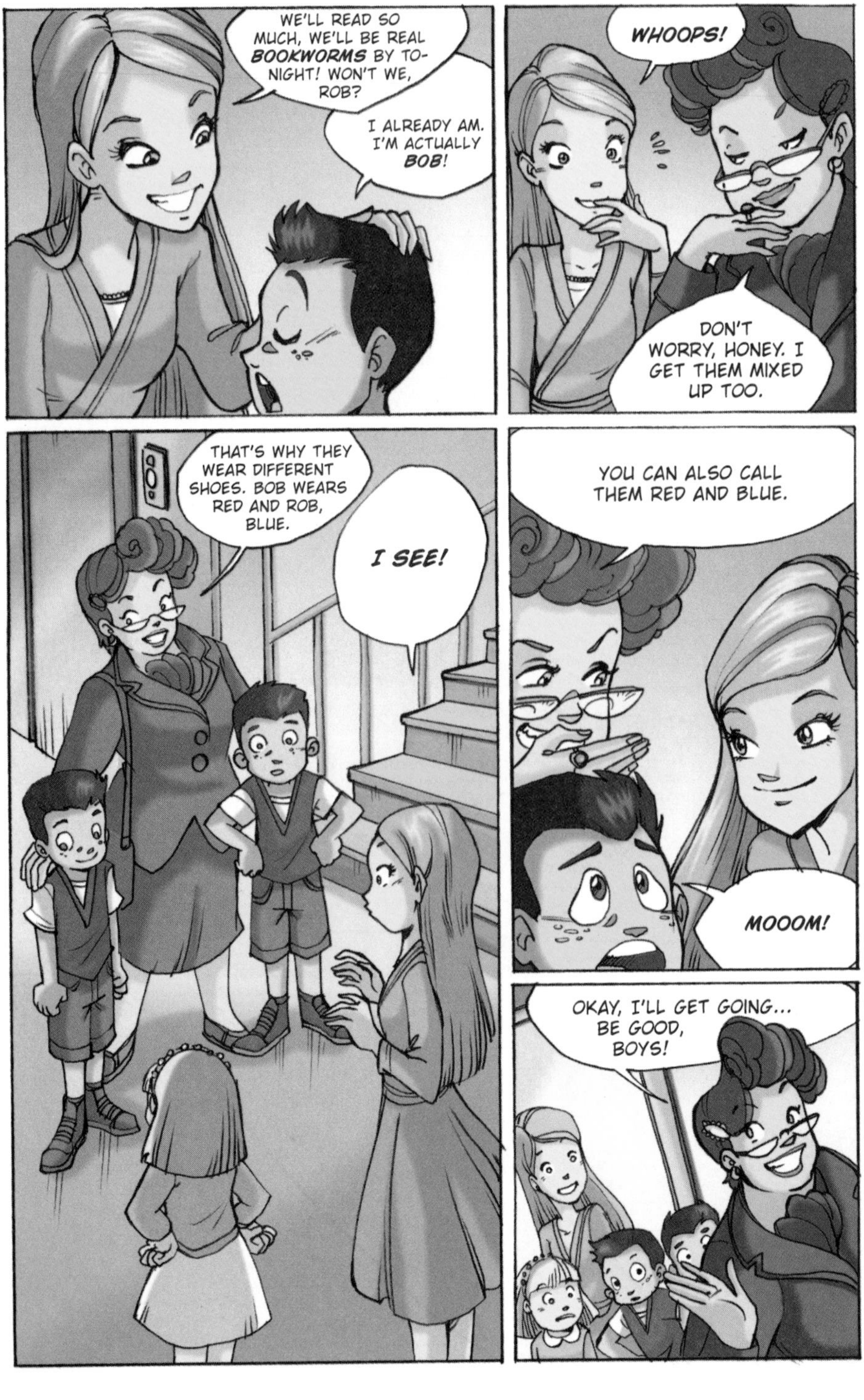
WE'LL READ SO MUCH, WE'LL BE REAL **BOOKWORMS** BY TO-NIGHT! WON'T WE, ROB?
I ALREADY AM. I'M ACTUALLY *BOB*!
WHOOPS!
DON'T WORRY, HONEY. I GET THEM MIXED UP TOO.
THAT'S WHY THEY WEAR DIFFERENT SHOES. BOB WEARS RED AND ROB, BLUE.
I SEE!
YOU CAN ALSO CALL THEM RED AND BLUE.
MOOOM!
OKAY, I'LL GET GOING... BE GOOD, BOYS!

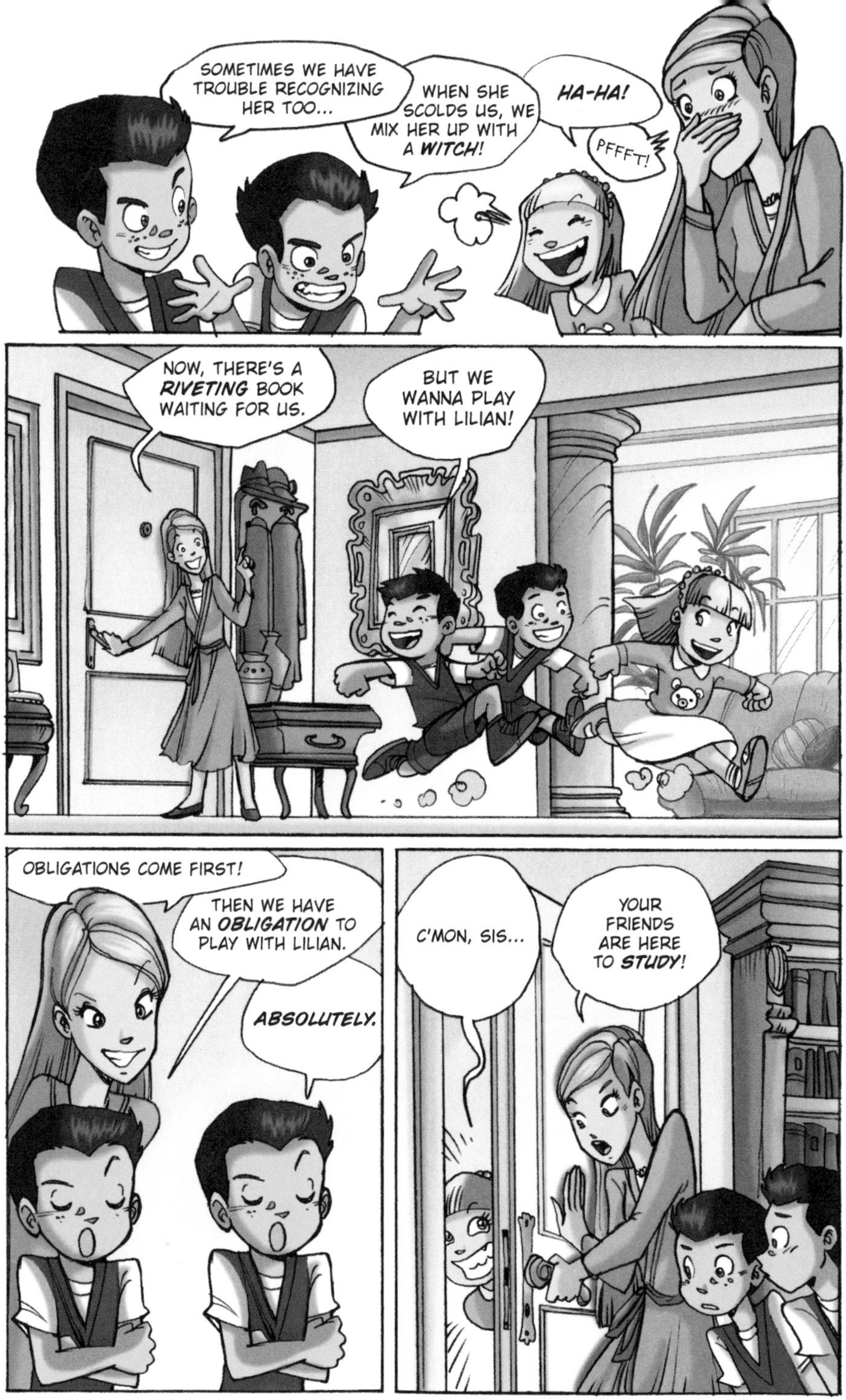
SOMETIMES WE HAVE TROUBLE RECOGNIZING HER TOO...
WHEN SHE SCOLDS US, WE MIX HER UP WITH A WITCH!
HA-HA!
PFFFT!
NOW, THERE'S A RIVETING BOOK WAITING FOR US.
BUT WE WANNA PLAY WITH LILIAN!
OBLIGATIONS COME FIRST!
THEN WE HAVE AN OBLIGATION TO PLAY WITH LILIAN.
ABSOLUTELY.
C'MON, SIS...
YOUR FRIENDS ARE HERE TO STUDY!

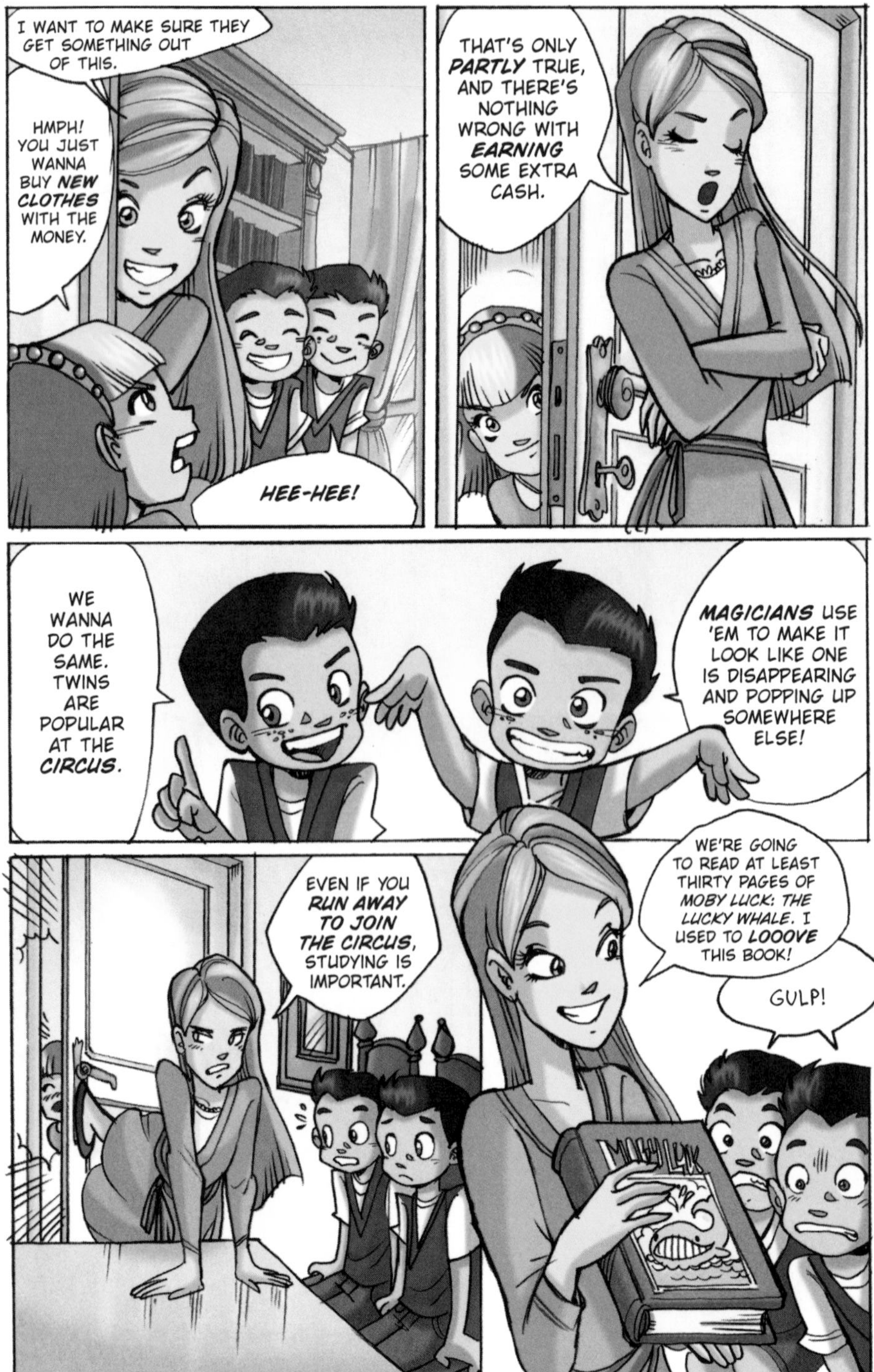

I WANT TO MAKE SURE THEY GET SOMETHING OUT OF THIS.
HMPH! YOU JUST WANNA BUY NEW CLOTHES WITH THE MONEY.
HEE-HEE!
THAT'S ONLY PARTLY TRUE, AND THERE'S NOTHING WRONG WITH EARNING SOME EXTRA CASH.
WE WANNA DO THE SAME. TWINS ARE POPULAR AT THE CIRCUS.
MAGICIANS USE 'EM TO MAKE IT LOOK LIKE ONE IS DISAPPEARING AND POPPING UP SOMEWHERE ELSE!
EVEN IF YOU RUN AWAY TO JOIN THE CIRCUS, STUDYING IS IMPORTANT.
WE'RE GOING TO READ AT LEAST THIRTY PAGES OF MOBY LUCK: THE LUCKY WHALE. I USED TO LOOOVE THIS BOOK!
GULP!
MOBY LUCK

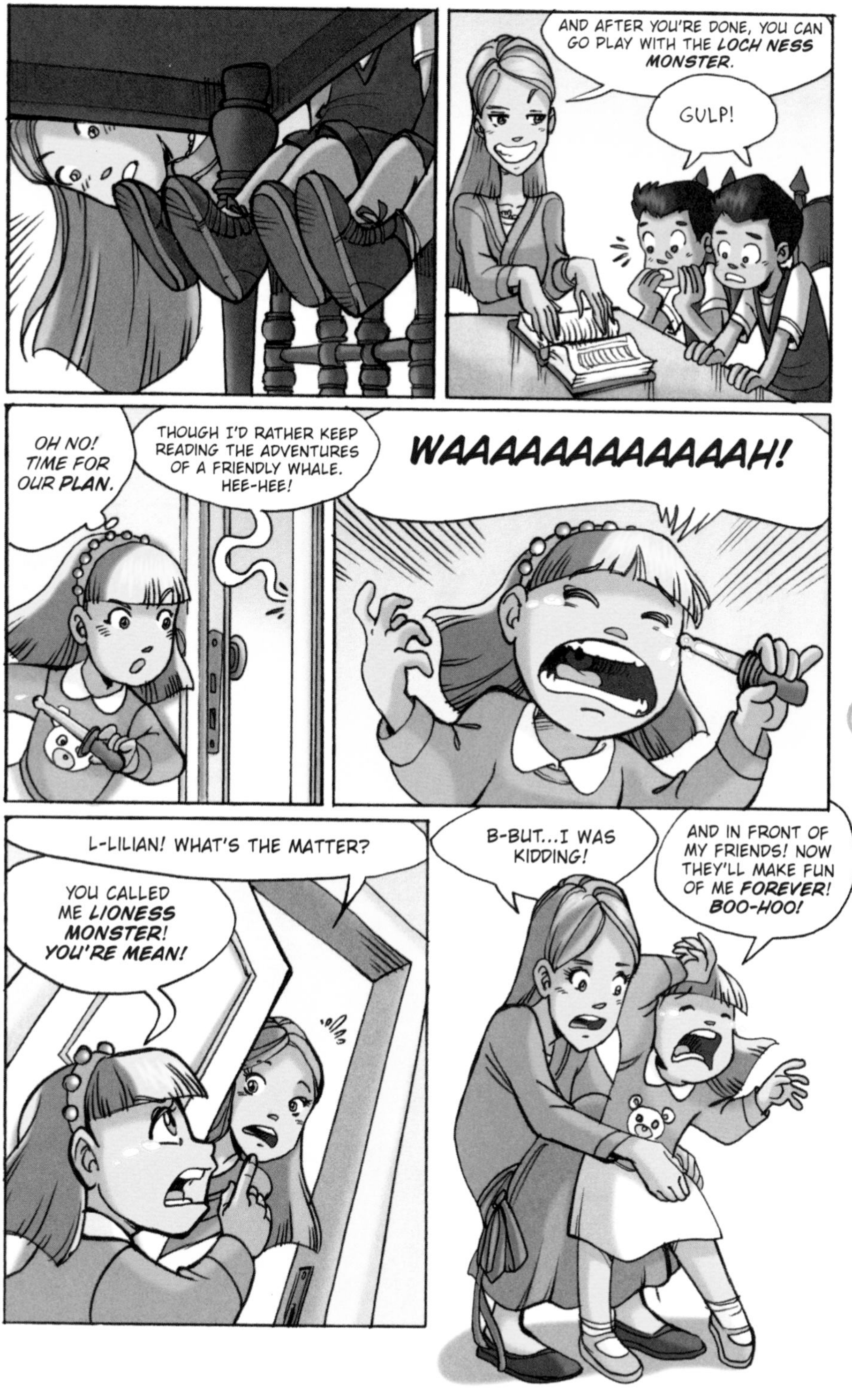
AND AFTER YOU'RE DONE, YOU CAN GO PLAY WITH THE **LOCH NESS MONSTER**.
GULP!
*OH NO! TIME FOR OUR **PLAN**.*
THOUGH I'D RATHER KEEP READING THE ADVENTURES OF A FRIENDLY WHALE. HEE-HEE!
WAAAAAAAAAAAAH!
L-LILIAN! WHAT'S THE MATTER?
YOU CALLED ME ***LIONESS MONSTER! YOU'RE MEAN!***
B-BUT...I WAS KIDDING!
AND IN FRONT OF MY FRIENDS! NOW THEY'LL MAKE FUN OF ME ***FOREVER! BOO-HOO!***

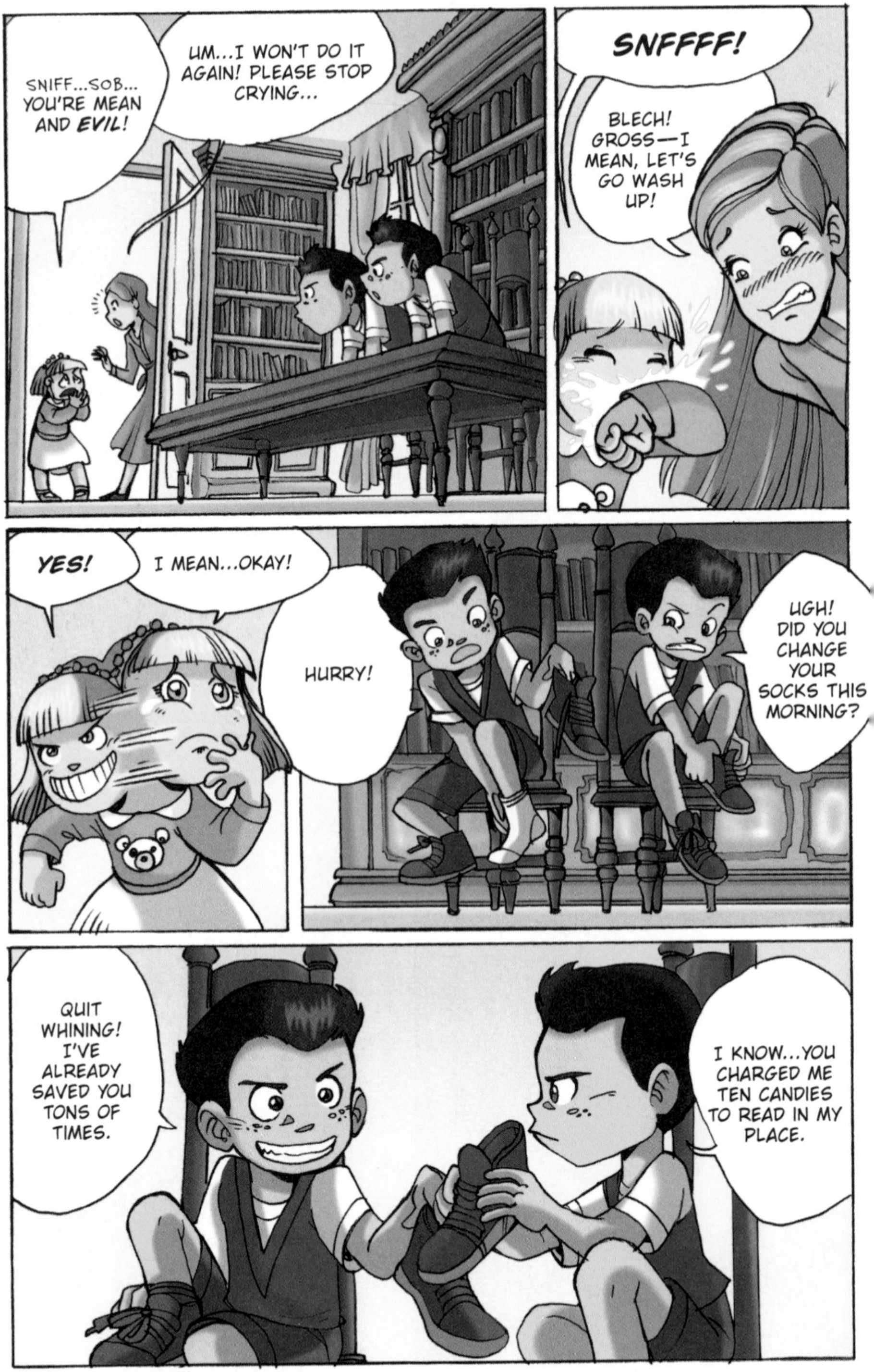
SNIFF...SOB... YOU'RE MEAN AND EVIL!
UM...I WON'T DO IT AGAIN! PLEASE STOP CRYING...
SNFFFF!
BLECH! GROSS—I MEAN, LET'S GO WASH UP!
YES!
I MEAN...OKAY!
HURRY!
UGH! DID YOU CHANGE YOUR SOCKS THIS MORNING?
QUIT WHINING! I'VE ALREADY SAVED YOU TONS OF TIMES.
I KNOW...YOU CHARGED ME TEN CANDIES TO READ IN MY PLACE.

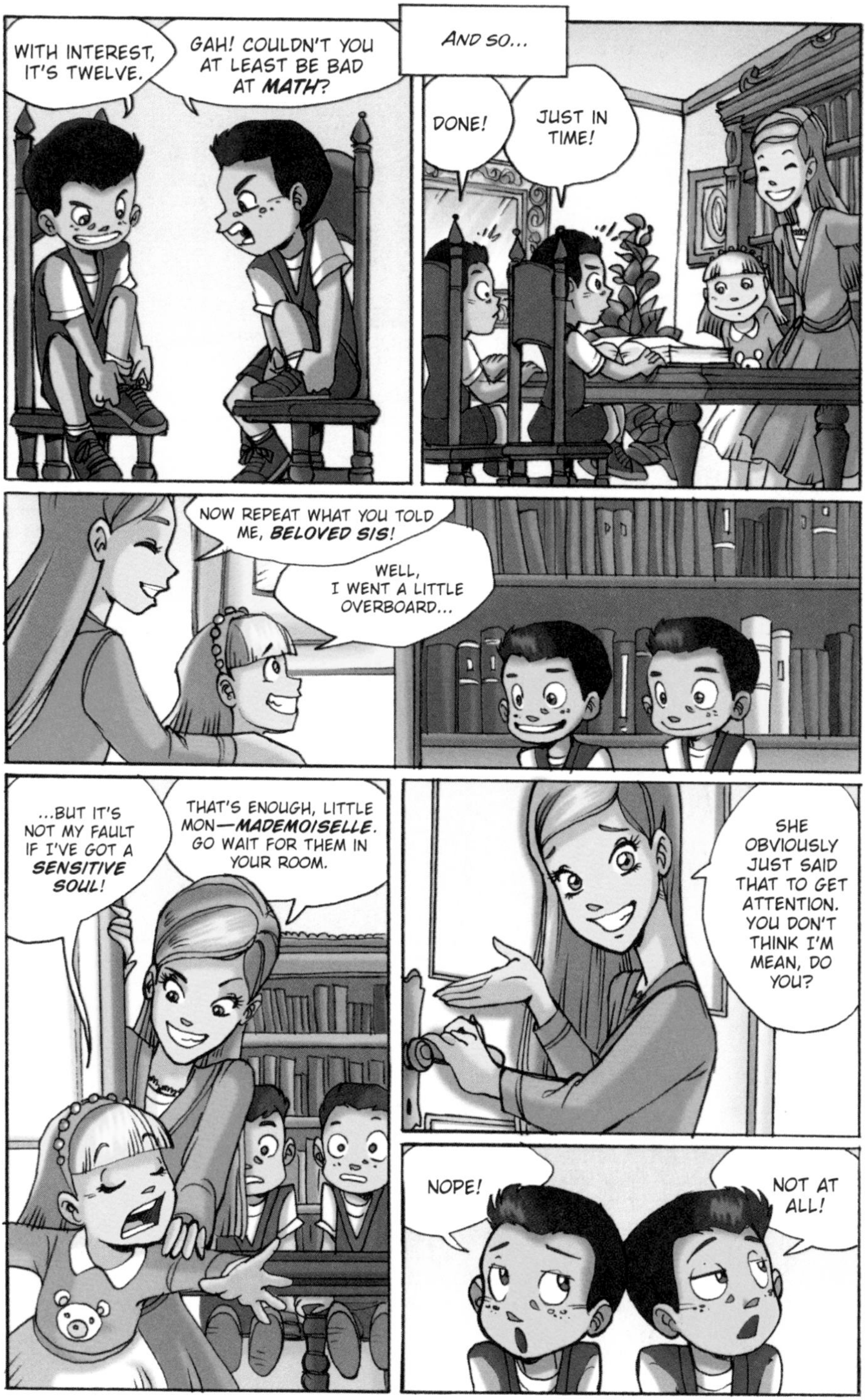
WITH INTEREST, IT'S TWELVE.
GAH! COULDN'T YOU AT LEAST BE BAD AT **MATH**?
AND SO...
DONE!
JUST IN TIME!
NOW REPEAT WHAT YOU TOLD ME, **BELOVED SIS**!
WELL, I WENT A LITTLE OVERBOARD...
...BUT IT'S NOT MY FAULT IF I'VE GOT A **SENSITIVE SOUL**!
THAT'S ENOUGH, LITTLE MON—**MADEMOISELLE**. GO WAIT FOR THEM IN YOUR ROOM.
SHE OBVIOUSLY JUST SAID THAT TO GET ATTENTION. YOU DON'T THINK I'M MEAN, DO YOU?
NOPE!
NOT AT ALL!

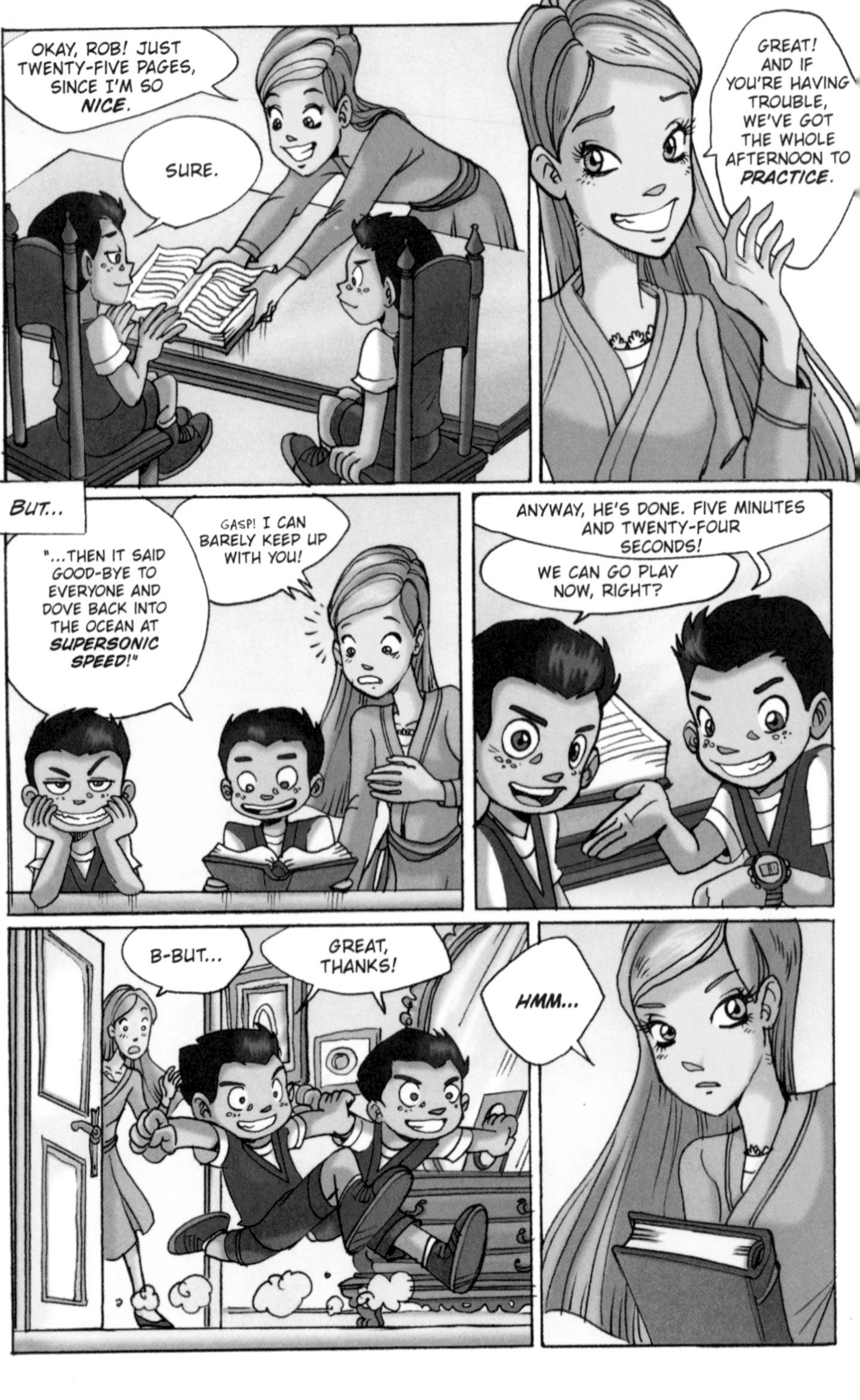

OKAY, ROB! JUST TWENTY-FIVE PAGES, SINCE I'M SO NICE.
SURE.
GREAT! AND IF YOU'RE HAVING TROUBLE, WE'VE GOT THE WHOLE AFTERNOON TO PRACTICE.
BUT...
"...THEN IT SAID GOOD-BYE TO EVERYONE AND DOVE BACK INTO THE OCEAN AT SUPERSONIC SPEED!"
GASP! I CAN BARELY KEEP UP WITH YOU!
ANYWAY, HE'S DONE. FIVE MINUTES AND TWENTY-FOUR SECONDS!
WE CAN GO PLAY NOW, RIGHT?
B-BUT...
GREAT, THANKS!
HMM...

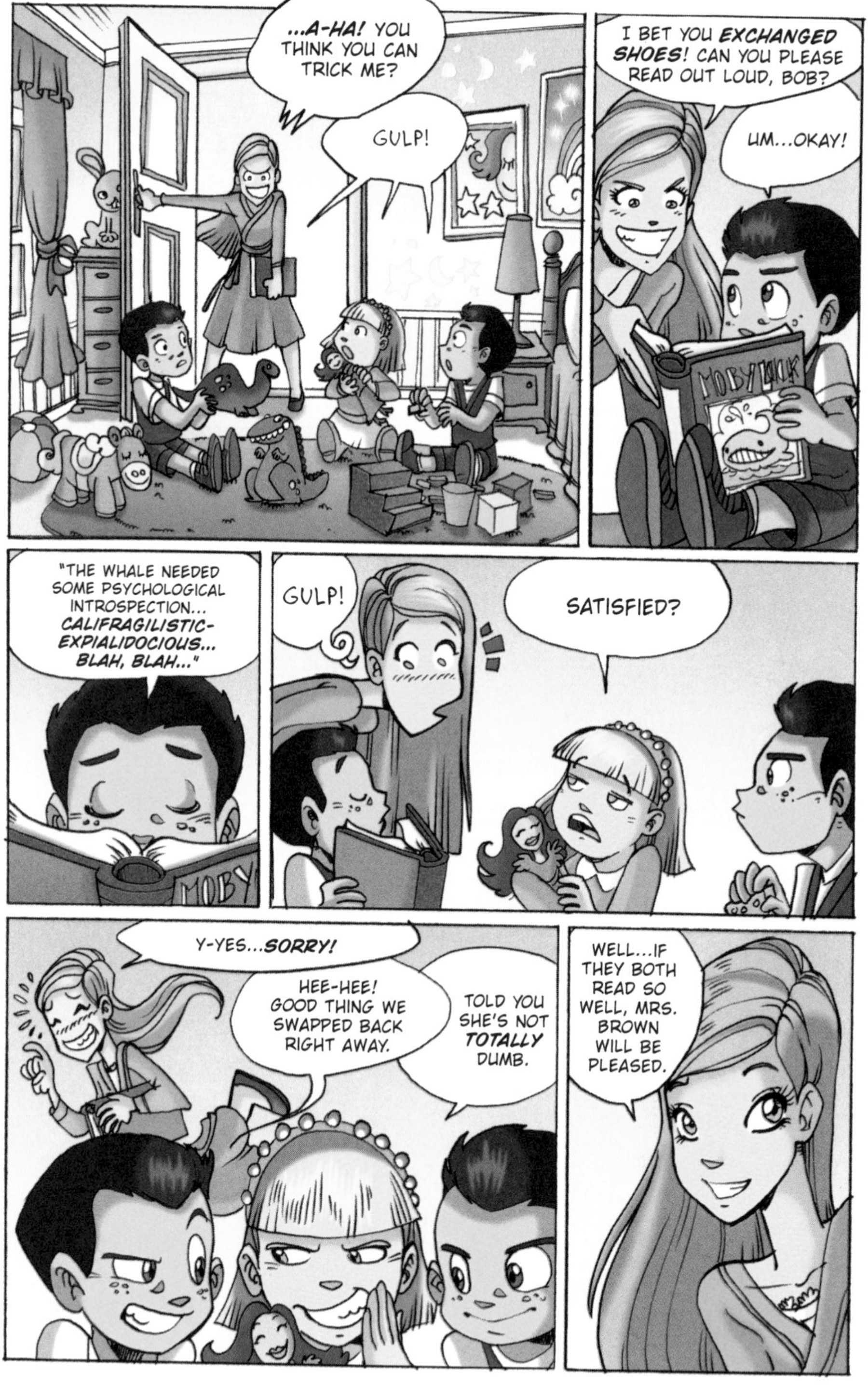
...A-HA! YOU THINK YOU CAN TRICK ME?
GULP!
I BET YOU EXCHANGED SHOES! CAN YOU PLEASE READ OUT LOUD, BOB?
UM...OKAY!
"THE WHALE NEEDED SOME PSYCHOLOGICAL INTROSPECTION... CALIFRAGILISTIC-EXPIALIDOCIOUS... BLAH, BLAH..."
GULP!
SATISFIED?
Y-YES...SORRY!
HEE-HEE! GOOD THING WE SWAPPED BACK RIGHT AWAY.
TOLD YOU SHE'S NOT TOTALLY DUMB.
WELL...IF THEY BOTH READ SO WELL, MRS. BROWN WILL BE PLEASED.

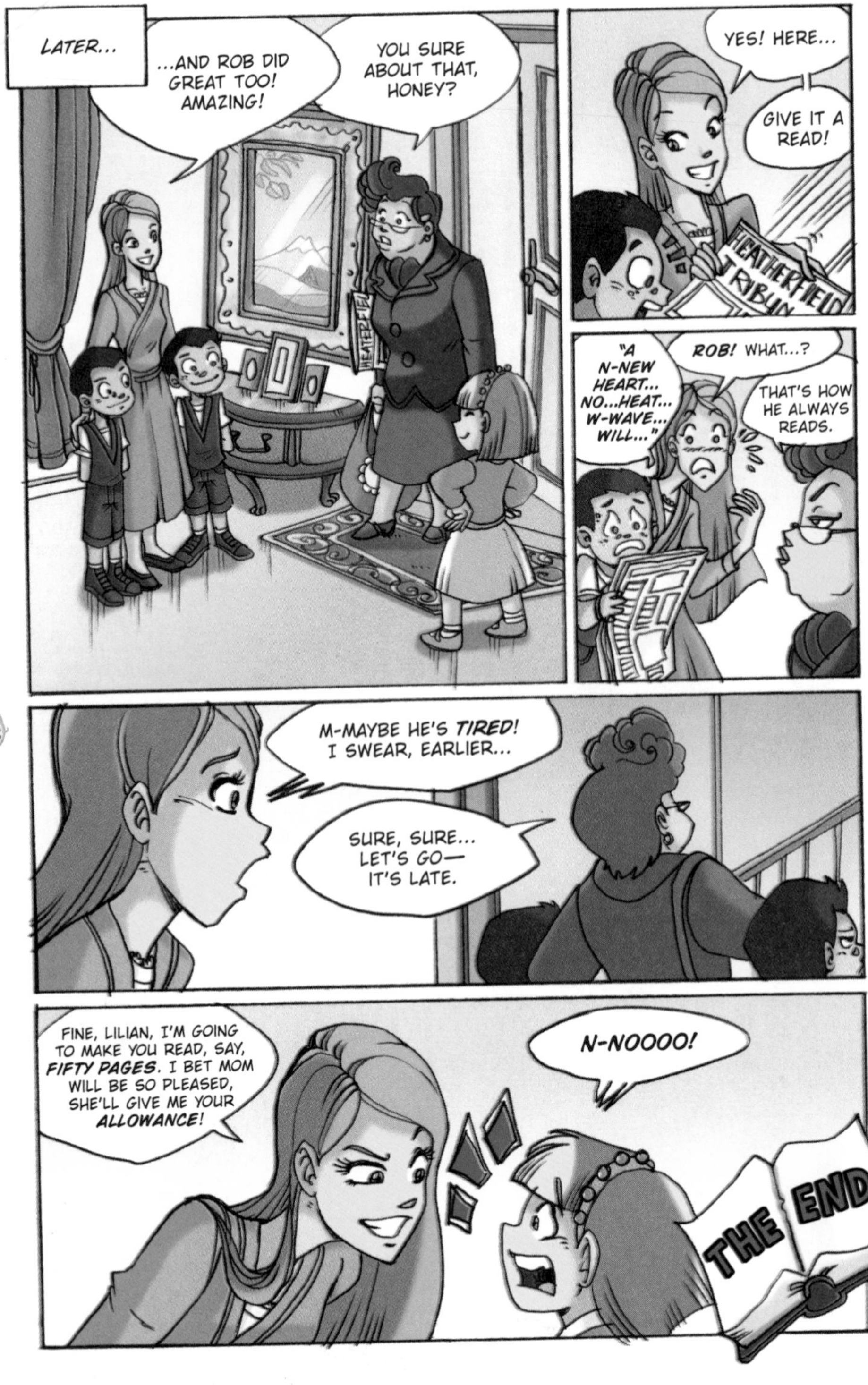
LATER...
...AND ROB DID GREAT TOO! AMAZING!
YOU SURE ABOUT THAT, HONEY?
YES! HERE...
GIVE IT A READ!
HEATHERFIELD TRIBUN
"A N-NEW HEART... NO...HEAT... W-WAVE... WILL..."
ROB! WHAT...?
THAT'S HOW HE ALWAYS READS.
M-MAYBE HE'S TIRED! I SWEAR, EARLIER...
SURE, SURE... LET'S GO— IT'S LATE.
FINE, LILIAN, I'M GOING TO MAKE YOU READ, SAY, FIFTY PAGES. I BET MOM WILL BE SO PLEASED, SHE'LL GIVE ME YOUR ALLOWANCE!
N-NOOOO!
THE END

Houston, We Have a Problem

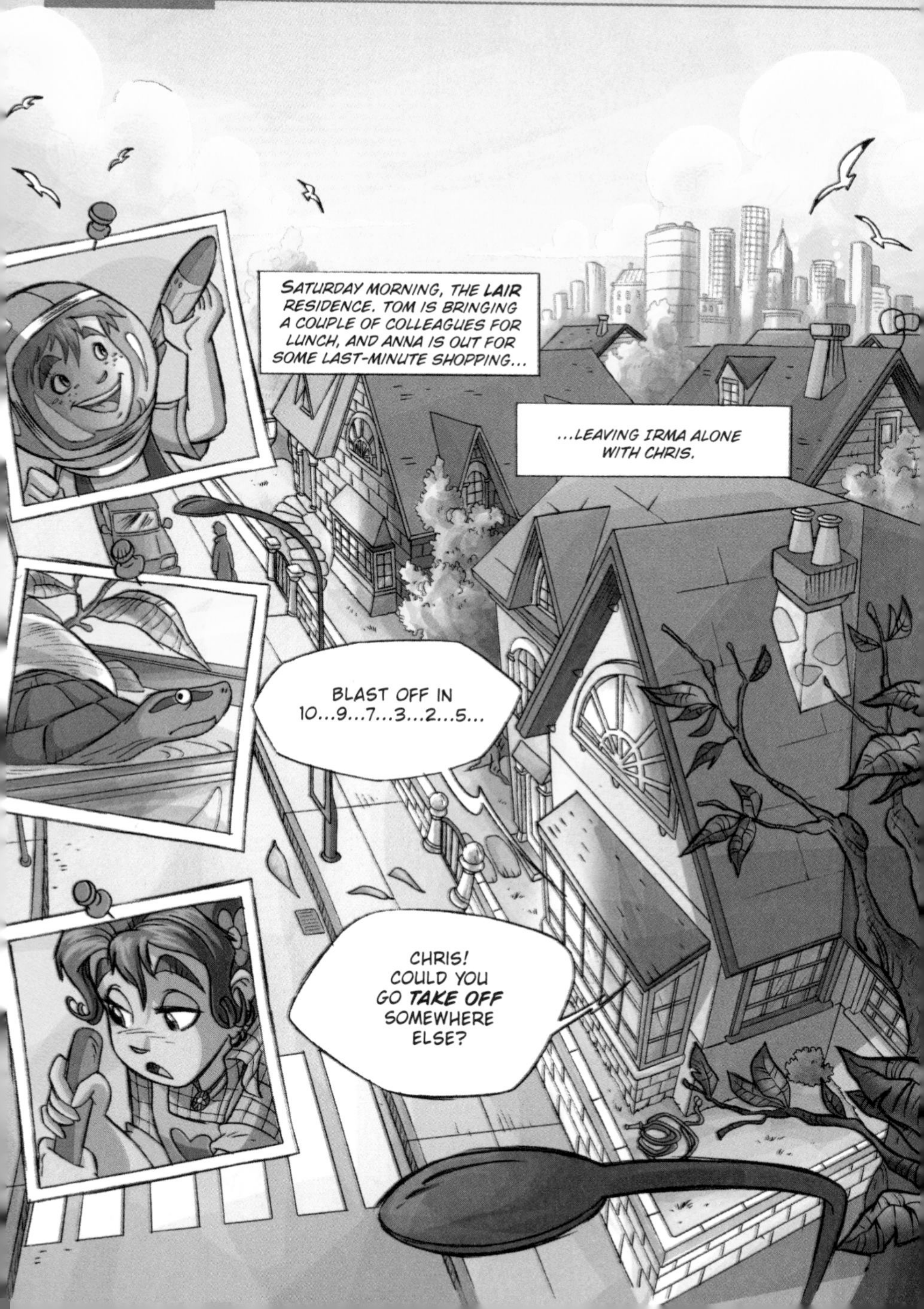
SATURDAY MORNING, THE LAIR RESIDENCE. TOM IS BRINGING A COUPLE OF COLLEAGUES FOR LUNCH, AND ANNA IS OUT FOR SOME LAST-MINUTE SHOPPING...
...LEAVING IRMA ALONE WITH CHRIS.
BLAST OFF IN 10...9...7...3...2...5...
CHRIS! COULD YOU GO TAKE OFF SOMEWHERE ELSE?

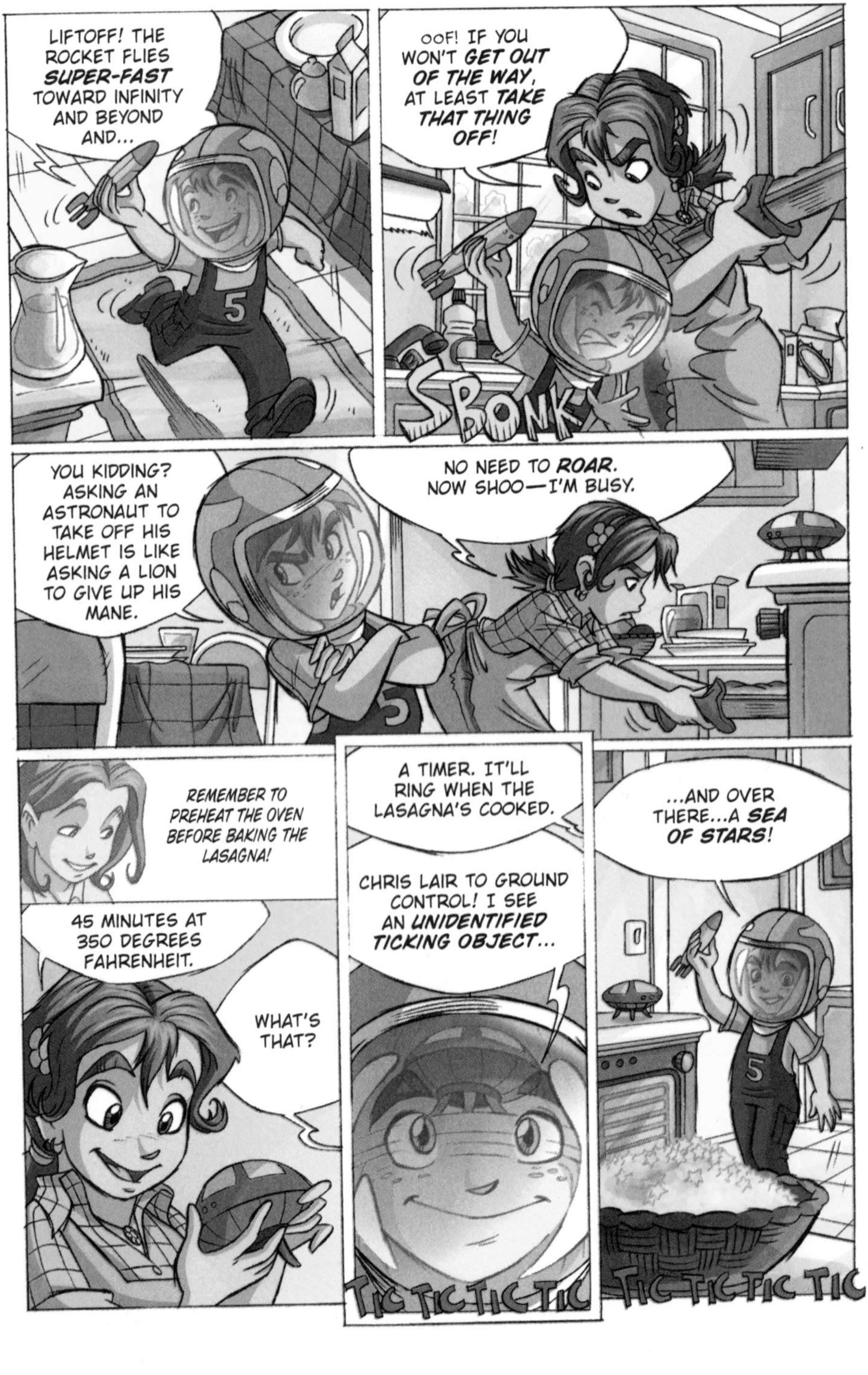

LIFTOFF! THE ROCKET FLIES SUPER-FAST TOWARD INFINITY AND BEYOND AND...
OOF! IF YOU WON'T GET OUT OF THE WAY, AT LEAST TAKE THAT THING OFF!
SBONK
YOU KIDDING? ASKING AN ASTRONAUT TO TAKE OFF HIS HELMET IS LIKE ASKING A LION TO GIVE UP HIS MANE.
NO NEED TO ROAR. NOW SHOO—I'M BUSY.
REMEMBER TO PREHEAT THE OVEN BEFORE BAKING THE LASAGNA!
45 MINUTES AT 350 DEGREES FAHRENHEIT.
WHAT'S THAT?
A TIMER. IT'LL RING WHEN THE LASAGNA'S COOKED.
CHRIS LAIR TO GROUND CONTROL! I SEE AN UNIDENTIFIED TICKING OBJECT...
TIC TIC TIC TIC TIC
...AND OVER THERE...A SEA OF STARS!
TIC TIC TIC TIC TIC

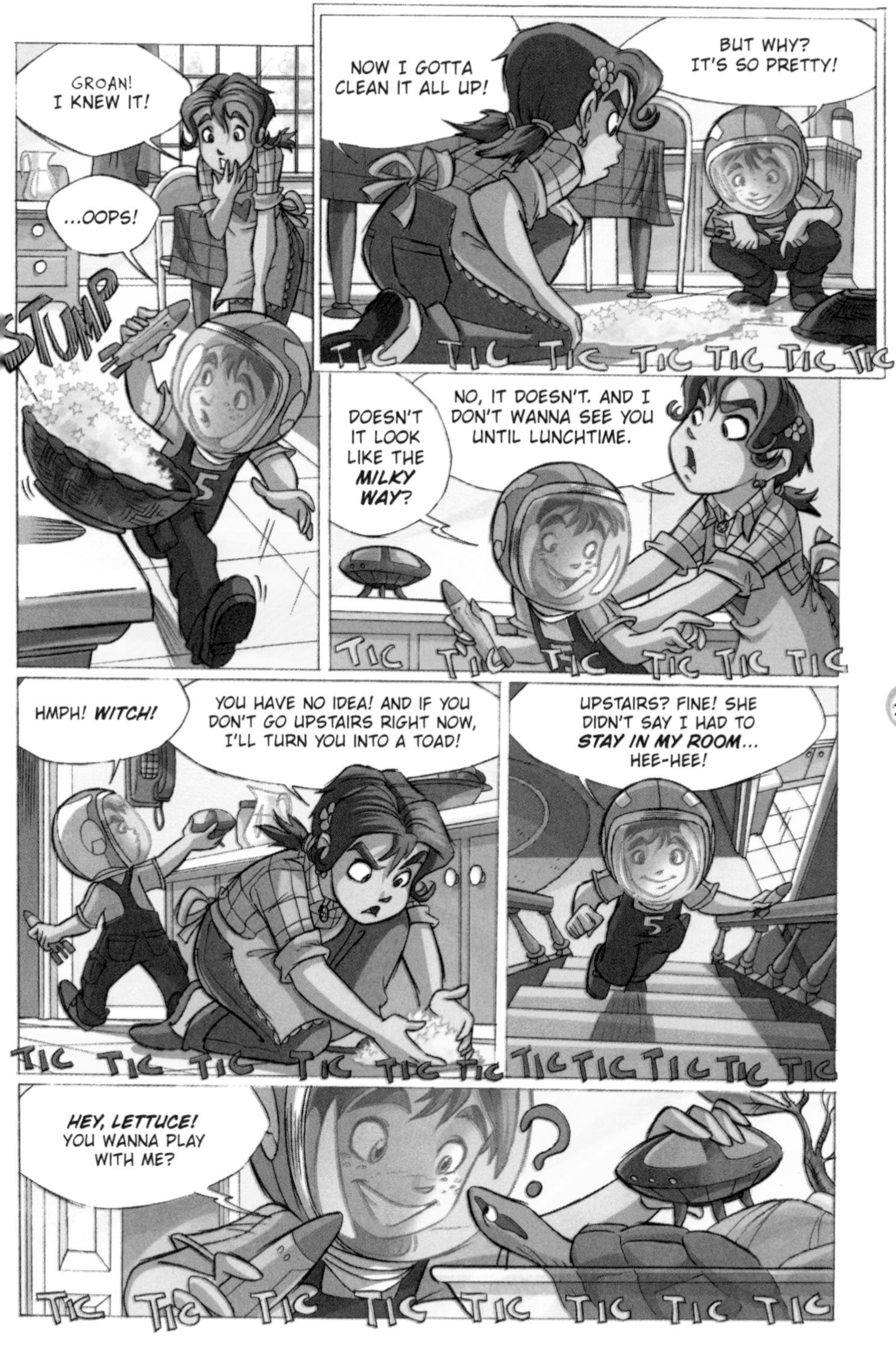
GROAN! I KNEW IT!
...OOPS!
STUMP
NOW I GOTTA CLEAN IT ALL UP!
BUT WHY? IT'S SO PRETTY!
TIC TIC TIC TIC TIC TIC TIC
DOESN'T IT LOOK LIKE THE MILKY WAY?
NO, IT DOESN'T. AND I DON'T WANNA SEE YOU UNTIL LUNCHTIME.
TIC TIC TIC TIC TIC TIC
HMPH! WITCH!
YOU HAVE NO IDEA! AND IF YOU DON'T GO UPSTAIRS RIGHT NOW, I'LL TURN YOU INTO A TOAD!
TIC TIC TIC TIC TIC TIC
UPSTAIRS? FINE! SHE DIDN'T SAY I HAD TO STAY IN MY ROOM... HEE-HEE!
TIC TIC TIC TIC TIC
HEY, LETTUCE! YOU WANNA PLAY WITH ME?
?
TIC TIC TIC TIC TIC TIC TIC TIC

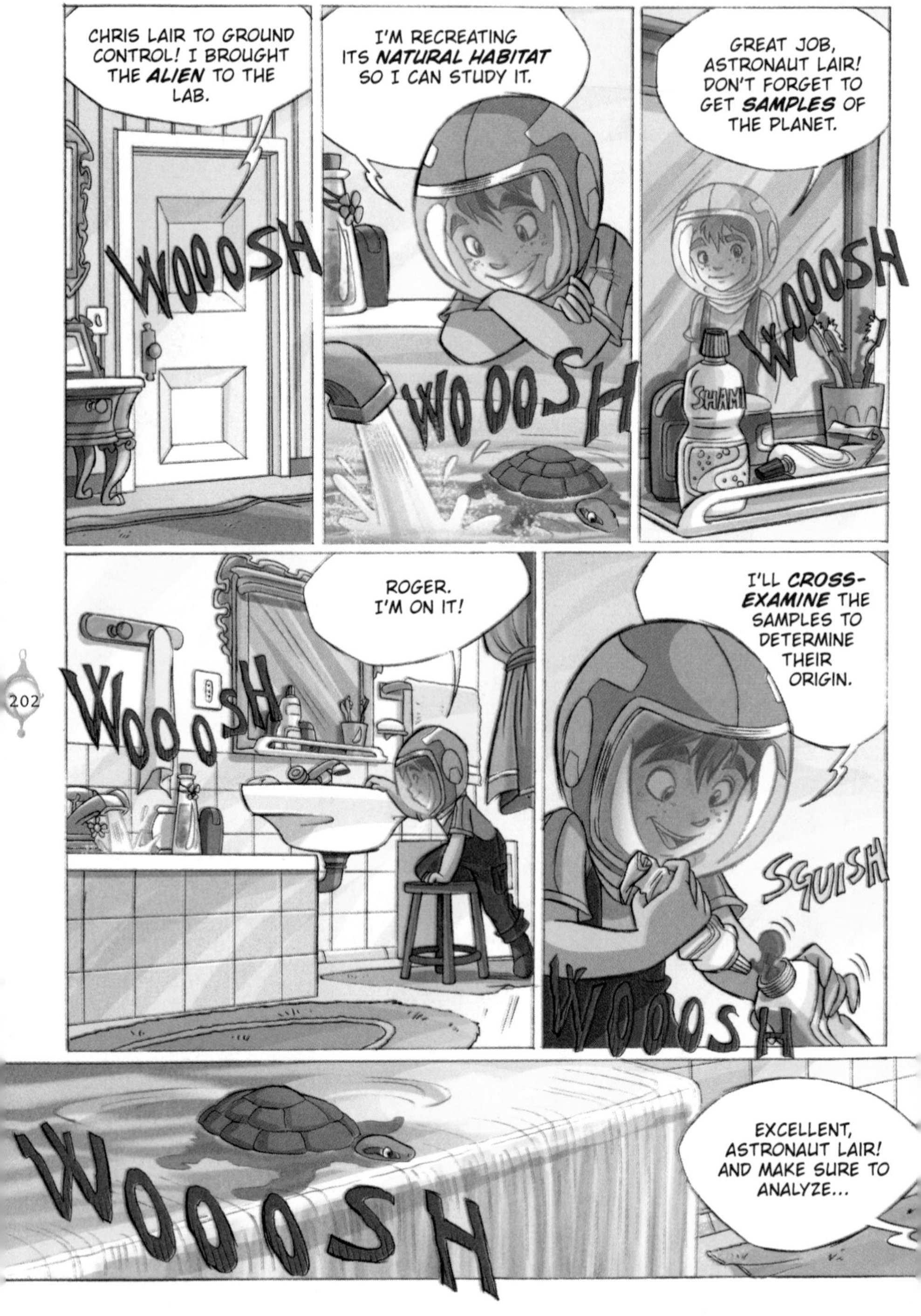
CHRIS LAIR TO GROUND CONTROL! I BROUGHT THE ALIEN TO THE LAB.
WOOOSH
I'M RECREATING ITS NATURAL HABITAT SO I CAN STUDY IT.
WOOOSH
GREAT JOB, ASTRONAUT LAIR! DON'T FORGET TO GET SAMPLES OF THE PLANET.
WOOOSH
SHAM
ROGER. I'M ON IT!
WOOOSH
I'LL CROSS-EXAMINE THE SAMPLES TO DETERMINE THEIR ORIGIN.
SQUISH
WOOOSH
WOOOSH
EXCELLENT, ASTRONAUT LAIR! AND MAKE SURE TO ANALYZE...

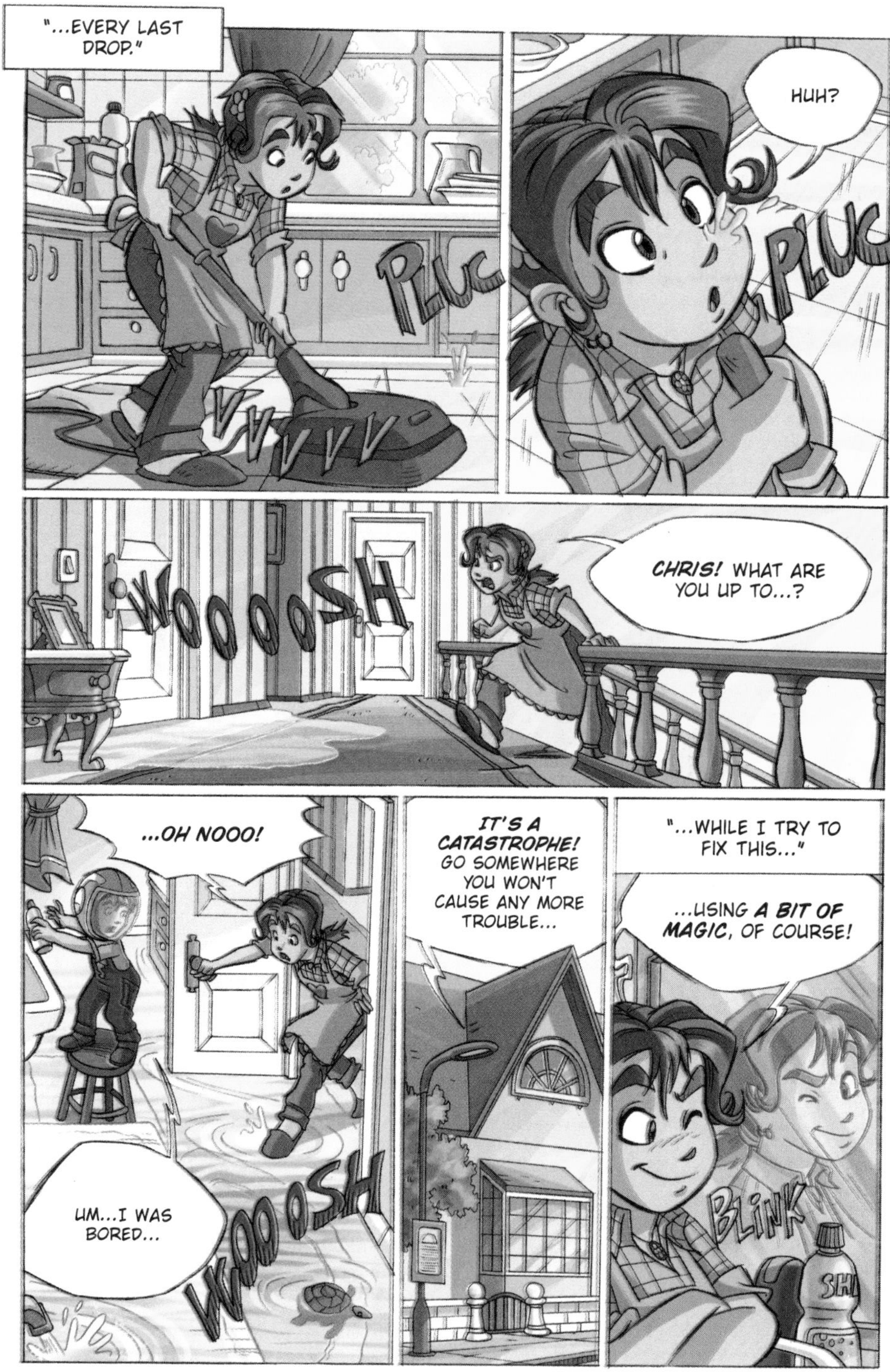
"...EVERY LAST DROP."
PLUC
VVVVVV
HUH?
PLUC
WOOOOSH
CHRIS! WHAT ARE YOU UP TO...?
...OH NOOO!
UM...I WAS BORED...
WOOOSH
IT'S A CATASTROPHE! GO SOMEWHERE YOU WON'T CAUSE ANY MORE TROUBLE...
"...WHILE I TRY TO FIX THIS..."
...USING A BIT OF MAGIC, OF COURSE!
BLINK

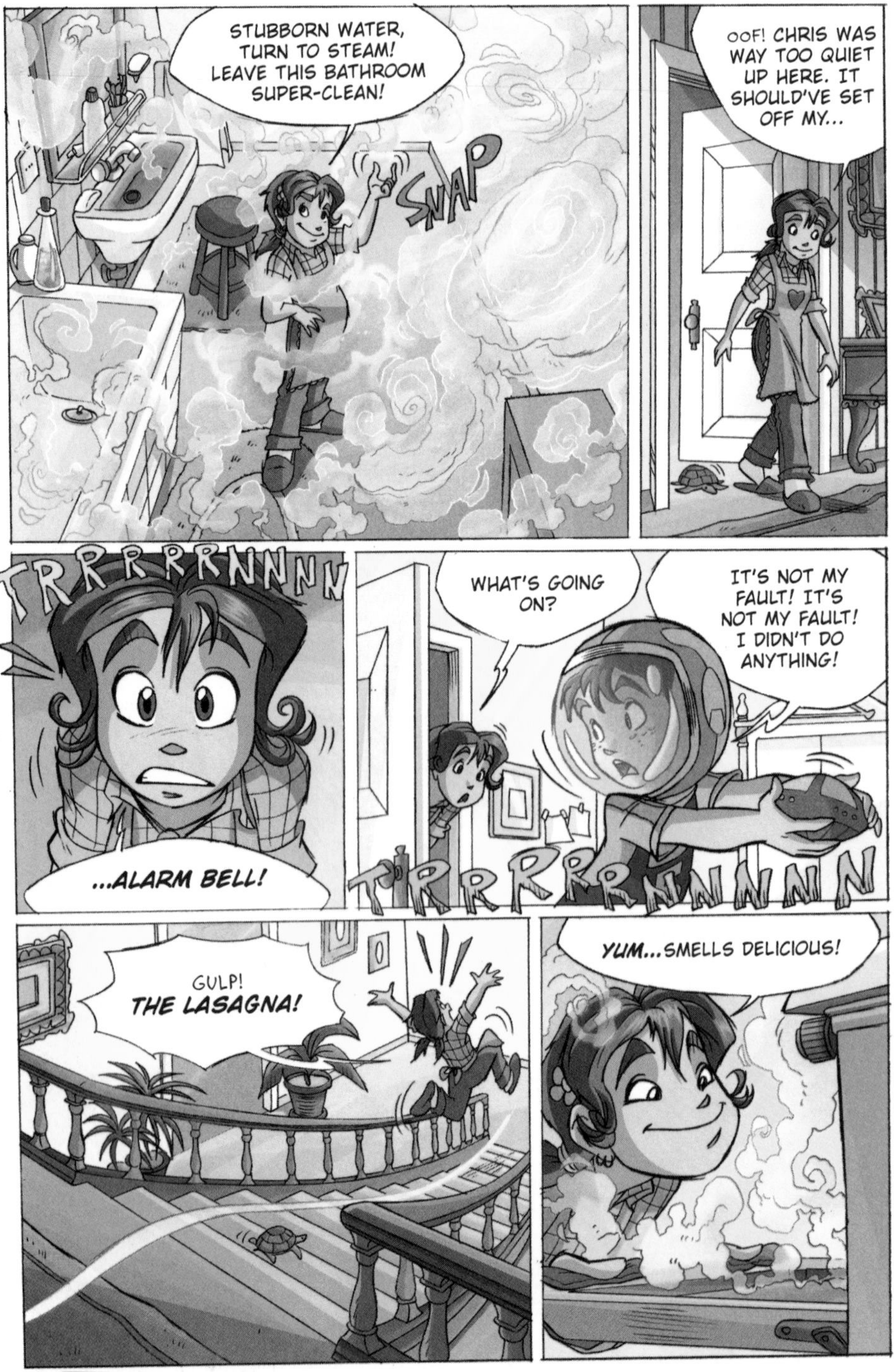
STUBBORN WATER, TURN TO STEAM! LEAVE THIS BATHROOM SUPER-CLEAN!
SNAP
OOF! CHRIS WAS WAY TOO QUIET UP HERE. IT SHOULD'VE SET OFF MY...
TRRRRRNNNNN
...ALARM BELL!
WHAT'S GOING ON?
IT'S NOT MY FAULT! IT'S NOT MY FAULT! I DIDN'T DO ANYTHING!
TRRRRRNNNNNN
GULP! THE LASAGNA!
YUM... SMELLS DELICIOUS!

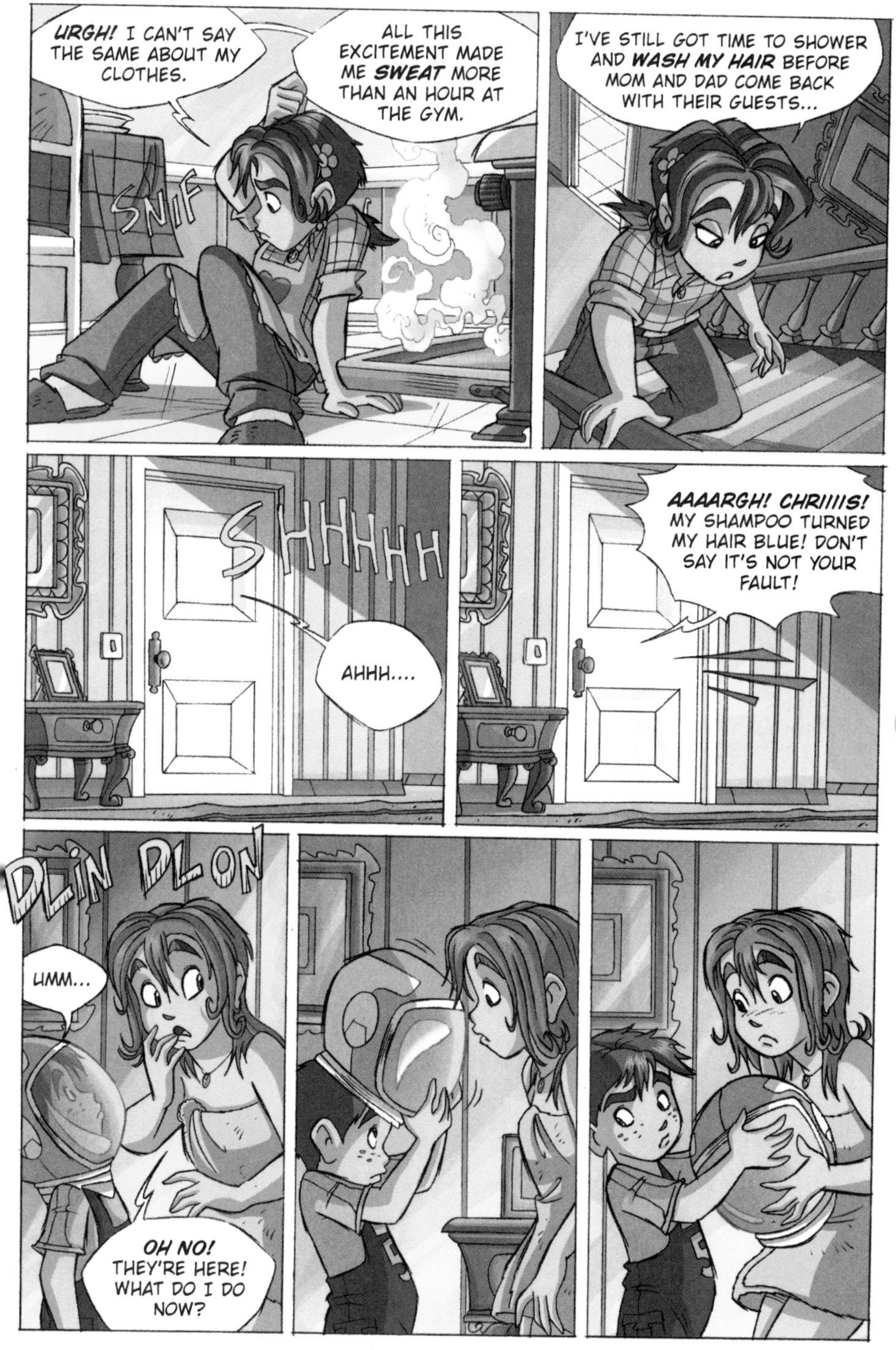
URGH! I CAN'T SAY THE SAME ABOUT MY CLOTHES.
SNIF
ALL THIS EXCITEMENT MADE ME SWEAT MORE THAN AN HOUR AT THE GYM.
I'VE STILL GOT TIME TO SHOWER AND WASH MY HAIR BEFORE MOM AND DAD COME BACK WITH THEIR GUESTS...
SHHHHH
AHHH....
AAAARGH! CHRIIIIS! MY SHAMPOO TURNED MY HAIR BLUE! DON'T SAY IT'S NOT YOUR FAULT!
DLIN DLON
UMM...
OH NO! THEY'RE HERE! WHAT DO I DO NOW?

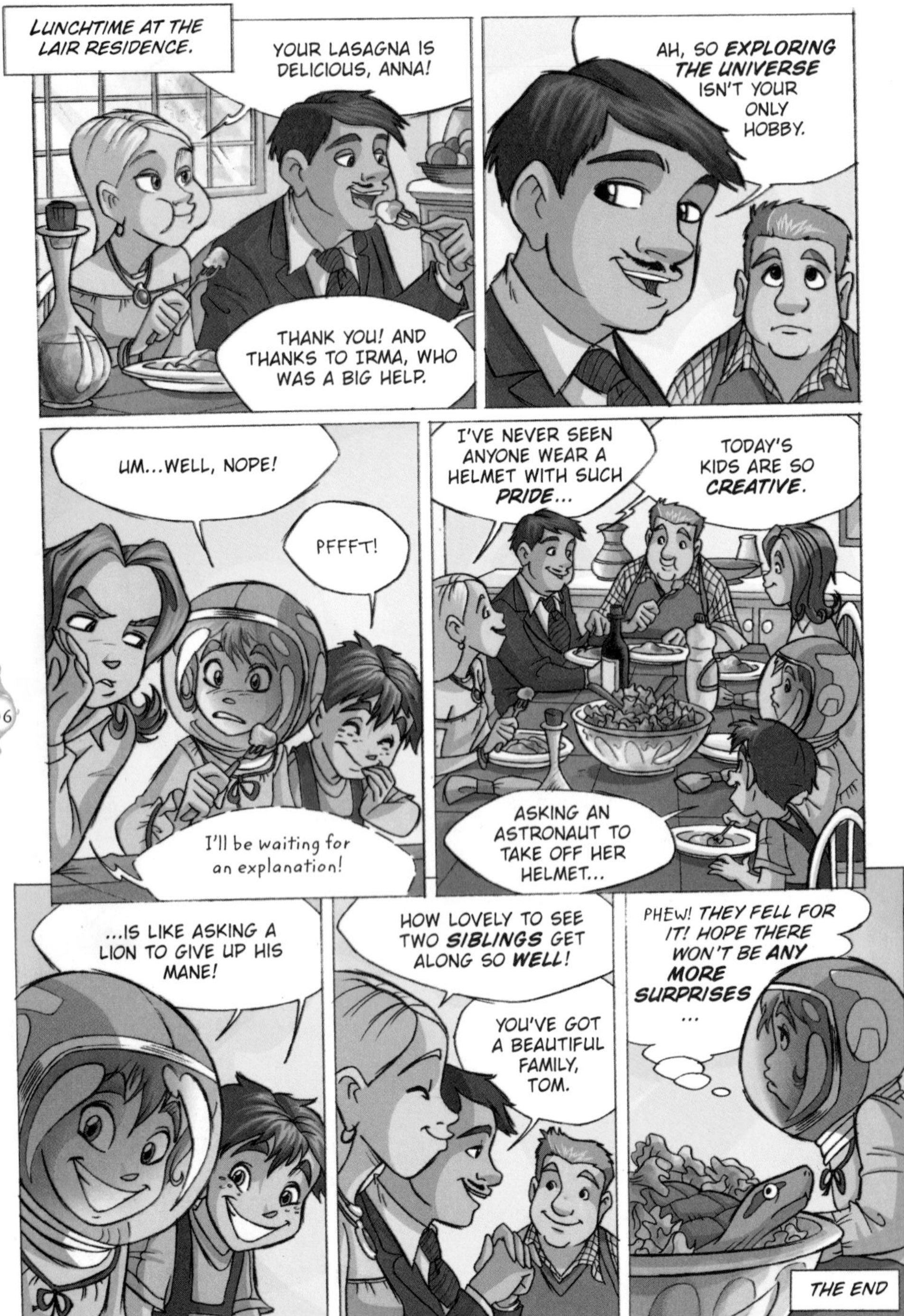
LUNCHTIME AT THE LAIR RESIDENCE.
YOUR LASAGNA IS DELICIOUS, ANNA!
THANK YOU! AND THANKS TO IRMA, WHO WAS A BIG HELP.
AH, SO **EXPLORING THE UNIVERSE** ISN'T YOUR ONLY HOBBY.
UM...WELL, NOPE!
PFFFT!
I'll be waiting for an explanation!
I'VE NEVER SEEN ANYONE WEAR A HELMET WITH SUCH **PRIDE**...
TODAY'S KIDS ARE SO **CREATIVE**.
ASKING AN ASTRONAUT TO TAKE OFF HER HELMET...
...IS LIKE ASKING A LION TO GIVE UP HIS MANE!
HOW LOVELY TO SEE TWO **SIBLINGS** GET ALONG SO **WELL**!
YOU'VE GOT A BEAUTIFUL FAMILY, TOM.
PHEW! **THEY FELL FOR IT! HOPE THERE WON'T BE ANY MORE SURPRISES**...
THE END

W.i.t.c.h.

Will Irma Taranee Cornelia Hay Lin

Read on in Volume 28!

Part IX. 100% W.I.T.C.H. • Volume 2

Series Created by Elisabetta Gnone
Comic Art Direction: Alessandro Barbucci, Barbara Canepa

W.I.T.C.H.: The Graphic Novel,
Part IX: 100% W.I.T.C.H.
© Disney Enterprises, Inc.

English translation © 2022 by Disney Enterprises, Inc.

JY
150 West 30th Street, 19th Floor
New York, NY 10001

Visit us at jyforkids.com
facebook.com/jyforkids
twitter.com/jyforkids
jyforkids.tumblr.com
instagram.com/jyforkids

First JY Edition: January 2022

JY is an imprint of Yen Press, LLC.
The JY name and logo are trademarks of Yen Press, LLC.

The publisher is not responsible for websites (or their content) that are not owned by the publisher.

Library of Congress Control Number: 2017950917

ISBNs:
978-1-9753-2323-3 (paperback)
978-1-9753-2324-0 (ebook)

10 9 8 7 6 5 4 3 2 1

LSC-C

· Printed in the United States of America

Cover Art by Giada Perissinotto
Colors by Andrea Cagol

Translation by Linda Ghio and
Stephanie Dagg at Editing Zone
Lettering by Katie Blakeslee

A SPECIAL LETTER

Concept and Script by Teresa Radice
Layout, Pencils, and Inks by Lucio Leoni
Color Direction by Francesco Legramandi

ZODIAC

Concept and Script by Augusto Macchetto
Layout and Pencils by Giada Perissinotto
Inks by Marina Baggio and Roberta Zanotta
Color Direction by Francesco Legramandi

IT WAS FATE

Concept and Script by Augusto Macchetto
Layout and Pencils by Giada Perissinotto
Inks by Marina Baggio and Roberta Zanotta
Color Direction by Francesco Legramandi

A FATHER'S HEART

Concept and Script by Teresa Radice
Layout and Pencils by Daniela Vetro
Inks by Marina Baggio and Roberta Zanotta

A TRICKY TRADE

Concept and Script by Maria Muzzolini
Layout, Pencils, and Inks by Paolo Campinoti

HOUSTON, WE HAVE A PROBLEM

Concept and Script by Teresa Radice
Layout, Pencils, and Inks by Ettore Gula